THE VILLA

Ruth Kelly has ghostwritten a string of *Sunday Times* top ten bestsellers – most recently *The Prison Doctor*, which sold over 250,000 copies, and *The Governor*, which went straight in at number one on the Amazon charts and number five in the *Sunday Times* bestseller list. *The Villa* is Ruth's debut thriller. She's drawn inspiration from her years working as a reporter for national newspapers as well as her experience writing for TV shows, most notably with Endemol, the creators of the original reality show – *Big Brother*. You can follow her on Twitter @ruthywriter.

THE
VILLA

RUTH KELLY

PAN BOOKS

First published 2023 by Pan Books
an imprint of Pan Macmillan
The Smithson, 6 Briset Street, London EC1M 5NR
EU representative: Macmillan Publishers Ireland Ltd, 1st Floor,
The Liffey Trust Centre, 117–126 Sheriff Street Upper,
Dublin 1, D01 YC43
Associated companies throughout the world
www.panmacmillan.com

ISBN 978-1-0350-0128-6

1 3 5 7 9 8 6 4 2

A CIP catalogue record for this book is available from the British Library.

Typeset in Sabon LT Std by Palimpsest Book Production Limited,
Falkirk, Stirlingshire

Printed and bound by CPI Group (UK) Ltd, Croydon, CR0 4YY

MIX
Paper | Supporting
responsible forestry
FSC® C116313

Visit **www.panmacmillan.com** to read more about all our books
and to buy them. You will also find features, author interviews and
news of any author events, and you can sign up for e-newsletters
so that you're always first to hear about our new releases.

For Mum, forever in my heart,
and for Michael

THE PRODUCER

Aruna, Balearic Islands

NOW

Broken glass crunches beneath my trainers as we move towards the pool. The sun is setting over the villa, the golden light that once bathed it in glory now a dull tarnished amber.

Detective Inspector Jose Carlos Sanchez lifts the blue and white police cordon and bows underneath. He raises it for me and I notice the forensic gloves he's wearing. Milky white – signposting me to what lies ahead. He stops and makes a visual sweep of the area.

'Tell me where all the cameras are located, señora.'

Despite the sea breeze, the heat is cloying. It's attacking me and I'm sweating in places I didn't know were possible.

'Señora?'

The locations. Every single one I know by heart. Months of meticulous planning had gone into designing and hiding the cameras. Positioning them in such a way we'd capture even the slightest nuance in the contestants' expressions.

There were no secrets on my show. I surrendered all of myself to create perfection – constructing the greatest entertainment show of all time.

I point to the magenta plant beside the sunlounger. 'Have a look in there.' The leaves are now dry and shrivelled – how quickly things die when they're not being nourished.

We walk in step towards it. He peers inside the terracotta pot and nods. Then he signals to one of the many officers guarding the crime scene from press and rubberneckers. Since the news broke, the villa's location is no longer my best-kept secret. I notice the camera's red 'recording' light has stopped flashing.

'Where else?' asks Sanchez.

'Over there.' I point up, into the palm tree shading the jacuzzi. 'There and there.' I reel off ten more locations.

'And the one closest to the pool?' he says. Drawing me towards her.

My stomach contracts. It's coming. We're almost there. I want to look away, but a morbid curiosity is pulling me in.

There she is. Face-planted on the hot stones. Her platinum blonde hair fanned around her head like a halo. Blood still leaks from her skull, seeping into the pool. Streaks of crimson run through the turquoise water, diluting into nothing, like a watercolour painting. If it wasn't so disturbing it would be beautiful.

'It's over.' I whisper the words as I stare at her.

Sanchez looks at me. 'What did you say?'

My gaze lifts and meets his. 'This wasn't how it was supposed to end.'

I shut my eyes, imagining how it should have played out. The fireworks exploding across the sky, perfectly timed to music. Their colours reflected by the ocean. Millions of viewers cheering from their living rooms. The pantomime handing over of the cheque.

I don't know what shock is but I'm certain that's what I've slipped into. My fingers and wrists tingle. The corners of my mouth prickle and I still can't tear my eyes from her.

'Miss Jessop, I need to know the location of the camera closest to the body.'

Body. Dead. No longer spoken of as a person with a name. She's become a thing to be processed. I swallow back the bile that's crept into my throat.

'It's in there.'

I point into the water, to the camera embedded in the side of the pool. Finally I divert my eyes away from the grisly scene.

Two men and a woman in white forensic overalls arrive. I watch as they put on shoe covers, as she tucks her hair into her hood. They approach the body like spirits who have come to collect the dead. They carry what resembles a cool box, but I know there isn't any finger food and chilled wine inside. They are the crime scene examiners and they have come to collect evidence.

Evidence. Crime. The words sink like rocks to the pit of my stomach.

A second white gazebo is being erected over where more blood was spilled. Now rust-coloured, peeling in the heat.

Two more officers arrive holding a stretcher and a black body bag.

3

'They're taking her away?' I turn to Sanchez. Of course they are, Michelle. Shut up. Use your fucking brain. *She's dead.*

She'll be the last contestant to leave the villa. That really will mark the end. The thought panics me more than anything. I don't want to let go.

'We'll need to perform an autopsy after the examination is complete.'

'Have her family been told?' I ask.

'They're on their way to Madrid.'

I feel sick at the thought of their grief.

'Anything else you need me for? I've so much to do, there's a lot I need to take care of.'

Catastrophe management. Reputation salvaging. I have an entire production team waiting for me to explain what's going to happen next. A press statement to prepare. I check my watch. Lost time fires up my adrenaline. Nerves prickle. *Move out of my way, Sanchez.* I turn to make my retreat.

The detective inspector holds up his hand. 'I'm afraid we need you to come with us to the police station.'

'What? Why?' I snap my head around, my veneer of patience and cooperativeness falling away. 'I've helped you with all I can.'

'You are the producer of the show.'

'Yeah, I'm the producer, but no, this isn't my fault.'

His eyes narrow. 'I'm afraid some might see that differently, señora.'

He turns, makes another hand gesture and two officers approach. 'You need to leave with us.'

4

He points me in the direction of the black and gold door. The same door that sealed in our contestants.

'Can't I answer your questions here?' Panic seizes control of my voice.

'I'm afraid not. This way.' The officers move either side of me, their posture stiffening in case I resist.

'Our boat is waiting,' Sanchez says again, his voice now thick with irritation. He isn't used to a strong personality like me. Someone who thinks what they do is equally important.

Our stand-off is broken by a thunderous whirring from above. We all look up at the same time and see a cavalier news channel breaking the airspace restrictions. The helicopter's flying much lower than it should.

This is a no-fly zone. I should know, it's why I chose it.

Their cameras are trained on me. Now I'm the one being filmed.

'We need to leave *now*, Señora Jessop.'

I relent. Sanchez steers me back underneath the tape, towards the next cordon that wraps around the entire villa. Shards of champagne bottles lie in our path. More smashed glass – on the bar and tables. Pool towels, strewn across the decking. Flies swarm around decaying food. The silver strands of a party wig flap in the breeze. A sudden gust of wind lifts the wig from its resting place, sending it cartwheeling into our path. What was once dazzling, now reminiscent of a Wild West film set.

My baby. My beautiful creation, decomposing before my eyes.

I turn to face Sanchez. 'It wasn't supposed to be like

this.' Tears rise. I stop dead. Rooting my heels into the ground. 'I'm not leaving.'

'Señora, the boat is waiting.' All pleasantries have gone.

'I'm staying!' This is where I belong. Here, in the world I curated, that I directed. I can't bring myself to face the reality. The judgement that's waiting for me.

Sanchez has had enough. There's no reasoning with me. He signals his officers to grab my arms.

CHAPTER ONE

THE REPORTER

The Record newsroom, London

EIGHT WEEKS AGO

Bingeing on coffee and sugary snacks had created the perfect storm in my stomach. The burn had risen to attack my throat. I swallowed hard but the pressure of meeting the deadline, and the guilt of knowing the harm my story would cause, was firmly lodged in my mind.

Mike Baron, retired England football captain and national treasure. As famous for his game off the pitch as his goalscoring. Back in the day, he was known for his partying, drinking, and womanizing.

But that was then. The 'real' Mike couldn't be more different from the headlines, from his 'lad' reputation. Loyal, kind, a father of two and a devoted husband. This Saturday would mark his twentieth wedding anniversary and he'd just found out his wife was dying of cancer. He didn't mean to tell me, it slipped out in our interview because he was grief-stricken. Because I had a way of getting people to talk. That was my gift. Although it didn't feel like a superpower now.

7

Having his heartbreak splashed across the front page of a tabloid newspaper would destroy him. I knew that – but the pressure to deliver was crushing my ability to reason.

My phone rang.

'Where is it, Peters?' He always used my surname when we were on deadline. 'I'm holding the page for you.'

My eyes were pulled across the newsroom, through the glass panel walls and into his office. Slouching behind his desk – my features editor, Ben Foster. Our eyes met and a tremor ran through me.

Holding my gaze, he said: 'Well send it the fuck over, then. What are you waiting for?'

He slammed the phone down. It wasn't meant as a question.

I stared at the screen, at my exclusive. The cursor blinking impatiently.

The interview with Mike had taken place on his sprawling estate outside London. Instead of showing off his trophies he'd talked about what really mattered to him. He couldn't keep the tears from his eyes as he reminisced over the day he first met his wife. As I'd got up to leave, Mike had pulled me into a hug and held me for a long moment. Seeking comfort after baring his soul.

His agent had stopped me on the way out. Aware Mike had opened up to me, wary I'd got more than I should have from the interview. He insisted on reading the story before it went to print. I couldn't look him in the eye when I promised I'd see what I could do. That was not something we ever did at *The Record*.

Destroying lives wasn't what I signed up for when I joined

the paper. They'd promised me investigative reports, stories that make a difference. Campaigns that raise awareness. Yet somehow, I'd been sidelined into writing celebrity exposés. Who's shagging who. Grubby journalism. It had become about tearing things apart rather than making a difference.

Every time I plucked up the courage to tell my boss I was fed up, he'd remind me I was still learning: 'You need to prove yourself.' He said the kind of stories I was after come later.

Five years on and I was still trying to show I was worth something.

Whenever I questioned why I didn't just leave, I came up against the same dilemma: what else was there for me?

I'd lost everything.

The job helped me to forget. If I kept running, if I kept chasing exclusives and deadlines, I wouldn't have room to think about *him* and how my life was supposed to turn out.

There was also that other teeny-tiny issue of *money*. I'd been struggling since I'd broken up with my ex, so quitting was not an option. In my most delusional moments, I'd daydream about how it would feel to win the lottery. The chance to turn the page and start all over again. What would I do for that?

You always have a choice. Listen to me, Laura, you can say no, the voice in my head told me. It didn't feel like something I could turn away from, though. None of it did.

The phone rang again. Unable to face another earbashing, I pressed *send*, my eyes shutting involuntarily as I did so.

*

By 9.30 p.m. we'd filled out the basement bar in London's Soho. My team – clustered beneath the arches of the vaulted ceiling. Colonel's was a dive. Wine stains soaked into the tables. The dirty floor hidden under a layer of sawdust. A patch-up job. Something we were very familiar with on the paper.

Jamie, one of the news reporters, appeared with another bottle of cheap Rioja, topping up my glass before I could say no. I wouldn't have turned it down anyway; I'd been gasping for repeat hits ever since I'd finished my exclusive. Relishing alcohol's divine ability to help me forget.

'Hey – and me!' Sarah from the celeb desk emerged from the gloom with an empty glass. We filled her up, clinked and said 'cheers' to the end of another fraught day.

'Do you reckon we can put this through on expenses?' Jamie ran his eyes across the receipt. 'I'm planning on getting monumentally wasted.'

This was how it always played out in Colonel's. As Sarah began to bitch about one of the other reporters, my thoughts drifted. Their conversation was drowned out by the drum of feet from above, by the bar's crappy nineties playlist, but mostly by my jealous thoughts.

I'd been watching him intently all evening as he worked his way through the group. Noticing the beer slosh over his glass because she made him laugh so hard. Kate, the new features writer, had caught his attention. I tried on several occasions to meet his eye, but he was too busy holding court, regaling her with stories of when he was a junior reporter.

In the low light, after four or so glasses of wine, there

was a small resemblance to George Clooney. Grey hair, greying stubble. Angular jaw. Seventeen years older than me, he wasn't my usual type but for some reason I was drawn to him. Perhaps it was his wealth of experience and knowledge. A mentor of sorts. That old cliché. I snorted to myself. The wine was really kicking in.

I was tired of feeling invisible. I stepped away from the group, ignoring the tuts and pinched looks as I pushed through the throng of city workers. With every step I took away from them, I felt lighter. That said it all really, yet still I persisted in ignoring what my body was telling me. I'd stopped trusting my intuition long ago.

Then I felt his touch on the small of my back.

'Where you off to?' he asked in that low tone he reserved only for me.

Or so I'd thought, until I saw the way he was chatting up Kate tonight.

'Toilet!' I said indignantly, the alcohol giving away my jealousy.

'Without me?'

A wry smile moved up his face, igniting the memory of the archive room. Last week in his lunch break – with the smell of old newspaper and the electrics humming as he took me up against the door. Despite my anger, I couldn't control the prickle that had spread across my skin.

Next thing I knew, his hand was around my waist and I was being guided into the disabled toilet.

There was nothing sexy about the small airless cubicle. The tang of excrement and vomit hung around us. The unforgiving bright light strobed overhead. I grabbed hold of the disabled rail to steady myself as he tugged at my tights from behind.

Every time I tried to part my legs they sprang back together. I kicked off my right shoe, stumbling as I slipped one leg out of my tights. His hand caught my waist, pulling me back upright.

It was all so urgent, pressurized, just like life in the newsroom. His breath, warm in my ear. He was rough but the pain made me feel alive. Noise from the bar drifted through the door while my temperature rose with every thrust. My knuckles turned white as I gripped the rail.

It was over in minutes. He'd zipped himself up before I'd turned around. I rushed to keep up – a quick wipe with toilet tissue before pulling up my pants. I twisted my tights into place and tugged my skirt down to my knees. Then I met his gaze.

He hooked his finger under my chin, lifting it to reach his mouth.

'You still turn me on.'

Said like a congratulations between boozy kisses. I was still dizzy with the abruptness of it all.

'See you out there.' He unlocked the door, checked the coast was clear and left.

I felt high, but at the same time utterly empty. It didn't help that I hadn't eaten for hours. I'd been doing the usual, putting self-care on the back burner. I fell against the wall, pressing into it as I slipped my shoe back on.

I couldn't bring myself to look in the mirror, fearful of the shame and guilt that would meet me in the reflection. Instead, I stepped back into the fray, returning to the group like a homing bird. Thankful for the alcohol numbing the rawness between my legs.

'Where've you been?' Jamie asked, handing me a shot of something dark and sickly-sweet smelling. I took it and knocked it back. 'You look—' He stopped short of the insult. Instead, he mimed a brushing action. Heat rushed to my cheeks as I smoothed my sex hair down.

No one in the newsroom had any idea what was really going on. It was our little secret.

'Laura,' his voice carried across the din. His tone much firmer than it had been minutes earlier. I turned to face my boss. 'Over here.'

Ben was in a booth, sitting opposite Mark Cush, the editor of the newspaper, who only graced us with his presence on very special occasions.

All of a sudden, I was hit with a rush of importance. I was being singled out. *Me.* I imagined all the other reporters had noticed and were glowering with envy.

I shrugged back my shoulders, lifted my head and catwalked towards them.

'Good work today, Laura,' Mark congratulated.

I pushed my hair from my eyes, trying to appear sober as I slid into the empty seat.

'You've made a sparkling addition to the team.'

'Oh, I don't know about that, but thanks.' I felt more like tarnished silver.

Ben and Mark locked eyes. 'We think you've got talent, but . . .' he paused, 'there's potential for more.'

If by potential he meant fucking people over, I didn't want it. I turned to Ben, willing him to give me one of his looks that showed me he cared. Nothing in his expression told of the intimacy we'd just shared. He lifted his pint to meet his mouth. The wedding ring catching in the booth's spotlight.

'Got a job that you're going to love,' he said instead.

I braced myself. 'OK.'

'You've got an audition for *The Villa*.'

'*The Villa*?'

'A new reality dating show.'

He waited for me.

'Haven't you heard the buzz?'

I shrugged.

'Where've you been, Peters? Gold tiles on Instagram ring any bells? With a silhouette of a palm tree? Midnight last Tuesday, thousands of influencers posting at the same time. It's grown some sort of cult following already. Models, celebs, they're all getting in on it.'

He fished his mobile off the table and began scrolling. 'Click on the tile and you get this' – he turned his phone around.

A glossy sun-drenched image filled his screen. A crowd of beautiful people on a beach, drinking champagne, dancing, having the time of their lives.

I looked away.

'The whole thing's been shrouded in secrecy. There's no official press release. It's all word of mouth and a slick social media campaign.' Ben returned to his phone and cleared his throat. 'But this is what people have been saying:

'*For one week only, a group of sexy singletons will be living it up in a luxurious villa in paradise, hoping to meet their ideal type, couple up and convince the public they've met their match in order to win the cash prize of £50,000.'*

He smiled as he read out the next bit. '*With time against our contestants, what lengths will they go to in order to win?*

'But the juicy bit is what they're promising: a unique VIP experience for the viewers.' His eyes were sparkling as he returned them to me. 'Wonder what that could be?'

What was Ben getting so excited about? *The Villa* sounded boring. Another trashy dating show featuring vacuous twenty-year-olds peacocking around in bikinis. Mind-numbing chat by the pool. I couldn't think of anything duller. And the prize wasn't even that much. As for the chances of finding love on a show like that – ha! All relationships were a waste of time anyway. I'd never allow myself to get hurt again.

Somewhere in the thrum of the pub I could hear my mum's voice ring out. 'It was *just* a break-up, it's not like someone died!' So why had it left such a deep stain on my life?

'Pegged as the entertainment of the summer,' continued Ben. 'Filmed in a top-secret location . . .'

It had ended so abruptly I'd been left questioning *everything*. Why? How? Was there someone else? My thoughts had spiralled so far from reason that at one point I thought I'd actually lost my mind. Instead of moving on, I'd spent the past three years blaming myself, trying to fix the things that were wrong with me, the flaws that made him leave. Maybe that was also why I'd stayed in this job. To prove to him *I am capable*. I'm not worthless. But why can't I hear the words? They still refuse to sink in.

'Laura, are you listening?' Ben's brow crumpled. 'Anyway, that's all we know for now.'

Tired format. Dwindling viewer ratings, did anyone actually watch this kind of show any more?

As for 'luxury villa', it was more like a zoo enclosure. The sort of place where secrets were prised out of you. Perfect tabloid fodder. The Rioja had blunted my senses but finally I caught up with what they'd done.

'Wait, an audition? You entered me for this show?' I looked between them. 'Without asking me first?'

'We plan to make history; be the first paper to get a journalist on the inside. Find out what really goes on in these shows. Are they fake? Are they scripted? Are the contestants really single? Unearth the lies. Let's expose the sham.'

The rapid fire of questions was making me dizzy. When I didn't reply, he sighed again.

'Do you realize how hard it was to get you an in?' He looked sideways at Cush. 'Our picture and graphics teams spent hours editing your photos.'

I blinked.

He handed me back his mobile.

'We sent these ones in, aren't they brilliant?'

He had my Facebook photos on his phone, only they now showed a heavily photoshopped version of me. Thinner, with flawless tanned skin and platinum blonde hair. They'd even superimposed me onto a beach in the Caribbean.

My head was spinning. They couldn't be serious?

'We'll also set you up on Instagram and TikTok. Under your new name, of course. We can't have them knowing you work for us.'

'New name?'

'Thought you'd be happy. You're always whingeing how I don't send you out on the good stories.'

I bristled, suddenly aware of how he was making me appear in front of the editor.

'I don't complain.' But my voice had shrunk to something small.

'Yeah, you do.' He exchanged looks with Cush. 'Far more than you should.'

Fuck you.

'This is your big break, Peters, we need this story,' said Ben, more forcefully. 'I'm trusting you with it, show us what you've got. I'm confident you'll win them over at the audition.'

The audition. My heart quickened at the thought of it. The idea of taking my clothes off for some beauty pageant parade filled me with dread. My body wasn't what they'd promised in the photos. I'm not who they think I am. If they knew what I was really like they'd never have entered me.

'Why me?'

Cush finally chipped in. 'Because you're the only one in the office who stands a chance of getting in. You're young-ish, slim, pretty.' He glanced to Ben. 'Can I say that?' They both laughed.

'You'll have to change your appearance to match our pictures,' said Ben. 'And you'll need a new ID.'

I let out a little gasp. Was that even legal?

'Like, a fake passport?'

'Just leave that to us. You focus on your disguise.'

'But, I . . .' My words fell away. 'How long have I got?'

'Audition is Monday.'

Monday! That gave me just the weekend to prepare. There must have been a way to say no, but with Mark Cush looking directly at me, with an assumption that I wouldn't let the team down, I lacked the strength to find it.

Ben's eyes softened for the first time since our conversation began.

'Blonde.' He grinned.

'What?' I frowned at him.

A hint of lust returned to his eyes. 'You're going to look cracking as a blonde.'

CHAPTER TWO

THE REPORTER

Figtree Studios, East London

'Hiya, I'm Iris. I'm thirty-one and I'm a dental nurse from Kent.'

I blew the camera a kiss.

Lie. That was the name Ben had come up with because it was 'showbizzy'. Something that would appeal to the TV mafia. He'd shaved a few years off my age to increase my chances of being picked. The dental nurse bit, well, that was supposed to sound 'wholesome'.

'And what's your type?'

I smiled coyly, 'I'm quite picky . . .'

Another lie. I wasn't choosey at all. Not recently, anyway.

'I would say, my type is . . .' But my words dried up as I thought back over my reckless behaviour. The hook-ups I could barely remember. Then Ben. I was having an affair with a married man and I hated myself for it. I never thought I'd be the kind of girl capable of doing something like that.

'What sort of guys *don't* you like?'

That was an easy one. Fair-weather boyfriends. Men who pretend they want to spend the rest of their life with you. What's that age-old saying? Why buy the cow when you can get the milk for free? I'm talking about a guy that gets down on one knee in the most romantic setting imaginable to ask if you'd be his wife and then two months later, out of the blue, dumps you.

He told me the spark 'just died'. He couldn't explain it, but he thought it was to do with my jealousy. He said my questions were starting to feel like an interrogation and that he couldn't build a future with someone who didn't trust him. It was my fault.

Guys who make you feel worthless. Oh yeah, I knew all about those types of men.

Too serious for a dating show? Definitely. Too bitter? Almost certainly. Iris was meant to be happy-go-lucky. Iris *is* happy-go-lucky. I thrust myself into character.

'I'm not interested in guys who are obsessed with their bodies. Don't get me wrong,' I giggled, 'I like someone who takes care of themselves, but nothing's more of a turn-off than a man who spends hours preening.' I laughed again as I searched for a final superficial anecdote. 'I don't want to be fighting my man for mirror space.'

Laughter rumbled from the back of the studio. We were in some dodgy warehouse in East London. I couldn't understand what all the hype was about. If the show was going to be anything like this, I wasn't going to get my hopes up.

'Can we get some more light in here?'

A technician emerged from the darkness and dived

between the cameras, hopping between the snake's nest of wires curled across the studio floor. He twiddled a few buttons and raised the reflective umbrella, unleashing a blast of light into my eyes.

'Do you have a type then?'

They weren't giving up on this question. And why should they? It was a dating show, after all.

I stared into the shadows as if the answer would be waiting for me there. It's then that I noticed him. Arms crossed, shoulders back. The silhouette of someone strong and athletic standing just outside the circumference of light.

His gaze was fixed on me, but something about the way he was looking felt different to the media circus going on around us.

We locked eyes and he passed me a small nod. As if to reassure me I was going to be OK. The moment was fleeting and at odds with everything else going on around us, but I grabbed hold of it with both hands and straightened.

Squinting into the glare, I embraced my reply with confidence this time. Drawing an imaginary boyfriend who couldn't be more opposite to the last one. 'One hundred per cent. He's got blonde hair. He's tanned. Blue eyes. And tall – I love a tall man.' I was getting into this now.

'And how's your dating past been?'

Car crash. My ex has left me suffering with panic attacks. Anytime I now feel overwhelmed, I forget how to breathe.

The current guy is married.

The emotions I'd been holding down surged to the surface and all of a sudden I was on the cusp of crying. I bit my lip to cancel out the pain and then drew another beaming smile on my face. 'Still looking for the one.'

'That's great, sweetheart. And now can you do something for the camera.'

'Huh?'

'Show us a bit of what Iris is all about. We want to see that cheeky Iris.'

'Oh, um,' I planted my hands on my hips.

'Little twirl for us?'

'Oh, like this?' I spun around, doing my best sexy spin in my bikini and heels. I felt like a piece of rotisserie meat on a spit.

'Love it! Give us more. With a bit more energy this time.'

I lifted my arms in the air and twirled again, my new platinum blonde hair extensions whipping around after me.

'YES, you got it! Do you think you're going to win?'

Win the show? £50,000 wasn't to be sniffed at. But they weren't to know the real reason I was auditioning. Smiling convincingly, I answered: 'One hundred per cent.' I looked directly into the camera. 'Watch out, girls!'

CHAPTER THREE

THE PRODUCER

Madrid, Interview Room One

NOW

I glare at the little white fan. Anger grabs hold of me as I watch it rotate – back and forth – squeaking left to right.

Beads of sweat roll from my neck down my back, seeping into my white vest. The heat has fired up my rosacea and my cheeks are burning. I want to plunge my face into an ice-cold bucket of water.

They're doing it on purpose. Positioning the fan so it just misses me. It's one of those messed-up torture techniques that push you to the limit. Forcing you to confess under duress, even if you're innocent.

I declined a duty solicitor – or the Spanish equivalent thereof – because they promised me it would be over soon, only a matter of crossing the t's and dotting the i's.

Anyway, I've done nothing wrong. And if I needed help, it wouldn't be from them. I'd call *him*.

Picking up the paper-thin cup, I gulp down more tepid water.

Jesus. Why is there no air conditioning in here?

Detective Inspector Jose Carlos Sanchez glances sideways at his partner before repeating the question, his voice thick with a Spanish accent.

'Michelle Jessop, you had no idea what was going on?' He leans forward, his fingers locking. His crisp shirt bunches at his shoulders.

How many different ways can I answer the same question? No. NO. Should I try in Spanish?

Shaking my head, my damp hair sweeping my shoulders, I say for the umpteenth time: 'No.' But it has turned into more of a whisper.

Sanchez sighs. Cool as a cucumber, even in that constricting shirt and tie. How does he manage it? Is it a special skill police in foreign countries have – to remain composed even when the heat is cranked up?

I should take notes.

He's a bulky-looking man. Short with broad shoulders, built like a rugby player. His black hair is thinning on top and flecked grey by his temples. His stubble is peppered silver. He survives off little sleep and coffee, just like me. His eyes are kind though. Wrinkles stream out from the corners. Sanchez looks like he laughs a lot, when he isn't doing this – interrogating people. He stares directly at me, those eyes now dissembling.

'Señora Jessop, as you can appreciate, it's difficult for us to believe that you had no knowledge of what was going on.' He looks down at his notes and, again, he asks me. 'You're the producer?'

Admitting I am will single me out. He'll only misinter-pret it.

'One of,' I lie.

'One of? How many producers are there on a television show?'

How can I even begin to explain to this man the dynamics of television? It takes more than one person to bring a show to life. We're a family. The familiar spike of adrenaline fires into my system – the same rush as if I were about to go live on air. I am wired. Permanently wired.

Agitated, I shoot back: 'This is,' I pause, '*was* going to be one of the biggest shows the world had ever seen. Many make the magic happen. Do you think I could pull it off all by myself?'

The heat was biting. I'm not normally this angry. This rude. He narrows his eyes. Sanchez doesn't get it. And why should he? He's not in showbiz.

'Explain it to me. Tell me exactly who was in charge of what.'

I nod, but Sanchez's expression hardens.

'Because, Señora Jessop,' he continues, with more acidity, 'someone on your reality show is dead.' He pauses for a moment, letting the word, the death, ruminate.

It works – suddenly I'm nauseous at the reminder of her. By the pool. Rigid because rigor mortis had set in. Her cold body. Her grey skin. The blood staining her bleached hair. Our show was meant to change lives, for those starring in it, for the millions watching it. Life-changing – just not this way.

Sanchez's partner's eyes are on me now. She's wearing

a short-sleeved white shirt with the Spanish national police emblem stitched onto the breast pocket. Her hair is stretched back into an unfussy bun. Her only jewellery is stud earrings and a plain crucifix on a thin gold chain.

'And from the way things appear,' Sanchez catches my eye, 'it's looking like you're the person responsible for what happened.'

'What?' I lift my head. 'You've got to be joking.'

Sanchez holds my gaze.

He can't be serious.

'I would never joke about something like this,' he says.

I look behind, to the officer guarding the door. Spanish police wear firearms. I stare at the gun holstered at his waist – and then back at the detective.

Another flash of heat. I fight to keep the emotion from my face.

How will I make him understand? I tug at an imaginary collar around my neck.

'I'll answer your questions. But please . . .' My fingers slip on my sweat. 'I need some fresh air.'

Because I can't breathe.

The room blurs. White rains down in front of my eyes and an image of her moves in.

The one person I wasn't able to control.

CHAPTER FOUR

THE REPORTER

Spain

ONE WEEK AGO

It was the fly. Buzzing chaotically around the sugary rim of the Bacardi Breezer. That was the first thing that shifted into focus.

I blinked. Refreshing my sore, dry eyes.

Without moving, I followed its path from the can to the whitewashed wall to the polystyrene carton overspilling with kebab shavings.

The first wave of nausea rolled in.

The fly took off again, rocketing into the air. Hurtling across the room. It hovered above before nosediving to my right, landing deep in the wiry thicket of hair on his sunburnt chest.

He made a deep guttural sound as he brushed it away and then rolled over onto his front. His arms splaying around the pillow.

I let out a breath I didn't realize I'd been holding. Relieved he hadn't woken. I didn't want Ben seeing me like this.

Incoming – the second swoop of sickness. Thick and fast. Spiked with adrenaline, I searched my memory, scrambling to piece together what had happened. That familiar feeling of unaccounted-for time. Big chunks swallowed up, in which I could have done anything.

The evening had begun in the bar opposite the hotel. We'd headed out for a drink to celebrate the impossible-to-get-my-head-around-fact I'd been selected for *The Villa*. Four of us, kicking off our night in Marbella. Bar-hopping our way around the marina.

Jamie usually wrote for the crime desk, but he'd 'sacrificed' his byline for a week in the sunshine. He would be my eyes and ears on the outside, gathering background on the show while I kept in character on the inside. Dan was our photographer. And Ben: he'd flown out to bed us in. To present me with my fake ID. I wanted to believe he'd made the journey over to be with me. The truth was, he was here to make sure I didn't back out at the last minute.

I'd arrived in Spain a few days early to see if I could dig up any dirt on the show. *The Villa* producers insisted on flying me out direct from the UK, but when I told them I wanted time to work on a tan, they were understanding, not even questioning my lie. It boded well for my reporting – security was going to be lax.

After knocking back our warm-up shots, I'd found courage to question the situation.

Turning to the team, I'd said: 'Don't you think it's weird I was picked? *Me?*'

'Why?' Ben quickly replied. 'You're the full package, when you want to be.'

'Seriously though, thousands must have applied. They could've picked anyone. Why me?'

'I don't understand where your head is at with this,' said Ben.

Features were always competing with the news team for the front page and often losing out to a breaking story. This was our chance, but still.

Pressure was even greater now the paper was under threat of closure. With the changing landscape of news, *The Record*'s future was looking uncertain. We were the tabloid lagging behind; the paper that needed to go the extra mile to stay in circulation.

I took another sip of my drink. 'All I'm saying is—'

'Fuck's sake, Peters, you're in. We did it! We fooled those arrogant TV twats. Just go with it and get us the story.'

Jamie and Dan had looked on awkwardly. I'd shut up after that.

The chat then shifted into strategizing. Overcoming our biggest hurdle – where was the villa? Its location had been shrouded in mystery to keep people like us out.

Uncovering secrets was what Ben lived for and he'd come alive as we talked through ways to infiltrate their security. All I'd been given was a date and a time to be outside my hotel for pickup. I could be taken anywhere.

Strangely, that part didn't worry me. Something about disappearing was appealing. Cathartic even. I should have been thinking about the show; instead, I was obsessing about Ben. As they picked at the tapas meats, I knocked back more sangria, fantasizing about how we were going to spend an entire night together. Excited to wake up in his arms for the first time instead of just a quick fuck and goodbye.

This was where my memory got hazy.

Ben sighed heavily as he rolled his head to the other side, his flattened cheek pushing his mouth into a ripple. He wasn't even attractive. Yet I still got a jolt every time I saw him. After all my longing and fantasizing about our night together, I couldn't even remember the sex. The telltale ache between my legs was the only indication it had taken place.

As usual, I'd overcooked it. While Ben revelled in the secrecy of our affair, hiding us from Jamie and Dan, the booze added fuel to my fire. I'd lost my temper. It was my fault. I shouldn't have let my disappointment get the better of me.

I could barely bring myself to look at him now. I was sure I'd done something embarrassing. The aftertaste of last night's sangria was bitter on my tongue. The burn in my stomach was intensifying, as were my feelings of self-loathing. Of all the nights to get drunk. Of all the mornings to be hungover.

Ben had told me to stop drinking, but I'd carried on defiantly. Enjoying my power – I was now his prized asset. He *needed* me.

More haze blotted out our evening. I remembered lashing out once Jamie left to go to the toilet. The loud music thumping, and me, yelling over it, my drink spilling as I lurched towards Ben, telling him I'd had enough, he was a bastard for using me when he'd never leave his wife. The alcohol helping me forget I was also to blame for our affair. 'It's over!' I'm sure I'd screamed that.

The sheer curtains rippled. A salty breeze swept through the balcony doors into my hotel room, refreshing my clammy skin. Staring out across the green and blue marbled sea, I bit down on my lip to stop tears of regret. The air was thick with smouldering charcoal and the smell of grilled meats as the tavernas fired up their barbecues for lunch.

My stomach heaved with the thought of food and then, with panic. Soon, the car would be arriving to whisk me off to the villa: 2 p.m. sharp, outside the hotel, and I was not to be late. They'd been very clear about that. I'd been warned filming would begin the moment we arrived at our destination. Wherever that was.

I peeled back the sheet and with ever so slight movements removed myself from bed.

The cold marble was almost painful against my bare feet. Hunching into myself, I wrapped my arms over my breasts and tiptoed across the tiles into the bathroom.

I glared at my puffy reflection in the mirror, barely recognizing myself.

My shoulder-length brown hair was now long and platinum blonde, thanks to the eye-wateringly expensive extensions I'd had weaved in. My eyelashes were fake. My tan, mostly fake bar the three days I'd had in Marbella sun. My nails were plastic and pointy with French manicure tips and my smile, false, because I'd had my teeth whitened and because I was forcing my lips to stretch over them.

'Hiya, girls!' A wave of hungover madness passed through me as I practised my grand entrance into the villa one final time.

'Nice to meet you. I'm Iris.'

31

Lie.

I stared at myself coldly, my smile dropping.

How the hell was I going to pull this off?

They'd find out I was a fraud. And then what?

My stomach clenched.

What would Iris do now? I searched my reflection.

I took a step back from the mirror. Projecting myself into the newsroom. Clearing my imaginary computer screen and starting my story again. She'd get her shit together. That's what she'd do.

Ben was awake by the time I emerged from the bathroom – transformed. A picture of the character he'd created.

I immediately busied myself. Moving around the room, snatching my dress, knickers and bra from the floor, shoving them into my suitcase – which was full to bursting.

I'd been gifted an entire new wardrobe. The material was cheap. The collection looked as if it had shrunk in the wash. *Fast fashion clothing.* But I was pleased with what I'd managed to sift out from the tat. Frayed-edge denim shorts, a sequin boob tube, a little black dress, off-the-shoulder tops, killer heels, wedges, flip-flops and lots of bikinis – one for every day of the week. I'd packed optimistically.

And for my grand entrance? A revealing bikini cut high up my leg and scooped low across my breasts. I'd paired it with canary yellow shorts and gold wedges. 'Wear as little as possible. We want maximum impact when you arrive,' someone from the show had instructed. She'd actually said that. Whatever happened to gender equality?

Women looking out for each other? I guess she was also following orders.

That was the one part of my undercover mission I was looking forward to. Unmasking the creator of such sexist bullshit.

The other girls would of course be stunning. I'd already created the 'competition' in my head. Model looks, enormous breasts, tiny waists, revealing bikinis and cut-out swimsuits. I still couldn't accept I'd been chosen. My figure was OK, but nothing to stop traffic with. I was nowhere as in shape as the models you usually see on shows like this. Unless – I paused my angry thoughts – the show wouldn't be centred on looks? I laughed. *Don't be daft, what other reason could there be?*

'Laura.'

I braced for my telling off. I had a lot to make up for.

But he was smiling. 'How's the packing going?'

'Look,' I paused. 'I'm sorry about last night.'

He laughed.

'What's so funny?'

He rolled onto his side, propping his head up with his elbow. Half-wrapped in the white sheets, three-day-old stubble – he looked sexy-rugged.

'You worry too much.'

'But last night, I—'

'Hey, stop, I like it when you do the hot mess thing.'

I looked away. Tears prickling.

'What I'm trying to say is,' his eyes softening, 'stop beating yourself up. Liking a drink or two isn't a bad thing and it'll work in your favour for the show. Everyone loves a party girl.'

I wasn't sure why, but I felt completely destabilized. Empty. Dirty. In need of a hug.

'I know the job is tough and demanding, but stories like this don't come along often. You've got this, you can do it.'

Last night I hated Ben. Today, I wanted to take back everything I said.

He ran his eyes over me and grinned. 'And this new look, wow, it suits you.'

I didn't want to leave. All of a sudden, I had an overwhelming urge to be held. To crawl back underneath the sheets and lie next to him.

I was in a foreign country, looking unrecognizable, about to be thrust under a microscope. The bravado of last night had worn off.

Ben got out of bed and slipped on his boxer shorts. He riffled around his suitcase, pulled something out and presented me with it. A teddy bear. I was completely thrown by the gesture. Even though it was tacky with cheap acrylic fur and a 'hug me' T-shirt, I was touched.

'For me?'

'Don't get all sentimental, Peters. Turn it over.'

I stared at him for a long moment and then did as I was told.

Running up its back was a zip, concealed within the long hair.

'Open it up.'

It felt like something I had to do cautiously. I pulled at the zip and reached inside. The candyfloss stuffing was scratchy. I felt my way around until my fingers touched something hard. I flashed Ben an 'Are you serious?' look and then pulled out the mobile phone. It was an old silver Nokia, the ancient model you could play Snake on. Small enough to conceal inside a teddy bear.

'As soon as you've got something, you call me. Press 1 – I've saved my number into speed dial. OK?'

I was still recovering from my foolishness.

'Hide it with your clothes and other girl stuff.' He was clearly pleased with his knock-off James Bond gadget.

'Hang on' – realization striking – 'how am I going to call you if we're being filmed?'

'You'll find a way. You won't be on camera all the time. That's not how these things work.'

'Right.'

Sensing my confidence drop, he walked over and took hold of my waist. This time, he looked right into my eyes before he kissed me. A confident kiss, full of passion, a hunger for me, and then he flipped me around, planting my face into the wall. The cold spread across my cheek, awakening my senses. I knew what was coming.

His fingers circled my skin, moving in strokes towards my bikini top. The feeling of being wanted, more powerful than anything.

'You need to go,' he sighed.

I nodded, straightened myself up and swallowed hard. Forcing down everything that had passed in the last twenty-four hours.

'You'll be brilliant. I'll vote for you.'

I managed a small laugh.

'Call me as soon as.'

When I didn't answer, he shot me a look.

'Yes,' I said, obediently.

I tugged my wheelie case out the door, forcing myself not to look back. Throwing on that 'I don't give a shit' shield. Today it was harder than ever to master.

The door closed softly behind me.

The corridor smelled of damp and a thick mildew was spreading up the wall. The familiar empty feeling crept over me. I'd never felt so lonely.

I should tell him. I should charge back inside that hotel room and confess to Ben I'm not up to the job – explain how I've been faking it. I suffer from panic attacks and claustrophobia and I don't know how I'll manage being locked up in a villa.

But I couldn't find my voice. Somehow, I'd been left feeling like I was the one who had to make up for something. Must try harder. My head hurt too much to ask why and how that had happened. It was easier to shut up, accept and carry on.

I turned and headed for the lift, the wheels of my suitcase squealing at me. Ben's voice in my head.

We're counting on you, Peters.

CHAPTER FIVE

THE VIEWERS

ONE WEEK AGO

Emma from London was cooking her signature dish – spag bol. Lauren and Kylie were around the kitchen table, scrolling through their Instagram feeds.

'Have you seen this?' Kylie thrust her phone under Lauren's nose.

Lauren took in the sun-drenched images and looked up. 'A reality dating show?'

'How epic does that look?'

'Because that's what the world needs, more fly-on-the-wall, house full of nutters, reality TV crap.' Emma was rolling her eyes as she turned to face the girls.

Kylie got up to show Emma the advert. A dozen models with perfectly worked out physiques partying hard.

Emma snorted. 'Seriously tacky. They're not *real* people with *real* bodies.'

'Trust you to be cynical,' Lauren said. 'You'll be the one who gets hooked.'

'Never! Where's it supposed to be, anyway? That ad tells us nothing other than they'll be fit people.'

'Don't know, somewhere exotic with a beach and hotties,' Lauren grinned.

'Sounds like a load of crap to me,' Emma blew on the spoon before trying the sauce.

'Ready in five.'

'Are you going to watch it?' Lauren said quietly to Kylie.

'For sure. I love all that. Takes my mind off things. Plus, they often get the contestants doing crazy shit.'

'Can one of you lay the table?' Emma said.

Kylie counted out three sets of cutlery and bowls. 'I'm the same,' she admitted. 'I tune in for the bitch fights and *drama.*'

'I'll have a fork and spoon with mine, please.' Lauren said.

'Not that I really care, but what's the show called again?' Emma casually asked.

A knowing smile appeared on Kylie's face now Emma had confirmed how their week would play out. Dinners in front of the telly. Character assassinations. Laughing at other people's misfortunes.

'It's called . . .' she paused, playfully building dramatic tension, '*The Villa.*'

CHAPTER SIX

THE REPORTER

Spain

ONE WEEK AGO

There was no shade outside the hotel. Not even a columned porch to shelter under. Singed shrubs book-ended either side of the entrance. Cars were congested along the main road outside.

The two-star Hotel Basilica was the best *The Record*'s expenses could afford for my pre-show nights in Marbella.

The drinks fridge of next door's 7-Eleven hummed loudly. Faded posters of ice creams hung in the window next to sweating salami.

I ached to crawl back through the hotel's revolving doors and return to Ben. I imagined our bed, the spritz of the cross breeze keeping us cool as we lay tangled together.

An involuntary giggle burst out of me. I was slipping into some sort of heat-induced delirium by the time the sleek black Range Rover pulled up to the kerb. The window buzzed down.

'Iris O'Donnell?'

It took a moment to remember that was me.

The door swung open and a stocky man jumped from the shadows onto the sun-baked tarmac. His skin was mahogany. Hair gelled into a man bun. He wore jeans and a black waistcoat over a white T-shirt. His eyes were hidden behind aviators.

'Here, let me help you with that.' He took my suitcase. I noticed the tattoos across his knuckles. The crucifix on his forearm. A thin chain dangled as he bent forward.

He disappeared with my case and before I had a chance to thank him, he'd returned to my side.

'Ready?' The Spanish accent was strong but his pronunciation, perfect.

'Ready as I'll ever be!' I put that practised smile to work.

He held out his hand. 'Your phone,' he motioned. 'Time for us to look after it.'

I stared at him for a moment and then smiled.

'Yeah, of course. Here you go.' I turned it off and placed it into his palm, forcing myself to keep smiling as a zip-lock bag emerged from his pocket. He slipped my phone inside and sealed it.

'And your watch.'

'My watch?'

The phone I could understand, but this was weird. I unstrapped it from my wrist and passed it over more hesitantly. 'Why do you need that?'

He sealed it inside another bag and then pulled out something similar-looking. A Fitbit.

'Put this on.'

'Why?'

He thrust it towards me.

'They will explain.'

I frowned. 'Can't you tell me?'

He turned, pulling open the passenger door. The cool air conditioning burst onto my skin.

'All will be revealed soon.' He motioned for me to get in.

Warily, I strapped on the device that monitors your heart rate.

Then I took a final lingering look over my shoulder at Hotel Basilica, where Ben was. The only person out here who really knew me, and soon he'd be gone too. A last glance up and down the street at the shops and bars that, all of a sudden, didn't seem quite so washed out. I drank in my final moments of freedom and then climbed inside the leather-upholstered ride that would take me to my new home. The door slammed behind me and – with a seamless click of metal – locked shut.

The Range Rover was dark and sumptuous, cocooning me in soft black leather and walnut panels. I ran my hand across the seat, soaking up the lavishness of it all.

A tinted screen separated me from the driver. The windows were also blacked out, but from the inside. I assumed it was part of the luxury experience – or to keep up the mystery of where they were taking me.

There was a television screen embedded into the panelling. I pressed the red button, hoping for a satnav image of our location. No such luck.

His voice travelled through the intercom.

'The temperature OK for you?'

'Yeah, fine thanks.'

'Beneath the arm rest there's something to eat and drink.'

I lifted the leather casing, releasing a bluish-white glow into the gloom. Inside were just two items. A bottle of Dom Pérignon champagne and a bowl of chocolate-dipped strawberries on a bed of ice. I immediately popped one into my mouth. The fruit burst from its hard casing, releasing sweet and bitter notes.

'You'll find glasses in the pouch in front of you.'

Just the thought of more alcohol turned my stomach. 'Where're we going?'

He laughed. 'Can't tell you that, Miss O'Donnell.'

'Why not?'

He didn't reply.

'How long until we get there?'

'Hours, so relax,' his voice, well oiled. 'Enjoy it while you can.'

While I can?

With little choice, I sank back, lazily casting my eyes around for more gadgets I could play with.

I hadn't noticed the folder resting on the seat next to me until now. Black, a matt finish with the words *The Villa* embossed in gold. It looked and felt expensive. I turned the hard cover, expecting a glossy brochure packed with panoramic photos of where we were headed. Instead, I was presented with a single page.

The Rules

They were numbered. One to eleven. I reached for another strawberry to get me through the literature.

Rule Number One:
Drugs or alcohol must not be brought on the premises.

Rule Two:
You must get up whenever you hear the alarm.

Great. There went my lie-in! I bit into another strawberry, catching the crimson juice before it dripped across the page.

Rule Three:
No contact with the outside world is permitted. This includes the internet, newspapers, phone calls and conversations with anyone outside the villa.

I shooed the thought of my secret phone away.

Rule Four:
All games are compulsory.

Games? Seriously?

Rule Five:
You must not threaten or use physical violence towards any other housemate. Any bullying or discriminatory comments could lead to serious consequences.

Consequences?

> Rule Six:
> There will be no evictions. The public will decide who will
> be crowned the winners.

So, nobody gets booted out? Hang on, I'm stuck in the villa
for the entire week?

> Rule Seven:
> You will be filmed at all times with our hidden cameras. Our
> state-of-the-art microphones will pick up your every sound.
> Any attempts to interfere with our transmission will lead to
> immediate eviction.

Hang on, that's not what Ben promised. He said I'd be able
to get away, that's not how these shows work. A wave of
anxiety swept through me.

> Rule Eight:
> You must not attempt to leave. The people who enter The
> Villa do so voluntarily. For security reasons, the front door
> is locked remotely.

Trapped. No way out.

> Rule Nine:
> We will remove you from the villa if you break the rules.

Rule Ten:
We reserve the right to change the rules at any time.

And then came Rule Eleven.

CHAPTER SEVEN

THE REPORTER

Spain

ONE WEEK AGO

Rule Eleven:
Each contestant has a safe word. The safe word will be
unique to you and given on arrival. It should be used during
the games when you feel that you can't carry on.

I read it over again. Something sharp spearing my insides.
And again. Can't carry on? What sort of games were they
going to make us play? I looked up, searching the cocoon
for answers. It was the first time that I'd looked, really
studied where I was. The dark space that had at first
protected me from the angry sun now suddenly oppressive.

I pressed the button on the panel, but the window didn't
move. I tried again, punching my thumb down. Still, it
wouldn't budge. I knocked on the glass in front.

'Everything OK?' the driver's voice travelled through the
intercom.

'The window won't open.'

I was met with a wall of silence.

'HEY. How do I get it to go down?' A flash of anger in my voice this time.

Still nothing.

'Er, Hell-oo?' I knocked again.

I thought I heard a sharp intake of breath before he spoke.

'Don't worry, miss, it's for your own protection.'

'What? Who are you protecting me from?'

'I've been instructed to keep the windows shut in case we have any paparazzi following us. I was warned they'll try to get the first pictures of you.'

I felt a prickle of guilt as I was reminded of the lie I'd cooked up. Of who I really was.

'Everything is OK, miss, I've been keeping a lookout. Please try and relax.'

There was a crackle as he cut away and I was left feeling strangely wrong-footed. Had I overreacted?

My emotions were yo-yoing – already. As I'd feared they would. *Must calm down, mustn't let things get out of control.* Not like before.

It was perfectly reasonable for the production company to want to protect their investment. *Remember, this is a TV show, people will be watching, nothing will go wrong.* I took a deep breath, closed the folder and placed it on the seat.

The drive seemed to go on forever. We'd been cruising at the same speed for what felt like hours. The sound of passing cars had petered out and I sensed we were alone on some big open road. At some point we began to twist and turn. It felt like we were climbing, curving around the side of a mountain. The faint sound of crashing waves on my left. Silence to my right.

I tried to log the sounds. Anything that might signpost where I was being taken. But the steady rhythm of the car coupled with the darkness was lulling my body into sleep. Finally I surrendered to my hangover. My head flopped to the side and my eyelids rolled shut like the shopfronts I'd left behind on the promenade.

An ice-cold blast of air conditioning woke me.

'Wakey wakey, sleeping beauty.'

I blinked. My eyes were dry and sore.

'Come on, princess, time to go.'

Slowly, I pushed myself upright.

'Where am I?'

My head was pounding and something was cutting into my thighs. I looked down – my shorts had ridden up. My bikini was twisted, barely covering me.

As I hurried to straighten myself out, the screen slipped down, releasing a beam of peachy gold into the back. The setting sun was so blinding I didn't immediately notice he was holding something out.

I stared at the chunky headphones. 'What are those for?'

'You need to put them on.'

'Why?' I tried to see past the glare. 'Are we here?'

'Almost.'

'Where's the villa?'

The driver jumped out of the front seat and opened my

door. Sunlight struck my face. I squinted, following where his finger was pointing. In the clearing, circled by rocks and a cluster of heat-ravished trees, was a helicopter. The man in the cockpit gave the driver a thumbs up.

'No way! Absolutely not. I'm not going anywhere in that.' I edged backwards.

'Come on, you'll be fine.'

'But I'm afraid of heights!'

'Put these on.' He thrust the noise-cancelling headset at me again.

I was so flustered I barely noticed his hand move to my lower back. How he gently steered me in the direction of the next leg of my journey. Before I knew it, I'd been hoisted into the cockpit with my wheelie case and the grey-haired pilot with tanned arms and sunglasses was instructing me to buckle up.

'Tower, this is 6525 Delta, over,' he said into his headset.

The radio crackled.

'Go ahead 6525 Delta, Tower Maya receiving, over.'

'Permission to take off to the north with a north-east turn out.'

Jesus, where were we going?

'Permission granted, over.'

With that, the pilot pressed more buttons and the propellers came to life, slowly building speed. The whirring grew louder and soon I couldn't hear anything but a heavy hum. I couldn't see for the dust cloud rising up around us.

We rocked left to right as the helicopter lifted off, hovering for a moment like a dragonfly over a pond, and then up we rose. I clutched my stomach.

Somehow, I managed to look down – in time to catch my driver's parting expression. The dust storm had stilled and he'd removed his aviators. He was gazing up at us, his brow lined with concern. I looked back, to reassure myself I'd imagined it, but he was already a speck in the sand. We were off, flying through the sky at speed. Past the edge of Spain, launching into an expanse of bright blue ocean.

The further we travelled, the more silence came to meet us. The noise of the blades had almost completely abated. Reduced to a gentle hypnotic whirring as we floated along. The sea had marbled into turquoise and emerald. My nerves had finally calmed enough to speak. To ask the pilot the question I'd been asking since I left the hotel.

'Please can someone tell me where the hell we're going?'

Cheerfully, the pilot responded: 'Aruna.'

'Aruna? Where's that?'

His eyes moved briefly to meet mine. 'Paradise.'

CHAPTER EIGHT

THE REPORTER

Spain

ONE WEEK AGO

It rose out of the sea like a rocky iceberg.

We banked right, curling over Aruna. From above it looked like a jigsaw piece, adrift in a blanket of topaz blue. There were dramatic cliffs, rocky outcrops and horseshoe bays with white sand. I'd only ever read about these kinds of private islands. The type you had to 'enquire' about because they were so exclusive. The pilot was right. It was paradise.

But as my gaze stretched back to the empty horizon, a small thought tapped on my shoulder. We were going to be completely and utterly alone out here.

Before I had time to deconstruct the terrifying thought, the pilot spoke into his headset and then began adjusting dials. The dashboard flickered. He pushed the control stick away and I felt my stomach lurch as we began our descent.

The ground rushed up at us. I tried to take in as much as I could. Mental snapshots that I could feed back to Ben.

An enormous white compound. *Snap*. An ancient yellow-stoned fort on the other side of the island. *Snap snap*. Between two rectangular Portakabins, presumably for the production crew.

An entire island to ourselves? This wasn't some budget dating show. What the hell had Ben got me into? Millions – I swallowed – *millions* had been spent on this set-up.

We landed on a similarly desolate clearing to the one we'd left from. Only this time there was a small army of people waiting.

'Head, down!' A woman with an earpiece and a clipboard ran towards me.

We bowed our way out of the wind tunnel. No sooner were we at a safe distance than the rotary blades sped up and the helicopter rose into the air. My only getaway off the island, vanishing.

Two more women, dressed in black combat trousers and T-shirts with walkie-talkies looped around their belts, approached. I was hurriedly frogmarched in the direction of the walled compound. A third woman trailed behind with my suitcase, battling with the terrain as she yanked it across the stones.

'Wait here.' The woman with the headset stopped abruptly.

Before me lay a red carpet. Unfurling like a lizard's tongue across white dust and rocks, leading all the way up to a gold-studded black door.

The woman with short red hair and a manic expression thrust her hand in my face. Her fingers stretched wide. 'Five minutes and you're up.'

I reached inside my clutch bag for my make-up. The tremor that had suddenly taken hold made me drop my lip gloss into the dust. I snatched it up and applied it hastily.

'Two minutes.' The woman in charge showed me her fingers. I counted down the seconds in my head.

Nothing about *The Villa* had seemed real until this moment. The cameras, the drama, actually seeing where I'd be caged – it was rushing at me faster than I could think.

Finally, the woman locked eyes with me. 'You're the first in, so make a splash.'

Splash?

'OK, and go. GO.'

Cameramen were appearing out of nowhere, their lenses trained on my face. There was an explosion of hot light. People were rushing around in the shadows, signalling directions.

Remember, you're beautiful. Fun. Desirable. You're the girl next door looking to meet a kind, funny guy who's tall with blonde hair and blue eyes – a perfect 10.

Was it too late to tell them? I'm an emotional wreck and sometimes I'm not in control of my emotions.

Listen up. You're Iris, Iris O'Donnell, a dental nurse from Kent, who loves animals and has signed up to star in The Villa *to find love.*

The wind whipped up behind, pushing me onto the red carpet. This was it. There was no turning back now. I kicked my legs into action and started walking.

CHAPTER NINE

THE PRODUCER

Madrid, Interview Room One

NOW

I'm not under arrest. I'm free to go whenever I like. I'm here to help them understand. The mantra I've been repeating since my little wobble.

I'm embarrassed I let myself go. I shouldn't have allowed them to see me panic like that. But it's made Detective Inspector Sanchez ease up. I knew he had a heart and it's clear now that he needs me, and my job is to help him see.

'Tell me everything about the villa,' he says. 'Why the island?'

Pride ignites.

'Those views for starters,' I say. 'The panoramic of the sea, the cliffs, no one around for miles. I knew it would look epic on camera.'

Sanchez leans in. 'So, you chose it because it was isolated?'

I look to his partner. 'It was perfect.'

'I see.'

The accusatory tone is back already and I'm overwhelmed with the urge to explain.

'We were offering our viewers an exclusive experience. VIP access to the villa. We couldn't let anyone take that from them. We couldn't risk any press leaks.'

The detective swaps another glance with the female officer.

'Millions had been invested. We had to protect that.'

Why are they still exchanging glances?

'We were also protecting the contestants.'

'Protecting them!' Sanchez rocked back in his chair and laughed. 'You did a good job of that, didn't you, señora? Perimeter wall, razor wire, security guards and dog patrols.'

Sanchez tapped his notes with the biro.

'That's not protection, that's a prison. Did you want the villa to be a prison, Señora Jessop?'

Idiot.

'We weren't holding them prisoner. It was to keep people out.'

'Keep who out?'

'Nosy reporters. Crazy fans. Nutters who'd do anything to get a selfie inside the villa. In 2018 the Big Brother House was broken into by two YouTubers. That wasn't going to be us.'

Sanchez looks at me blankly. I suppose he thinks he's above watching reality TV, but shows like mine offer a unique insight into human behaviour. Revealing how we respond under pressure. The lengths we'll go to in order to win. Not too dissimilar to the workings of the criminal mind. He could learn a lot from me.

'People will do anything for content,' I say instead.

'Including yourself?'

A silence sits heavily on the room. I sip my water; the swallow is loud in my ears.

'Tell me more about the villa.'

I want to be honest. I want to lay myself bare, but he's weaponizing everything I say.

'The architect who designed the villa is famous for his ultra-modern creations,' I pause, thinking of something that might please him. 'And we only used local contractors to build it.'

It gets a small nod from Sanchez. See, we're not some evil corporation. Figtree Studios had given Spain a landmark to be remembered by. That had been my vision. It had been his vision, too. Our sponsor.

'And the cameras? I want to know everything about them,' he says.

I let out a little breath. Relieved Sanchez hadn't thought to ask where the funding had come from.

The cameras. What reality shows are famous for. Ours were state of the art. We'd almost blown our entire budget on them.

'Ninety-two of them,' I explain. 'Motion sensitive.'

'Everywhere?'

'Mostly everywhere . . . except . . .'

'Except?'

'Not in the toilets. Jeez, nobody wants to see that.'

My laugh dies in my throat when I see Sanchez isn't joining in.

'We need to see the recordings. The camera inside the pool is a priority.'

'Of course.' Although even I haven't seen that footage yet. There wasn't time, not after the alarm was raised.

'All the recordings,' he stresses.

'Not a problem.'

I didn't see it as withholding information. I didn't think it was relevant because it wasn't 'officially' *The Villa*. Floating in the ocean. Tucked out of sight in the bay – our love boat.

Cameras were also hidden there.

CHAPTER TEN

THE REPORTER

Aruna, Balearic Islands

DAY ONE, *THE VILLA*

It had a smell of forensic newness. As if the protective covers had been ripped off moments earlier. The paint was still drying. The surfaces had been washed down and the wooden decking was soaking up its final coat of wood stain. The aroma of turpentine hung around me like a low mist, but none of that mattered as I gazed back at my new home, dazzling in the setting sun.

The door had opened into the garden and I could have been teleported into the future. With its chrome and white surfaces, sharp angles, dramatic floor-to-ceiling windows, the villa was stunning in its stark simplicity. It was spread across three floors. Three rectangular blocks stacked and staggered towards a cliff edge.

Aside from the palm trees, the pointy cypresses and the rainbow plant beds, the garden was almost entirely made of decking.

The garden was broken into terraces. At the top was a

hot tub with panoramic views across the ocean. The middle terrace boasted an enormous dining table with transparent thrones for chairs. The centrepiece: a golden bowl over-spilling with grapes and exotic fruits. It reminded me of the banquet table in *Beauty and the Beast*.

Nearby was a fire feature. One of those ultra-modern designs, encased in a glass box with a matt black flume tipping smoke into the sky. Purely decorative as I didn't feel any heat coming off it.

I made my way down the steps towards the sea. *This is more like it*, I smiled, *this is where I'll park myself for the entirety of my time here*. Stretched out before me was an infinity pool. Sleek, pristine, dissolving into the ocean. Another sharply executed design.

Nearby were oversized beanbags and rattan chairs pitted with pink cushions. There was also a bar and a ping-pong table and a gym zone. Somewhere I wouldn't be venturing. As far as I was concerned, I was on holiday for a week bar the odd report back to Ben. He'd parachuted me into this drama. He could take what he got. A flicker of rebellion returning.

Now I'd reached the furthest I could go, with only a shoulder-high transparent wall separating me from the thirty-foot drop to the sea below. Cupping my hands over the edge, I gripped on tightly. I'm cautious of heights, always have been. The time I froze on the Eiffel Tower and had to be helped down by security will be for ever burned into my memory. Thankfully there was a wall to protect me now, and I had to trust in it. *Trust* – something I also struggle with.

Lifting onto my toes, I peered over the barrier.

The cliff face plunged into the ocean so cleanly it could have been sliced with a cheese wire. There was no sign of the white sand beaches I'd seen from the air. Only rocks and hostile choppy water.

I tore my eyes back to the horizon. To the spectacular fading sky before me – glowing orange and red like dying embers in a fire.

I take it all back, Ben. A hint of a smile crossing my face. This was far better than I'd ever imagined it would be. I revelled in being the first to set foot inside somewhere untouched. Somewhere without a past. A place I could be someone entirely different. For a brief moment, I forgot about the twelve-foot solid steel perimeter wall that penned me in. I dismissed the cameras that were lurking. For the briefest moment, I actually forgot I was in a game show and that I had a job to do. It was just me, at the end of the earth, catching my breath.

'You have got to be kidd-ing me!'

I spun around as the door was closing and a twenty-something blonde woman was sashaying across the decking. Her sculpted bronzed legs shimmered. Her enormous breasts bounced violently in her triangular bikini, her high heels making a loud clonking noise across the wood.

She stopped. Looked around her and exclaimed: 'This is unreal!' Shielding her eyes from the sun: 'Un-real.'

An overwhelming desire to pretend I hadn't seen her took hold.

Ben. His face, always swimming back into my view. The

pressure to not let him down returning. I wasn't going to get him his exclusive being a wallflower. I forced myself to wave enthusiastically. 'Hey, over here.'

She startled, fluttering her hand theatrically. 'You scared me, babe!' She pinned on a smile – an even whiter, more practised one than mine – and headed over.

'Wow, you're stunning! Love your bikini, it's gorgeous.' She introduced herself with a light lip-brush of my cheeks. 'Hiya, I'm Becky.' Within seconds her eyes had left mine and were searching for something more interesting.

'Is that for us?' She zeroed in on a bottle of something on the bar, swimming in a white ice bucket. 'Yaaass, gimmie some of that!'

She tore off, her blonde hair swinging across her back. Her bum, so pert it didn't jiggle once. She was a younger, thinner and much prettier version of me. That's all I could think as I caught my reflection in the floor-to-ceiling windows, striding to keep up.

She pulled the bottle from its bath. Becky eased off the cork with an air of confidence. Her kohl-ringed eyes twinkled as she turned to me. 'Let's get stuck in!'

My stomach turned at the sight of the froth brimming in the neon pink flute. I wanted to scream *no* but then, out of the corner of an eye, I noticed the red light. Fixed to the ceiling. Blinking.

I took the flute from her, flexing my smile.

'Cheers.' We clinked glasses.

'Hashtag, new besties!' Becky giggled, tipping back her drink.

Besties? We didn't even know each other. She was

everything I'd feared I'd be cooped up with for a week. Fake, vacuous. Ben was going to love her.

She brushed her poker-straight hair from her eyes. Her lips were plumped with filler and overdrawn with liner and gloss. Most of her face looked like it had been 'enhanced'. A crying shame, because her natural features were delicate. Despite being irked by her arrival, I felt a maternal pang, wishing someone had shaken some sense into Becky before she went under the knife. She couldn't have been more than twenty-five.

This was my moment. If I was reporting on a breaking story, this would be when I'd charge in with questions. Superficial ice-breakers swiftly followed by something much more probing to peel back the layers. *How are you feeling? How does being here make you feel?* I'd try and find out who Becky really was.

Instead, I was panicking about the logistics. Where were we going to sleep? What were we going to eat? What were we going to do all day? What were the games? *Safe word. Rules.* The otherworldliness of what I'd been thrust into had paralysed me. Instead of leaping into action, I stared at her dumbly.

'What are you looking for?' she said.

'Oh,' I reddened. 'Nothing, sorry.'

'Nothing?' she laughed. 'Think you've come to the wrong place, babe.' A twinkle in her eyes. 'What are you looking for in a guy, you know, what's your type?'

I had this one covered. 'Well,' I smiled coyly, 'I'd like to meet someone tall, who's got blonde hair and blue eyes.'

Her overplucked eyebrow lifted.

'Who's got a good body.'

She nodded approvingly.

'Who's funny, and kind, and—'

'Bless. My sister's mates are all looking to meet someone *kind*. I guess that becomes more important when you get older.'

Older. Ouch. The stab felt deliberate.

Her manicured fingers tightened around her drink. She stared at me, wide-eyed, willing me to reciprocate with a question.

What I really wanted to ask was why someone as pretty as her needed to go on a dating show. But I stuck to Ben's script. 'What sort of guy are you looking to meet?'

The moment she'd been waiting for. She shook her hair like a show pony before straightening, determination filling her face.

'Where do I start? So, I've this epic checklist when it comes to men. They must be smart, funny, fit – obviously – loyal, and they've got to love animals. I've two dogs and they'll always come first.' Her voice fell into a simper. 'Two cockapoos, my babies!' She leaned against the bar. 'I've had boyfriends – but they only last six months; that's around the time I get bored.'

'Six months is the longest you've ever been with someone?'

She laughed. 'I'm a bit of a diva, me. Never been dumped. I actually don't know what I'd do if I was.'

The information didn't come as a surprise. She reminded me of the popular girls at school. The ones who commanded all the attention. Always the prettiest girl in the room. She would never have entertained an affair with her married boss. Becky wouldn't have been dumped by her fiancé. I turned the anger I felt at myself onto her.

'Are you nervous about meeting the guys? What if they don't like you?'

She snorted. 'I've got this, babe!'

She knocked the remainder of her drink back with an air of insult. I parted my mouth to speak, regretful of the bad feeling I'd created, of the bitterness I'd let escape, and then, the door opened.

Her curvaceous body was silhouetted by the lights. The camera flash illuminating her outline like lightning in an electrical storm. There they were again – the shadowy figures – rushing back and forth. Then the huge metal door, as dense as a bank vault's, slammed shut.

CHAPTER ELEVEN

THE REPORTER

Aruna, Balearic Islands

DAY ONE, *THE VILLA*

She stood perfectly still.

Becky leapt into action. 'Babe!' She waved. 'Over here.'

Blinking like she'd woken from a long sleep, the woman by the door searched for us.

Becky bounced, arcing her arm through the air. 'Come join the paaar-ty, hun.'

Our new housemate slowly came to life as if she was putting the pieces of herself back together.

She was petite with a sexy hourglass figure. Her shiny black hair was long and tousled into loose waves. Her brown skin popped against the bright fuchsia of her swimsuit. She wore matching pink flip-flops and a turquoise sarong, knotted at the hip. Its tassels jangled as she moved towards us.

I could tell by the way she carried herself she was less confident than Becky. Reserved and classy. She wasn't who you'd typically expect to see on a show like this. But then, nor was I.

She arrived with a hesitant smile and Becky immediately proffered a drink.

'Get this down you, girl.'

While she took a hesitant sip, Becky charged in with compliments, identical to the ones she'd handed me.

'You look incredible,' Becky said.

She avoided eye contact as she replied. 'Thank you.'

'What's your name?'

'Angela.'

'Where're you from?'

'Basingstoke.'

'Yeah, but where are you *originally* from?'

My insides curdled.

'My family are from Turkey.'

'Oh nice. What do you do?'

Angela's gaze lowered again. 'I'm a solicitor.'

There was a strained, competitive pause and then Becky quickly turned the conversation back to herself.

'I could have been a barrister, but Mum said I was too pretty for all that. I'd be wasting my looks so that's why I got into fashion.'

'You're a model?' I asked.

'An influencer.'

I knew what that was. Half the people I wrote about for the paper were the new breed of celebrity, but Angela clearly had no idea. Only adding to Becky's growing feeling of inferiority.

'Where do you think we are?' I changed the subject.

'Who cares!' Becky snorted. 'We're on an island and it's hot. That's all I give a shit about.'

Wow, this was hard work. I returned to Angela. 'So! How about you? Are you looking for love? Is there a type of guy you're after?'

'Just *a* guy would be nice,' she replied.

'Oh really? What's your story?' Becky moved in on her.

Angela will clam up. Someone as reserved as her won't fall for Becky's one-upmanship.

But to my surprise, she was desperate to tell her story. As if she'd been bottling it up to breaking point.

'Been single for three years and had my heart broken too many times to count.'

'Oh, babe.' Becky clutched her heart.

'I'm always let down on dates. It's never what I expect. We don't get on. We don't have any common ground.'

'Think you could be too picky?'

'It doesn't help that I'm always working. I don't have time to meet anyone. When I do go out it usually ends up being some bender which I barely remember when I wake up. Lately, I've been going for women.' She paused. 'There's so much chaos in my life. God. I'm too old to be living like this.' She shrugged. 'I don't know, maybe I should just have a baby.'

Wow. Angela was more all over the place than me. It was ashamedly reassuring.

'How old are you? If you don't mind me asking?' said Becky.

'Twenty-eight.'

A pang of anxiety.

'That's plenty of time to meet a guy. Or a girl.'

'Maybe. I don't know what your mum and dad are like,

but having pushy parents isn't helping. They're always on my case. "You're twenty-eight, you have to get married, you need to start a family. You've got three years left before no one wants you."'

There it was again. Talk of being on the shelf. A stabbing reminder of what I'd lost. While Becky and Angela swapped advice, I found myself picking at the old wound. The life we'd mapped out together. I thought back to that crisp wintry morning he'd woken me at the crack of dawn, dragged me out of the cottage we'd rented in Cornwall to show me the sun rise above the ocean. I was wearing my brushed cotton PJs. The frosted earth had crunched under my slipper boots. As he'd distracted me with the view of the lighthouse, he'd silently dropped to the ground, one knee ploughed into the ice-crusted footpath. 'Will you marry me?' A diamond ring shaking between his thumb and fore-finger. It had been so perfect in its cheesy imperfection.

I shut my eyes, pressing the feeling of loss away.

'. . . Anyway, so that's why I'm in here, to meet someone before my parents pick out a husband for me.'

Zoning back into the conversation, I caught the tail end of Angela's story.

'You're actually hoping to meet your future husband in here?' Becky couldn't hide her shock.

It was obvious why Becky was on the show – to find sponsorship deals. To get people like me to write stories about her. But who was I to judge? I was hardly being genuine. Scratch the surface and you'd find all kinds of secrets.

'Why else would I be here?' Angela said innocently.

There was a sudden bang behind us. We all turned.

'Heeey ladies!'

Oozing with confidence and much older than any of us, our new housemate clearly didn't seem to care about revealing her lumps and bumps. She catwalked the boards in a size-too-small red bikini, her face shaded by a wide-brimmed hat and oversized sunglasses, waving as if she was serenading her fans on the red carpet.

'Hell-ooo, gorgeous girls. Annie is *in* the villa.'

It seemed a pantomime performance for the cameras, but her arrival instantly lifted the mood, cutting through the tension that had stagnated around us.

'I'm here for one thing, and one thing only, to find myself a gorgeous young hunk of a man,' she announced in a faux posh accent. 'As long he's got a six-pack and knows how to mix a good martini, I'll be happy.'

Becky didn't even need to put a glass into her hand. Annie yanked the bottle from the ice bucket and, with an air of ceremony, lifted it to her lips, taking an enormous swig, her eyes enlarging as the bubbles slipped down her throat.

She was overdone. But magnetic. At that moment it occurred to me what an unlikely but explosive combination we all made. Despite being polar opposites, I had this strange feeling there was something that connected us. Something we all had in common. I couldn't put my finger on what though.

Annie held the bottle at me with her outstretched arm. 'You next,' she gave me a nod of encouragement.

We passed the champagne between us like a rite of

passage. With every swig, our camaraderie grew. Any initial unease, any reservations we'd had about each other, seemed to dissolve as we grew more and more light-headed. We were putting the world to rights. All thoughts of heartbreak and dating disasters – pushed aside. We were lost in belly laughter when the mechanical grinding shook the villa.

'Hey, what's going on?' Annie swung around.

'Shhhh, quiet.' My eyes searched the gardens.

The noise swelled, frightening the birds out from the branches. They scattered like confetti across the fading sky.

Up it rose from behind the pool. Sliding into the sunset. The vibrations sending ripples across the water.

'What is it?' whispered Becky.

'I have no idea,' Angela said.

'Are we supposed to do something?' Becky looked to me.

I shook my head. 'I don't know.'

'This is a game,' Angela said.

'What makes you say that?' said Becky.

'Didn't you read The Rules on the way over?'

'Contestants!' A woman's voice hushed us into silence.

'Oh my God, who's that?' Becky's hair whipped my face as she jerked around.

'Contestants . . . gather by the pool.'

CHAPTER TWELVE

THE REPORTER

Aruna, Balearic Islands

DAY ONE, *THE VILLA*

Her voice was everywhere – circling us, weaving between us. Sweeping through the villa with the ocean breeze.

Annie was first to confront her. 'Come on, girls,' she said, turning and striding towards the cinema-sized screen.

I had to concentrate on where I was placing my feet. The welcome drinks had gone to my head, and looking around, it seemed we'd all fallen victim to the champagne's potency. We formed an unsteady line along the pool edge. Becky took hold of my waist, jerking me into her. I bristled, my hands curling into tight balls. I wanted to push her off, but I could sense whatever was approaching would be a key moment. I could feel the cameras trained on our faces. I remained in character and gave Becky a friendly squeeze and smiled.

THE VILLA exploded onto the screen in bold gold lettering and someone along our line cheered. Becky snaked her hips, knocking me sideways.

As music blasted, the letters shattered, slowly fading

from view. There was a long pause and then, from the darkness, a woman's face emerged.

She looked similar to Becky. Barbie-like, only she was entirely computer generated. Her voice was husky, a low sexy growl that lingered on vowels.

'Wel-come, ladies.'

There was another stunned silence and then came the hooting. Annie punched the air, yelling at the screen as if she were watching a sports match. Becky joined in, bouncing up and down. I rooted myself, determined not to let her take me with her.

'Ladies, are you buzzing?'

The women shrieked, they clapped.

'Are you gagging to meet your love match?'

There was a 'hell yes!' from Annie.

I stood quietly. Giddy, mesmerized by how lifelike this woman's face was.

'Well,' she smiled, 'I'm almost ready to introduce them.'

'Give us the boys!' Annie demanded.

The presenter winked at Annie. Could she see us? How were they doing this?

'There's something you must know first,' she said. '*The Villa* is making history. We're the world's first reality show to stream our content live on the internet. Great Britain, the world, is watching everything you do, twenty-four hours a day with our unique VIP viewing experience.'

My stomach knotted.

'With the press of a button our viewers can move between our cameras. Zoom in on their favourite characters. They can follow you *everywhere* you go.'

Is she serious?

'There're no regulatory boards to spoil our fun. No Ofcom rules. So, you can drink as much as you like. Say what you like. You can do. Whatever. You. Want.'

'This is insane!' Becky looked between us. 'She's having us on?'

'Are we being filmed now?' I said.

'Correct, Iris. The livestream began on your arrival.'

'Can we really do whatever the fuck we like?' Becky shouted rebelliously.

'Ladies,' the presenter replied, 'a little reminder. No one leaves the island until the show is over. You will face challenges. The most loved-up couple wins. The audience decides who will be crowned winner.'

On the word *winner*, jet flames spewed out of the ground around us. A force of heat hitting us from all directions.

'LET THE GAMES BEGIN!'

With that, her image shrank into a crackled line. The screen slipped back into its pocket, returning the ocean view to us.

While the others exploded into celebration, I found myself quickly feeling sober. Studying the villa with fresh eyes.

The sunset had sunk into a bruised purple, only a muted red lingering on the horizon. The trees had become a mass of black. The girls had also turned into silhouettes, twirling around the pool in the twilight, high on alcohol and the bombshell that the mystery presenter had delivered.

No regulations. *Freedom.*

The words hummed in my thoughts as I quietly removed

myself from the party. My body, drawn back to the ocean, which had deepened even further, into an inky purple. I managed to mute the girls' shrieks and tune my ears into the waves' frequency. The faint lapping against the rocks.

It was then, within the stillness, before the vast Mediterranean seascape, that I first felt it.

A current of unease that was so fierce it made my hairs stand on end.

CHAPTER THIRTEEN

THE VIEWERS

FIVE MILLION VIEWERS

Carly from Brighton had planned for a quiet night in with her boyfriend, but he'd let the boys talk him into inviting them over. Jason had a fifty-inch flatscreen TV and his friends had hijacked the controller.

'Found her!'

'Yaasss, bro. Show me.' Phil tried grabbing the phone off Dan.

'In a minute. Oh my God,' Dan's eyes stretched wide as he scrolled through Becky's Instagram page. 'Check this out,' he held up a photo of Becky in a lacy red bra and thong. The caption beneath read *Never stop exploring* with a wink emoji. 'How banging's that?'

Carly crossed her arms, shooting Jason a look, but as usual, he was too busy fawning over his mates to notice her silent protest.

'Hey, never mind the Gram, look what you can do with this.' Phil's laptop was linked to the TV and with silver membership he'd unlocked the feature that allowed viewers to swap between rooms. There were little pulsing red icons showing the contestants' heart rates and Phil had even worked out how to pause a livestream and zoom in on an image.

He zoomed in on Becky's breasts.

'Whoa, look at those!'

Closer, until they filled the entire screen.

'Pervert!' Carly hissed.

'Oh, get over yourself. She's asking for it with Instagram pictures like that. Jason thinks it's funny, don't you, mate?'

Jason averted his eyes.

Carly glared at her boyfriend as if to say, *Stand up for yourself, for me. Just once.* For some reason, watching the show was stirring up deep unresolved anger. She turned to the boys.

'Press play, *now*.'

'OK, OK, chill out,' said Dan.

He returned to camera eight near the swimming pool – in time to catch Annie's entrance into the villa. No sooner had the forty-seven-year-old appeared on screen, the boys were back with their running commentary.

They exchanged looks and sniggered.

'Are you serious?' said Dan. 'Nobody wants to look at that. We want fit birds. Who's going to cop off with her?'

'If you put a bag over her head, maybe,' Phil said.

'Any hole's a goal,' Dan snickered.

Carly stood up.

'Where you going?' Jason said.

'I'm not listening to this.'

'Don't get all wound up, it's only a stupid show.'

'Come on, Carly,' said Dan. 'We're just messing. Why are you so bothered, it's not like these people matter.'

'I'll be upstairs.' Carly made a point of slamming the door on her exit.

Jason let a few minutes pass and then turned to his friends.

'Iris is fit, can you zoom in on her?'

CHAPTER FOURTEEN

THE PRODUCER

Madrid, Interview Room One

NOW

'Why stream the show on the internet?' The detective sits back heavily in his chair. 'In my country, we also have reality productions like *Big Brother*, but they appear on TV.'

Big Brother is nothing like *The Villa*.

'The whole point of *The Villa* was to produce something fresh and exciting,' I fight back. 'Audiences want more from their viewing experience. The round-the-clock access and unprecedented control of the stream and decision-making feed their insatiable appetites.'

He looks disgusted.

'I wanted *The Villa* to be a game changer in livestream entertainment. We broke the world record for the most watched show – did you know that?' I say proudly.

'Or,' he carries on, disinterested, 'is the real reason you chose to stream because no network was interested?'

I snort. 'No.'

'Really?' Sanchez baits.

'Why jump through Ofcom's hoops when I didn't need to? This way, our viewers got real entertainment in real time. Access to all areas. Like I said, VIP treatment. That's what everyone wants, isn't it? To feel special. And the best bit? Our viewers didn't even have to get dressed up to take part, they could be a VIP from the comfort of their living room.'

I clear my throat.

'And then there's the *insane* amount of money we were earning from our subscription fee – you wouldn't get that from TV. Pay per view,' I clarify with a nod to the puzzled-looking detective. 'People paid to watch what our contestants were getting up to, around the clock. On top of that, there's our membership scheme, with gold patrons being awarded the biggest concessions.'

'Concessions?'

'The power to vote in real time.' I smile. 'To influence.'

It really was a genius idea of mine.

He's frowning again. It's OK, I didn't expect him to catch on.

'*The Villa* was printing money!' I move on quickly. 'We were earning from the subscriptions, the voting and sponsorship deals. You wouldn't believe how much we got paid to feature those pink champagne flutes. *That*, Detective, is why we chose to livestream.' I sit back.

Sanchez laughs. 'You're missing my point.'

I frown. 'I am?'

'Where did the start-up money come from? Without a television contract you had no collateral.'

I'm still frowning.

'Who paid for *The Villa*?'

I'd wondered how long it would take for him to ask. I won't tell. The only person to believe in me. 'What do you mean?' I shrug.

'Funding, señora. Who bankrolled your little show?'

Little. *Little*. And then I notice the slight curling of his lips. The enjoyment. *I see what you're doing, Sanchez.*

'Investors.' I leave it there.

'Who does the island belong to?'

I stare at him.

'Who built the villa?'

I blink.

'I can find out.' He pauses. 'Are you protecting someone?'

Sanchez leans in.

'Is he Spanish?' He laughs.

My eyes narrow.

'You think you can keep it a secret? There're records for things like that. And I'm willing to bet whoever owns Aruna funded your show.' A look of disgust returning. 'But for what reason someone would want to do that, I'd very much like to know.'

CHAPTER FIFTEEN

THE REPORTER

Aruna, Balearic Islands

DAY ONE, *THE VILLA*

We'd found Aladdin's cave. A sparkling white bathroom with our very own make-up stations, brimming with lipsticks, glosses, highlighters, plus every hair styling tool you could ever want.

The mirrors were ringed in bulbs. Old Hollywood glamour-style. But that's where the nods to the past ended. Everything else was modern, minimalist and hotel-clean. White marble countertops. Rolled towels stacked into pyramids. The fresh scent of cedar pine pumping through the ventilation. The showers were vast and unleashed rainfall amounts of water.

Cheesy dance classics belted out, shifting the mood back to fun.

'What do you reckon the guys will be like?' Becky asked, reminding us all that tonight wasn't just about us.

'Lookie what I've found,' Annie marched into the room with a fresh bottle. 'There's an entire champagne fridge out there waiting to be drained. It's not Bolly, but it's drinkable!' She worked her way around the room, topping up our flutes. 'There's more fridges with food but they can't seriously expect us to cook for ourselves, can they?'

'I'm on a diet,' announced Becky.

'Of course you are, darling. Nobody's interested in solids when we have this to get through.' Annie made a toast. 'Eating is cheating! So! What have I missed?'

Becky's nose was pressed up to the mirror. She gazed intensely at her reflection, carefully drawing a feline flick across her eyes. 'We're wondering about the boys.'

'They better be fit and mind-blowing in bed. *And*, blessed with huge . . . ahem.'

'Hands?' Becky finished her sentence.

They both erupted into laughter. Annie fell back onto the chaise longue. 'I could do with a man right now, feeding me grapes while I lie here like this.'

She sprawled across the red velvet fabric.

Angela cast me a look. 'Here, this will look pretty on you.' She smiled and handed me a pink lipstick.

'I'm not used to wearing something that bright.'

'It'll suit you, try it on.'

Out of the corner of my eye I noticed Annie heave herself up and move in our direction. She sat down heavily on the stool next to me. Planting her elbow on the counter, her chin cupped in her hand. She leaned in.

'So, girls! What are you talking about?'

Angela passed me another weary look. 'Nothing, just swapping make-up.'

'Code for "we've got gossip". Darlings, come on, you

can't keep secrets from Annie.' Her eyes latched onto me. 'Tell me a secret, something you haven't told anyone. What do you do when you're not starring on shows like these?'

My face burned under the spotlight of her drunken interrogation. Did she know? What if she were here under the same guise as me? Two journalists – no, that would be ridiculous.

'I look into people's mouths all day long. Not very glam. I'm a dental nurse.'

She pulled away. 'Grim. Bet you've seen some real *filth*?'

Why did everything Annie say have to sound so deviant? And it seemed forced. Like it wasn't really *her*.

'Where's your practice based?' Angela asked.

I hadn't prepared for this question. *Shit*. I didn't think anyone would actually care. I said the first thing that fell into my head. 'Lydd.' Somewhere I once wrote a story about. A seaside town in Kent with a pebble beach. So tiny, nobody would have heard of it.

'Oh! I've a client down there!'

I looked away. Hiding my face from Angela. She mustn't see the lies I was frantically pulling together. She was clever, and like me, Angela made a living from reading people.

'Do you know the Tea Cabin on the Parade? The coffee's excellent there, and the cinnamon rolls, to die for.' Her hazel eyes were bright, expecting me to share something with her. 'It's so peaceful, looking out on the sea—'

'Never heard of it.' Forcing an abrupt end.

She recoiled, a look of disappointment moving across her features, and I immediately felt bad.

'Well, you should go sometime,' she said more softly.

Annie thrust herself between us. 'Come look at the rooms. They're sublime!'

I'd been so caught in panic I hadn't noticed she'd gone and come back. The interruption was a chance to catch my breath, work on my story.

'The rooms are open?' Becky tore herself away from her reflection.

They were locked when we first entered the villa.

'Wait up, I'm coming,' she said.

We followed Annie's lead. As we were leaving the bath-room, Angela stopped. 'Hey, who's that for?' She pointed to a fifth dressing table.

Becky shrugged. 'Come on, let's go.'

We marched in a clumsy line, the click-clack of our heels echoing into the corridor. The bedrooms were to our left. A view of the sea to our right. The sunset had melted away and I couldn't see anything except a mass of black pricked with stars. I wondered how we must appear to passing boats? An illuminated cube on a cliff edge. Like a lighthouse warding them off the rocks. Only, this place felt far from safe.

'This is me!' Annie peeled off. My room was next to hers. Iris, looped in pink marker across a solid white door. I turned the handle, relieved I had a space for myself.

The smell of newness rushed towards me. Followed by cold air and then the blinding brightness of the white décor.

In the centre of the room was a large double bed. Suspended from the wall, it gave the illusion of floating inside the big empty space. It was dressed up in a thick white duvet to combat the fierce air conditioning and decorated with scatter cushions. A white fur throw was folded neatly at the end and opposite the bed was a cupboard. Next to that, my suitcase. Open on a rack and – empty.

The bear. The phone. I searched around me.

Quickly crossing the room, I slid the cupboard door to one side. My clothes were all there, ironed, arranged along the rail. But no bear. I moved the door across and a small whistle of relief passed my lips. There, pushed inside a shelf, was Ben's secret weapon.

Wow. I'd shocked myself with how frightened I'd felt.

Regaining composure for the cameras, I turned back to face the room.

This time I noticed there was a basin set into the far corner on which all my toiletries had been laid out. Above the sink was a small square window. Now night had fallen – a black hole in a stark white room. The contrast was so severe it could have passed as a piece of modern art on the otherwise naked walls.

Although the room was luxurious with its expensive fabrics and spotlessly clean surfaces, it felt unfriendly. Chillingly representative of some sort of secure hospital unit.

Hang on, there was something else. On the pillow, how could I have missed it?

A red envelope.

I peeled it open and pulled out the black and gold card. It was thick, crisp, and expensive, like a wedding invitation. Only there was significantly less writing on the page. Five little words:

Your safe word is Ellemara.

I felt a jolt of recognition. I couldn't place why, or from where. The word carried no obvious significance, yet it was eerily familiar, lurking at the periphery of my memory.

Was I meant to keep it a secret? What would happen if I said it?

I was still holding the card when the girls breezed in. Becky's eyes fell to my hand.

'You've got one too! Mine is Cocoa. My dog's name. What's that about?'

'Not sure how I feel about this.' Angela pushed to the front. 'It's weird.' She looked around at us. 'Anyone else think so?'

'What's your safe word?' I asked.

She gave a dismissive shrug. 'Something stupid.'

'Chill, it's just a bit of fun,' Becky said.

'Mine is cock.' Annie's plummy voice made it sound even more farcical.

'Seriously?' I couldn't disguise my eye-roll.

'You'll stop for cock, will you?' Becky encouraged.

Annie pulled a face. She reminded me of a child desperate for attention. 'It's Heather. My daughter.'

'You're a mum?' Becky appeared shocked.

'You'd think the creators of a show like this would be able to come up with something a bit more imaginative than *Heather*,' she said to the cameras, crossing what felt like forbidden territory. 'Anyway, I won't be needing a safe word. I'll be the one *gagging* for more.' She snaked her hips as she said it. Still clutching the neck of the bottle.

A week of this attention-seeking behaviour? My body instinctively tightened. How was I going to survive?

It was as if the villa heard my pleas for an intervention. The music stopped dead. There was a brief moment of restorative silence before the voice travelled through the speakers.

'Contestants!' It was the show's presenter. 'Gather by the pool.'

Becky immediately sprinted from my room to the corridor with the windows.

'Oh my God, they're here!' She turned back to face us. Trembling with excitement. 'The guys. They're here!'

CHAPTER SIXTEEN

THE REPORTER

Aruna, Balearic Islands

DAY ONE, *THE VILLA*

The patio doors slid open, revealing a garden lit up as brightly as a Christmas tree. Fairy lights looped around branches and tea candles clustered on rocks, flickering in the evening breeze. Halogen beams sliced through the pool like lightsabres. Our path to the screen was illuminated like a runway.

We held hands, because that's what we'd been told to do. We'd stripped off to our bikinis and heels because that's how the production crew had instructed us to dress. *Look sexy. Pretend you're best friends. Viewers want girls having fun.* The sweat from Annie's hand leaked into my palm. She was barely keeping it together from all the alcohol she'd necked.

In front of the pool were four men. Poised like soldiers with their hands clasped behind their backs and their legs splayed. It was hard to make out any other features except their strong shoulders, backlit by the silver lights.

'Oooof, there's my six-pack!' Annie said.

The screen came alive – shining light across their faces. They were blindfolded.

My throat tightened with the realization: I had to couple up with one of these guys whether I liked it or not.

'Hola, girls!' the blonde presenter welcomed us.

'Hola!' we parroted.

'Meet your new housemates. Blake, Charles, Adam and Cameron.'

'Hell-ooo boys!' Annie hollered.

Second from right, the guy with the tattoo crawling up his neck grinned harder.

Never had I missed Ben so badly. Ordinary Ben, with his ordinary looks. These men were too preened for my liking.

Was he watching? *I hope he's jealous*. It hadn't occurred to me until now – *I can use the show as a weapon to make him want me*.

'Get ready, girls! It's time for your very special introduction.'

But something about the way the presenter said *special* left me cold.

'Our viewing platform has been soaring since you lovely ladies arrived on our screens. As part of our VIP experience, our viewers will decide your future.'

Hang on. What?

'The nation has been voting. Our audience has spoken.'

Wait, slow down.

'For your first game . . .' she paused, building tension. 'Get excited to play MIX 'N' MATCH.

'Ladies, it's time to get up close and personal with our lads. TONIGHT, you'll be making cocktails, only you won't be using a shaker to fuse your drinks' – another theatrical pause – 'but your mouths.'

I looked around in horror. Annie was beaming. Becky seemed into it. If Angela minded, she was hiding it well.

'Remember. The viewers will be watching and they will be judging. They will decide who sleeps in whose bed tonight.'

I should have seen it coming. No rooms marked out for the boys. No name tags on the doors. I just assumed we'd be the ones choosing.

'And if you need reminding what you're playing for . . .'

A gold £50,000 filled up the screen. Followed by cheering.

All control had seemingly been handed over to the viewers. They had the power to decide what happened to us tonight. Was that OK? It didn't feel OK. But everything was moving so quickly. Before I had time to take in what it meant for us, the narrative unfolded more.

'Saucy, playful, fruity, your first cocktail will be – Sex on the Beach.'

I could feel it coming.

'Iris – take a sip of your first drink.'

'Iris! Iris!' the women chanted.

I picked up the glass brimming with something pale yellow. It smelt harmless. Sweet, like pineapples. But I knew it would be lethal.

'Down it! Down it!' The men had joined in now.

'Take it in one, sweetie,' cackled Annie.

Charles. That's who I had to make Sex on the Beach with first. His name was written on a sticker stuck to his bare chest, the sort of tag kids wear on their first day at school. Ironic, considering he looked like he'd come from boarding school, with his floppy blonde hair folded to the side and his hairless chest, with his preppy pastel shorts. He had a silver coin on a chain slung around his neck. Leather bracelets and an old festival pass on his wrist.

'Go on, girl, get stuck in!' Becky's voice took over.

Someone wolf-whistled.

Charles blindly felt his way to the glass on the table. Then, in some show of bravado, he tipped the entire contents into his mouth. Slamming the empty tumbler down. The dark liquid shining across his chin.

You've kissed worse. Far worse. But I couldn't soothe myself. I took a sip of the pale liquid and, with it clasped in my mouth, I stepped towards him.

As I drew nearer, I noticed Charles wasn't muscly like the others. He lacked their natural confidence, too. His lips were thin, which, in the half-light, appeared to distort. I couldn't work out if he was smiling or smirking.

He stretched out his neck on hearing my approach.

'Kiss, kiss, kiss!' chanted the ladies behind me.

They were really starting to piss me off.

I parted my mouth and pressed my lips to his.

His tongue thrust inside me and the cocktail surged – a tidal wave of vodka, cranberry juice, saliva. The warm liquid spilling over the corners of our lips. I pulled away, gagging.

'Ha-haaa, she's going to chunder,' Annie celebrated while I folded over into a coughing fit, my nose burning from where the alcohol regurgitated. There was no dignified way around it, I had to use my hand as a tissue. My nose, my face, across my chest – wipe.

No sooner had I straightened up than the taunting started again.

For Dutch courage, I necked most of the next cocktail: sweet and potent, it instantly numbed my throat. I drained the last of it, this time holding on to it as I stepped in front of Adam.

He was the tallest at around six foot five. Lean with the body of an athlete, a shaved head and a strong angular jaw that he wouldn't stop clenching. His skin was dark and the tattoos cloaking his body made parts of him appear petrol black.

A phoenix on his left shoulder. A buxom waitress in stockings and suspenders on his forearm. But it was the tiger crouching on his chest that transfixed me. Intricate black inkwork except for the yellow eyes. So vivid they glowed from beneath his skin. I followed the tiger's tail, curling past his neck up to his ear. In the shadows, it almost appeared to swish back and forth.

'Come on, darling, get on with it! Snog him!' Annie broke into my thoughts. But her barbed tone told me she wanted him for herself. *Well, she could have him.*

Adam didn't bother to stoop, he made me work for it. I lifted onto my toes, stretching, fighting to keep my mouth tightly sealed and then, all of a sudden, two strong arms wrapped around my waist. In one sweeping movement he lifted me into the air. I was a worm speared on a hook and, in my fight for survival, I did the only thing I could think of to stop me flailing around – I locked my legs around his waist – at the very moment he decided to go in for a kiss.

There was a roar of excitement from behind. The screaming drilled my ears as the cocktail washed into my mouth. All my senses felt violated.

Adam was putting on a crowd-pleasing performance. The viewers will think I'm into him!

Shit.

If I don't do something, we'll be spending the night together.

I planted my hand onto his chest, wrenching myself from his grip. With my bikini bottoms riding up between my cheeks I took the most humiliating of dismounts. But I was free, that was all that mattered. For any viewers still in doubt whether I enjoyed our kiss, I ratcheted up my performance, turning and retching.

'Becky. Take a sip of your first drink.'

She was hot on my heels.

The cocktails had hit me hard and I was having trouble focusing. Recently I had been living for this feeling. That moment when the booze cradles you in its warm arms. But there was no soothing numbness now. *What was in these drinks? Triple measures?* I stumbled towards my next introduction.

Blake could have been a Viking with his wavy shoulder-length hair and chiselled features. He seemed best of the lot – I took a swig of cocktail and sashayed my way towards him. *The audience will decide. The viewers will judge.* I grabbed the waistband of his pillar-box-red board shorts and pulled his body to meet mine. He coughed with surprise, barely managing to keep hold of his drink. I teased my hands across his chest and locked them around his neck. Then, in for the kill. The ground shifted beneath my feet as I forced myself into our kiss.

Stumbling back, I caught Blake's grin. *Good. Job done.*

I moved towards the final contestant with a sense of relief; this would all be over soon.

Cameron was the only guy who'd covered up. He wore a Hawaiian shirt, roughly rolled up to his elbows. Long denim shorts and sunglasses clipped into his front pocket. *I am pissed* – all I could think was Lego hair as I stared at his perfect quiff.

I knocked back the cocktail.

His aftershave was musky, heady and familiar. Too familiar. Jean Paul Gaultier. That's what my ex wore! Why does he keep coming back to haunt me? Thrown by the association with my past, as our lips were about to touch, I steered my mouth away, grazing Cameron's cheek.

I instantly regretted it. There was a tense pause followed by a flash of something in his expression. He took a step back and lifted his hands to his face. For a moment, I thought he was going to rip off his blindfold. But then, slowly, he smiled. I'd seen that look before on other men. It was the practised smile of someone hiding who they really are.

A wolf.

CHAPTER SEVENTEEN

THE PRODUCER

Madrid, Interview Room One

NOW

The door opens but they finish up their conversation in the corridor. Just out of earshot. She's managed to say something funny. Sanchez is laughing and from the way he's leaning into her, I'd say he likes his deputy. I feel a stab of jealousy – how dare she try and steal attention from me.

She flashes him a parting look and disappears from view. He peers into the room, at me, and his face drops. That's OK. At least I have him to myself now.

I remind myself that he needs me.

He takes a seat. Blows on his coffee before taking a sip and then presses record on the tape player.

'Where were we?' His earlier aggression has left him. He checks his notes. 'Si, si. The contestants.'

'What do you want to know?'

'Why them?'

Does he want the abridged version? We'll be here for

days if I get started on explaining the epic amounts of work that went into selecting my golden eight.

'We chose them because we knew they would make good – no,' I can't help but smile at all the hard work I've put in, '– *great* entertainment.'

'And what sort of a person makes *great entertainment*?' He taps his chest. 'Would I, for example?'

I laugh. 'No.'

'Why not?'

Jesus, he actually looks offended.

'Because you're . . . um . . . I don't know.' I shrug again. 'Too serious.'

'Too serious!' he chortles. He clears his throat and leans in, his stare turning cold. 'I suppose you're right; I am serious. Very serious about finding out what happened. I ask again, why them?'

The abridged version it is then. I scratch at the back of my head. The sweat has made my scalp insanely itchy. My fingers rake back and forth, nail on skin feeling good. Pain is my release.

'For starters, they're attractive. The viewers want fit guys and girls wearing as little as possible. Secondly, they were extroverts. They craved attention and we were confident they'd put on a show-stopping performance.'

If Sanchez has an opinion, he keeps it buried this time. 'What else?'

'It's good to throw different backgrounds into the mix, values that might clash.'

'What else?'

'They showed strong signs of competitiveness and ruthlessness, which is what you need in a game show.'

'Ruthlessness?'

'They'd do anything to win.'

'Anything?'

I'd walked into that one.

'I suppose so,' I say, more warily.

'And who would be the most ruthless of them, would you say?'

The cuts on her feet. The bruises marking her arms like stains. Purple and angry. She's all I can see now.

'Señora?'

It's not going to reflect well on me if I tell him. He won't understand, not yet, he's not ready. I have to protect myself. He'll have his answer soon – when he watches the tapes.

He's studying my eyes for the answers. When he can't unearth them, he digs some more.

'How did you find them?'

'They replied to our advert. Others we discovered through social media. Their Instagram, TikTok profiles.'

'You must have had a screening process?'

'Of course.'

'How did you decide?'

'From their audition. Did they sparkle? Would they turn your head? How big was their social media presence? What are their followers saying about them?'

I'm excited now. Psychology fascinates me – especially working out what makes people tick and how you can use that information.

'If they generate a high engagement rate you know they'll

be popular in the villa,' I continue. 'If the comments are savage, well, chances are they will wind someone up.'

'You can tell this all through social media?'

What planet has Sanchez been living on?

'And obviously you wouldn't choose someone who was getting negative feedback?'

'Hell no!' I laugh. 'Bitch fights get ratings.'

Sanchez looks repulsed and I remind myself why I'm here. Why I'm sitting in this sweatbox of a police station. The last person to leave the villa is dead.

'Everyone loves a villain, they keep the viewers interested,' I say with less enthusiasm.

'What exactly was the screening process?'

'We checked for criminal records. We did blood tests to make sure they weren't using or had any serious health issues that might affect filming.'

There's a knock at the door.

The officer reappears, hands Sanchez a Manila file and promptly leaves. He opens the folder, his eyes scanning through a mass of stapled A4 sheets. His face is emotionless, although I'm getting better at reading him. His tells. When he scratches his temple, he's spotted something significant. He's doing that now. It's part of my job, reading people, and that's what I've been trying to tell Sanchez. I'm a producer, psychologist and a detective all rolled into one. I could do his job.

He snaps the folder shut and returns to me.

Sanchez will come around. I'll make him understand. I just need time.

He takes a seat, and a moment. Gearing up. I know what he's going to ask and this time I'm prepared.

'Cameron Walker . . .'

Here it comes.

'Señor Walker has a criminal record – grievous bodily harm against his ex-wife.'

He locks me in his stare as he says: 'A very dangerous man. Tell me, why did you choose someone with a history of violence to star on your show?'

CHAPTER EIGHTEEN

THE REPORTER

Aruna, Balearic Islands

DAY ONE, *THE VILLA*

The blindfolds had been removed and now their eyes were sliding up and down our bodies like airport scanners. It reminded me of the meat-on-a-rotisserie-stick feeling I'd had at the audition and I had an overwhelming urge to grab an outdoor blanket and hide myself.

We'd been instructed to remain apart while the votes were counted. Boys on one side of the pool, watching the girls perform across the water.

The women looked clumsy and uncoordinated as they turned the decking into a dancefloor. Annie was moving between the tables, draining leftovers from glasses. Angela was propping up Becky, the pair swaying out of rhythm to some hectic club music that blasted out while we waited. Becky had changed into a dress, the sequins shimmering with fragmented light. Her straps slipping further down her shoulders with each jerk and stumble.

Slowly I moved towards an oversized beanbag. Somewhere I could rest, close my eyes and stop the world from spinning.

But the viewers had plans for us.

The presenter spoke from the darkness.

'The votes are in!'

Who was she? I wondered if there was a real person behind the artificial voice, smirking as they read out the lines. I imagined the viewers at home. How titillating her words must sound from the safety of their sofas. It was the kind of thing I'd write for the paper. Who's going to be shagging who? That's what she was implying, after all.

'Gather around for the big reveal. It's time to find out who will be sleeping with whom tonight.' She echoed my thoughts.

Eight names appeared on the screen before shattering. IRIS, now in pieces. All of us reduced to tiny gold fragments floating through darkness like dust motes in an attic.

We were transfixed, anxiously waiting for our identities to be pieced back together. I could feel my pulse thumping with the uncertainty of who I would have to spend the night with.

'An incredible £50,000 up for grabs for the winning couple!' she reminded us.

'£50,000' echoed as the pieces slowly reassembled, as I watched the list of couples appear.

It took far longer than it should have to digest what had just happened. I couldn't understand it.

What the . . . ?

A hand touched my arm and I startled.

'Are you OK?' Angela said quietly. Charles hung back, waiting for her to join him.

I was still gazing at the screen.

'Iris?'

'I don't understand!'

'He seems nice,' she said, shrugging. In an even lower tone: 'I think I'd rather be with him than . . .' She pointed to Charles with her eyes. She gave me a little squeeze and then slipped away with him into the shadows of the garden.

How could this happen? Why wasn't I with Blake? Why did Becky get to have him?

I looked enviously at the others. Everyone else seemed content with the viewers' decision. And Annie, she was ecstatic. Her hand planted on Adam's bum. Already marking him as hers. The couples drifted to corners of the villa to begin getting to know each other while I remained frozen by the pool.

Cameron was strolling towards me. His shirt catching in the breeze, billowing behind him. The rage had lifted from his face. He was smiling but his eyes told another story. There was something hidden behind them – I was sure of it.

'Hey, gorgeous.' He swooped in to kiss my cheek, once again assaulting my senses with his aftershave.

Why had the viewers matched us? It was obvious we didn't have chemistry. It must be something else. A dark thought struck me. Did they have something else planned for us?

Had I been paired with Cameron *because* we didn't get along?

*

Swarms of midges circled the lights, darting into our eyes.

'It'll be better down there. Come on, follow me,' Cameron said, pointing down the terraces to the cliff edge. He rose to his feet, picked up our glasses and led us away from the others to where two chairs overlooked the ocean. I followed quietly while he tried to make conversation.

'What do you think of this place?'

I shrugged. 'Impressive.'

'Meh, I'm not so into private islands.'

I stopped. He turned around and grinned. 'This view's not too bad, though. Come on.'

'It's pitch black. We won't be able to see anything.'

'Yeah, we will. Your eyes will get used to the dark.'

Cameron sat down and handed me my drink. He adjusted the pillow behind him and then nestled into the chair, while I perched stiffly, the rattan weaves pushing grooves into my bare legs.

'Relax, I'm not going to bite.' He lifted his glass to mine. 'Cheers.'

Perhaps I was being hard on him? He was clearly trying, even if his jokes were crap, whereas all I'd given him were clipped replies.

'Cheers,' I said, putting a little more heart into it.

'I guess we haven't drunk enough for me to ask what our bed's like?' he said, a smirk unfolding.

I threw him a look.

'Ooof, tough crowd.'

'I've got a question for you,' I retaliated.

He leaned forward. 'Go on, then.'

'Have you slept with anyone famous?' Ben would like

that question. Direct, potentially explosive. The *Record* journalist coming out in me.

He frowned. 'What makes you ask that? Pretty savage when you're getting to know someone.'

I swallowed. 'Sorry.' I could hardly tell him the real reason I was being so abrasive. 'I guess I'm conscious of how little time we have. I want to know as much as I can about you.'

He fixed me with his stare, his peaty-brown eyes unblinking. It was enough to make me pause. Playfully, I added, 'Because I already know what you do.' He was a web developer. 'And, where you live.' Leeds. 'And that Sex on the Beach is your least favourite cocktail.'

'Wow, you make me sound so interesting. Summed up in two sentences.'

He laughed a little.

'I'm just trying to find out what your type is.'

He leaned in and in a low voice said: 'I'll tell you when you tell me something.'

Playing me at my own game. He had a bit more 'oomph' than I'd first thought. 'OK, what do you want to know?'

'Hmm, let me see.' He glanced over my shoulder, a smile developing. 'Do you like the other girls?'

It was so direct, the question threw me. I probably hesitated for too long. 'Yes.'

He smiled. 'Really?'

'Yeah, really,' I said more insistently. 'Why wouldn't I?'

'It's just . . . you seem different. I mean,' he said, trying to read my eyes, 'I realize I've only known you for five minutes but I can tell you're nothing like them.'

Shit. I was supposed to be blending in.

'Different in a good way?' I said, hesitantly.

He paused, looking serious as he considered my question. I swallowed.

'Of course, in a good way,' he laughed.

I gave him a playful shove.

A heat rose between us then. Something so intensely sexual it knocked me off my guard.

Quickly, I said: 'That's me. Now your turn.'

'No.'

'No?'

'The answer to your question about whether I've shagged a celeb. That's what you were getting at, wasn't it?'

'Oh right, that,' I blushed.

His grin then shifted. The jollity suddenly washing away. As if he was considering his next words carefully. Softly, he said, 'Does a divorcee put you off?'

The revelation took me by surprise. I didn't know why. Maybe I thought he looked too young or too much of a player to be the type to settle down.

'How long were you married?' I said.

'Three years.'

'Kids?'

He moved his eyes from me into the distance. 'We wanted them, but . . .' he sighed with what I sensed to be pain. 'It didn't work out.'

'It wasn't right of me to pry. Sorry.'

'It's fine. You should be curious about my past. We're on a dating show, after all.' His gaze was still fixed ahead and while he searched the ocean I took the moment to study his profile – the creases around his eye as his frown deepened. His slightly receding chin. His long nose. Cameron wasn't conventionally good-looking but, put together, his features gave his face character.

The air had become thick with grief. A feeling I was all too familiar with. It never leaves you – some days you think it's gone but it's still there, lying dormant, waiting to spring up when you're at your most vulnerable. I don't think I'll ever move on from my ex or stop searching for those unanswered questions as to why he stopped loving me. Why he gave up on us. I wanted to change the subject but before I could, Cameron moved his eyes back to me.

'Things weren't easy. Camilla, my wife, she suffered from depression. The doctors said it was a chemical imbalance and put her on a load of meds. But the drugs were only masking the problem, not fixing it. If you ask me, it all stemmed from what happened to her when she was growing up.' His face hardened. 'I could never get her to open up to me about it, though.'

I kept silent. Letting him speak.

'We'd have good spells and bad ones and then, she got pregnant. That seemed to change things. Give her hope. *Us* hope. You know?'

I sensed something terrible on its way.

'But she miscarried and then . . .' His voice choked up.

He looked at me, but I couldn't read his expression any more. I felt compelled to reach out, to touch him. I placed my hand lightly on his arm.

'You don't need to revisit this . . .' I said, guilt prickling at me for intruding.

'I thought I'd be OK talking about it but, I guess it's still too fresh.'

'Honestly, I understand.'

He drew in air and then straightened.

Despite myself, I was desperate to know how his sentence would have ended. The way he held back, the gaps he left, his mysteriousness had left me wanting more.

There were so many more questions: how long ago did they separate? Was his wife OK? Was he over her and why did he want to star in *The Villa*? To find love, I suppose. I assumed their loss broke their marriage for good. I could relate to that – burying pain by thrusting yourself into a world that leaves you little space to breathe and think. Perhaps we were more similar than I'd thought.

I wasn't sure what motivated Cameron to disclose such personal information to me, and to everyone else watching. Perhaps a credit to my reporting skills? Whatever the reason, his honesty drew me in and to my surprise I found comfort in the silence that had now moved between us.

How strange, I kept thinking, as I looked out across the ocean. That someone could be so intimate so quickly and for it not to feel weird. In the 'real world' Cameron's abrupt confession would be unnerving. Yet here, on *The Villa*, it seemed normal.

Out of the corner of my eye, I saw Becky and Blake falling onto the daybed, their bodies tangled. Across the pool, Angela and Charles were deep in conversation. Annie was grinding with Adam to the club classics. Her hands gripped around his bum. She didn't seem to have a slow-down button and he didn't seem to mind.

'Want to get out of here?' Cameron asked, seeming to sense my agitation. Everything was happening so fast.

'Please.'

'Unless . . .' he looked across the garden, his humour returning. 'You fancy a dip in the hot tub?'

My expression must have been one of horror.

He laughed. 'I thought so. Come on, let's go.' He pulled me up and I stumbled. The cool evening air had done nothing to sober me up. I reached out to Cameron for support and he immediately took me into the nook of his arm. Warm, soothing and protective. Suddenly all I wanted was my bed and I didn't mind I'd be sharing it with him. His cuddle reminded me of what it felt like to be close to someone. The touch of Ben still fresh on my skin. Ben – I hoped he was watching and that our intimacy was making him jealous.

Cameron wouldn't be the first stranger I'd spent the night with. Anyway, he wasn't a stranger any more. He'd opened up to me. He seemed honest and transparent about his past. That was more than I could say for myself.

CHAPTER NINETEEN

THE PRODUCER

Madrid, Interview Room One

NOW

'Everyone's got a past.'

Sanchez is silent, waiting for me to quantify that.

'I bet even a nice bloke like you has a skeleton or two stashed away. Something they'd rather keep secret.'

He doesn't flinch.

'People make mistakes. I believe everyone deserves a second crack at life and so did Cameron.' I hear the emotion creeping into my voice and I'm quick to control it. 'The assault was some time ago and he paid for it. He served his sentence; he went through therapy. When we spoke about the assault, which we *did*, he said he was deeply sorry for what he'd done – and I believed him.'

'You *believed* him?' Sanchez's eyebrow goes up again in that fucking irritating manner.

'Yeah, I saw his remorse. It was genuine.'

He stares coldly at me before returning to the file in front of him. Reading from the report, he says:

'Twenty-fourth of August 2015, 2.15 a.m. Camilla Walker rang the emergency services reporting that her husband, Señor Cameron Walker, had attempted to strangle her. She dropped the charges three days later. On the nineteenth of September, neighbours called the police after hearing screams. Mrs Walker was found on the landing with three cracked ribs and a four-inch laceration from where a mirror had been smashed over the back on her head. One week later, she miscarried. She wanted to drop the charges, but the CPS went through with the prosecution. Señor Walker was sentenced to five years.' Sanchez closed the file. 'He served half of that. X-rays of Señora Walker revealed healed breakages indicative of multiple past traumas.' Sanchez's eyes harden. 'I don't believe the reports filed were the only incidences of abuse. Camilla Walker was too afraid to speak the truth and suffered years of violence.'

I have to admit, it makes for heavy listening. I hadn't known the ins and outs of all the charges until now. I look away.

'You thought he would make good television, so you forgot about all of this' – his hand flitters across Cameron's file – 'isn't that right?'

'No,' I say, sharply.

'Who cares if he's potentially dangerous? He's good on camera.'

'I did care.'

Sanchez shakes his head.

'I cared. But I believed in him.' I don't add that I know all about trying to amend for past mistakes. 'Anyway, we had a trained professional on hand to help.' I pause. 'Dr Alexander.'

'I was just coming to him.'

'A trained therapist on the island on twenty-four-hour standby offering counselling and advice to any contestant who might be feeling overwhelmed by starring in *The Villa*. We cared, *OK*. If there was a problem with anyone's behaviour before the . . .' I can't bring myself to say it out loud. I swirl it around on my tongue, trying it out, but I can't unleash it yet: '. . . the incident, Dr Alexander would have seen it and intervened.'

'So you're telling me that Dr Alexander never had to step in while the contestants were in the villa?'

I look down at my hands, locked into a clasp.

'Señora, answer the question.'

CHAPTER TWENTY

THE VIEWERS

EIGHT MILLION VIEWERS

In South Shields, South Tyneside, sisters Amanda and Liz Dean had something to say about the contestants' first night in the villa.

'Watching them makes me want to fake tan and get my hair done,' said Liz. 'Look at those high-rise bikini bottoms.'

'I want one,' said Mandy.

'Don't be daft. We wouldn't look like them,' said Liz.

'I would in my head.'

'How jealous was Angela when the couples were announced?' said Liz. 'It's obvious she's after Cameron. You're a fake, love!' Liz shouted at the screen. 'Don't blame her for fancying him, though. Cameron's fit, and he's a decent sort. Sounds like he's had it tough. How refreshing to have a guy who's being honest for once.'

'I didn't get that vibe about Angela – she's genuine, trying to be nice to Iris,' Amanda argued.

'Are you serious? Angela gave her the death stare! There's something not right about her. She's too quiet, I don't trust her.'

'I'm not picking up on that. Think it's Becky we got to watch out for,' said Amanda.

Liz opened a fresh Google search on her mobile. 'She said she was a solicitor?'

'Think so.'

'Angela Akbas?'

'Yeah, maybe.'

'I've found her. Works at Duncan Charles family solicitors in Basingstoke.'

'So she's legit then,' said Amanda. 'God knows why you'd risk your job to go on a show like this.'

'Hey, what's this?' Liz turned her screen around. 'It came up when I searched under photos.'

'Is that *her*?'

'Posted ten minutes ago.'

'Fucking hell!'

'She won't have a job to go back to now.'

The sisters swapped horrified faces.

CHAPTER TWENTY-ONE

THE REPORTER

Aruna, Balearic Islands

DAY ONE, *THE VILLA*

The temperature in my bedroom had plummeted and I couldn't find a device of any kind to push it back up to normal.

I checked under the bed to see if the remote had fallen there.

'This is weird,' I searched around angrily.

Cameron appeared by my side with the white fur throw wrapped around his shoulders. He looked like a yeti. 'Who you calling weird?'

A small smile escaped me. 'What's going on with this air con? Can you fix it?'

He moved closer, pulling me into another of his bear-like embraces. He rubbed my back. I couldn't help but giggle.

'What are you laughing at?'

'How absurd this is.' My teeth were now chattering.

'I suppose we'll have to snuggle to keep warm,' he said.

Ah. The penny dropped.

Cameron began unbuttoning his shirt.

That's why the air con is on full blast.

He shrugged it to the floor, revealing an athletic, but not gym-obsessed body. The fact he hadn't been as showy as the others was attractive.

'Boxers on, I promise,' he said with a grin, unzipping his shorts.

I looked to the corner of the room, to where the beady eye of the camera was watching. The temptation to stick my fingers up at it almost got the better of me.

Cameron lifted the corner of the duvet and bounced across the mattress before diving underneath. He pulled the covers up to his nose. Only those dark eyes were left showing.

'Brrrr, it's freezing in here too.' His voice was muffled through the bedding.

'I can't hear you properly,' I said over my shoulder.

'Hurry up and get in!'

I'd turned to face the wall. Hiding from Cameron and the camera as I removed my bikini. The process took far longer than it should. The cocktails had really gone to my head. I cupped one arm over my breasts as I used the other to rummage through the cupboard for my nightshirt.

'Getting frostbite! Can't feel my hands . . .'

My fingers ran over the teddy bear. Feeling for the rectangular lump. *Relief*, it was still there. I pushed him deeper into the alcove.

'Pretty close to death now,' he said.

'OK, I'm here,' I announced, arriving by his side.

He stared at my oversized nightie. 'What the heck is *that*?'

'What does it look like?'

'And you were hoping to score in *The Villa* wearing *that*?'

'Shut up!' I nudged him to move over and slid under the covers. The sheets were warm from where he'd been. He immediately slung his arm around my waist, pulling me into a little spoon. I slapped him away.

'Oi! No funny business.'

'OK OK, best behaviour.'

It came out more as a whisper. Hot in my ear. He backed off, but only slightly. I could still feel the heat of his body and his breath on my back.

Despite his proximity, I trusted him not to try it on. I was enjoying the attention, the thought I could be making Ben jealous. The intimacy was comforting – I was cold and Cameron was warming the bed. *Viewers: your underhand games to push us together will not work.*

Will not work. They were the last words I silently proclaimed before I finally drifted off, after what felt like the longest day of my entire life.

He lingered in the room long after he'd left. His scent marking the sheets. He'd had sex with me, getting his fix before delivering the news that the engagement was off. We were over.

He didn't feel the same way any more. I was suffocating him. He didn't want to have to deal with my jealousy. All the blame – shifted onto me. And what did I do? Instead of putting my side across – that I wasn't going mad, he had been behaving suspiciously – I took it. He slapped me with a stream of put-downs and I accepted them. I even said how sorry I was for doubting him. Please could we try again? Never in my life had I sunk to such levels of desperation, but I couldn't stop myself, I would have slid even lower if that's what it would take to make him change his mind. When I look back at it, nothing makes sense. My paranoia about his cheating, nothing.

The smell of my ex had become so vivid it was like he was next to me. *Am I dreaming?* I could feel tears hot on my cheeks. *Burning.* I was burning up . . .

I startled awake.

Where am I? There was sweat between my thighs and my stomach was cramping.

I blinked into the darkness. As my eyes adjusted, my bearings slowly returned – to the soulless, sterile room.

Why didn't I eat something earlier? Annie had said the fridge was full. I shifted, sliding one leg in front of the other, drumming up the energy to go hunting for food, and then came the tug to my waist.

It didn't register at first. I was still resurfacing from my nightmare. Still blinking the memory of my ex away. I tried moving again. Stretching my toes towards the cool air outside the duvet.

The tug was unmistakable this time.

I looked over my shoulder to find Cameron's face inches from mine. His eyes were closed but the moonlight through the window showed me something more.

While I'd slept, he'd manoeuvred us back into spoons. His arm had returned to my waist. The smell of my ex crowding me. That explained the dream and why I was burning up then.

I lifted his arm. It was heavy and limp, how you'd expect it to be if he were asleep, but as it dropped back onto the bed I thought I caught a hint of a smile as he groaned and slung it back to where it had been.

I bristled with irritation. I wanted – needed – my space. I wriggled, caring less about waking him this time, only I couldn't move because his grip had tightened.

And that's when I felt it. His erection. Pressing into my lower back.

Before I had time to say anything, Cameron came alive, pulling the duvet up and over our heads.

We were thrust into darkness. A humid, airless space reeking of sweat. I could hear my pulse accelerate.

Thud. Thud. Thud.

'Let go of me,' I hissed.

He didn't say a word.

'Hey, I'm not messing around. Let go!'

Nothing. Just his breath, hot on my neck.

'Hey!'

I tried prising off his fingers but they immediately curled back around my forearm.

'If this is some joke, it's not funny.'

I twisted my head around so he could see the full force of my threat. His eyes were wide open, ink black and gleaming.

'I *will* scream.'

He watched me, unblinking, and then it came, the darkening of his expression. The flash of rage I'd seen earlier returned. His muscles contracted around me.

It was low and dangerous. A whisper. Just for my ears. 'I know you want it.'

Adrenaline spiked my blood, activating all my fight or flight responses. I raised my knee and kicked back, smacking his shin. The surprise was enough to loosen his grip.

I rolled out of the duvet and onto the floor, the cold rush of air snatching my breath away. I scrambled to my feet and without thinking, grabbed Ben's bear from its cubbyhole. I held him fast against my chest as I sprinted for the door. The sense I was trapped in some sort of hospital asylum returning.

The handle. *Shit*. It was jammed. I couldn't bring myself to look back. I imagined him pulling back the duvet and taking slow, measured steps as he crept towards me.

Shit shit shit. The door was still stuck. All reason went as blind panic took over. I shook it and rattled it and yanked the handle so violently that, when it finally opened with a click, I fell backwards with the force of it.

It sounded like a catch releasing. Had we been locked in? I didn't have time to think about it. Without looking back, I lurched from the dark into the moonlit corridor. My bare feet smacking the stone as I rushed towards the girls' bathroom. The only place I could think of where I could call Ben and demand he get me the fuck out of here.

CHAPTER TWENTY-TWO

THE REPORTER

Aruna, Balearic Islands

DAY TWO, *THE VILLA*

It was 4.32 a.m.

My hands were shaking as I read the time on the phone. The dance music had stopped and an eerie silence had settled over the villa. My shuddering breath now the only sound.

What had Ben got me into? My fears were snowballing as I pressed speed dial.

Pick up, please pick up.

'Hi, it's Ben, you know what to do . . . *bleep.*'

No, no, no. I tried again. Punching redial.

Making a quick scan of the toilet for cameras, I ran my fingers across the wall, burying my hand inside the fern behind the cistern. The cubicle was black and gold. Even the toilet paper was custom designed, embossed with the *Villa* logo. I prayed it was safe to talk but there was no way I could be certain.

Hunched over on the toilet seat with my left arm clamped

across my chest, my right foot nervously tapping the floor, I waited again for Ben to pick up. My hope of reaching the outside world was dying by the second.

'Yeah, hi?' It was more of a croak than anything.

I was so relieved I couldn't say anything.

'Laura! Is that you? Are you OK?'

My chest was tightening. My ribs crushing my lungs.

'Laura?'

'Not OK!' I forced the words out.

'Talk to me!'

'The guy I'm coupled up with . . . he . . . he . . .'

I heard a rustle, as if Ben was pushing himself upright in bed. 'Did he hurt you?'

'No. Yeah . . . I mean . . . he tried to.'

'Jesus.' He cleared his throat. 'I wasn't watching. Well, I was, and then I turned it off.'

'You turned it off?!'

'You were having a moment together, so, I left it.'

'You thought we were having a *moment*?' My voice climbing.

'It looked that way. The two of you, going for it under the covers.'

An awkward silence came between us. Was Ben jealous? It was a surreal moment to glow, but through my panic, a warmth spread.

'Well, I'm not *into* him,' I stressed. 'Ben, I'm frightened.'

There came another pause, but for a beat too long.

'Look, it'll be OK, stay calm and see what happens.'

His words struck like a slap to the face.

'OK?' he confirmed.

The sting intensified, spreading across my entire body.

'OK?'

I felt dizzy.

'Laura, you still there?' he sounded almost impatient.

'I'm not OK,' I managed to reply. 'What are you saying?'

'Something might come out of this. There could be a story in it for us. You need to take a breath, calm yourself down and look at it another way.'

'Look at it another way?'

'Now we can't run a story saying the show's scripted, we need a new angle, and this could be it.'

I heard more noise as he moved around.

'I'm thinking we'll lead with an "I survived *The Villa*" headline.' His voice now alert. Excited. 'Your exclusive, your first-person account on how you escaped a sexual predator. If you could push it a bit further, there might be an even better story there.'

'Push it further?'

'Get him riled up. Meanwhile, we'll work on his backstory. We'll do a bit of digging this end and try and find out who he really is. Maybe he's done more dodgy stuff. This could be huge!'

I couldn't believe what I was hearing. This was what I was here for? As BAIT? He didn't give a shit at all.

'Tell me you're joking?'

'Iris.' Her voice ricocheted off the tiny space.

I froze.

'Who's that?' Ben said.

'Iris O'Donnell . . .'

It was the *Villa* presenter.

'Oh shit,' I whispered.

'Iris, could you make your way to the therapy room.'

'Therapy room?' Ben parroted.

Oh God, they were going to take my phone away. My lifeline.

'Shhh, don't say anything in case they can hear. Listen, stay calm, it'll be OK,' Ben said soothingly. 'If what you said really happened, tell someone.'

IF? Is he crazy? Of course I was going to tell them.

'Iris – the therapy room is on the ground floor. The entrance is in the living room beside the Picasso painting.'

My stomach twisted. I didn't want to end the call. As long as I stayed on the line I had a protector, albeit a half-hearted one hundreds of miles away.

'I'll be watching you,' Ben promised. 'We'll come and get you out if we have to.'

There was a softness to his tone now, but it was too late. How could I trust him after what he'd just said? Christ – did he even know where I was? The Nokia Ben had given me was so old it didn't have internet, let alone GPS tracking.

I had a sinking feeling we were off the grid and whoever was in charge wanted us to stay hidden.

'Iris.' The voice was much more forceful this time.

I was a schoolgirl being summoned to the headmistress's office. That's how it felt. I may have even let out a tiny whimper as I removed the phone from my ear.

A final silent moment with Ben and then I forced myself to hang up.

CHAPTER TWENTY-THREE

THE REPORTER

Aruna, Balearic Islands

DAY TWO, *THE VILLA*

You wouldn't have known the door was there, it blended so seamlessly into the white walls. I ran my fingers around its edges, across the surface, searching for some sort of hidden handle or button.

It sounded like an airlock releasing in a compression chamber. The sudden noise made me startle. A reinforced door slowly swept outwards, revealing a violet-lit room with walls made of white padded diamond shapes. There was also a white armchair dressed up with a blood-red cushion. A glass coffee table and a jug of water.

Cautiously, I stepped inside. I made sure to hug the bear, conscious I had to portray some sort of deep attachment to it.

It was probably too late for that, though. I'd been outed. Why else would I have been singled out?

I perched on the edge of the seat, every one of my muscles tight, my shoulders aching with the tension. But I wasn't ready for my reflection in the wall-to-wall mirror. Dark shadows had spread beneath my eyes and all colour had drained from my face. I looked dead.

My fingers dug into the bear's fur. Why hadn't Ben believed me? I searched around, looking for something to happen.

Finally, the woman spoke again, her voice circling me. 'Iris.'

'Uh huh.'

My eyes swept the room, trying to pinpoint the source.

There was another pause before her tone changed to something much softer. 'Are you feeling OK?'

It sounded so caring it threw me off guard.

'No, NO, I'm not OK,' I blurted. 'Cameron's a psycho! He tried to suffocate me, he pushed me under the covers and he wouldn't let go of me. You need to get him off the show, he's a lunatic, he's dangerous!' With every breathless word, my voice climbed higher. I hadn't realized my hands were trembling until I looked down.

There was a painfully long silence before she spoke and I noticed her tone had changed once again. This time, detached: 'We've examined the recordings and we can't see anything untoward.'

WHAT?

The glass of the mirror transformed into a screen, coming to life with an infra-red night image. It was my room, *me,* under the covers. A mound, moving around in such a way it looked like . . . Oh my God.

I shook my head and pointed. 'No, it's not true. We're not having sex.' I searched around me for someone real to explain it to. 'It might look that way but that's what he wants you to believe. It didn't happen. He wouldn't let me go. He said I wanted him, but I didn't, I'd never want someone like him!'

The recording continued to play.

'He threatened me.' I nearly choked on the words as they finally came out: 'He was going to rape me!'

There was another lengthy pause before she spoke. 'We haven't been able to pick up any dialogue from the recording.'

'Yeah, of course you haven't!' My anger was stinging. 'That's why he pulled the covers up – so no one could hear or see what he was doing. Can't you see what he's trying to do?!'

When her reply didn't arrive, I marched on. It felt like I was having to build a case in my defence. But for some reason, the more I explained, the less confident I became.

A new image appeared on the screen. Cameron and me – making our way to the villa after our chat in the garden, his arm wrapped protectively around me.

Ben's words came back to haunt me – *It looked like you were having a moment* – as I watched my arm clasp around Cameron's waist. My suggestive smile as I gazed up at him. I was doing it to make Ben jealous. I remember thinking that at the time. Didn't I?

'It appears a considerable amount of alcohol was consumed.'

She leaves the statement hanging.

'I don't think I need to tell you the allegations you are making carry serious consequences,' she continued. 'You must be absolutely certain, or you could face legal action for defamation of character.'

The playback continued and I watched as the camera zoomed in on me. I was hugging Cameron, nuzzling into his shoulder as he helped me through the patio doors. Leaning on him the entire way to the bedroom. Laughing. It certainly looked like I was flirting.

'The nation agreed you were having a good time. Iris and Cameron were the top trending words on our social media platforms tonight.'

While she spoke, streams of fan comments were appearing: #gettingup2allsorts. #SEXONTHEFIRSTDATE #easycomeeasygo #IRISandCAMERONtoWIN

The screen switched back to a live feed from my bedroom: to Cameron, sleeping like a baby.

'Are you going to evict him?' My voice had slipped to something brittle.

Instead of answering the question, the woman said: 'We're concerned you might be feeling a little,' she took a breath, 'overwhelmed.'

The next clip showed me stumbling from the bed, grabbing my bear. While Cameron remained under the covers. He didn't stir once. As I watched myself battle with the door, I realized the footage made me look manic.

'We think it might be a good idea if you spoke to our therapist, Dr Alexander.'

'Therapist? There's nothing wrong with me,' I insisted.

But I was losing my grip on my anger. My conviction was diminishing – as it so often did.

I had this sense of déjà vu. Like I was reliving the same confusion I felt when my ex told me I was going mad.

'Our therapist is on hand, twenty-four hours a day, to

offer support to our contestants. We are aware that appearing in a reality show is an extreme departure from everyday life, which is why we are offering support. All interviews are conducted in the strictest confidentiality and will not be filmed for the viewers.'

'You need to remove Cameron, he's dangerous. Listen, I'm telling you the truth.'

I could hear how small my voice had become.

'Iris,' she replied, her voice now cold and devoid of any emotion. As if *I* was the problem. 'Would you like to leave *The Villa*?'

CHAPTER TWENTY-FOUR

THE REPORTER

Aruna, Balearic Islands

DAY TWO, *THE VILLA*

It was exactly how I'd imagined a therapy room in Harley Street might look. Pristine white. Minimalist. Only there were no lofty windows or washed-out watercolours on the walls. It felt like we were in a chamber buried deep beneath the villa. I was trying to work out what other secrets this place might have when an airlock hissed open. A strikingly tall man breezed into the room through a different door to the one I had entered from. He was handsome, in a Scandinavian way. Late thirties, tall, lithe but muscular.

It took a moment to register. *It's him.* The man who was at my audition.

'Iris!' he greeted me with a set of straight white showbiz teeth. 'I'm Dr Alexander Scott but everyone around here calls me Dr Alexander.'

His hair was cropped short to his head, sandy-coloured and combed to one side. He was clean-shaven and his eyes were bright blue. Almost an exact colour match with the sea surrounding the island.

'You've got nothing to be afraid of, try and relax . . .' He gestured to the closest chair.

I lowered myself, tugging my nightshirt to cover my knees.

The doctor immediately turned and disappeared through the hidden door, reappearing moments later with a woolly blanket, handing it to me without saying a word.

I looked at him warily. 'Thanks.'

He nodded appreciatively and took a seat. It was then that I noticed how exhausted he appeared. As tired as I felt. I could sense his entire body sigh into the fabric of the armchair opposite. It must have been around 5 a.m. Maybe later.

He crossed his long legs and folded his hands across the notepad, holding it in place on his lap.

'I want you to know, Iris, anything you want to say – or not say – I'm here to listen. In confidence.'

Oh wow. I didn't bother disguising my eye-roll. At least come up with something original, *Dr Alexander.*

'What are you? One of those TV doctors? Don't tell me, you do all the breakfast shows?'

He looked back at me calmly. 'Too shy for all of that. I'm more of a behind-the-scenes man. And I'm here to offer help and support.'

'I don't need your help.'

'OK, if that's how you're feeling,' he said.

The warmth of his smile only angered me more.

'Did they tell you I was attacked?' I could hear the doubt again.

'I was given your account of events.'

I crossed my arms, folding the bear into my chest. 'You don't believe me either?'

'I'm here to listen.'

'I'm not crazy!' But saying the words out loud made me feel like I was going mad. Why had I been sent to see a therapist? Because they thought I was unhinged? Could they see them too? *The flaws* – my ugly side he'd grown to hate.

'No one is saying you're crazy.'

But instead of reassuring, the repeated word only filled me with more uncertainty.

I lifted my gaze to the ceiling. 'Who's watching us?'

'Our time together is not being streamed for the viewers. This is patient-doctor confidentiality.'

'You didn't answer my question.'

I noticed his jaw clench. Like he was about to or wanted to say something.

'But are we being watched?' I nodded to the centre of the oval room, where a black sphere was flashing red.

He nodded. 'We must keep a log of everything.'

Dr Alexander had a softly spoken way about him. There was a hint of a regional accent but I couldn't quite place it. Northern, maybe? It sounded like he'd had elocution lessons to try to stamp it out. He shifted in his chair, the open neck of his shirt widened and I caught a glimpse of bronzed skin.

'We don't have to talk about anything,' he said, but his eyes lingered on my bear.

'Great, because I'm not feeling very chatty.'

'There's something important you should know though,'

he stressed. 'The people in charge won't let anything happen to you. *I* won't let anything happen to you.'

Even though he spoke for everyone, there was something in his tone which seemed to create a distance between himself and the rest of his team.

'Will you be OK?' he said.

'Can I go now?'

'Of course you can.'

I stood up to leave and then he said, 'I heard you were told about the prize money.'

I bristled. My whole body stiffened as his words dragged me back to those final moments before I came for my therapy.

Iris, do you want to leave The Villa?

Her words, now ringing in my head.

She hadn't let me answer, though. Before I could say anything, while I still had a choice, she pressed on with her news, announcing there'd been a change in the show, something I should know before I decided whether to leave.

'Iris, the prize money has been revised – our winning couple will now walk away with £250,000. Does that make it easier to decide?'

It was put so casually. As if it were £100 rather than £250,000. But we both knew the difference was life-changing. It was the kind of money I'd been dreaming about when stuck behind my desk writing yet another trashy story for the paper. It was the key to moving on. I could begin again.

A quarter of a million pounds.

While I sat in shock, processing the information, numb and confused, the presenter explained that, because of 'the circumstances', I was the first to know about the increase.

Singling me out. I'd suddenly felt special.

Then, she asked me again if I'd like to leave *The Villa*.

It wasn't just the money. Instantly, everything became easier – the focus had shifted to the prize and I could stop thinking about Cameron and what may or may not have happened. When had I become so exhausted by life? Someone had handed me an easy way out.

She'd bought my silence. She knew it. I knew it. And so did Dr Alexander.

'Iris?' The doctor tore into my thoughts. 'Are you OK?'

I swallowed hard, pretending not to hear him. As I reached for the door, he touched my arm. It made me jump.

'Sorry, I didn't mean to frighten you.'

I rubbed where his hand had been, as if that might soothe my nerves. But his touch had left a surprise prickle behind.

'You don't have to share a bed with Cameron.'

I turned around this time and his eyes were waiting to fix me.

'If the audience vote for you and Cameron to remain a couple, there're plenty of daybeds outside where you can sleep – *alone*.'

Again, he spoke as if hidden among his words there was a message, just for me, and for a fleeting moment I felt it was just the two of us. Lost together on a deserted island. It took me by surprise – the flush of heat.

He smelled fresh like hotel linen.

'Really, I'm fine,' I said, trying to sound more certain than I felt.

Now he was closer, I noticed there were chips in the

veneer. Three small divots running up his earlobe; closed-over earring holes. Were these hints of a wilder side?

I pressed the strange feeling away.

I turned to leave, but Dr Alexander had one more thing to say.

'Iris, don't let the money drive your decisions. Don't let it push you to do anything you don't want to do. It's just money.'

Easier said than done.

'Remember, I'm here whenever you need to chat.'

'Thanks,' I said, not really taking it in. My mind was saturated.

But as I slipped through the hidden door, returning to the villa and the people I was locked up with, I noticed his words had taken effect. They'd left an aftertaste. Something bitter and unpalatable that left me questioning everyone's motives. Including my own.

Now the stakes had gone up, what lengths would the other contestants go to in order to win the prize money?

CHAPTER TWENTY-FIVE

THE PRODUCER

Madrid, Interview Room One

NOW

'Dr Alexander Scott is his full name?' Sanchez looks at his notes.

'It's a showbiz thing. Dr Alexander sounds more *catchy*.'

'And you had to call on him for help?'

I let out a little laugh. 'It was more the case of *them* calling on him. How can I put this?' I smile. 'Dr Alexander has this way of fixing his gaze on you, making you feel the most important person in the room. Word got out that he was a shoulder to cry on and pretty soon all the women were putting in requests. Reality shows have come under fire for not having adequate support networks. I wanted to be the forerunner in offering the best support and aftercare plan.'

'So you're saying it was your idea to employ him?'

'That's what I've been trying to tell you. I only ever wanted the best for the people starring in the show. Dr Alexander Scott is hugely experienced and respected for his work at the Trinity Hospital in North London. He's clever, caring and gentle in his manner, but he's also enigmatic. You need that energy for TV. Yes, he was behind the scenes, but we still needed to keep that vibe through every part of the experience.'

'And the victim? Did she ask for his help?'

I wish he wouldn't keep doing that. Dredging her back into my thoughts.

'He spoke with her,' I admit.

Sanchez looks down and reads from his notes.

'It was reported that she was acting in a disturbed manner. Distressed. Not long after she arrived.'

He looks up, waiting for me to answer.

'Well, a show like *The Villa* takes some getting used to.'

'Was your doctor unable to calm her down?'

'It's hard to say.'

He blinks. 'Why?'

'We all wear masks. It's easy to hide what's really going on underneath.'

'Such as with Cameron Walker?'

I ignore him.

Sanchez returns to his notes. 'There's something very important I need to discuss with you now, in relation to the victim.'

I look across the table to where he's underlined, twice. I don't need to decipher his scrawl to see what he's written.

'The final prize amount – can you tell me why you kept increasing it?'

A silence sits between us while I try to answer this, delicately.

'A device to get them to do what you wanted?' he pokes.

I shift in my seat.

'The more they stood to win, the more extreme things they were prepared to do.'

He's saying it like it's news – when money has been a motivation since time began.

The words leave me before I have time to filter them: 'Everyone has a price!'

He sits back, laughing at his small victory.

'When you say price, you mean an amount they would do anything for?'

I nod. Let's run with this, Sanchez.

'That they would . . . kill for?'

CHAPTER TWENTY-SIX

THE CONTESTANT

Aruna, Balearic Islands

DAY TWO, *THE VILLA*

I woke up to the feeling of my skin burning.

I must have kicked the sheets off the daybed during the night, exposing my arms and legs. It was dawn but the sun was already searing everything in reach.

I say sleep, but it had been something much more broken and disturbed. When I'd managed to drift off, I'd been woken by a jolt. A falling sensation.

Dark, confusing thoughts had been chasing me. Mostly the uncertainty over what had happened.

I'd entered the therapy room pumped with adrenaline and crystal clear about what Cameron had done. And then, somehow, I'd left feeling utterly exhausted with a muddled order of events and what felt like someone else's version of how the night had unfolded. How did that happen?

That someone had been important though. The voice – she'd spoken with authority. A tone that forced you to listen. Now I felt nervous of saying the wrong thing.

Consequences. Her warning was the one thing that hadn't distorted. It rang out, clear as a bell.

And then there was Ben, someone who knew the *real* me. Even he thought I was into Cameron. *Leading him on.* They couldn't both be mistaken. Could they?

The images of my crazed behaviour, running from one room to another, were back, casting shade over my memory. Perhaps I had misheard Cameron?

Every time I went over what had happened to find some semblance of me, *my truth* in everyone else's words, I became more lost. That had to be a sign to leave it well alone. This was about *my* hang-ups. *My* trust issues.

It wasn't the first time I'd felt like the crazy one. My ex would always tell me how I'd got things wrong, how I'd misread the signs, I'd leapt to conclusions *again*. Ben was always warning me that I complained too much. That I should be more grateful.

Their angry voices swirled together and the dizziness returned. *The Villa* was supposed to be an escape. A chance to try out being someone else. To *become* Iris. But old ghosts had followed me and were prowling within the walls of the compound.

Day two and I was already exhausted. I rubbed my eyes, trying to rinse away the feeling. Instinctively looking to my wrist for the time. Only to be reminded there was no way of knowing. A neon pink Fitbit where my watch should be. The screen still black – it must be broken. That's when I saw it. A flash of movement. A figure stalking past the villa's patio windows.

I could just about make out an outline of someone, short

and petite, who had Angela's unmistakable long dark hair. There was a faint *slap slap slap* of sandals on a hard surface as she started up the stairs, disappearing from view. Her movements were stealthy. The quick steps of someone who didn't want to be seen.

My conversation with Dr Alexander in the white room came flooding back. Had Angela also been summoned to see him? Why would she need to speak to a therapist? Had she also been told about the new prize amount?

Suddenly there was a deafening noise. Blasting from every speaker inside the villa came the promised wake-up alarm.

'Rise and shine, contestants! Make your way to your bathrooms, where you will find everything you need for today's game.'

I wasn't in the mood for games.

'And for those that are hungry, breakfast is served.'

Across the garden, I was met with the sight of a table laden with treats. Croissants, muffins, a towering cylinder of pancakes, all artfully arranged on gold platters. The smell of buttered bacon rolls and freshly brewed coffee catching on the air.

The production team were like ghosts. They seemed to float in and out of the complex without anyone noticing. Just the thought of it gave me the shivers.

'You have one hour,' the presenter warned. 'At the sound of the next alarm, everyone must gather by the pool.'

Cameron. I wasn't mentally prepared to face him yet. With my bear tucked under my arm, I slid from the bed and darted inside. I took the stairs, two at a time, bowling through the bathroom door.

'Oh, it's you!' said Becky, startled.

She was in front of the mirror, wearing pointed-toe heels and a leotard that was so high cut you could see her hip bones. She practised her catwalk turns. Hand on hip, rotating this way and that. On a counter was a pile of gym wear. Next to that, a box brimming with beads and flower hairclips. What sort of game was this? Becky didn't seem at all curious as she obediently dressed herself. I caught her looking at me in her reflection.

'How was your night, babe? You and Cam looked cosy.' There was a wink as she said it.

My skin crawled at the mention of his name, but last night's warning had taken root. *Accusations carry consequences.* Before I could decide what I should say, Angela emerged from the bedroom stretching and yawning, making a big show as if she'd just woken. Only I knew she hadn't.

'Morning, sleepyhead. How was your night?' Becky was on the hunt for something salacious.

Angela shrugged.

'Oh?' Becky picked up on her disappointment.

'Nothing to report. I kept to my side of the bed. He kept to his.'

'He didn't try anything on?'

She shook her head. 'Guess he wasn't that into me.'

Angela spoke as if the rejection came from a much deeper place. Her wounds as open as mine.

'What about you?' Angela turned to Becky. 'You looked like you were cracking on with . . . What's his name again?'

'Blake. Yeah, it was fun. We may have had a bit of a kiss,' she said coyly.

'And . . .'

'And nothing.' A smile building as she moved the flower clip around her hair. Tilting her head and pouting every time she repositioned it.

There was a sudden surge of noise from outside. Stamping of feet. Laughter. Cameron's voice, ringing out. I recoiled from the door, even though I knew they weren't coming in. Moments later there was splashing and shouting coming from the pool and in the midst of my fear it struck me how quickly the guys had fallen into friendships while we were still jostling for position.

I peeled off into a toilet cubicle and pulled out the phone. Four messages from Ben.

'Laaaae-dies!' Annie's voice filled the bathroom. 'Good morning! Where's that filthy animal, Iris?' she called out.

I tried to block out her voice while I read the first text:

> Nothing yet on Cameron but we've got a lead on two of the girls. Done some digging and it turns out Becky shagged Premier League footballer Martin Kloss.

I glared at the screen.
Second message:

> We know posh boy Charles is lying about how rich he is. So what's his motive to win?

Laughter erupted from the other side of the cubicle door. Third message:

And we might have something on Angela. She got
herself into debt at uni, she might have more reason
than anyone to win the show. All coming together from
our end, so stick to the plan we agreed.

Agreed?

Final message. Missing you. He'd typed a smiley face:
colon, bracket, because the phone was too old for emojis.

I could sense the softness coming through but it was
too late.

I began a reply and then stopped myself. Had nothing
I'd said to him last night mattered? All Ben cared about
was the story, and his desperation to get the front page
had made him lose all perspective. He could piss off!

There was only one reason I was sticking this out now.
Money.

My anger wouldn't last, I knew that. But until then I
was going to keep Ben waiting for my reply. Holding on
to that crumb of power for as long as I could, I tucked the
phone away and unlocked the door.

'There she is,' said Annie, embracing me theatrically.
'I've been dying to know – what happened last night?'

'She slept outside,' Becky spoke for me.

I moved towards the tower of clothes.

'That's a lie, I saw you two lovers sneak off to your
room.'

'We're not lovers! And I slept *alone* on the daybed,' I
said, trying to keep the emotion out of my voice.

'Really?' said Annie.

I turned around. 'Yes, really.'

Annie eyed me mistrustfully. And then came the painted-on smile. 'Come on, you can tell us, darling. Bonking like rabbits all night long, weren't you?'

I glared.

She pulled a face as if to say *what a bore*. 'How frightfully dull.' She turned, raising her voice so there'd be no mistaking what she had to say. 'I spent the entire night fighting Adam off.'

Her announcement had Becky's full attention.

'He's into me, that much is obvious. He kept saying how sexy I am and what an incredible body I have.'

'So why fight him off then?' said Becky.

'We still have six days to go and making them want more is the only way to keep them interested. But, as you can imagine, darlings, it's been utter torture.' She wagged a finger at us. 'Don't get any ideas. He's mine.' She laughed but the sting in her tone gave her away. It was a warning. The entire conversation had seemed strained and it was hard to tell if it was us or herself that she was trying to convince of Adam's affection.

I was struggling to cope with her aggression, but at the same time, I couldn't help feeling worried for her as I studied her in the morning light.

Her face was swollen from her drinking, her eyes had sunk into their sockets. She'd had extensive work done to make her look younger. Botox, cheek implants, chemical peels and lifts. I wondered what was driving her insecurities. Ben seemed to have found secrets on everyone. Was there something Annie was hiding?

She caught me looking and cast me a sharp stare. With

an air of insult, she shrugged her lace nightie to the floor and walked naked to the showers.

'Twenty minutes until the games begin.' There was our reminder.

I grabbed matching green hot pants and crop top and a string of orange beads. My shower would have to wait – I needed to get the phone back to my room.

Angela was by the door as I was leaving. Debt? That's what Ben said in his message? As I slipped out of the room, I remembered how secretive she'd appeared earlier that morning, stalking the staircase.

'Hurry, hun. We don't have long,' Becky called after me.

My back was to the door as it opened. All three women appeared in my bedroom but there was something different about them. A frisson of threat hung between us.

A big shift in mood to the breezy chat in the bathroom moments earlier. Becky held a croissant in her hand, she was picking at the pastry.

For a moment they didn't speak, holding me in their icy stare.

'Is everything OK?' I said.

Annie leaned against the doorframe.

'So, turns out you have to fuck someone to win?'

I looked between them. 'What?'

'She's playing dumb again,' Annie said to the others.

I laughed. 'I have no idea what you're going on about.'

'Of course you do, darling. And surprise surprise, you're in the lead. You and Cameron are officially the nation's sweethearts. You must have really put on a show.'

'It's on the screen,' Becky joined in. She cast Annie a wry smile. 'Cameron's been telling everyone what an epic night you had. That you "put out".'

I pushed past them into the corridor, to the long windows that gave a view across the garden. They weren't making it up. There was my name, at the top of the leader board alongside Cameron's.

My eyes were drawn down, to the man poised at the edge of the pool. Confidently he pushed off, the crystal water breaking around him. The splash rained across the screen, across our names. Cameron emerged from the water, his hair slicked back from his face, grinning.

'He's been telling everyone what you did,' Becky said, in an amused way. Implying I was cheap.

I spun around. 'Well, he's lying!'

'We don't believe you, darling.' Annie stepped in. 'And now you're the favourites to win.' She made a step towards me. 'So! What we would all like to know is – why you lied to us? I thought we were all friends, and friends don't keep secrets.'

'I didn't *lie*.'

She laughed. 'That's hilarious.'

'Is this yours?' Becky picked up Ben's bear from my bed. Her grip tight around his tummy. Her nails dug into his fur as she shook it from left to right. 'He's just the cutest. He reminds me of my pup.'

I felt a flush of heat.

She pressed her face against him. The glitter from her make-up sprinkling his fur. 'I'm missing my Boo now.'

Put him down.

'Oh my goodness, he is A-dorable!' Annie exclaimed. 'Wherever did you find him?'

The whole of me was prickling. 'I didn't find him, he's a present.'

'You packed your teddy bear on holiday?' said Annie.

They were all looking at me in fascination. Annie and Becky moved closer.

'Darling,' Annie smiled, 'it's so cute you feel you can be yourself in here.' She turned to the girls. 'Isn't it ADORBS that Iris doesn't feel embarrassed to bring her teddy to bed with her?' She took the bear from Becky. 'A present, you say?'

There was an intensity in the way they were staring at me. Animals eyeing up their prey.

'Was he a present from someone special?' Becky said.

'No,' I cut her off, snatching the bear from Annie's grasp.

Annie raised her eyebrow to the girls. 'I didn't mean to upset you.'

'You didn't.'

A smile was building. 'Are you sure?'

'Really, I'm sure.' I held her gaze for a second longer to make sure my message had impact. Her eyes were sparkling. She shrugged. 'Well, if you say so.'

Every inch of me wanted to scream *Get the fuck out.*

I didn't need to – the alarm did the job for me.

The games were starting.

Although, it felt like they already had.

CHAPTER TWENTY-SEVEN

THE CONTESTANT

Aruna, Balearic Islands

DAY TWO, *THE VILLA*

His name was Flying Cheetah. He sat cross-legged in a string vest with a small red dot planted on his forehead.

'Namaste, contestants.'

He pressed his palms together. He was the first real person we had seen on the screen. A video link all the way from a studio somewhere in London.

The audience had decided we'd start the day with couples yoga, which meant I was trapped with Cameron.

A quarter of a million. Think about the money. Focus on that.

I swallowed my fear and sat down.

We were arranged in a semicircle, sharing mats rolled out across the decking. I could still sense the hostility from the girls.

Flying Cheetah spoke: 'I'd like us to come together in our breathing. To feel at one with the beautiful nature of the island. Close your eyes. Breathe in for four counts. Exhale for six. Let us join together on our mats.'

I kept my eyes open so I could keep an eye on everyone. I took note of their amused smiles, their sniggers. Only Blake seemed to be taking it seriously. He actually looked spiritual with his long, tousled hair.

The men had got off lightly with their gym wear – white cotton drawstring trousers – while we had been made to wear next to nothing. Annie was the only one who hadn't tied her hair back into a sporty ponytail. She wore it loose and backcombed from her crown.

Flying Cheetah also wore drawstring trousers, only they were bright orange and spotted with yin-yangs. His head was shaved. He was thin and wiry with leathery, sun-worn skin.

'And breathe out,' he said.

There was a burst of shared laugher from Becky and Adam as they locked eyes across their mats.

The yoga instructor touched his earpiece. 'We're having our highest viewer engagement. They're thrilled to see you take part in something more spiritual. And four more deep, calming breaths in.'

Becky's shoulders were shuddering – she was trying so hard to stifle her fit of giggles.

'Tune into the sounds around you. Listen to nature's vibration,' he said. 'What do you hear?'

Cameron breathing. In and out. Just as it had been on my neck. What could I feel? The temperature, clawing at me. The lycra, squeezing the air out of my chest. The air was completely still. Not even a hint of a breeze to move the heat away.

'And when you are ready, come to a standing position at the top of your mat. Placing your hands into the prayer position.'

Obediently, we rose to our feet while the instructor produced a large white card on an easel with two hand-drawn figures. The yoga position was not one I recognized.

'This is a beautiful asana or "position" for all you new yogis to start off with. It's called *trust*.'

We had to face each other, bend forward and form a prayer with our partner's hands. The trust part came from the threat of falling. If someone didn't apply equal pressure, the other would fall.

'Come on then, you,' Cameron said cheerily, behaving as if nothing had happened. He held out his palms, waiting for me to come to him.

I didn't want to give Cameron the satisfaction of knowing he frightened me. I forced myself to lean in and our palms touched. The feeling of his skin against mine made me flinch.

'Wonderful, yogis!' Flying Cheetah clapped enthusiastically. 'Now breathe into your pose.'

Cameron smiled.

'Lean forward and press into your partner's hands.'

The grin rose. Signalling there was something between us.

'Use your intuition, and *trust*.'

Every part of me felt stiff, awkward and unyielding.

'Relax,' Cameron whispered in that same low tone.

I drew my hands away, letting him fall to the mat.

'I'm sensing a vibration to my left. Is everything OK, yogis?' the instructor said.

'No!' I snapped. *Everything's not fucking OK.*

'Yes!' Cameron said quickly.

'She pieing you off, mate?' Adam laughed. 'Lost your touch already?'

'Not at all, *mate*, just a bit of fun.' Cameron looked at me sharply. 'What's up with you?' he said to me under his breath.

He doesn't know?

Cameron frowned. A look of confusion taking hold. Christ, he really thinks everything is OK between us? What's wrong with him?

'Let go of your egos, yogis, this practice is not about showing off,' said Flying Cheetah, glossing over what was unfolding. 'Moving on to our next pose, we have a variation of the downward dog. If the men could find a position, like so . . .' The instructor folded in two. Speaking from under his armpit, he said: 'If the ladies could place their feet on their partner's back, forming a downward dog above him. This is challenging, I know, yogis, but I sense your chakras are open and ready.'

'Chakras,' Charles said. 'What are those?'

At least I didn't have to look Cameron in the eye for this one.

There was laughing and squealing as we attempted to mount our feet onto the base of our partner's back. The position was intense. Blood rushed to my head. My wrists ached with the weight of my body pressing into my hands. My feet slipping on Cameron's sweat. There was a thud followed by a clap of laughter and I peered from under my arm to find Angela rolling around on her back in hysterics. It was the first time I'd seen her laugh, really laugh. Charles quickly leapt to her side, checking she hadn't hurt herself.

'OK, yogis. Feedback from our viewers. They're loving the vibe from Charles and Angela right now. Although they would like to see something a little,' he paused, 'more hands on. Adam, if you can't straighten your legs in downward dog, you can add a slight bend in the knee. Don't feel embarrassed, this position is always more challenging for men.'

'I can do it!' Adam nettled.

'They aren't feeling the energy from Iris and Cameron. Has someone stolen your zen this morning? The viewers want more of the performance you put in last night.'

'You mean put out,' Becky said under her breath.

Flying Cheetah touched his earpiece again. 'Beautiful energy, people. More requests are coming in from our viewers. They want *to see less clothing*.'

He broke away. I glanced up at the screen and I thought I saw something strained in his expression now.

'OK,' he said, his voice now slightly uneven. 'Our viewers want you to free yourself of your burdens and enter a new kind of practice.' He touched his earpiece again, more nervously this time. 'If you feel comfortable with the idea, you may remove all clothing from the top half of your body.'

I laughed to myself. This had to be a joke.

'We already have, mate,' Adam shouted. Casting around to drum up some laughs.

'And namaste.' The instructor smiled through the disruption. He kept smiling until they quietened down, smoothing over the impact of what he'd asked of us.

Topless yoga? Nobody will fall for this.

The connection to London was suddenly replaced by a gold number running across the entire length of the screen: £250,000.

'What the . . . ?' Cameron jerked around. 'Guys, look! The prize money's gone up!'

Screaming broke out, a fresh energy instantly building. I watched how their expressions quickly changed from shock to excitement to something much quieter and withdrawn. A subtle narrowing of their eyes as if they might be scheming their next move.

I felt a prickle of anxiety. I preferred it when it was just me who knew the stakes had gone up.

Then, Becky's hand shot up.

'I'll do it.' She reached for the sky, waving her hand around like a child desperate to win the teacher's approval. 'I'll take off my top.' She grinned as she looked around her. 'They cost me enough, I might as well show 'em off.'

I thought she was messing around. But then, to my astonishment, Becky began undressing. A stunned silence fell as she slipped the straps of her leotard from her shoulders. She peeled the lycra down, all the way to her waist, slowly revealing two perfectly shaped breasts.

'Oh my God,' Angela gasped.

Becky lifted her arms up and twirled.

The silence stretched as we stared at the spectacle. I didn't know whether to admire her confidence or pity her.

The whole thing was so bizarre, it took a moment to bring me to my senses.

This is wrong. Really wrong.

Surely someone was going to step in? I looked to the instructor, who was back leading the class.

Nothing.

It was Adam who eventually broke us out of our shock, wolf-whistling through his teeth.

Anger. Jealousy. Rage. The shades visibly rose across Annie's face but then, as if remembering the cameras, she drew on a smile, calmly rose to her feet, flicked her hair over her shoulder and began undressing.

'I think I'll join you, darling,' she said, pulling aggressively at her boob tube. She reminded me of a caterpillar trying to wriggle free of its cocoon, her hips jerking from side to side as she wrestled with her top.

When she did finally get it off, Annie felt it needed celebrating. She raised the boob tube into the air and swung it around, her breasts flouncing while she lassoed. Laughing as it crossed the air, aimed directly at Becky's partner, Blake.

The top planted onto his face. Our breaths held, waiting for his reaction.

Blake was grinning as he pulled it away.

'You can return that to me later,' she winked at him.

It had been made clear. Annie and Becky had entered into some sort of game of their own. If Annie had a glass of champagne in her hand now, she'd have raised it to Becky.

'I can do tree pose,' Becky retaliated, rushing into the yoga position.

'That's easy, darling. But can you do it with your eyes shut?'

'What a great idea,' said Flying Cheetah, trying to take back control of his class, his tone uneven. 'If everyone could move into tree, otherwise known as Vrikshasana.'

'Vrika-what?' Adam said.

'Vrikshasana,' Blake repeated with a sigh. 'It's ancient Sanskrit.'

We followed our instructor, lifting one foot and pressing it to our inner thigh. Hands into a prayer. Holding ourselves perfectly upright. Tummy in.

'And breathe.'

We were told to focus on something ahead. The horizon. To act like everything was normal. But Becky and Annie's nudity had stolen the gaze of all the men.

The sun continued to beat down. The temperature had soared five degrees, or at least it felt that way. I longed for the breeze to come in and sweep everything away.

'Lovely, yogis. And as we come to the end of our morning's class . . .'

My prayer had been answered. 'Oh thank God,' I said on my exhale.

'If we can return to our seated position.'

I wondered how Becky and Annie would feel later. Once the dust from their duel had settled. I'd be mortified to know thousands, maybe millions, had seen my breasts. There's no coming back from something like that, is there? You can't unsee things.

A sense of calm arrived as we ended with a prayer. I closed my eyes this time, relieved the game was finally over.

'And namaste,' our instructor said, bowing out.
'Hang on!'
Her voice was unmistakable. Clear as a bell.
Annie stood up: 'I'm not done yet!'

CHAPTER TWENTY-EIGHT

THE CONTESTANT

Aruna, Balearic Islands

DAY TWO, *THE VILLA*

'Game's over, Annie,' Becky said, laughing at her in a way that people do when someone misses the punchline.

'Don't be such a spoilsport,' Annie said jovially. 'There's many more positions we can try.'

Dread hit me.

'Ones that will *really* loosen you up.'

Oh God, I could feel it coming.

'What about the Dog? You know, doggie style. You're all familiar with that position, aren't you?'

She winked at Blake again.

'Ladies, move into downward dog. Gentlemen, support your woman from behind.'

She cast around as we stopped and stared.

'Lighten up, people, it's just a bit of fun! Who's joining me then?'

Nobody knew what to say or do.

'OK, I'll have to show you.' She stepped off her mat.

'Before you bend over, I suggest you find more length in your body, really stretch out those calves.'

I looked to Flying Cheetah. Do something! He was hiding behind a faraway look. Why wasn't he saying anything? Only his eyes were moving, blinking rapidly. Gagged. I got the sense strongly worded instructions were being fed into his earpiece.

I opened my mouth to call out to him and then the transmission cut out. Our one link to the real world – gone.

A tremor ran through me as I cast around. *Someone, do something!* Angela must have been thinking the same as she looked back at me fearfully.

Annie was now in charge.

'You can call me Guru,' she said, moving across the decking to where she'd parked her high heels. She strapped herself into them and sashayed back to the mat. Commanding attention with every hip thrust.

Annie hooked her finger at Adam. 'Come close behind.'

Obediently, he followed.

'Clo-ser,' she purred over her shoulder.

He glued himself to her back. A look of excitement growing. Sweat shimmered like glitter across his dark skin.

Nobody knew what to do. One look at her determined expression and you could sense something terrible was advancing.

'This is the best bit,' she said, taking her time as she bent over. Pressing her bum cheeks into Adam's groin, her breasts hanging like udders.

There was a slight buckle of her knees as she reached

for the mat. The extra height on her heels made it almost impossible for her to fold into a downward dog. What could have been vaguely sexy suddenly looking clumsy and amateur. Like a drunk stripper clambering about on stage.

The fact it wasn't alcohol fuelling her behaviour this time made it all the more alarming. Annie really didn't have any sort of off switch. She seemed willing to do anything for attention.

Adam put his arm around her waist and hauled her back onto her feet.

'Thanks, darling. I was just getting there myself.'

I spotted the flash of anger in her eyes. Determined to keep her heels on, she resumed more of a bent-over position.

'What else would you like to see?' she said through her thicket of hair.

'Nothing! You're a headcase!' Becky shouted back. She raised her hands like a flag, announcing she was standing down. The game had gone *way* too far.

I searched around. Where was the presenter? Or Dr Alexander – surely he should step in? Where were they now?

The air had become charged with sex and I noticed the predatory look filling Cameron's eyes.

'What else do you want to see?' Annie said more loudly. This time it was clear she hadn't been addressing us. 'Come on, darlings, I'm waiting.'

This was no longer about one-upmanship. It had become about winning over the viewers. She was offering herself up for votes.

'Oh God,' Angela whispered.

But it was impossible to tear my eyes away. None of us could. We were all mesmerized. Watching, waiting to see how much worse it was going to get. I knew the viewers were doing the same.

But while Annie waited for her response, the boys' interest began to wane. Until eventually, Cameron's attention was diverted to the kitchen.

'Champagne, lads?' he announced.

'Yaass, bro!' Adam released his grip on Annie, preferring the challenge of hunting down booze to their sex position.

It felt like we should look away to spare her embarrassment. Annie straightened and stepped off her mat, pretending to still be in full control of the situation.

Determined to be the one in charge, she grabbed the bottle of champagne Adam had found from out of his hand and tipped it back. Then she wiped her mouth and turned to face us.

'And that's how it's done, girls,' she said triumphantly, aiming her barbed look at Becky and me.

With that, she turned on a point, trying to look sexy as she headed for the hot tub.

A stunned silence followed her exit. Nobody knew what to say. How do you follow on from that? Finally, after what felt like a very long time, Blake said:

'Fucking hell!'

A typhoon had struck our little island. Turning our sense of what was right and wrong upside down.

Cameron offered up his bottle. 'Drink, anyone?'

*

There was an immediate drop in tempo after Annie left, the guys and the girls splintering into two groups to digest what had happened.

Again, I noticed how tentative Charles was with Angela. How he lightly touched her arm to check if she was OK. Eager to know he hadn't upset her. Charles was the only one to show any remorse over how he'd behaved. In the sobering aftermath, he clearly regretted being led along by the pack. Out of nowhere, it sprang. A stab of jealousy at the tenderness he was showing Angela. *I missed Ben.* I knew he'd return to my thoughts; I just didn't think it would be so soon. Suddenly I was craving everything normal.

'What was she trying to prove?' Becky said to us. 'That was mental.' She lowered her voice to a whisper: 'And I can't believe how Adam behaved.'

Becky was so distracted by her jealousy that she'd forgotten to dress herself. Bitching away while her leotard remained bunched at her waist. Angela and I couldn't find the courage to say anything.

There was a splash from behind us. The boys were done with their chatting and were taking it in turns to bomb the pool. Waves of water threw up over the sides.

'This is too weird,' Angela said. Her face was flushed with stress. 'What do you think?'

The boys were shouting and laughing. They washed away their behaviour like it never happened.

'I want to know why nobody stepped in.' I looked around as I said it, addressing the phantom presenter.

'Maybe one of us should have said it?'

'Did you see how Annie was cracking onto Blake?

Desperate. As if he'd be interested in her.' Becky turned to Angela. 'Said what?'

'The safe word.'

'You can't say it for someone else. It has to be when *you* can't handle it.'

'Well, I couldn't deal with it – I was really uncomfortable,' Angela said.

'Why didn't you speak up if you felt that freaked out?' Becky said coldly.

'I wasn't sure if I should . . . or, if I could . . . This is all so weird. Doesn't anyone else think something messed up is going on?'

'Stop being so serious all the time. Have a laugh!' said Becky, apparently forgetting how appalled she'd been at Annie's behaviour.

'I'm worried about the next game. If yoga can turn into that then—'

'Babe. You're getting too worked up. Fuck's sake, chill.' Becky squinted into the middle distance. 'Hey, who's that?' She pointed across the garden to the black and gold door.

With all the drama, nobody had heard him arrive.

Becky lurched forward and stopped. 'Oh my God. New housemate.' She turned back to us, shrieking: 'Fresh meat!' She spun around again, waving her hands at him from across the pool, her breasts bobbing up and down. 'Hey! Over here!'

He was tall with strawberry blonde hair. A medium build and wearing board shorts and a sky-blue T-shirt. Normal looking.

Despite the heat, a chill ran through me. Because our

new housemate wasn't a stranger. He made my fear of Cameron pale in comparison. The man walking towards us knew my true identity.

He knew me, better than anyone.

CHAPTER TWENTY-NINE

THE VIEWERS

ELEVEN MILLION VIEWERS

Katie and Beth were best friends from Solihull in Birmingham.

Katie had recently broken up with her boyfriend of eighteen months. What started out as a distraction from her heartbreak had spiralled into an addiction. Consoling herself by watching other people's car-crash lives.

'This is so shit, but it's SO good!' Beth leaned forward, reaching closer to the screen. 'Annie's mental. She doesn't give a toss what anyone thinks.'

'That's a man in women's clothing right there,' Katie agreed.

'But we need people like her in *The Villa*, otherwise it's boring. What else can we make her do?'

They studied the contestants' heart rates, noting how Iris's Fitbit reading was spiking.

'Where's Iris going?' Katie remarked.

'New guy's arrived and Iris is doing a runner. Why? Quick – follow her. Camera five, quick. Six, press six!' Beth squealed at Katie. 'Give me that.'

Beth nudged her friend aside, taking control.

'Hey!'

'That's a girl on a *serious* mission,' Beth said. 'Maybe she wants to get tarted up for the new guy.'

'Nah, she's not into him.'

'How can you tell?'

'She'd be sticking around. I'd say she's trying to avoid him. Christ – look at her heart rate now.'

'Do you think there's more to this?'

'I'd say,' said Katie.

'He's noticed her though. Look! Talk about a stalker stare.'

'There's definitely something going on here. If you ask me, she's frightened. You don't get a heart rate like that unless you feel in danger.'

'This just got interesting!'

'Savage!' exclaimed Katie.

Beth tittered. 'Don't tell me you're not enjoying yourself?'

Katie looked offended.

'It's taking your mind off you-know-who. Hang on, where's Iris going now?'

CHAPTER THIRTY

THE CONTESTANT

Aruna, Balearic Islands

DAY TWO, *THE VILLA*

Don't run. Keep calm. Don't let anyone see how frightened you are.

My heart thundered as I tried to soothe myself, my eyes dodging the cameras as I quick-stepped past the pool.

Why is he here?

A flush of heat spread up my neck at the thought of what was to come. The shaming. The embarrassment. I imagined the bemused smile he was wearing as he watched me flee.

I need to call Ben. He'll rescue me. Get to the phone.

Inside the villa, the cold pinged the soles of my feet. Striking like small electrical shocks. Then an even more frightening thought hit me.

Can Ben rescue me? And would he, even if he knew my location? The word BAIT going off like gunfire in my head. The thought of putting all my trust and hope in a man who wanted to put me in jeopardy – who'd disappointed me countless times before – was terrifying.

Slow down. Small steps. I can't let anyone see yet. But despite my efforts to hide my panic from the cameras, I could feel my face contorting. The deep worry groove between my brows was caving inwards.

Through the patio doors and up the stairs. I counted my steps by way of a distraction. Fighting the urge to break into a run.

It's a coincidence. Yeah, that's it. He was randomly selected to star in The Villa.

Shut up, Laura. Coincidences like this don't just happen.

The temperature in the room had returned to normal. The bed was as Cameron had left it. Duvet strewn messily. A half-empty glass of water on the table. No, wait. Something was different. My nightshirt, which I'd left on the floor, had been folded neatly and placed on my pillow.

Someone had been in my room.

My pulse took off. I hurried towards the cupboard. Who'd been in my room? The girls? No, they'd been outside all this time. Who, then?

Too much uncertainty was hurtling towards me. Fear of *him*, of the shadowy figures who worked behind the scenes. Worry about the trouble I was in.

A small hysterical laugh broke free when I saw the bear exactly where I'd left it. Middle alcove, pushed to the back.

My line to the real world was still there. Thank God.

Never had I been so happy to see a cheap soft toy.

Whatever was headed my way, I'd be able to deal with. Ben might be an utter dick, but he wouldn't leave me stranded. The newspaper had a responsibility to get me out of the mess they'd thrown me into. Calmer, more rational thoughts began circulating as I headed for the toilet. My breathing slowed. My pulse steadied.

Through the hall window I could see everyone was still outside, and the girls had crowded around *him*. Becky had managed to dress herself. Annie had returned from the hot tub wearing a kaftan. What was he telling them? Whatever it was, they were listening intently.

Call Ben. Hurry up. GO.

It took all of my restraint not to sprint the last few metres of the corridor. I marched into the bathroom and locked myself in the toilet. Finally, alone, and in what I hoped was my safe space, I unzipped the secret compartment.

The news would come as a shock to Ben. Despite our physical intimacy, he barely knew me.

I wish I could say the same, but I knew everything about Ben's family. His wife's name, that she worked as a nurse in a care home, that they had three boys, all primary school age. In one of my low moments, I'd spent an evening googling everything about him. Pathetically searching for holes in his happy home life.

I shook the thought loose. None of that mattered now. Not now my past had come calling.

I reached my hand inside the toy, threading my way through the rough fibres. Burrowing deeper and deeper, clawing away at the padding until I reached all the way to the fabric on the other side.

The phone – it had gone.

CHAPTER THIRTY-ONE

THE CONTESTANT

Aruna, Balearic Islands

DAY TWO, *THE VILLA*

There was no way out.

They know.

I was trapped on the island.

They must have taken my phone while we were doing yoga.

Trapped with them. With *him*.

My whole body tightened, my muscles contracting. I crossed my legs and curled into a ball, trying to make myself as small as possible. The way an animal would do if it were cornered by predators.

Only no one was attacking me. Nobody had come to flush me out – at least, not yet. Maybe if I hid here for the rest of the day, it just might all go away.

And then, all of a sudden, I couldn't stop the tears. Hot with rage. *Fuck you, Ben, for getting me into this situation.*

I didn't know whether I wanted to kick down the door or shrink into a tight ball.

Never had I felt so confused. So alone.

I'm not sure how many more minutes passed while my emotions yo-yoed. Because time had been snatched from us the moment we stepped inside the villa. Had that too been turned into a weapon to control us?

Nothing was making sense.

Yet the small part of me that was still functioning recognized I couldn't hide forever. I had to accept the situation. Either I must go out there and stick to my story – or confess.

What choice did I really have? I took a deep breath and slid open the lock.

They were crowded on the other side of the pool. Close to the sea. Huddled in low, threatening conversation.

I was having another out-of-body experience. As if I'd become the viewer looking on from behind my screen. Watching myself take small, nervous steps towards the enemy. I imagined the strain on my face. The stiffness across my body as I watched myself perform as Iris, one last time.

There's still time to change your mind.

I slowed to a stop. The hot planks burned my feet. The sun was first to punish me while I hung in my indecision.

Go back. Now, before they see you.

But as I turned, a chorus of laughter rung out.

'Hey, Iris!'

I pretended I hadn't heard and carried on walking.

'Hey! Where you going?' It was Cameron's voice. 'Hey!'

I stopped and stood perfectly still, knowing I had to turn – I couldn't not, now I'd been seen. But I was terrified.

More than anything, I was afraid of facing *him* and the power he held over me.

Slowly I forced myself around. Steeling for the confrontation.

Angela stepped from the group. 'Where'd you go? We were all worried about you.' She looked genuinely pleased to see me.

The splish-splash made both of us jump. Blake had thrown Annie into the pool and dived in after her. The pair frolicked, slapping the water in each other's faces. Flirting like teenagers.

They don't know. He hasn't told them.

'Hey, you OK?' Angela said.

I'm safe. I'm going to be OK. Relief wrapped its blanket around me.

I rearranged my expression. 'You don't need to worry,' managing a smile. 'So, what have I missed?'

'There's a new guy.' Becky pointed.

On hearing himself mentioned, he broke away from his conversation with Charles and headed over. Everything so familiar – the confident stroll. That affable smile.

I, on the other hand, was a rabbit in headlights.

His eyes met mine and for a brief moment I imagined everything would be OK. Just like the good old days when I'd have panic attacks and he'd hold me until my heart slowed and I felt calm again.

Projecting his voice so there would be no room for misunderstanding, my ex, *my* Matt, greeted me with a casual: 'Hi, Laura.'

CHAPTER THIRTY-TWO

THE PRODUCER

Madrid, Interview Room One

NOW

'At what point during the show,' he leans in, 'did you find out Laura was a journalist?'

I roll my eyes. Seriously? Now he's insulting my intelligence, and that offends me.

'Can I get a top-up?' I say, waving my plastic cup at him.

'No. Answer the question.'

I sit back into my chair. 'You can't deny me my rights. What time is it?' It feels like the middle of the night.

'It's 5.10 a.m. I'll get you water in a minute. First, answer the question.'

'Don't you people sleep?'

He ignores me.

Sulkily, I let out a sigh and say: 'I knew from the very beginning.'

Of course I bloody knew. That's what my researchers were there for.

'Laura's application was a perfect fit for *The Villa*. She quickly made the shortlist and then the researchers got to work carrying out the usual background checks. Who is Laura? What does she do in her spare time? Who's she shagging? All the stuff I mentioned before that makes someone a good candidate for a reality show. Don't look at me like that, Detective. We had to know, and Laura barely covered her tracks. It didn't take too much effort to work out she wasn't who she said she was. That she had all sorts of questionable morals, like having sex with her married boss.'

'And that she worked for a British national paper.'

'Exactly.'

'So . . .'

'So? I thought, what's she playing at? It really pissed me off. There we were, trying our hardest to produce something entertaining that also helps people find love. And all that trashy tabloid wanted to do was ruin us. Infiltrate my show. Sabotage it with their sleazy stories.' *How dare they try and hurt my baby.* 'Their smug editor, Mark Cush. I met him at a drinks party once, so full of himself. Misogynistic prick.' I snort. *Deep breath.* 'I actually felt sorry for Laura. She was just another one of Cush's disposable soldiers. He was using her.'

Sanchez laughs. 'And that's not what you were doing? *Using* your contestants for entertainment?'

'I'll square with you. After I got over my anger, I saw an opportunity in Laura to attract more viewers. That phone she brought in had to go though. As soon as she left her room, I had one of the crew fetch it.'

'It was exploitation!' he comes at me.

'I was trying to create something beautiful. I wanted to help people find love.' I pause, sadness creeping in. 'Lasting love.'

He casts me another sceptical look before returning to his pad. He licks his finger and thumbs his way back through the notes. While he does so, my mind drifts. Way, way back to the caravan park in Wales. Our conversation about love and relationships has unboxed a memory.

At the time, I believed her. That's what seven-year-olds do; they trust everything that comes out of their mum's mouth. She told me it was going to be our special holiday. To make up for all the shit that had gone on before. The neglect. The poverty. The nights I spent alone watching cartoons while she had another of her 'special friends' around. She always made sure she turned the volume up so I wouldn't hear them fucking through the paper-thin walls. But I always heard.

She'd rented a static caravan on a cliffside in Wales. Our special girly weekend together. The caravan was a shithole. The inside walls were blackened with mildew. The cupboards were hanging off their hinges. The toilet didn't flush, so every time I needed a piss I had to run across the mud to the concrete building where the strange men hung around.

Our girl-time barely lasted two minutes. Mum took off to the local pub where she could get wasted and pick up a job, i.e. a man who would pay her thirty quid to fuck her. She did him outside the caravan, up against the door. Banging away. He followed her inside with a gaze I'll never forget. Eyes half-closed with drunkenness. Unshaven. His head pressed to his forearm as he leaned against the door. Flies still hanging open. 'Night, baby,' Mum said and gave him a sloppy kiss. 'You dirty bitch,' he smiled as she closed the door on him. She stumbled into the kitchen area and glared at me like I was her biggest regret. 'Whad'ya looking at? I did it for you, didn't I. Ungrateful bitch.' They were the last words she spat out before collapsing on the mustard couch that wrapped around the table.

I couldn't sleep that night. I hid under the blanket on the pull-out bed, listening to the storm raging outside. The rain hammered, drumming the roof like gunfire. The wind shook the caravan so violently I imagined us being pushed right off the edge of the cliff, smashing on the rocks below. I couldn't breathe, I pulled the blanket away from my face.

Mum. It was all I could think with the fear. As usual, I'd already packed away my disappointment from the evening's events. I crawled out of my nest in search of a hug, only to find she'd moved from being sprawled on the couch to slumped over the table. All her drug paraphernalia, scattered in front of her. She must have woken up at some point, tried to shoot up but been too pissed out of her skull to see it through. It was my chance to stop her.

I crept across the caravan, on tiptoes, while the windows rattled in their sockets. I held my breath. The tips of my fingers trembled as I reached across the table for the needle. Stretching. And then, all of a sudden, her eyes opened and she grabbed my wrist, squeezing it so tightly I thought it was going to snap.

'You're hurting me,' I cried.

'You evil child.' She tightened the hold on my arm and

then came the fist. Smack. A haymaker to my right eye. So hard it knocked me off balance and I fell into the kitchen counter.

'Stop crying, pathetic bitch!'

I crumpled, curling into a ball, folding my arms over my head to shield me from the onslaught of punches that was headed my way.

'NEVER' – smack – 'take' – smack – 'my gear away!' Smack, smack. I thought my eardrum had exploded.

The reservoir of painful memories leaks into my eyes. *Stop.* Tears are for the weak. I slip my hands under the desk and begin pinching the skin around my wrists to counteract the pain growing inside my chest. Just how I used to do with the scissor blade.

'Señora, we need to speak about Matthew Taylor,' he says, but I can barely hear him. I'm concentrating instead on swallowing back the hurt.

'Through your *research*, you discovered he was Laura's ex-partner and you invited him on the show?'

I manage a small nod.

'Why would you do something like that?'

I keep my gaze low, not wanting to let Sanchez see I'm upset.

'I wanted to reunite them. Laura came across like a lost soul. Underneath the fake smiles, she was rudderless.' I know because that was once me.

Sanchez notices. 'Are you all right?'

'I'm fine,' I snap. 'The show was about people finding "the one".'

His eyebrow goes up.

Love. Why won't he believe that all I'd wanted to produce was love?

'Did you know that almost fifty per cent of couples who break up get back together again? *Fifty per cent.*'

'And the prize money. What amount was Señor Taylor told he could win if he came on the show?'

I blink.

'An extremely influential amount of money, wasn't it?'

I don't say anything.

'Did Cameron Walker and Señor Taylor know of each other prior to *The Villa*?'

CHAPTER THIRTY-THREE

THE CONTESTANT

Aruna, Balearic Islands

DAY TWO, *THE VILLA*

'You're a journalist?' Adam came nearer still. Repeating my confession. 'A sneaky gutter press reporter.' A vein was visibly bulging from his temple. He spat at the ground. 'Lying bitch.'

They'd formed a wall around me and it was tightening.

Cameron planted a hand on Adam's shoulder, indicating he was taking over. 'What have you told your paper about us?'

My voice had been reduced to a whisper. 'Nothing. I didn't tell them anything.'

'What a load of shit.'

It was just as I'd imagined. Them as the jury. Casting judgement. Me, choking on my words because there was nothing I could say in my defence. I glanced behind, hoping a magic portal would open up and teleport me somewhere safe.

But all that waited for me was the fierce drop into the ocean.

'Look, I'm sorry, I was doing as I was told.' But as soon as I said it, I realized how pathetic that sounded. 'I swear, I didn't give them any stories on you.'

Shit. Why did I open myself up to that? Please don't let them know about the phone.

I looked pleadingly to Matt, but he was staring at his feet, anxiously biting his bottom lip. He'd thrown the grenade and then backed away. As if by order.

'Liar! You can't believe anything she says,' said Cameron, moving his eyes around the group.

'Oh darling, you really have got yourself in a frightful mess,' Annie said, looking triumphant.

'What paper did you say you worked for?' Blake said.

Warily, I replied, '*The Record.*'

I felt dirty just saying it.

Adam crossed his arms and shook his head: 'Like I said, gutter journalism.'

I shrank away some more, until my back hit the wall. With nowhere to go I looked to Angela, the only person in here who I could vaguely call an ally, but her gaze was fixed low to the ground.

'What have you got on us, then?' Cameron said again. This time, I noticed the tension in his voice, an apprehension lurking behind his incessant questions. 'What stories have you been making up? That's what you do, isn't it? Make shit up! I despise your kind.' He said it with such bitterness, such hatred. The anger in him was palpable. He stabbed a finger at me. 'Scum like you ruin lives.'

'Hey mate, bit savage, ease up,' Blake said with a laugh, attempting to defuse the situation.

'I'm not asking you,' Cameron snapped his head around. 'You'll know when I want your opinion.'

Blake held up his hands and took a step back.

Matt, please. Do something.

My eyes were shooting looks at him, praying he'd pick up on my cries for help. That he'd confront the damage he'd caused. *Look up.*

Finally, Matt lifted his head. His brow had become lined. His mouth moved open but then just as quickly closed.

A small part of me died.

With no one else to call on, I searched around, into the vast emptiness. Pleading with the presenter to step in. Barely believing it had come to this. All my hopes now pinned on a virtual being.

And then – I remembered.

Of course. The ace up my sleeve.

That's what the silence has been for. She's been waiting for me to say it. Yes, that's it. Fine. I'll shout it out and let the whole fucking world know I've had enough!

But as I parted my lips to speak, the word got caught in my throat. The sudden realization snatching my breath away.

Jesus.

The hairs on my neck stirred.

It all made sense now.

This, all of it, had been planned.

My safe word was the name of the lodge where we'd stayed in Cornwall, the weekend Matt had proposed. I'd buried it with all the other memories of Matt. So deep underground it had taken this level of anguish to be exhumed.

Matt must have told them *everything* about us. But why? Why go to all this effort to humiliate me?

Spearing my anger into the air, I fired the word out. 'Ellemara.'

Now get me the fuck out of here.

I crossed my arms and waited.

When nothing happened, I tried again, 'Ellemara!' Just in case there had been some confusion.

Soon I'll be home. If only I'd thought of it earlier.

More seconds passed. I cast around for a sign of something happening. For the screen to emerge. For the door to swing open. Something. Anything.

But all that met me were sniggers.

Becky giggled. 'Think you've lost the plot, babe.'

'ELLEMARA!' Even louder, sharper. More desperate.

Still there was nothing. Why isn't anything happening?

Matt was looking at me as if he had something urgent to say. His freckly face flushed pink with stress.

After what felt like an eternity, contact with the outside world was made.

'Laura,' she said.

The presenter's voice had taken on a headmistress tone. 'Laura, you've disappointed us.' She paused. It felt deliberate, as if she wanted me to feel guilt.

It had the desired effect. Like a scolded child, I bowed my head.

'Lying about your identity is a breach of our house rules.'

'I know, I'm sorry.' There was nothing else I could say.

'You have broken rule number three. Contact with the

outside world is forbidden. This includes the internet, news-papers, phone calls and conversations with anyone outside *The Villa*.'

Adam whistled. 'Little Miss Naughty.'

'You now face eviction from *The Villa*.'

I lifted my head. Great! Yes! This wasn't how I thought the safe word worked, but as long as I was leaving . . .

'Good riddance,' Cameron jeered.

'However . . .' the presenter interrupted their celebra-tion. She waited for another theatrical silence to settle and that's when I knew. It wasn't over. 'We like to include our viewers in our decision-making.'

I was back on the rollercoaster, slowly chugging up the track. The big drop, only moments away.

'Laura . . .'

'Yes,' I murmured.

'The audience will decide whether you will be evicted from *The Villa*.'

My stomach dropped.

'What the actual fuck?' Becky mouthed.

'Voting is now open,' she said breezily. 'You can register on our website, app and all our social media platforms. Text messages will be charged at standard network rates. You have twenty minutes to decide whether Laura should stay or leave *The Villa*.'

CHAPTER THIRTY-FOUR

THE CONTESTANT

Aruna, Balearic Islands

DAY TWO, *THE VILLA*

'Laura . . .'

It had all been a lie. More smoke and mirrors.

'Yes,' I said, my voice barely there.

There'd never been a safe word and now I was at the viewers' mercy.

'Pack your things. You must be ready to leave *The Villa* immediately if you're evicted.'

If? Was there any doubt the public would boot me out? I was probably the most hated woman in the UK right now.

Like some playground bully, Cameron began clapping: 'Out! Get her out! Out!' Adam, Becky and Annie were only too eager to join in. That's all they were, overgrown school bullies.

They're just words, harmless little words. Yet I still felt myself shrink at their cruelness. It was the rejection, the humiliation of it all.

Angela and Charles looked increasingly uncomfortable

and had drifted to the edge of the group to be with one another.

Soon you'll be in the helicopter, soon this will all seem like a bad dream.

Cameron and Adam didn't want to let me pass so I shouldered my way through.

I was breaking for freedom when I felt something warm clamp down on my arm. I spun around, instinctively raising my hand, ready to defend myself from another attack.

It was Matt.

'Sorry,' he pulled away. 'I didn't mean to surprise you, I just—'

'You just what?' I roared. I could feel myself losing it. The needling, the taunting, I'd been pushed too far.

'Give me a minute to explain,' he said, his voice suddenly urgent. 'Please, there's something I need to tell you.'

I stared at him. He couldn't be serious? *Now* he wanted to speak up. 'What could you possibly have to say that's worth listening to?'

All the hurt I'd buried was being exhumed. I could feel it rise in my chest. My throat tightening with rage.

Becky smiled gleefully. 'This is too good.' Her enjoyment, building.

The mood in the group had shifted from aggressor to voyeur. A look of delight passed between them. They were now staring at us, enthralled.

'What's going on between you two?' Becky giggled. 'Wait' – she glanced from me to Matt – 'are you two shagging?' She was in her element. The popular girl, cruelly picking people apart for her own entertainment.

Matt held my gaze, pretending not to hear the taunts.

'Oh, you *are*,' she reeled. 'This just keeps getting better.'

He'd become flustered. 'Laurie, the thing is . . .' he said, and then stopped. It reminded me of how nervous he'd been in those moments before he'd proposed. Matt clenched his jaw and then, with a sudden look of determination, he blurted, 'I'm here to tell you how sorry I am. So sorry I hurt you!'

I could hear their gasps. I could imagine their stunned faces. But I couldn't take my eyes from Matt.

I didn't know what to say. But a dull ache had begun drilling through my temple.

Matt looked around nervously as if searching for some sort of approval. He moved his eyes back to me and said: 'I acted like a total prick. I stupidly thought the grass was greener. That I'd be better off without you. I fucked up. Laurie, you're amazing. You're beautiful, talented . . . it's always been you.'

I rolled my eyes.

'No, really. I'm an utter twat for thinking I'd be better off without you.'

Jesus, he looked like he might cry. His words came across as scripted, yet something deep within me stirred. Buried emotions. *Go away.* The pain in my head grew.

'I shouldn't have walked out and left you like I did. It was cruel and I'm so sorry for that. Like I said, utter twat.'

He shook his head, brow furrowed with sincerity. He appeared genuinely upset.

Matt turned to address the others. 'For the record, we were together for five years. I ended it with Laurie thinking

I'd be better off, and I've come here to admit I was wrong.' He moved back to me. 'Give me another chance?'

'Is he serious?' mocked Cameron. 'Why would anyone in their right mind want to date *her*? You were right to bin her, mate.'

For the first time since I could remember, I felt in control. Matt was begging *me* for forgiveness. I'd longed for this moment, and now it had arrived I couldn't quite believe what I was hearing. It couldn't be? Could it?

Matt took another tentative step towards me. His hand lifted as he tried to reach for mine.

His familiar scent devouring the space between us. Drawing me in. The smell taking me back, invoking lost memories. Helping me reach into the past.

'Don't do it, mate,' Adam joined in. 'She's a compulsive liar. There's still time to turn back.'

Matt cast them a pointed stare. 'Ease up, guys, Laura's a good person, she'd never deliberately hurt anyone. If she came in here as a journalist, it would've been because someone pressured her into it.' He looked at me, really looked at me this time. 'I know her, and she wouldn't hurt a fly.'

It was true. Matt was the only one who got me. Who *really* understood what made me tick.

His fingers brushed mine and I flinched. But I wasn't sure if it was the surprise or because I felt something. A spark. Then came the three little words.

'I love you.'

Becky's mouth fell open.

I stood perfectly still. Confused. Disorientated. Moments

ago, I couldn't have been more desperate to get off the island. Distraught at my ex's treachery. Now I didn't know what to think.

The presenter had another announcement for us. 'Ten million viewers have voted so far.'

'Ten million!' Charles echoed. Cameron made that irritating low whistle again.

I'd been so caught up in what Matt had to say, I hadn't noticed how the mood around us had shifted. As if Matt's proclamation of love had turned the competition on its head. There were now ripples of jealousy. An undercurrent of threat had drifted in.

'Laura . . . it's time to find out whether you will be evicted from *The Villa*.'

CHAPTER THIRTY-FIVE

THE VIEWERS

FOURTEEN MILLION VIEWERS

The Villa had made a splash across the pond and the sorority girls in the University of California's Alpha Xi Delta had set up a cinema in their front room. A sign 'No Boys Allowed' was hanging from the door in case any boyfriends showed up unannounced and tried to crash their villa party.

'Keep her in.'

'I vote, out!' said Ruby.

'No, *in*, it'll be funny, keep her in,' Skyla stressed.

Marsha returned carrying two giant bowls of popcorn. 'I say *in* – we need to know if Laura gets back with her ex.'

'What a phoney – anyone can tell that dirtbag is lying,' Krystal, the new girl, joined in.

'Actually,' Daisy yelled across the debate, 'THAT IS THE MOST ROMANTIC THING I HAVE EVER SEEN!'

'Oh, stop! Come on, Daisy,' Kelly cut her off.

'No, seriously, if my boyfriend fucked up and then told

the entire world how sorry he was and how much he loved me, like, oh my God, I would so take him back.'

'Yah, but you went back to your ex twice after he cheated, so, what does that say?'

'Fuck off, Kelly. You don't have to be such a bitch all the time.'

'GIIIIRLS!' Jade stepped in. 'Helloooo, why are we fighting over some stupid little British show?'

'It's not stupid, the show is insane and I'm OBSESSED!' announced Skyla.

'*Totally obsessed.*' Agreement rolled around the room.

Kelly moved off the couch and stood in front of her sorority sisters like she was making some presidential speech.

'Here's what I think. We keep Laura in because, even though she's a lying snake, now her ex is back on the scene we can totally have fun coming up with stuff that will wind them up.'

'Isn't that a bit . . . cruel?' But Daisy faltered as she sensed the mood shift.

One by one, the girls turned and glared at her. 'I mean . . . just because she lied, she doesn't deserve anything bad to happen to her.'

'Shut up, Daisy,' Kelly, the self-appointed ringleader, cut her dead then turned back to her squad. 'OK, girls, we need to have a bit of fun. Let's keep Laura in, but the first chance to fuck with her head, we take it. Are we all agreed?'

A look of glee spread like wildfire across the sorority.

CHAPTER THIRTY-SIX

THE CONTESTANT

Aruna, Balearic Islands

DAY TWO, *THE VILLA*

We'd been sitting in silence for five minutes. Dr Alexander waited patiently until I was ready to talk.

The sterile room had been given a splash of colour – bright red tulips swimming in a slim rectangular vase on the table between us.

His expression hadn't changed since my last visit. There was the same weariness in his eyes. I sympathized with how he felt. The show was an energy vampire. He seemed genuinely happy to see me, though.

'So,' he said, in that measured way of his, 'I'm glad you felt you could come and chat.'

He'd prepared a blanket for me. Neatly folded over the back of the chair. I shook it free and wrapped it around my shoulders. Then, with shaky hands, I took a sip from the glass of water he also had ready. My throat almost seized up as the cold liquid slipped down.

The doctor was dressed more casually than before,

wearing a white cotton polo shirt, denim shirts and Converse trainers. Sunglasses pushed back. He looked ready to step out into the sunshine. I felt a sting of jealousy at his freedom.

What I wouldn't give to be able to leave the villa. To go exploring. Find that beachy cove I'd seen from the helicopter and just lie, stretched out on an oversized towel in a warm spill of sunshine.

Instead, I was trapped, going around in circles in a goldfish bowl. And that's why I'd come to speak to him.

'Are you relieved?' he asked.

I didn't know how to answer that yet.

'When it was announced that you were saved from eviction, instead of celebrating with Matt, you came to see me. Do you want to tell me a bit more about why you did that?'

I looked to my hands. To the ring I'd been twiddling around my finger.

Finally I spoke: 'I had to clear my head.'

'That's good, it's important to step back and look at the bigger picture.'

'One minute I was being attacked, made to feel a monster and all I could think about was getting off the island. The next, I was being told that *millions* of people wanted me to stay.'

'Of the viewers who voted, eighty-two per cent were rooting for you,' he reminded me. The eviction result had been shown on the big screen. Their glowering eyes were still vivid. Their jealousy had stalked me indoors. 'How does that make you feel?'

He sounded like me. It was the sort of question I'd ask the people I interviewed. How do you *feel*? I was in the hot seat now, unpicking my emotions.

I closed my eyes and exhaled. I felt numb. I was still in shock. 'I've gone from being what felt like the most hated person on earth to being, I don't know, loved? On top of that, Matt told me he was sorry for screwing me over and that he loved me. Talk about a brain fuck.'

I sighed.

'It was too much. I couldn't breathe. I wanted to just . . .'

'Talk?'

'Yeah. Talk.'

'It must be a good feeling to know you're wanted, though?'

He smiled kindly. Dr Alexander was kind and gentle and . . .

Wake up! What are you thinking? You can't trust him. Not after the way the show stitched you up. I pulled the blanket tightly across my chest.

'Did you know?' I glared. 'When I was last here, did you know I was a journalist? That they were bringing Matt in?'

He shook his head. That weary look returning. 'The Agenda is kept secret from staff on the ground.'

The Agenda. Jesus. It sounded sinister.

'I'm not here to hurt anyone. I want to offer my support and I can assure you, if I'd known about Matt, I would have warned the team how dangerous a game they were playing. How a stunt like that could provoke heightened levels of anxiety. I'm actually,' he paused, his mouth suddenly a tight line, 'quite angry about it all.'

He spoke as if it were directed to the camera, not me.

'But would you have warned me if you had known?'

My question made him uncomfortable. 'I can't answer that. Legally I'm contracted to keep that information to myself.'

I sat back heavily in the chair.

'Let's return to you,' he said. 'Most importantly, are you happy with your decision to stay in the game?'

'Game?'

'Sorry, I meant *The Villa*.'

I pressed the heels of my hands into my eye sockets. 'I don't know,' I shook my head. 'I am, but then I'm not, because . . . I'm frightened.'

'What are you frightened of?'

I lifted my head and removed my hands. 'Being hurt again.'

There was concern in his eyes. 'Trust your gut. Let it be your guide.'

'My instinct is warning me off.'

'What are you doubting, Laura?'

I shrugged. 'Whether Matt really loves me. He was so brutal when we broke up. He didn't seem to give a shit at all. Five years together and I meant nothing. It's hard to believe he's had some huge fucking epiphany.'

Dr Alexander tilted his head to one side, opening himself up to me. This time, I accepted.

I described the dark place I was in when I'd met Matt. I told Dr Alexander how Dad had left Mum for the waitress at the local where he'd stop for a pint on the way home from work. Young, blonde, big breasts – she was as clichéd as you could get. I'd met Matt at the gym. I was an angry person. Furious at Dad. And even angrier at Mum. I blamed her for not doing enough to hold Dad's attention.

'Horrible and unfair, I know,' I confessed, shaking my head.

I explained how, for whatever reason, Matt wasn't put off by my bitterness. By my barbed replies. He listened to my ranting and persisted with asking me out on fun dates to distract me. I giggled as I remembered the crazy golf somewhere in the middle of nowhere that we got completely lost trying to find.

'Eventually I softened, I let him in.'

'He was your knight in shining armour?'

'Ha! Wouldn't call him that, exactly.'

'But he saved you?'

I shrugged.

'And he's here to save you again. Or it seems that way.'

I blinked.

'You just need to work out whether you need rescuing.'

The words hung in the cold room.

'How do you feel about the competition now? The audience have shown their appreciation.'

The money was more on my mind than I dared confess. £250,000. Now that my reputation had been trashed, winning, and the thought of buying myself a new life, had become almost everything.

My gut twisted with the guilt. I was doing exactly what Dr Alexander had warned me not to do.

But then, how could he possibly understand? With his

well-paid TV job. His doctor salary. He's never known what it's like to struggle.

There was a buzzing noise. The doctor frowned as he fished into his pocket. While he read his mobile, his face became lined with concern.

'What?' I said. 'What is it?'

'I'm sorry we don't have longer together.' He looked frustrated. Angry even at whoever sent the message.

'Why don't we have longer?'

'You're needed outside. There's going to be another announcement.' He looked up at me, pressing his lips together in a condoling way.

My stomach plummeted.

'You know, I didn't mean any of the stuff I said earlier.' Becky had been outside this whole time, waiting to ambush me. 'Were you talking to that therapist?'

'Dr Alexander,' I corrected her.

'What's he like? I hear he's smokin'.' Quickly, she added. 'Unlike the others, I haven't needed to see someone about my mental health.'

'Which others?'

'Annie for one, she's been to see him. Angela definitely has *issues*. Anyway,' Becky looped her arm through mine, forcing us together. 'I want you to know I'm not really a bitch. OK, I admit I was pissed off when I found out you'd lied to us, but when I saw what you and Matt have, I was like, go girl! He's nice.' A wry smile reappeared. 'Cameron's not happy about it, though.'

We emerged back into the daylight.

'You can tell he's jealous. Hey, what do you make of Annie and Blake flirting?' She glanced sideways at me. 'Don't tell me you haven't noticed? Hands all over each other. Throwing her in the pool.'

I opened my mouth to speak.

'It's all for show!' She flicked her ponytail over her shoulder. 'To wind me up.'

'Do you think?' I said.

'Seriously?' Becky laughed. 'It's obvious Blake's using Annie to make me jealous. Bet she gets used by men all the time—' She stopped herself from saying something even more vicious.

'Anyway. Cam is looking bangin'. And now you're with Matt, you wouldn't mind me cracking on with him, would you? Just to get even, you know?'

Crack away. But before I could reply, the noise of the screen rising up cut our conversation short.

'Contestants – stop what you are doing!'

'What's happening now?' Becky whispered in my ear. She clutched my arm more tightly. I caught Annie looking at us suspiciously and I wondered if that had been Becky's intention.

'The viewers have chosen.'

'Here we go,' Becky sounded amused, but my stomach was in knots.

'Matt and Laura – you will spend the night together *alone* on our luxury boat, *Barco Amore.*'

Becky tensed and freed her arm from me. Across the garden, Matt was beaming.

'And our viewers have also voted for Blake and Annie

to have a romantic dinner for two at our sea-view table inside the villa.'

I could almost feel the vibration caused by Becky's jealousy.

'Cameron, as Laura has been coupled up with Matt, you are now single.'

He stood up from the sunlounger and glared at me: 'Fucking joke!'

'Cameron, you do not have to leave the island, *but* you are now vulnerable. To be crowned winner of *The Villa*, you *must* be in a couple.'

My brain was struggling to keep up. Cameron despised me. I was going to spend an entire night alone with Matt. I wasn't sure how I felt – about any of it. But things were developing so rapidly I was struggling to process my feelings.

Or was that the idea? To make you unsure of yourself?

Cameron shrugged. Poorly disguising his rage, he said: 'Won't stay that way for long.'

With all the commotion, I didn't hear Angela approach me. 'Can we talk?' she whispered. With the same tense expression as earlier. 'It's important.'

She gestured towards the chairs furthest from earshot.

'What's going on?' I mouthed.

But whatever Angela needed to tell me was going to have to wait.

'Laura and Matt. Get ready to leave the villa for the love boat.'

CHAPTER THIRTY-SEVEN

THE VIEWERS

FIFTEEN MILLION VIEWERS

In Hong Kong, China, the time difference had made it difficult to stay on top of the drama. Li Mei was catching up on the show's highlights. She had a weakness for the British accent, especially floppy-haired posh-speaking boys. Luckily, she'd found some juicy gossip on Charles in a British newspaper:

THE VILLA'S CHARLIE IS
LOOKING FOR CASH NOT LOVE
Shock truth about the hunk

By Ben Foster

THE VILLA's toff Charles Barrett-Jones has been disinherited from his multimillionaire family fortune.

The 23-year-old blonde hunk is the son of the pasta king, Henry Barrett-Jones, and was sole heir to the family's fortune.

The family made their money through dried pasta empire Barrett's, and their fortune grew when they sold their firm in 2010 for a whopping £200 million.

In the past, Charles made no secret of his luxurious lifestyle, posting photos with wads of cash, sports cars, private yacht and skiing trips.

But rumour has it a family rift has led to him being cut out from his fortune. Close friends reveal that cash-strapped Charles has been begging for handouts from his mates and has no interest in finding love in *The Villa*. They claim he's faking his love for Angela and the only reason he's come on the show – is to win.

CHAPTER THIRTY-EIGHT

THE CONTESTANT

Aruna, Balearic Islands

DAY TWO, *THE VILLA*

A side door opened and Matt and I walked in silence through the dimly lit tunnel, snaking away from the villa. I tugged at my short black dress, feeling increasingly self-conscious. Matt was wearing shorts, a T-shirt, flip-flops and sunglasses for our date. That was so typically him, though. He wasn't one to be led by trends and expectations. It's something I used to love about him.

'Think we're here,' he said, as we emerged onto a rocky footpath.

The villa was illuminated behind us. A huge expanse of sky and sea lay before us and hundreds of steps, zig-zagging down the cliffside.

Slipping off my high heels so as not to trip up, I dangled them by their straps. The sensation of my skin touching the island's elements brought a feeling of freedom. I nodded to Matt. 'You first.'

'I'll be guinea pig then, shall I?'

There it was. The playful banter we used to have. It was a relief to be in the shade, and, at long last, to have silence.

The more distance I put between me and the villa, the calmer I felt. I could tell my doubts about Matt were beginning to subside. It was just us now, and the iridescent ocean. Even the crashing waves sounded less threatening. A restless breeze had picked up, sweeping the salted scents towards us.

Matt was loving playing the gentleman, leading the way, offering me his hand whenever we crossed a slippery patch. At first, I declined, but the further we moved away from the threat of the villa, the more I relaxed. When I did finally take his hand, the touch felt charged. Little sparks of electricity flew between us. I could tell he'd noticed, too. His eyes wouldn't stop smiling.

Yes, there were still cameras. Eyes on stalks, documenting our journey down the cliffside. But somehow it didn't seem so invasive. The glowering looks of our housemates were far worse. I felt like it was just him and me and the vast seascape.

The bay was mostly pebbles and boulders. We navigated our way around the rock pools and the slippery patches of seaweed. Beige-coloured crabs ran from our shadows, diving between the crevices. Ahead was a long wooden jetty that led out to sea. Moored at the end, our love boat.

It was jet black with a gaudy gold finish. *Barco Amore* painted across the hull in glittery swirls. But it was plush. And, best of all, it was away from *them*.

I glanced behind, my eyes drawn back to the villa. White

and formidable. From below, it looked almost alive. A crouching animal, peering over the cliff edge. Keeping a watchful eye on us.

'Hey,' Matt snapped me from my thoughts. 'How many islands like this do you reckon are out here?' He cast his gaze out to sea. 'It feels like we're the only ones left on earth.'

The thought made me shiver.

Matt was right. Despite the beauty, we could have been starring in an apocalyptic film. The last ones standing.

'Maybe they should have called this show *Survivor*,' I laughed, but something inside prickled as I said it.

'No keys,' Matt said. His head bobbed up from behind the helm.

'You didn't seriously expect they'd leave them in the engine? They were probably terrified we'd flee the island in their multimillion-pound boat, never to be seen again.'

'How epic is this though?' He'd crossed the deck and was now running his hand across the crème leather couch that curled around a table. Another neon-lit bucket brimming with crushed ice, spirits and champagne was waiting for us.

'Somebody wants us pissed.' Matt looked delighted.

That couldn't happen. I'd lose control and then I'd let him back in. I wasn't ready for that.

Matt rustled up some gin and tonics.

'Just the way you like it, my dear,' nodding as he handed me a frosted glass.

I wanted to neck it, anything to take the edge off.

'Cheers,' he toasted. 'To us.'

I clocked the first camera. Dead ahead.

'Cheers!'

My eyes quickly slid from Matt, scanning the rest of the boat. Three more orbs. One above the table. Another between the spotlights. There was even one inside the fish tank embedded in the wood panelling. A ribbon of red in the water. Reminding us we weren't alone.

The world was watching, waiting to see if I'd get back together with Matt.

I took a much larger gulp than I should have and within minutes I realized I'd drained the glass. Matt poured me another, this time adding a sprig of rosemary and peppercorn. Whoever prepared our *love boat* had paid close attention to detail. There was also a bowl of chocolate-coated strawberries and a platter of oysters bedded in ice. Matt slipped one down his throat.

I winced. 'Don't know how you can do that.'

'They're an aphrodisiac.'

Ignoring the suggestion, I added, 'They can stay where they belong, in the sea.'

'God, you look stunning.'

'Oh, come on.' But I could feel myself blushing.

'No, really, with the light falling on you like this.'

The sun was setting, coating everything in a buttery yellow light.

'Cut it out, Matt. It's cheesy.'

He rubbed his hand back and forth through his hair. 'You never believed me when I told you how pretty you are.' He looked away. 'It was kinda annoying, actually.'

'Oh, sorry, I didn't mean to offend you,' I said quickly.

He shrugged. 'It's OK. Just learn to take a compliment, hey.'

'Sorry.'

'Cheers,' he raised his glass again. This time I knocked the entire drink back. I felt my throat working hard to get it down. The bitterness of the gin was as comforting as old slippers. I smiled vaguely as the warmth of the alcohol started to wrap its arms around me.

Several drinks later, I had enough Dutch courage to interrogate Matt.

There was no beating around the bush. I wanted to know exactly why he was on the show.

'Totally out of the blue!' Matt exclaimed. 'This woman got in touch saying you were going on some dating show. At first, I couldn't believe it was true. *You*, on a dating show. Then I freaked out that she knew who I was and that we'd gone out. It was so creepy; she could even tell me how long we'd been together. And then I remembered all my old Instagram pictures. I hadn't deleted them. I couldn't.'

After we broke up Matt had removed me as his friend. It felt satisfying to know he hadn't erased me all together.

'I didn't take mine down either,' I confessed.

'The woman was very persuasive.'

'Who was she?'

He shrugged. 'She kept telling me you'd changed and how incredible you looked now, and kept pushing for me to go on the show. She then showed me a picture of you.

I couldn't believe it.' He took a step back, his eyes travelled up and down my body. 'I mean, WOW! You always were a babe, but this new look – blonde really suits you.'

I frowned but, remembering his earlier scolding, quickly rearranged my expression.

'Something inside just went off. I had to see you. Next thing, I was on a plane to some mystery location, nobody was telling me anything—' He stopped. 'I'm not sure we're allowed to talk about this.'

I nodded conspiratorially. Remembering the rules we'd been warned of at the start. Everything must be kept a secret.

'Anyway,' he touched my arm, 'as soon as I walked into the villa and saw you, I knew I'd made the right decision.'

I took another slug of my drink. Topping up my courage.

'Has there been anyone since us?' Such a stupid question. Three years had passed, of course there had been. I wondered if they'd had more fun together. Him and this phantom woman, *women*. If she'd been better than me in bed. I looked away, ashamed of myself. How quickly I'd returned to being needy. 'Don't answer that,' I said, quickly.

He reassured me anyway. 'No one who mattered.'

My stomach still twisted at the suggestion he'd been intimate with someone else.

'Are you telling me the truth?' My old friend, mistrust, coming to get me.

He held me in his gaze. 'Yes. One hundred per cent.'

But I couldn't stop. 'Are you seeing anyone?'

'I'm here, aren't I? Trying to win you back.' I was sure I saw a flash of apprehension as he said: 'And you? Is there someone "special" in your life?'

With one small shake of my head, I erased Ben. I hoped he was watching. I wanted Ben to know what it was like to feel insignificant. That didn't make me an evil person, did it? Finally, my life was falling into place. I couldn't believe it had taken a reality show for that to happen. I guess I did have Ben to thank for something.

The alcohol was doing a fine job of bringing down my guard. Before I could think it through, I'd reached out and pressed Matt's freckled cheek.

'Ouch! What you doing?'

'You're really sunburnt! I've got some moisturizer with me, that should help.' I bent down and rummaged through my tote bag. As I straightened to face him, Matt lurched, planting his lips on mine. It was frantic and clumsy. He immediately pulled away and apologized.

But the atmosphere had altered and there was no changing it back.

CHAPTER THIRTY-NINE

THE CONTESTANT

Aruna, Balearic Islands

DAY TWO, *THE VILLA*

Two hours later, we'd moved below deck. Matt had brought another bottle with him. I lay on my back on the bed, gazing numbly at my reflection in the mirrored ceiling.

The room was a tarted-up sex den. A mahogany walled cavern of plumped pillows, sumptuous bedding sprinkled with petals, fur throws, candles, and more mirrors. There was even one of those retro shag rugs.

Matt threw himself down beside me. 'What's this?' He rolled onto his side and plucked a black and gold box from the side table.

'What's inside?' My words came out slow and slurred.

I propped myself up with my elbow. He was holding the box. Not saying anything but grinning.

'Well?'

He was waiting for something. Inviting me to get involved.

'If you won't look, I will.' But as I made a grab for it,

Matt switched the box to the opposite hand. Waving it from my reach. Teasing me.

'Very funny,' I said, pushing myself onto all fours. With a roguish grin he continued to wave it around. Side to side. Taunting me. Willing me to just . . .

A hiccup flew from my mouth as I slid my leg over him. Next thing I knew, I was straddling Matt. Pinning his wrist down. Suddenly, out of the corner of my eye, I saw something move. Someone was in the room with us. I almost screamed with shock but then, as I peered through my curtain of hair, I realized the only thing moving was *me*. My swaying body. Car Crash Laura reflected in the cupboard mirror opposite. God, *I'm drunk*.

'Cooo-eee.'

Matt rattled the box. There was definitely something hidden inside. Like a dog being egged on to chase a ball, I charged for his hand, thumping my body onto his chest. I fought for my prize.

Laughter, real happiness flowed through me. A feeling I'd forgotten existed. Eventually Matt let me win and released his grip. I snatched the box away. Straightened. Still breathless and giggling as I opened the lid.

I didn't know what I was expecting. But not that. I jerked my gaze from the box back to Matt. My eyes stretched wide. If the air hadn't been charged with sex before, it was now.

The little black box was full of condoms. Sealed in red foiled packages. Buried underneath was a tube of lubricant. To begin with, Matt looked as surprised as me, and then came the look of lust.

'I think someone is *definitely* trying to tell us something. First the oysters and champagne. Now this.'

He grinned. I was swimming somewhere between feeling vulnerable, intensely awkward and aroused.

'What do you think, Laurie?'

He was studying me. He seemed fascinated. As if he liked this new wilder side – the hot mess I'd become after he dumped me. Our eyes locked and I watched his pupils dilate.

'Think about what?' I knew what he wanted but I was too afraid to say it.

'That we're being led into . . . you know . . .'

My heart started to pound. The room spun. All I could see was myself, dancing around in the mirrors. I slid from him onto my back, my arms falling limply by my side. He immediately rolled on top. His face so close to mine now, I could feel the heat of his breath. His musky aftershave awakening memories of the sex we used to have.

I closed my eyes, waiting for the kiss to arrive.

The air between us cooled. The pressure from my chest lifted. I blinked my eyes half open. Matt had moved back onto his haunches and was wearing a concerned frown. Earnestly, he said: 'I've never seen you like this.'

'Hey, come on, I'm absolutely fine,' I slurred.

'No, you're not. Let's get some food in you.'

He moved away.

Don't go.

'Really, I'm OK. I liked what you were doing.' My arms and legs felt leaden. I was having a sensation of sinking, right through the bed.

The next thing I heard was the noise of his flip-flops slapping up the stairs to the deck. I was left with the whir in my ears. The sound of blood rushing.

I gazed at myself in the ceiling mirror. I was looking but not really seeing *me*. It was as if the air between us was as thick as fog. And then, out of nowhere, I thought of Dr Alexander. Of what he said. Spoken so quietly into my ear just as I was leaving. As if he was trying to conceal something. Had it been a warning? '*I want to help you see clearly.*'

During our final minutes of therapy, I'd told Dr Alexander I'd been the one to destroy my relationship with Matt. I'd convinced myself he was cheating on me. That he'd fallen out of love. That I wasn't enough. But every time I confronted Matt about my suspicions, he always came back with a reasonable explanation.

'I make that sound like he was twisting the truth, but that wasn't the case,' I'd told the doctor. 'I was losing it. Because of my dad being a cheat, I've half expected all men to behave in the same way. The more mistrustful I became, the less time he wanted to spend with me. Until he'd finally had enough – and who could blame him really? I was so obsessive I'm not surprised he wanted rid of me.'

What was Dr Alexander trying to tell me? What was I not *seeing*?

I felt the bed move down and then the warmth of his skin back on mine. Matt had brought the chocolate strawberries with him.

'This was all I could find. Open up,' he teased.

I propped myself up and snatched the fruit away. 'I'm not a baby,' I said, as the juice squirted down my chin.

'Oh no?' He plucked another from the bowl. 'Looks to me like you need help with that.' He placed the strawberry in his mouth. Inviting me to bite it from him. I took the bait.

The sweetness. His tongue soft as he followed through. It was a heady mix. Nothing like the rough foreplay I had with Ben. This was soft and gentle. The Matt I'd been in love with.

'You're looking a lot more perky,' he said as he pulled away. Gleaming with mischief.

I smiled lazily. If I wanted it to stop, if I wanted the control back, I didn't fight very hard. We kissed, his fingers stroking me. His hand moved from my leg to my stomach and carried on up, brushing my nipple through the fabric of my dress.

My memory snatched me back to all those frantic quickies with Ben. How I would beg him to fuck me and then feel horribly empty after he left me.

That's what Matt's going to do. Bin me after he's got what he came for.

Matt wouldn't do that. He wouldn't be that cruel.

Perhaps that's what Dr Alexander had meant. For me to *see* that something good was finally happening and for me to, just once in my fucking life, stop worrying and enjoy myself.

Next thing I knew, we were underneath the duvet. My dress, unzipped. I could feel Matt pressing against me and the heat of him. His arousal.

'Matt, I don't know if—'

He kissed me again. Hard and excited. Pulling the sheets right up and over our heads. Hiding us from the cameras. Just as Cameron had done. Only this time I wanted it. Well, I did and I didn't, and then I just couldn't bear the torment of deciding any longer so I closed my eyes and let things be.

Matt wouldn't hurt me. Not again.

CHAPTER FORTY

THE PRODUCER

Madrid, Interview Room One

NOW

What's going on out there? Officers are charging in and out of the room. Raised voices are echoing outside. The skeleton shift have been reinforced by fresh blood. That must mean it's morning already. Sanchez no longer seems calm or in control.

Have they finally made an arrest? Then they can stop wasting my time.

'Is there a problem?' It's not my place to ask. I can't help myself, though. I always have to know what the crisis is.

Sanchez is having an animated chat in Spanish with a male officer. He turns and looks back at me.

'We have a situation.'

'Oh,' I say, and then something inside me ignites. Excitement – the anticipation of drama. 'What sort of situation?' I bury my smile.

He walks across the interview room and plants his

fingertips on the desk. Reminding me who's in charge. *But I see beneath your veneer, Sanchez. Something's rattled you.*

His reply is not what I expect, though.

'There are protestors outside the station. They've come for you.'

'For me? Why?'

He looks mightily pissed off with the situation. 'Because people are angry about your show. They want answers. News has got out that we're holding you here.'

He breaks to shout instructions to the officer at the door.

'We have to issue a press statement soon.'

He returns to me.

I'm confused. Blindsided by what he's saying. Also, they aren't *holding* me. I'm cooperating with their inquiry. And I've given them far too much of my precious time already.

'I don't get it,' I say angrily. 'Why would they be mad at me? There's been a mistake, I haven't done anything wrong.' I sit back, crossing my arms. 'I'm the one that created the show that only two minutes ago they couldn't get enough of.'

The show that had them on the edge of their seats. That attracted twenty million viewers to a livestream platform. A world record.

'If anything's being said about me, it should be that I've got hero status.'

Oh boy. Sanchez looks seriously pissed off now. 'Señora. Have you forgotten that someone has died? People are angry, they want justice.'

Jesus, I'm hardly going to forget something like that.

'Who's out there? A handful of crazies?' Bet Sanchez is

making more of this than he should. He's trying to rattle my cage.

'Three hundred or so.'

'Come on!'

'Waving placards. Seeking justice.' He turns his back to me. This time speaking to the officer in English. 'We need to call for back-up. And prepare the communications team for the press statement.'

I stare at him in disbelief. I'm so shocked that it's only now I notice the new file in his hands.

He sits down and flips it open.

'The autopsy report has come in,' he says.

My mouth is suddenly bone dry.

'She was found to have blood *and water* in her lungs,' he says.

An expectant silence fills the room as Sanchez waits for me to ask him what that means. I know what it means, Detective.

'The blow to her head didn't kill her,' he goes on. 'She was unconscious when she went in the pool. It was the water filling her lungs that cut her life short. Death by drowning.'

I can't look at him or the photos he's pushing across the desk.

'She would have lived, señora, if she'd been rescued in time.'

CHAPTER FORTY-ONE

THE CONTESTANT

Aruna, Balearic Islands

DAY THREE, *THE VILLA*

We were a power couple. That's how it felt as we held hands and walked in step.

I could sense their heads snap around as we returned to the villa. I could feel their eyes following us, but I didn't give a shit. I was with Matt. He wanted me back and that's all that mattered. I gave him a squeeze and he looked at me. There was a fresh intensity to his gaze. Feeling loved by Matt was what gave me confidence. I was nothing without it.

Cameron and Adam were sweating it out in the gym zone. Cameron was on his back, groaning under the strain of a barbell as he pressed it above his head. Adam was watching his biceps intently as he pumped the free weights.

Annie was first to say something. 'You're back. Hurrah!' she cried with false excitement.

There was a clang and thud as Cameron dropped the

weight. Adam wiped himself down. The towel was slung over his shoulder as he strutted over.

Becky won the sprint to my side. My new best friend. Breathless and excited, she grabbed my arm, tugging me from Matt.

'OK, you need to tell me *everything*. I want all the deets.'

'Not before she tells me,' Annie came between us.

I flashed Matt a 'save me' look.

'So, did you do *it*?'

Protectively, Matt took my hand back. Matt, my saviour. Sometimes it takes a little longer for things to fall into place. Be patient. That's the lesson *The Villa* has taught me. I looked back at the girls confidently. *You can't hurt me now.*

'Oh, don't be such a bore. We're dying to know,' said Annie. 'Foreplay? A fumble under the sheets? A little slap and tickle?'

'First base? Second base?' Adam joined in. 'Come on, mate, we're bored. Entertain us.'

A voice boomed from the other side of the pool. 'No secrets in *The Villa*,' Blake shouted. 'Spill!'

Annie smiled knowingly. 'I think it was much more than second base. My guess is our star reporter went all the way.'

She watched me closely for a reaction. I kept my gaze fixed ahead. Avoiding everyone's eyes. *This was our secret. Nobody would ever know.*

'As she was quick to spread her legs with old Cam, there's no chance she would deny her ex.'

I could feel Matt bristle.

'No chance of Matt putting in a performance like mine.' Cameron couldn't resist.

Matt's grip on me loosened. For a moment I thought he was going to swing around and punch Cameron. And part of me hoped he would.

Instead, Matt pointed his finger at Cameron's face and hissed, 'Why don't you piss off.' Each word pronounced. I'd never seen him like that before.

'Ooooh, hit a nerve, have I?' Cameron sniggered.

'Leave it,' I whispered.

I could feel Matt straining under my grip.

'He wants you to start a fight. Be the better person.'

'Ha, thought so,' Cameron laughed. 'Knew you didn't have it in you.'

I squeezed Matt tightly. I'd have to explain everything to him, but later.

Where was Angela? I cast around the garden. She'd been wanting to tell me something.

'Hope you're not feeling too cut up about this, old Cam.' Annie began toying with him instead. 'Are you sure you're OK, darling?'

I'd noticed the screen was raised when we returned but something was happening now. While they gossiped, our names were being reshuffled. Everyone was too busy needling, they hadn't noticed.

I was about to say something and then Becky pointed: 'Look!'

'It's the leader board, votes are IN,' Annie said, cocky and confident their strip yoga performance would have secured her and Adam first place. They'd clearly done all sorts while we'd been away to keep the viewers' appetite whetted. The viewers' attempt to set her up with Blake hadn't worked, then.

The thought of how much money was at stake had electrified the air. I'd ruled myself out, of course. I'd only just survived an eviction and there was no way I could – or would want to – compete with Annie.

Matt squeezed my hand as our names spun around in a tornado of fragmented light. One by one, the pieces reassembled. The apprehension building. Matt fidgeted beside me, shifting from foot to foot. I thought I could feel his pulse, thumping into my palm. One by one, we were put back together. The unexpected result caused a shock silence.

And then, Matt erupted in my ear with a: 'Fuck me, Laurie!'

He didn't waste any time, guiding us away from the group. When he was sure we were out of earshot, he stopped and pulled me close. Brimming with excitement, he whispered, 'We're in the lead! We actually have a shot at winning!'

I could feel them watching. Their eyes boring into the back of my skull.

Angela and Charles were in second place. Annie and Adam coming in at third. Becky and Blake, fourth. And Cameron, he wasn't even on the board.

'You and me, king and queen of *The Villa*, imagine?'

There was no mention of the prize – he didn't need to. The air was already charged with the promise of money. Matt kissed my forehead and I felt my heart quicken as the thought of winning a quarter of a million took hold.

£250,000. *Fuck*.

Something inside me was stirring. Something danger-ously competitive.

Matt led us back to the group. In those few moments we'd been away the mood had darkened. Bitter stares. Treacherous whispers. Even Charles, who'd appeared gentle up until now, was glaring. I reminded myself of the stakes, that he and Angela were close behind us in second. And then came Annie's astonishing reaction. Instead of her usual snarky put-down, she turned abruptly and made a beeline for Matt and me.

'What the—' Matt exhaled.

She powered through us, forcing our hands apart. We weren't her target, though. Adam was.

Annie removed the towel from around his neck. Whipped it into a tail and hooked him by the waist. Like a fisherman reeling in its catch, Annie pulled him in. Not even flinching when his sweat spilled over onto her. She latched on to his lower lip and sucked, hard. He reciprocated by cupping her face with his hands and then sank his tongue into her mouth. They kissed like angry people. A rough power play of tongues, darting between their mouths. It was grotesque.

'Get a room, Christ's sake!' Becky said.

'Let's get out of here,' I said quietly to Matt.

As we turned to make a quick exit, something moved. The vault door swung open.

The familiar explosion of harsh white light spilled into the villa, camera flashes that signalled the arrival of someone new.

Only once they had died down could we see that it was

a woman – and she was making confident strides towards us in platform heels and a silver glitter bikini.

Waving enthusiastically, she looked beside herself with happiness to be entering the villa.

'Hiya! I'm your new housemate,' she announced.

CHAPTER FORTY-TWO

THE CONTESTANT

Aruna, Balearic Islands

DAY THREE, *THE VILLA*

Jessica, or Jess as she introduced herself, was young and bouncy with a gym-sculpted body. She had brown, shoulder-length hair that spiralled, a tattoo of a bird flying out of a cage on her upper left arm and fake breasts. Two hard balls stuck onto a bed of muscles.

She wore a fixed smile as she moved between us, greeting everyone with the same kiss to the cheek. Everyone except Matt.

I thought I noticed a flicker of something else as she brushed his cheek. Her face – it seemed to light up.

Matt's back was to me, I couldn't see how he responded. But all of a sudden, I needed to know.

It was happening again. Matt and I had been back together less than twenty-four hours and already my head was swimming with jealous thoughts.

She's just one of those pushy girls who thinks it's OK

*to make eyes at unavailable men. She's probably deeply
insecure and desperate to be loved.*

For fuck's sake, Laura. Listen to yourself. I looked away,
ashamed.

This was the sort of behaviour that broke us before.
And poor Matt didn't seem the least bit interested in her.
In fact, he appeared more bored than anything. He kept
nudging me, trying to lead me away.

I rearranged my thoughts. If anything, it was a good
thing Jess was here. The mood in the villa had dramatically
lightened. There was a new toy for them to play with. Matt
and I were off the hook.

More insistently, Matt said in my ear: 'Can we get some
food. Please, I'm starving.'

As we slipped away from the group, a hand brushed
my arm.

'I didn't get to say hi to you yet.'

Up close, I noticed how made up she was, with her
cartoonish, drawn-on eyebrows. Jess was clearly a sun
worshipper – her youthful skin was already starting to
line. The beginnings of wrinkles were creasing around her
mouth and neck. It was then that I noticed the beautiful
gold chain with a heart locket that lay along her collar-
bones.

Oddly, she didn't even acknowledge Matt this time.

'We were feeling a bit tired coming back from the boat.
Sorry.' I smiled. And then lied. 'So nice to have another
girl in here.'

Her head lolled to the side. 'I just wanted to say hi. And'
– she glanced back at the leader board – 'congratulations. I

was watching the show before coming in. I saw what happened to you when . . .'

I felt a twinge in my chest.

'Anyway, I think you're really brave, coming out with the truth like you did, and to turn it around like that.' She looked to Matt. 'You're a lucky guy.'

Matt smiled awkwardly and brought my hand into his.

'I hope I can find someone to couple up with. It's hard meeting someone you gel with. Who gets you, I mean, really understands where you're coming from. I'm confident about one thing though, when I do find him, I'll know.'

'Oh?' I said.

'I'm a bit spiritual like that. I've always believed, you know when you know.'

'Um, right.' Matt was uncharacteristically short with her.

She stole a glance over her shoulder at the others. 'Wish me luck.'

What should have been a natural end to a conversation seemed to linger on. A second passed and then another as Jess continued to loiter. There was an intensity to her gaze. A strange sexual vibration to her. In the way she was standing that little bit too close to me. Thrusting out her breasts. She wanted to be noticed. What was she waiting for? I sensed Matt was as uncomfortable as I was.

Eventually Jess spoke. 'I guess I better head over there, then.'

A roar of laughter erupted, followed by some more chanting. 'Down it! Down it!' Voices shouting over each other. The boys were starting up a drinking game.

'Guess so,' Matt said.

I flicked him a look.

'Good luck,' I said, sympathetically.

As she left, I hissed at Matt. 'That was really rude.'

He shrugged.

'It can't be easy, coming in when everyone's already in cliques. I don't envy her. Cameron's the only properly single guy in here and I wouldn't wish him on anyone.'

The fact it was such slim pickings suddenly struck me. Had the casting gone wrong? It was almost as if the contestants had been chosen for some other reason.

As I watched her walk away, I realized what was bothering me. Despite her confidence, Jess had a vulnerability about her. She was hiding bruises underneath that mahogany tan.

'She seemed nice,' I said. 'I actually feel a bit sorry for her.'

Matt had a faraway look about him.

'Hey! What's up? What are you thinking?'

'Nothing.' He turned to face me, but he still seemed preoccupied. 'OK, there is something on my mind. I was thinking how nice it would be if we could go back to the boat. Just the two of us.'

Him wanting me all to himself immediately made me forget about our odd encounter with Jess.

He gave me a playful tug. 'Come on.'

'What about the food? Where are you taking me?'

But before I could find out, the presenter had stepped between us. She was back on the big screen with another announcement.

'Tonight, to welcome Jess, there will be another game. The dress code is . . . white and glamorous! Contestants, please make your way to your bedrooms – immediately – where you will discover what we've prepared.'

'Woooohoooo! Party – hell yeah!' Becky cheered.

'And remember, contestants, in order to be crowned winners of *The Villa*, you must be coupled up.'

As soon as her voice faded, there was a booming 'Let's get fuuuucked-up! Another round, lads!' Followed by a 'Down it! Down it!'

I shuddered at the thought of how tonight was going to play out. At least I had Matt by my side. We were a *real* couple. While I considered whether we might actually be the only genuine people in the villa, something strange happened. It felt like someone had walked over my grave.

I looked behind and there was Jess – staring, with the same silent intensity as before. I gave her a small nod and smile and she waved back cheerily. But as I turned to head indoors, a shiver crept up my spine. Despite the heat, my whole body had turned cold.

CHAPTER FORTY-THREE

THE VIEWERS

SIXTEEN MILLION VIEWERS

Gavin from Milton Keynes couldn't tear his eyes away.

It was love at first sight. He'd never seen anyone so beautiful in his entire life. He moved towards the screen, lightly brushing her cheek with his fingertip. He edged closer so his mouth was almost pressed up against hers. He wanted to peer into her soul, because he knew it must be so. She must feel the same way about him.

He parted his lips, ready to confess. He knew she'd be able to hear him.

'I love you,' he told her.

He took a step back, taking her all in.

'I love you. I love you. I love you.'

Then a smile.

'You will be mine.'

CHAPTER FORTY-FOUR

THE CONTESTANT

Aruna, Balearic Islands

DAY THREE, *THE VILLA*

It was more beautiful than I'd imagined.

A crescent beach of pure white sand, protected by granite cliffs. They stood tall and impressive. Soldiers, guarding us from the elements.

The sea had calmed with the change of tide and was gently lapping the beach. The moon burned boldly through the fading light. Only a small dash of sunset was left, simmering red on the horizon.

I slipped off my high heels so I could feel the sand. It was still warm from the sun.

The cove had been lit up with flaming torches, Roman candles buried into the sand and hundreds of tea lights in jars. There was also a firepit ringed with stones. It was the most romantic thing I'd seen in my life.

Matt looked sophisticated in a three-piece linen suit. I'd never seen him so smart. In fact, all the men looked sharp with their white tailored shirts. Blake was particularly handsome. He'd tied his hair back. His cheeks chiselled by the evening shadow. His sun-kissed chest peeking through the open-neck shirt.

Finally, it felt like we were on holiday.

Yet, for some inexplicable reason, my eyes were pulling me back to the villa. They roamed the cliff's edge, searching. But it had completely vanished from view. Not even a glow of lights was visible. We'd been guided to a new part of the island. One that felt like the end of the earth. There was so much beauty you couldn't see the cameras.

Tonight it was just us and Aruna's raw beauty.

The girls were so delighted to be off camp that they'd briefly forgotten about being bitchy.

'GLASSES!' Annie shouted. 'Who's seen the glasses?' Annie had been first to the alcohol. She was bent over the pirate treasure chest packed full of spirits, her white sequined 1920s flapper dress hitched over her knee so she could get stuck in.

'Oi! Put me down!' Becky squealed. Cameron had her in his arms and was running for the water. 'Stop,' she giggled. Smacking at his legs as he plunged them into the surf. Her feet kicking the air. Her knickers on show as her tiny dress rode up to her waist. He spun her around and she screamed with delight.

'I feel old saying this.'

I startled. 'Oh, it's you!'

'Sorry, I didn't mean to frighten you.' Jess looked back at the ocean. 'I was just thinking out loud. How old I feel watching those two muck about.'

'You're kidding? You can't be much older than twenty-five?'

Her face fell. *Shit*, had I insulted her? 'Did I say something wrong?'

She shook her head, but her expression was strained. She moved her hand to her gold necklace and began running the locket back and forth along it.

Jess was wearing an embroidered toga dress. Its heavy folds of fabric swept the sand. The front dropped into a deep V, accentuating her bulbous breasts. She'd styled her hair to be big and wild, wavy like a mermaid's. There was also something wild about her eyes tonight. They were red-rimmed. Haunted. All her earlier enthusiasm had leached away. Jess looked like she'd been crying.

'Hey, is everything OK? I'm a good listener,' I said, lightly touching her arm.

She bit down into her lower lip.

'I know it's hard to trust people in here, and I don't come with the best track record,' I said, making a little laugh. 'But I promise, you can.'

Her eyes slipped up and down me, her gaze settling on my breasts.

My dress was translucent in the sunlight. A silk floor-length gown that scooped at my neck and at the base of my back. A dress that forced me to go braless. Jess was staring at my nipples.

I folded my arms. Smiling awkwardly.

'Not ideal that we didn't get to choose our own clothes.' I made a joke of it.

She blinked at me with those big wounded eyes of hers, her voice not much more than a whisper. 'You're beautiful. And kind, for wanting to help.'

Her eyes had shifted again. This time she was gazing at something past my shoulder.

I turned to see what she was looking at so intently, just in time to catch Matt larking around with the boys. They were cracking open beers and working on the barbecue. The smell of chargrilled steak and chicken swept through the cove on the breeze. He caught my eye and grinned, and then his whole expression changed.

'Laura,' Jess said, urgently. I turned back to face her, and her eyes were now full of concern. And then, without warning, she pulled me in for a hug. 'Thank you,' she softly said in my ear. As she draped herself over me, I could feel the heavy weight of her mood. We stood there hugging for an uncomfortably long amount of time.

I was more than grateful when Angela interrupted us.

'Mind if I steal her?' Angela said, passing me a look.

'Thank you,' I mouthed my relief.

As Jess pulled away, she brushed the hair from my eyes. 'Catch up with you later?'

'Yes,' I swallowed. 'Sure thing.'

It was only as Angela led me away that it registered – Jess wore the same perfume as me. My signature scent. I'd been wearing it since I was a teenager.

'That looked intense,' Angela said under her breath.

'Yeah, you could say that.'

'Do you think she's into you?'

'Nooo – no way.' I frowned. 'Don't think so.' It hadn't crossed my mind until Angela brought it up but maybe, now she mentioned it . . .

'Physically, she's my type. Amazing body. Clearly works

really hard to look like that, but, I don't know, there's something weird about her, something loopy in her eyes.'

'I think she's feeling left out, that's all.'

'Hmm.'

Angela stopped marching us from the group and turned, looking at me squarely, her wispy cotton dress streaming behind her in the breeze. She looked ethereal in her hippy gown, flowers planted in her braided hair.

'Look, there's something I need to talk to you about. Everyone is pretending like it never happened, which is freaking me out even more. And then,' she lowered her voice, 'I saw him doing something even more scary.'

She checked over her shoulder.

'I can't keep this to myself any longer.'

'What is it? Tell me.'

'It's Cameron,' she whispered.

CHAPTER FORTY-FIVE

THE CONTESTANT

Aruna, Balearic Islands

DAY THREE, *THE VILLA*

He was manning the barbecue while the rest of the boys taught Becky and Annie the rules of a new drinking game. He took slow, measured sips from his beer can, flipping the meat.

'Cameron scares me.' Angela stared across at him. 'He's got a temper. The way he lashed out when you told us you were a journalist was not *normal*. He took strips out of you, and nobody said *anything*. I wanted to talk to you about it before you left for the boat but we didn't have time. Once you were gone, he completely lost his shit.'

'What do you mean?'

My stomach clenched as I remembered that look in his eye. His determined expression when he thrust me under the covers. Hearing Angela voice what I'd been bottling away was a huge relief. I *knew* it wasn't in my head.

'After you left, I went and sat by myself on the daybed near the kitchen. I needed to clear my head; I was feeling so weirded out by everything. I couldn't have only been there more than five minutes when Cameron came storming over. He was muttering, opening and closing cupboards noisily. I don't think he saw me and at first I was really pissed off that he'd interrupted my quiet time but then . . .'

'But then what?'

'I heard something smash.' Angela held her hands to her chest, as if the memory still panicked her. 'I looked over as he was picking up another glass and he smashed that too! I think he was angry, jealous – at losing out to Matt. He just kept going and going, pulling the pots and pans down, flinging them across the kitchen and then' – her eyes widening – 'he punched the fridge! He actually took his fist to the door! Have you seen the dent? It was mental. Really insane behaviour, and all because he couldn't handle a bit of competition. If he can lose it like that now,' she whispered, careful not to let anyone hear. 'What will he do if he thinks he's going to lose the prize money?'

The secret I'd been keeping suddenly felt like it was going to explode out of me.

'I need to tell you something . . .'

'What?' Angela looked frightened.

'That night everyone thinks I slept with Cameron. That's not what happened.'

'Oh God, no, don't tell me he—'

'LAURA.'

The presenter cut in. An eerie echo moving through the darkness.

'Laura and Angela.'

Our names ricocheting off the cliffs. The presenter's voice was stern. Scary-sounding. I felt my body recoil.

'Laura and Angela, you must go to the firepit *immediately*. There will be an announcement.'

We exchanged nervous glances. Angela and I had been singled out as the naughty kids. And we'd been silenced.

Angela threaded her arm through mine, whispering in my ear: 'What do you think's going to happen to us?'

My stomach was doing flips. Since entering the villa I'd been stuck on some loop of adrenaline.

'What did we say wrong? We haven't broken any rules, have we?'

I shook my head. 'Don't think so.'

'I was just speaking the truth.'

'I know, so was I.'

'I haven't revealed anything people watching wouldn't have seen.'

'Exactly,' I agreed. Although I wasn't so certain any more.

The warning I'd been given about Cameron was lodged firmly in my mind. *Accusations carry consequences.* Had we gone too far?

Angela and I were greeted with some 'oooh-ing' and sniggers as we rejoined the group.

'What have you done now?' Annie tittered.

I felt Matt's arms wrap around me. He kissed me on the cheek. 'Everything OK?'

'Not sure,' I said quietly.

'What were you girls chatting about?'

'CONTESTANTS!' the presenter interrupted me again.

Now I was in the light of the fire and candles, I could see how the speakers were arranged around us. And the cameras. They were everywhere.

'I have something very important to reveal to you all . . .'

'Oh goodie,' Annie looked around, making sure she caught my eye. 'I love secrets.'

'Firstly, as a little incentive, you'll be thrilled to know we've increased the prize amount to . . .'

Music started blaring from all around us. Loud, intrusive, as if we were suddenly at some rock concert.

'£500,000!' she shouted over the noise.

'Fuuuuck,' Matt said in my ear.

While everyone around me celebrated, I felt something crawl down my spine.

'Yes, that's right people, half a million pounds could be yours!'

'There's more,' she interrupted the celebration. 'As you know, our viewers watch *everything* that you do.'

The knot in my stomach tightened.

'There are no secrets in *The Villa*. The viewers have been reacting to what they've seen. And they've been voting . . .'

And tighter.

'Our audience has decided. *Tonight*, you will be reliving your teenage fantasies. Tonight's game is . . .'

CHAPTER FORTY-SIX

THE VIEWERS

SEVENTEEN MILLION VIEWERS

Stephen and his husband Daniel had barely left their living room in Maidstone, Kent, since *The Villa* began.

'Hey, listen to this.'

'I'm trying to watch the show, I'm on the edge of my seat here, would you look at Laura's heart rate now?!' said Stephen.

'You'll want to hear this. Breaking news, just in,' said Dan.

'What's the game going to be this time? Annie's bound to get her boobs out again.'

'It's about Angela.'

'No! I like her. What is it?'

'She's been keeping secrets from everyone.'

'I can't take any more suspense.'

Dan cleared his throat and began reading *The Record*'s latest exclusive. '*The Villa*'s *Angela Akbar was an escort with a £2,000 a week cocaine habit.*'

'NO!' Stephen gasped.

'*The solicitor has been hiding a seedy past of sex and drugs.*'

'It's always the quiet ones!'

'There's more,' said Dan. '*The news comes as a revenge porn photo of the reality star surfaced earlier this week. A former "client" of the Oxford graduate posted a nude photo of the solicitor on Snapchat and the picture went viral.*'

'Have they printed the picture?'

'It's been pixelated,' said Dan.

'She seems so sweet. I feel so sorry for her.'

Dan read on. '*A fellow law student, who was in the same year as Angela but wants to remain anonymous, said it was well known that cash-strapped Angela offered her services to pay for her cocaine habit. Another friend has since contacted the paper and said Angela has been through rehab and will be devastated the news has got out. Her law firm declined to comment.*'

'I'm speechless!' said Stephen. 'You have to wonder though, with a past like that to hide, and a decent job now, why would you risk coming on a show like this?'

'Maybe she needs the money more than anyone realizes.'

'Poor thing,' Stephen shook his head.

'Question is – if she's in debt, how far will she go to win?'

CHAPTER FORTY-SEVEN

THE CONTESTANT

Aruna, Balearic Islands

DAY THREE, *THE VILLA*

It felt like a séance, the way we huddled together in a circle. The fire behind us. Our faces half-amber, half-shadow in the soft light of the candles.

'Who's going first?' Charles looked between us.

There was a mix of groans and excitement.

I shifted. Edging closer to Matt.

Charles began the preparations, patting flat the sand in the centre of the circle. He placed the empty wine bottle in the centre and fell back.

The five shots the viewers had made us neck before the game were kicking in.

'Me! I'll go,' Becky announced.

Blake frowned. 'Let the new girl go first.'

She ignored him, snatching the bottle into her hand.

Spin the Bottle with my boyfriend. The definition of hell. The thought of watching Matt kiss another girl filled me with dread.

'OK, here goes!' She spun it.

My stomach knotted as I watched the neck of the Chardonnay flit between us.

Please don't let it be Matt. My prayers on a loop as I watched it go round and round. I wanted to reach across and grab his hand. Mark him as mine. But how needy would that look? We were in the lead. We were on track to win half a million pounds. I must appear confident and unthreatened. *Hold it together, Laura, for fuck's sake.*

There was a crescendo of cheers as it slowed to a stop on Charles. Angela was trying to hide the strain as Becky moved onto all fours. Her knees ploughed the sand as she crossed the circle towards Angela's man.

'Come here, babe.'

Becky puckered up. A collective 'oooooh-ing' rattled around the circle as Charles leaned in to meet her.

Angela blinked and then tore her eyes away.

'You're missing the best bit, honey,' Annie taunted.

Becky's pillowy lips engulfed Charles. Playing to the gallery, she put on her most sensual performance. Cleavage out, bum lifted into the air. But, try as she might, her tongue wasn't getting in because Charles had locked his mouth shut.

Becky was scowling as she pulled away. There were sniggers but the darkness hid their identities.

'SHOT!' Annie decided. She hobbled around the group clutching a bottle, her stilettos driving into the sand. She demanded everyone held up their glasses, the Sambuca sloshing everywhere as her aim missed. 'On three,' she said, necking it before the count.

'That wasn't a *real* kiss.' Annie was pointing at Charles. 'From now on, only with tongues!'

'No way!' Angela blurted.

Annie snapped around.

More quietly, Angela said: 'We shouldn't do anything we don't feel comfortable with.'

Annie laughed. 'Don't listen to her. Who's up next?'

My fingers balled into fists.

'Contestants!' The presenter was back. 'We've been inundated with requests; ninety-three per cent of our voters have expressed a desire to see something more . . . *intimate*.'

'I told you,' Annie chimed. 'Nobody wants PG! So, who's next?'

Nobody moved.

'Anyone?'

'I'll go!'

Jess caught me by surprise. Until now, she'd been the one hiding in the shadows. So quiet and pensive, I'd been worried about her.

'New girl wants some action. Here,' Annie filled her glass to the brim. 'You'll need this.'

Jess winced as she knocked back the shot. She took the bottle and gave it a firm spin.

'Ooooooooooh,' the noise rolled around.

Matt planted his hand on my leg reassuringly. I was relieved, but also slightly embarrassed at how transparent I was.

There was laughter as it finally came to a stop. I didn't register it at first. I'd been so preoccupied with Matt, I'd forgotten I was also part of the game.

'That doesn't count,' I said, staring at the neck of the Chardonnay pointing at me. I looked around. 'Spin again.'

'Oh, it counts!' Annie said. The ringmaster. 'And don't forget, *it's a French kiss.*'

'Piss off,' I snapped at her. But I was met with a wall of resistance. I was suddenly feeling very uncomfortable. Outnumbered. Was Matt grinning, too? I couldn't bring myself to look at Jess.

'Always had you down for a prude,' Cameron smirked.

'Oh, for fuck's sake, just get on and kiss her,' Adam joined the needling.

Annie whispered something to Becky. They sniggered.

I glared back at her. *Fuck it. It's just a kiss. And if anything, it'll make the viewers like me more. Think about the money.*

Casually, I said: 'Where's my shot then?'

'Attagirl,' Adam said, clapping.

Matt looked taken aback. Impressed even. I flashed him a small smile and then necked the Sambuca.

The chanting fired up as Jess walked the circumference of the circle to my side. It felt less schoolyard and more tribal ritual with the flames and the echo. The distant hiss of the ocean. 'Kiss. Kiss. Kiss.' The words shuddering the air like a drumbeat.

Jess looked like a Greek goddess walking barefoot, her dress billowing behind her. She nestled into the sand beside me and, with a light sweep of her fingers, brushed the hair from my eyes.

The chorus rose, louder, sharper.

KISS KISS KISS.

Jess drew nearer. The smell of rose petals, *my* perfume, filling the air. I closed my eyes.

Her lips were soft. Her kiss, tender and sensual. Her tongue sliding gently into my mouth. It felt hot.

There was cheering, excited, drunk, thunderous noise as we kissed.

In those few passing seconds I couldn't help thinking maybe Angela was right. Jess was interested in me.

She pulled away, blinking her eyes open. Passing me another of her intense stares. It was enough to give me goosebumps.

'Jesus, I'm feeling turned on,' Adam said.

I felt Matt stir.

'Cameron, you're next.'

Annie headed his way with the Sambuca. Just as things were gathering pace, we were interrupted for a second time. She was back – our reminder we weren't alone in a deserted cove. *They* were always watching – the real ringmasters of this game.

'The rules have been changed,' the presenter announced. 'Cameron . . .'

He looked up.

'Your turn will have to wait . . .'

'Huh?'

'The viewers have chosen. Jess to go again.'

'Hey, not fair!' Cameron was about to kick off.

'The audience has spoken,' she repeated sternly.

We immediately hushed, passing one another looks. Jess leaned forward and took hold of the bottle for a second time. I couldn't explain why, but dread had risen inside me.

The boys had grown rowdier. Pounding their fists into the sand.

Kiss. Kiss. Kiss. Kiss.

The bottle spun.

The words drilled through me.

Kiss. Kiss.

'Oooooooh, savage!' someone said as it came to a stand-still.

I didn't even have to look to know where the neck was pointing.

Matt stiffened as Jess rose to her feet. Without so much as a consolatory glance, she planted herself between me and Matt, forcing me to make room.

I had a front-row seat to the worst show imaginable.

All I could hear was Becky and Annie's laughter as Jess moved in.

At least Matt looked terrified. His body was stiff, his arms were folded across his chest. Nothing about him wanted this, I could tell.

Jess cupped his face with her hand and pressed her lips onto his.

My throat tightened. I didn't want to watch, yet I couldn't tear my eyes away.

She was trying hard to engage him. Small kisses across his lips, building up to something much more.

Matt's eyes were still wide open, his brow, furrowed. *He doesn't want this*, I thought. *He's not into it.*

But she just kept on going. Determined to win him over.

My eyes were burning, I was staring so intensely. I blinked but when I looked again, everything had changed.

Jess's tongue had slipped inside his mouth, Matt's eyes had closed and he seemed to have moulded into her rhythm. Worse still, I noticed *the look*. That same excitement he shows me when he's turned on.

I wanted to reach out, grab hold of him. Yank him back to where he belonged.

The corners of her lips were curling as she kissed. Suppressing a smile. The vulnerable woman I'd met earlier – gone. It was clear to everyone enjoying the spectacle, Jess was into Matt. Worse still, it looked like he was into her.

She kept her gaze on him as she pulled away. Still blanking me. She handed him one of her long lingering looks.

Anger burned inside. Rage. *That bitch*.

While she floated back to the other side of the circle, Matt looked sheepishly ahead. Avoiding eye contact with me.

I felt humiliated, jealous and insecure, all at once. I prayed for the game to end.

Was there something going on between them? Not in that way – they'd only just met. But was there a spark? It was hard to brush this one off as being in my head. I'd seen the electricity with my own eyes. I felt sick at the thought of Matt being attracted to *her*.

I could feel their eyes. The others, the viewers. Watching, waiting for my reaction. *I'm not going to give them the satisfaction of seeing me upset*. It took all my strength to stop myself from crying. *Fuck all of you*. I swallowed down my sobs.

'Who's next, then?' I said, smiling tightly, trying but failing to keep my tone light.

The game continued for a few more rounds before it disintegrated into drunken chaos. Thankfully I was spared from kissing anyone else. I don't think I could have handled Cameron trying to ram his tongue into my mouth.

Annie was pouring shots directly down throats. The boys were rugby-tackling each other into the sand. Jess had become Becky's new best friend. The pair were huddled by the firepit, sharing a blanket, every so often throwing me glances and laughing.

'It was just a game,' Matt said, breaking the long heavy silence we'd been wading through since *the kiss*. 'Come on, Laurie, don't be in a mood. I didn't have a choice. I could hardly push her off me, could I?'

I bit down on my lip. There was so much I wanted to say to him. Such as – why did you have to kiss her like *that*? He tried to take my hand, but I snatched it away.

'We'll talk about it later,' I hissed. 'When we're in our room.' *Away from these vultures waiting to feed off my distress.*

There was a scream from the darkness. A misjudged rugby tackle had shoved Angela head first into the sand. Adam barely noticed. He charged at Blake again. Charles went for their legs. The three of them fell into a tangled knot of limbs.

'Contestants!'

The boys were on their backs, laughing hard.

'There's been a change to tonight's schedule.'

They were so drunk they barely heard her. But I was listening. I don't know if it was something I'd picked up in her tone. Or the creepy way her voice swept like a ghost through the cove. But something in my gut was warning me.

Angela sensed it, too. Her worried eyes met mine.

'Tonight there will be a recoupling.'

All the hairs on my neck prickled.

'Tonight, the audience has decided one couple will swap partners.'

I already knew what was coming.

CHAPTER FORTY-EIGHT

THE CONTESTANT

Aruna, Balearic Islands

DAY FOUR, *THE VILLA*

I was haunted by the image of them in bed together. By Jess's final passing look before she disappeared through the door to the love boat with Matt.

He'd promised me all the right things. As Matt had hugged and kissed me goodbye, he'd repeatedly told me I had nothing to worry about.

'Trust me,' he said.

Trust. Such a tiny word that had the ability to cause such unparalleled pain when broken.

He held me by my shoulders, forcing eye contact. 'I love you, silly. Why would I make all this effort to come here only to fuck things up for us? Think about it, it doesn't make sense. Laurie, are you listening to me?'

I could barely hear him over my internal monologue. *Liar. You fancy her. You're going to sleep with her.* It was deafening.

Somehow, I managed a smile. To pretend to him I wasn't

insecure. To show all those viewers, who'd been on my side only twenty-four hours ago, that they couldn't get a rise out of me.

But I could feel my charade cracking as soon as he vanished from view.

It was now the middle of the night. Hours had passed since he'd left with her and the images of their bodies tangled on that bed were torturing me. The candles, the condoms, the soft lighting. He was reliving it all over again with *her*.

I brought my hand to my mouth, tracing my lips with my finger. The feeling of her kiss still tingled. Her sensual touch bleeding into the memory of watching how *they* kissed. I saw how Jess turned Matt on. *That's what she's doing to him now. Pressing his buttons. In ways I never could.*

I threw back the sheets from the daybed.

Cameron had laid claim to my bedroom. He'd said I should join him to help forget about Matt. Still trying. Still hoping we could win together. Like that was going to happen! So instead, I'd been tossing and turning outside with the mosquitos and the midges, listening to the rustle of the night animals as I cooked up every worst-case scenario. The breeze would whip up and I'd think I could smell her perfume. Swept from the boat up the cliffside. Mixed with the scent of sex.

Like the insects, I needed to return to the flame that I knew would burn me.

I crossed the garden, slipping from the protective glow of the villa to where land met the sea. I peered over the wall, raking over the ocean. I'd seen the villa from the boat, so the reverse must be possible.

I needed to know.

The sea was the colour of lead. The moon, hidden behind a mass of pillowy clouds as black as factory plumes. Nothing like the star-filled night *we* had on the boat. Ha! A small victory. I rose on tiptoes, peering as far over as I could. Was that a light?

I could just make out the glow from the spotlights, ringing the vessel like a halo. But the gratification of finding them was quickly replaced with a rush of dread. Actually *seeing* the boat made my fears ten times more real. I was now panicking – what was going on below deck?

At first, I didn't notice it creep up on me. That I wasn't breathing normally any more.

I was too busy glaring down at the boat. Consumed with hatred. With jealousy. Envy. The fresh fear Matt might choose Jess so he could win the half a million. All the while, small shallow breaths whistled through my lungs.

I hate every one of you bastards who voted for them to be together. Don't tell me you're not getting off on watching them crack on, leaving me stuck up here to imagine the worst.

My chest tightened.

You're loving seeing me fall apart, aren't you? AREN'T YOU? Was this what you wanted?

What sort of show tortures people like this? The cameras, the voyeurism, the voting. Taking away our right to choose. Suddenly I was struck with how wrong it all was.

Jesus. I can't breathe.

The sea, the night, the vivid white of the villa – was now swirling. I gripped the wall but my legs had already turned to mush. My hands and feet were prickling, the way they do when blood stops reaching them.

I can't breathe. I CAN'T BREATHE.

My legs folded and I slumped to the ground, hyperventilating.

I was having a panic attack.

I had to slow myself down. Control my breathing and count. Four breaths in, four out. Just like the doctors taught me to do. *Come on, you've been here before, Laura, you've got this.*

My shoulders sagged. My head rolled into my hands. But this attack seemed worse than the others.

In, deep breath. Out, deep breath.

It was almost impossible to keep my mind trained on my count.

In. Out. My chest heaved.

It was almost working, but not fast enough.

And then, just like when I was feeling vulnerable on the boat with Matt, he bulldozed into my thoughts. Dr Alexander.

He's a doctor. He'll help me.

With the last of my energy, I pushed my palms into the ground, wrenching myself onto my feet. I was wobbly but I could walk. I staggered the length of the pool, past the kitchen, towards the therapy room.

Somehow the air had become thicker. The temperature had risen.

As I struggled to keep moving, I realized I wasn't the only thing changing.

The island was heating up.

CHAPTER FORTY-NINE

THE CONTESTANT

Aruna, Balearic Islands

DAY FOUR, *THE VILLA*

'I'm worried about you, Laura,' said Dr Alexander.

'Can you give me something?'

'When did these panic attacks start?'

'What's it called? Diazi-something? How about Valium? Something to slow me down,' I wheezed.

'When did you last eat?'

'Sleeping tablets? If I could just *sleep*, I'd feel calmer.'

'Laura! Are you listening to me?'

It was the first time he'd raised his voice, yet it was still full of concern. He leaned forward. Elbows on knees, searching for my eyes. For a moment I thought he was going to take my hands. To my surprise, part of me wanted him to.

'Have some water, it'll help.'

I did as I was told. He spoke softly, but Dr Alexander had a way of commanding authority. He smelled of suntan lotion and the outdoors. Coconut and sunshine.

'Is that better?' he said.

I nodded. My breath finally began to slow and deepen.

'You're going to be OK. It will pass.'

I nodded again.

'Take your time, there's no rush.'

There was nothing extraordinary about what he was saying, but his words had a power to soothe. Like a thick cool ointment that melted into your skin. It must have been the reassurance that I was now in the care of a qualified doctor.

'Better?'

'Yeah, better.'

'Do you want to tell me what's been going on?'

My eyes flared again. *I mean, where do I start?*

'Laura.' His voice shuddered. 'Calmly.'

'OK.' I nodded. *Calmly.* From the beginning. Or from when things began to fall apart.

This time, I didn't hold back.

I confessed to Dr Alexander about my dark thoughts. Matt and Jess in bed together. How I'd role-played the entire conversation we were going to have when they got back to the villa. I would be dumped for her. Just when my life was coming back together, it would be snatched away – again.

'Is that what the show wants? To fuck with people's heads?'

I was using the word 'show' like it had become an institution. A firm of shady, faceless characters.

I thought I saw a flicker of something in his expression. A confirmation?

I couldn't stop. Just like the last time I was here, some-thing about Dr Alexander was prising me open. At what felt like 100 mph, with tears streaming, I told him everything about my clusterfuck of a life. How badly I wanted to get married. How much I hated my job. The random guys I'd slept with. I even confessed to my affair with married Ben. How low I'd stooped, shagging him in a filthy pub toilet. Filth – that's what I was. And then, after I'd tipped my life into his notebook, I finally opened up about what had happened on the boat with Matt.

I closed my eyes, the memory so fresh it still made my skin tingle. The places he touched me.

'I knew I shouldn't have done anything. I had this feeling of dread, right here,' I clutched my stomach, 'but what did I do? I ignored it. I got drunk. Because then I didn't have to think about what my gut was telling me.'

'So rather than taking control, you let yourself be controlled?'

'I just got pissed. It was easier that way and – I'm such an idiot.' I sobbed. 'He treated me like shit and I let him back in. What have I done?'

'Did you enjoy yourself, though?'

It was so direct, it made me stop and look up. I couldn't read his expression, but his blue eyes were suddenly smoul-dering. Instead of answering, something inside me made me ask:

'Did you watch us?'

He held my gaze. For several beats.

'No.' He cleared his throat. 'No, I didn't.'

But I could tell he was lying. Probably to spare me the

embarrassment. But to my surprise, I wasn't blushing. The thought of the doctor seeing me like that – it was strangely arousing.

'Yes,' I confessed. 'It was wonderful. Everything felt so much more intense because of what happened in the past. And that's what scares me. The fear I could lose it again. Will it be OK?'

I was surprised at how quickly I'd become dependent on his reassurance.

'Just breathe, Laura.'

'God, I must seem like a car crash to you.'

'Not at all.'

'A terrible person for having an affair?'

'We're more complex than that. People aren't all good or all bad.' There was a trace of something in his tone as he said: 'There's shades of grey between.'

'But what will the viewers think of me after this?'

'They'll love you even more for being genuine. For showing your vulnerability. What person can't relate to what you're going through?'

Again, an edge to his tone. As if he didn't like what the show was doing to me. As if he wanted to say more.

His next question came out of nowhere. 'Can you remember the first time you felt rejected?'

I frowned. 'What?'

'Is there a memory that stands out?'

'Do I have to answer that?'

He nodded. 'I feel it might help with our therapy.'

'OK.' I blew out my cheeks. 'Well, umm . . .' But finding the answer wasn't as difficult as I'd imagined. In fact, it was sitting there, right in the forefront of my memory. I don't think I'd ever packed it away properly.

'I was six or seven and I'd been given a bike for my birthday. Pink without stabilizers. A big girl's bike,' I smiled. 'Dad had promised to come home at lunchtime to teach me how to ride it, and all morning I'd been buzzing. Finally, I'd be like the other kids. I could keep up with them. I sat for two hours outside on the porch, waiting. He never showed up. I didn't say anything when he came home that evening, but he sensed my unhappiness and was quick to turn it around and make me feel like it was my fault for imposing such a commitment on him.' I laughed while I wiped my tears away. 'Saying it out loud makes it sound stupid, so trivial, but at the time I was heartbroken because I felt it wasn't about the bike, it was about me. *I* was the problem.'

Dr Alexander nodded and listened.

'That's how it's always been with Dad. He's made me feel like an irritant. He wouldn't show me love unless he thought I'd earned it. I needed to achieve something first and then I could have my reward.'

'Which was?'

'Some off-the-cuff "Well done". I'm not saying he wasn't generous; he did buy me stuff. Gave me money for my birthday, that sort of thing, but I always felt that came out of guilt rather than love.'

'I see.'

I snorted. 'I never did learn to ride that bike. It stayed in the garage. Parked up against the wall. Collecting cobwebs.'

More tears appeared, replacing the ones I'd wiped away.

Dr Alexander offered me another tissue, smiling encouragingly.

'Why do you think it is that you're attracted to unavailable men?' he said.

I laughed nervously. 'Am I?' But I knew the truth.

'I put it to you, it's not so much them not liking you enough, more that you choose partners who will never be yours. That way, when it doesn't work out – which inevitably it won't, with a married man, such as Ben, or a guy who wants no-strings-attached sex – you can say' – he parted his hands – 'I told you so. Your fear of rejection is so great, you sabotage your own happiness. A defence mechanism to protect your heart. Tell me, Laura . . .' He locked me back into his stare. 'Why do you feel you don't deserve to be loved?'

I sat there, silent. The truth hurting.

'You are enough. A ring on your finger won't make you feel more loved.'

A deep, dull ache was spreading across me.

'Have you considered maybe Matt isn't up to anything with Jess? Perhaps he's telling you the truth?'

I looked at him blankly.

'Jess might have her own agenda, such as thinking she could win the show with Matt. But Matt might not be playing along.'

He was right; trusting Matt hadn't been something I'd ever considered.

Dr Alex was doing his best to reassure me, but the mention of *them* was enough to kick off my nerves again. The anxiety button had been reset. I needed to know.

I stopped staring at my hands and looked squarely at the doctor. *I'm an idiot. Why hadn't it crossed my mind to ask him earlier?*

'Can you see what they're doing on the boat?' I said, urgently. 'Do you know if anything's happened?'

He sighed heavily. The weight of the world back on his shoulders.

Oh God, he did, that's definitely a yes. I leaned forward. 'Tell me!'

'I can't, I'm not allowed to.'

'Please, Alex.'

He noticed how I'd dropped the 'doctor'. He glanced up to the camera above us. His face strained. Conflicted. 'I'm sorry. I can't.'

Every last bit of calm flushed from me. I shot to my feet. 'I need to get out of here.'

'Laura, calm down.'

'I have to see him. The not knowing while everyone else can see what they're doing, is killing me.'

He caught me as I rocketed for the door.

'Hey, get off!'

Dr Alexander kept hold of me until he'd pressed all the fight from out of my arms. After one final burst of energy, I gave in and let the doctor guide me into him, my head coming to rest on his chest. I could feel his muscles as they shifted beneath his shirt.

His mouth was close to my ear. 'I'm on your side. You know that, don't you?'

I could hear his heart thudding. His pulse was also racing.

If I could have managed a reply, I would have said yes. He seemed like the only genuinely *normal* person in the villa.

'I won't let you out of here until you show me you're OK. I'm worried about you.'

Gentle and steadfast.

'OK?'

'OK,' I sighed into his chest. 'OK.'

'All right, then.' He released his grip. 'You're going to be just fine.'

I looked at him like I was seeing Dr Alexander for the first time. I'd been too worked up to really take anything in until now. His eyes were bluer than I remembered. A beat passed, neither of us saying anything.

'Well, you're looking a little perkier,' he said quickly, as if he too felt something within the silence. I then caught him looking nervously at the camera.

'I guess I'll have to just put on a brave face. Give Matt a chance.'

He pressed out a sympathetic smile. 'If you feel panicky again, come straight to me this time.'

There it was again. Something in his eyes sharing a hidden message. But what?

It had become clear. Dr Alexander wasn't going to give me the answers. I was to work them out for myself.

'Sometimes, Laura,' he said as I was about to leave, 'it's better not to know everything.'

He was still trying to be reassuring but the suggestion of *not knowing* triggered me again. This time, though, I hid it from him.

A strange new energy was humming. Unloading my past

had opened Pandora's box and untamed emotions were now flying around the room like poltergeists. Angry, destructive thoughts. Things I couldn't even share with the doctor.

What would I do if I *knew*? If I found out something had happened between Jess and Matt on the boat?'

I couldn't tell him because the answer frightened me.

CHAPTER FIFTY

THE PRODUCER

Madrid, Interview Room One

NOW

'You engineered her breakdown.'

The statement is left floating around the room, untethered and dangerous.

The autopsy report is still open. The photos of her are laid out in front of me. He's pushed them right under my nose. There's no escaping it. This is what he wants, of course. For the image of her dead body to be burned into my thoughts.

I hadn't noticed before – her eyes. They're misty and cold like a frosted window. Bruno had eyes like hers. My beloved teddy bear. Mum knew that, of course, so he was the first thing she'd use when she decided I needed punishing. At first, it would be small acts of cruelty. Mum would place him somewhere just out of my reach. I'd gaze up at him longingly – sometimes weeks would pass before he'd be back in my arms. But when she noticed how strong I'd grown, how I'd conditioned myself to pain, she moved things to another level. That was Mum all over. She fucking loved to find chinks in your armour. One day, when I wouldn't stop crying after she'd smacked me, she snatched Bruno from my arms and cut off his ears and legs with the kitchen scissors. She laughed as she scattered his body parts around the living room.

I think of Bruno when I look at *her* eyes.

Sanchez doesn't realize how this special power numbs me to violence and pain. I don't feel anything as I take in her injuries. Nothing, as I stare at the cuts, the blood, the slices of pinky flesh.

I look up at Sanchez in a way that says, *So what?*

'You engineered the love triangle between Matthew, Jessica and Laura, didn't you?'

'No.'

'Yes you did. You created it for "drama".' He wraps air quotes around the word.

'I didn't.'

'One moment Laura is with the man she loves, who you've reconnected her with, and the next, she's all alone, imagining what he's doing with another woman.'

'I had no idea she'd react so badly to it all.'

'What normal person wouldn't?!'

'It was the viewers who voted for Matt and Jess to spend the night on the boat. Not me. I didn't engineer that.' I say it again. I'll say it a thousand times if I have to. *Are you listening, Sanchez? It's not my fault.*

'But the viewers wouldn't have had the option to choose if you hadn't given it to them. So with whom does the responsibility lie?'

He stares at me.

'We had a trained therapist on board twenty-four hours a day to offer support if it was needed,' I say, trying to reason.

'Jessica Carmichael, let's talk about her,' the detective cuts in. 'How did you find her?'

'Well, I didn't. She found us, actually.'

'Oh?'

'She'd been watching the show and rang in. She begged us to bring her into *The Villa* as a surprise newcomer.'

'Begged?'

'We had her booked on a flight to Spain within hours.' I feel a spark of pride as I think back over the logistical nightmare we managed to navigate. The flights, the hotel, the chopper to the island. The twenty-four-hour turnaround.

'That sounds very unusual. You didn't do that for anyone else.'

'She was different to the others.'

'How so?'

'She said she was Matt's girlfriend.'

CHAPTER FIFTY-ONE

THE CONTESTANT

Aruna, Balearic Islands

DAY FOUR, *THE VILLA*

I'd been keeping watch for what seemed like hours.

Nothing Dr Alexander had said to calm me down had stuck. I was back on the hamster wheel, chasing my worst fears. I wanted to return to the therapy room. To run through it all over again until I felt calm, but then I might miss their grand entrance, and I couldn't do that. I had to see the look in Matt's eye. I needed to know.

More agonizing time passed and then, finally, the side door to the sea opened.

I saw her white dress before anything else. Last night's party clothes, swishing. *But hang on, they're not holding hands. That has to be a good sign. And they're not making eye contact – maybe they didn't . . .*

Jess looked tanned and beautiful, and *happy*. Striding a step ahead of him. Flicking her hair off her shoulders in a way that suggested she had something to be confident about.

My stomach heaved. I couldn't bear it.

It had all got too much. Cameron, the threats to keep me silenced, the humiliation of being outed as a journalist, Matt coming back into my life and then ditching me the night after . . . far, far too much . . .

And yet I couldn't stop myself from watching them.

Oh shit. He's crossing the garden with a determined expression. Someone's told Matt where I am. Go away. I don't want to speak to you. I don't want to hear it – the rejection speech.

His footsteps on the stairs were quick and urgent. *He needs to tell me something.* My whole body was braced as he emerged into the upstairs hallway.

But to my utter surprise, Matt arrived smiling. Showing off that warm, friendly grin – as if nothing was wrong.

'Wow, it's getting hot out there.' He fanned his shirt from his chest. His skin was red from a morning on the boat. With *her.* 'I think there's a heatwave on the way,' he said.

When he noticed I was looking haunted, he slowed his approach.

'Everything OK?'

I couldn't believe he was acting like nothing had happened.

'Hey?' He stepped towards me, more gingerly this time. 'Are you going to say something?'

I couldn't bring myself to meet his gaze.

'Laurie, come on, don't be in a mood. You're being silly.'

Silly.

'Really over-egging it.'

Over-egging it? My hands balled into fists.

'Well, do you like her?' I could see the spittle fly as I said it.

He sighed impatiently. 'No.' He paused. 'She's a nice enough girl, but I don't like her like *that*, if that's what you mean.'

'Did something happen?'

'Nothing happened, Laurie.'

Stop using my pet name as if you have a right to it.

Finally, I turned to face him.

'We just had a laugh and then went to sleep. Nothing went on apart from a bit of drinking. Swear on my life.' He shook his head. 'I sound like a kid saying that, but really, I swear.'

I stared at him, trying to read his eyes. 'You're lying.'

'Jesus, I'm not.'

He shoved his hands deep into his pockets, his body stiff and awkward.

Liar.

'Please, listen to what I'm saying.'

I pivoted so I could look at her from the window. Jess had regrouped with Becky and Annie, who'd been sunbathing by the pool all morning. They were laughing so hard that Becky spilled her drink.

'I didn't ask to be stuck on a boat with her. We were forced into it.'

Their heads almost touching as they spoke in whispers. My stomach plummeted. *She's telling them a secret.*

I whipped back around to face him.

'Stop lying to me!' Adrenaline flushed my veins. 'Tell me what happened *now*, or I'm going to lose it!'

He held up his hands. 'OK, OK, calm down.'

I couldn't. Some sort of madness had taken hold. I looked down. My hands were trembling.

'She tried to kiss me, OK. But that was it.'

'What do you mean *that was it*?'

'She got drunk, made a move, I told her, "NO, absolutely no way, I'm with Laurie, stop making a tit of yourself." And that was the end of it.'

'Do you seriously expect me to believe that after the way you kissed her on the beach? The way you were all over her. What kind of an idiot do you take me for? How drunk did you get?'

'Umm, I dunno,' he shrugged, 'I had a glass or two. It was quality champagne. I wasn't *drunk* per se.' He met my eyes. 'I wouldn't do that.'

I was confused. My head and heart were pulling me in different directions.

'If anything, I felt sorry for her. She's a tad desperate.'

'So you pity-fucked her?'

He raked his hands through his hair. 'You're not listening to me.' And then, his expression changed. His mouth flattened into a hard line. 'God,' he sighed. 'You haven't changed at all.'

I flinched.

He stared at me. Not saying a word.

'What do you mean, I haven't changed?' I said.

My voice had grown less certain.

'Seriously? Laurie, you're doing it again.'

'Doing what?' But I knew what he was referring to and a sickness was swelling inside.

I stopped talking and waited for him to tell me what was wrong with me.

'Being jealous. Distrusting. Making up shit.' He shook his head. 'This is why we broke up.'

'No, it's not the same, that's not what's going on here.' The sound of my own words had become like thunder in my head. Noisy and destructive. Suddenly they didn't make any sense at all.

'What about Spin the Bottle, the kiss?'

He rolled his eyes. 'Not that again. Honestly, you're the most jealous person I have ever known. You haven't changed and you never will.'

I began wringing my hands, using the sensation of movement to try and calm myself. In the blink of an eye, the balance between us had tipped.

Matt sighed. One of those scolding 'What are we going to do with you?' sighs.

More softly, he said: 'I'm really worried about you. Are you still taking your pills?'

Pain spread across my sternum. His low blow felt like an actual punch to the stomach. How could he? My secret. The anti-anxiety pills I'd had to take when things became too unbearable towards the end with Matt. How could he?

'I tried to be there for you then. I did everything in my power to reassure you. I told you over and over how much I loved you. Fuck, Laurie, I even proposed to you. But still you wouldn't believe me. I'm here for you now and you don't see it, but . . .'

He shook his head. He looked exhausted. *I've exhausted him. That's how draining I can be.*

'But what?' I whispered.

'But if you're going to keep behaving like this then I don't see how we can have a future together.' His expression had hardened. 'I don't know what else to say.'

Shame washed over me. An all-too-familiar feeling. Matt was right. I'd taken things too far.

'Are we breaking up?' I didn't mean to, but I started to cry.

His eyes were full of irritation.

'No, but . . . this can't carry on.'

I nodded. Overwhelmed with relief that he hadn't said yes. Matt was right. I must change.

'I'm sorry,' I said.

CHAPTER FIFTY-TWO

THE VIEWERS

EIGHTEEN MILLION VIEWERS

It was breakfast time in the quiet suburbs of Auckland, New Zealand, and Millie and Noah were getting ready to leave for their banking jobs in the city.

'No. No. No! You stupid thing!'

'Hey, ease up, you'll break it.'

'It's my work laptop, I don't care. I've got to know what happens,' Millie exclaimed.

'What are you on about?' Noah stopped pouring milk into his cereal bowl and came over.

'Laura's ex Matt is on the love boat with Jess and it looked like they were about to get it on before this friggin' piece of crap cut out.'

'Shouldn't you be getting ready for work?'

'I've been up all night; I can't leave it now. This show's insane, why don't we have anything like this over here?'

'What show?'

'*The Villa*. It's some British reality dating show on the

internet and we get to tell the contestants what to do, that's crazy, right?' Millie smashed the refresh button again. 'Come on! I need to know if Matt cheats on Laura!'

'You're enjoying this.' Noah cast his fiancée an unimpressed look.

'No! But who doesn't love a bit of drama?!'

'Here, let me look at it.' Noah took control of the keyboard. He closed the live feed and reopened it in another browser and then frowned. 'Sorry, hun, I think you'll have to forget about this and get ready for work.'

'Why?'

'It's not your computer. It's the show. Look, they've cut transmission.'

'You're having me on. Why would they do that?'

Noah shrugged. 'Maybe something happened? Something so bad they couldn't show it?'

CHAPTER FIFTY-THREE

THE PRODUCER

Madrid, Interview Room One

NOW

Sanchez carries a silver laptop in one hand, a mug in the other. He places the computer on the table, takes a seat and a noisy sip of his drink. The fan sweeps the bitter smell of instant coffee my way. He doesn't say anything.

Seconds later, the female officer enters the room. Oh great – *she's* back. I preferred when it was just the two of us.

She takes her time getting comfortable, arranging her features into another scowl.

What are they waiting for? I'm exhausted, we've been on this witch-hunt all night. *Come on, Detective, I've given you far too much of my time as it is.*

She throws him a look. Clearly she's in on whatever he's planning. I scratch the nape of my neck, the intense itch won't leave me alone.

'What is it?' I finally say. The silence is killing me. 'Just tell me.' I'm used to noise, panic and chaos. When things fall quiet, that means the shit's hit the fan. I can smell it now. I bite down on my rising anxiety.

Detective Sanchez opens his laptop and slides it across the table.

A knot tightens in my stomach. 'What's that?'

'I think you know what it is.'

He takes another sip of coffee. His eyebrows lifting as he does so.

'We've managed to retrieve the video footage from the boat.' Another sip. 'It's very . . . enlightening.'

A sudden flare of heat strikes me.

The screen is split into four. Paused recordings from the cameras I had planted on *Barco Amore*. The deck. The bar area. The bathroom and the bedroom.

Sanchez shuffles his chair around to be next to me, nice and close. He reaches across. He stinks of coffee and cigarettes and a cheap aftershave he hoses himself with to conceal his vices.

He presses a key, shrinking the four screens to one.

'Only one recording was deemed to be relevant to our case,' he says. We are taken below deck, into the bedroom.

He presses *play*.

The bed is made. The rose petals are scattered. The candles are flickering. Everything is prepared. It's beautiful, I can't help thinking.

And then Matt appears. Strained and exhausted. He sits down heavily, his shoulders slumped, his head bowed.

Seconds pass and Jess comes charging in. Her eyes are wild and frenzied. He's shouting something at her. He's running his hands through his hair. He's signalling for her not to come any closer.

'We couldn't retrieve the sound,' Sanchez says. 'That's OK, it's our little silent movie.'

How dare he? Making out like I've obstructed his investigation. He didn't ask to see the tapes from the boat. As soon as he did, I made sure he had a copy.

He directs me back to the screen as Jess explodes. She's yelling. Her face is twisted with rage. She's pointing at something on her neck. He continues to stonewall her and eventually she turns her back to him.

For a moment there's some semblance of calm. I grab the chance to take a breath.

'There's more,' Sanchez says.

Jess is breathing heavily. Wringing her wrists in a repetitive motion. And then, without saying anything, she begins to strip off.

She peels off her dress, letting it fall to the floor. The swathes of white fabric ring her feet like a spotlight. She's not wearing any underwear. Her body is sculpted. Tanned and toned. She's a vision. Jess holds herself perfectly still, demanding Matt's attention.

I look sideways. I want to see if Sanchez is getting off on watching this. *Don't tell me my show isn't entertaining – I know you're enjoying it.*

'Señora,' says Sanchez, guiding me back to the screen.

She trails her fingers across her breast, guiding Matt's eyes down. I'm no master at lip reading but even I can work out what she's saying.

Fuck me.

Matt leaps up off the bed. Scoops the dress off the floor and shoves it into her chest.

She stares at the fabric in her hands and then – then comes the rage. She flings the dress across the room, whipping off her mask. Her expression veering from sexy to manic. She lunges at Matt, thumping him so hard he falls back across the bed.

'This next bit is very interesting,' Sanchez says.

I can't admit it, but I too am riveted. Sanchez would hate me for saying this, but it was a crying shame we had to cut the transmission when we did, because this would have made for epic viewing figures.

Jess has Matt pinned by the wrists. He isn't trying very hard to get her off. In fact, from the way he's staring at her breasts, I wonder if he's enjoying her breakdown. But the moment doesn't last because Jess kicks off again. She screams into his face, something so vile that it triggers Matt.

Sanchez presses pause.

'This is why you stopped the live feed,' he states.

I stare at the frozen image. A shiver prickles me.

'Answer the question.'

I tear my eyes away and look directly at Sanchez. 'We cut the transmission from the boat much earlier, as soon as . . .' I take a breath. 'Jess broke the rules.'

'The rules?'

'Rule number five: No violence or abusive behaviour towards another housemate. I'd thought the chance of winning *The Villa* with Matt would have kept her in check.'

'In check?'

'Look, yes, we brought Jess in – at great trouble and

expense – hoping for fireworks. But we thought she'd drop her bombshell of a claim she was Matt's girlfriend the moment she arrived. I have no idea why Jess waited to be alone with Matt. That she had something else planned all along.' More softly, I say: 'I hadn't counted on her being such a nutjob.'

'She clearly became distressed by the situation.'

'So it seems.'

'It would be understandable that she's angry. Don't you think?'

Why's he feeling sorry for her?

'Jessica was as fame-hungry as the rest of them. It was her chance to show the nation she could win over her man. She was overly confident she could steal him back into her bed.'

'Still, her behaviour is understandable?'

He blinks as he waits for me to answer. I stare back at him.

'Her so-called boyfriend appears in front of the nation declaring his love for someone else. Those are the kind of things that piss people off. That push people to do extreme things.'

The body we pulled from the water. The image smacks me like a punch.

'Nothing to say?' He inches closer, resting his chin on his hand as he watches my reaction. 'Laura – she too was inconsolable.'

'You can't say that about Laura. I was doing her a favour. The poor girl needed some closure. Either it worked out with Matt or it didn't, but I was opening her eyes to who he really was.' *That's right, Detective, I was* helping.

Call me the fairy fucking godmother. But I can tell I'm losing control. I'm losing this battle to make him understand. I shut my eyes, scrunching them tight.

The scratchy noise the computer makes as Sanchez pushes it across the table wrenches them back open. He's placed the screen right under my nose.

'Matthew Taylor' – he taps the frozen image of Matt, bringing it to life, his hands wrapped around Jess's throat – 'was a ticking time bomb. And I think you knew it.'

CHAPTER FIFTY-FOUR

THE CONTESTANT

Aruna, Balearic Islands

DAY FOUR, *THE VILLA*

I traced my finger across the delicate lace, the fabric soft and yielding to my curves. I rotated in the mirror, admiring the matching red suspender belt and knickers. The only sexy lingerie I'd packed. Matt was in for a treat.

I released my hair from the clip, letting it tumble past my shoulders. I outlined my lips with pencil. Filling them in with pillar-box-red lipstick. I kissed away the residue into a tissue, admiring the perfectly shaped crescents I left behind. I stroked blusher across my cheeks. I passed the mascara wand over my lashes. I had the feeling I was performing a ritual. As if I was getting ready for something final.

I couldn't explain why I was feeling uneasy. Especially since Matt had been faultlessly attentive. Our argument had cleared the air and he'd spent the entire day showering me with kisses and cuddles. Whenever he sensed my anxiety rising over the looks *they* were casting us, he'd take me into his arms. Like a guard dog, he hadn't let me out of his sight.

We'd found a quiet corner of the villa and Matt had stopped anyone from coming near, from polluting our love.

Perhaps exhaustion was to blame for my unease. Last night's panic attack had left me drained. The memory of not being able to breathe had attached itself. The fear it could happen again was draining me.

I slipped the red silk dress over my head, gently shaking my hips from side to side to help it slide down the length of my body until the fabric grazed the floor.

I had my bedroom to myself. Matt had been so insistent I kept away from the others that he'd managed to talk Cameron into letting me have it while I got ready for tonight's Bond-themed dinner party. Cameron's hatred for me had waned since he'd seen a prospect in Jess. He'd spent all day flirting, trying to win her over. It had been tiring just watching him prance and preen, a last desperate bid to still be in with a chance of winning.

The door creaked open, making me jump with fright. This on-edge feeling was starting to pervade every part of me. It was only Matt.

'Wow! You look incredible.'

'You're not so bad yourself,' I said.

I admired the tailoring of his dinner jacket. The sharp line of his suit trousers. But his lopsided bowtie, his sunburn, and those flip-flops he insisted on wearing made him more adorable than hot. My Matt.

'I wish we didn't have to go out there,' he said, coming up behind me, the warmth of his chest spreading into my back. The heat of his breath touched my ear as he murmured: 'All I want is to get you into bed.'

They shouldn't have, but his words made me flinch.

I'm tired. I need to snap out of this mood.

I cupped my hands over his and tilted my head to the side, offering up my neck for him to kiss.

His lips met with my skin and I pushed down my doubts.

Tonight will be amazing. We'll show them what a strong couple we are. Nobody can break us.

The *ting ting ting* of cutlery on glass filled the air.

'I'd like to propose a toast,' Annie announced. It was her third of the evening. An entire afternoon knocking back cocktails with the girls had left her unsteady on her feet. 'Here's to new friends' – she turned to Adam – 'and lovers.'

There was a collective 'Oooooing'. Most people humoured her and raised their glasses.

My fingers were clammy around the champagne flute. The day's heat hadn't abated and there was no sign of it letting up. Not even an ocean breeze to sweep the humidity and unspoken tension away.

I tipped back more than I should have. The bubbles pricked my throat.

Matt caught my eye.

I love you, he mouthed.

Charles stood up. 'I'd also like to make a toast.'

He pivoted to face Angela. There was genuine warmth in his expression. Something scarcely seen since entering the villa.

'Angela . . .' he fumbled over his words. '. . . I'm so glad I met you.'

'Come on, Charlie boy, you can do better than that,' said Cameron, cruelly parodying Charles's plummy accent.

Charles shot him a hard stare, but the bully jibe had worked. He tried again. 'Angela, you're an incredible woman. Honest and pure of heart. Most of all, I admire how genuine you are.'

I noticed a quiver of sadness. As if Angela might be on the cusp of tears. She quickly rearranged her expression to a smile, clinking glasses with Charles.

She was barely recognizable as a blonde. Her timidness had gone, she was oozing sexy. The vivid red of her lipstick contrasted beautifully against the platinum blonde wig she was wearing. A knockout – Angela won the prize for being the best Bond girl.

'You could have worn one, too.' She caught me staring. 'There's a trunk of dress-up stuff in the bathroom.' She rolled a strand of nylon hair between her fingers and laughed. 'Just a bit of fun.' I could hear the note of disappointment, though. I knew she would have liked us to get ready together.

Ting ting.

Blake rose to his feet. 'Another toast, if you will.'

He pretended to be stiff and formal. His back was to the sunset. Purple, orange, red, smudging around his broad shoulders. He held up the glass and a beam of sunlight shot through, turning his champagne into liquid gold.

I squinted into the glare. I was one of the few not wearing sunglasses at our banquet table.

'This one's to Becky,' he said, but he was looking at Cameron. 'Here's to you. You're an absolute babe. A rare gem.' He tucked his sun-bleached hair behind his ear, finally meeting her eye. 'For every yin there's a yang, and in the words of Jerry Maguire: You complete me. Cheers and namaste.' He bowed his head.

Becky clutched her heart. 'Babe, stop it,' she said, casting around to see who was marvelling at her. 'You're the best.'

It smacked of desperation. Each of them taking it in turns to outdo each other. Persuading the audience they were the most loved-up couple. The most deserving of the prize money.

Still, their competitiveness had left a mark. Part of me wanted Matt to get off his arse and pledge his love.

I could feel the weight of her stare. I glanced across the table at Jess. She was silently watching. I drained my glass, placed the flute down and immediately poured myself some wine.

'Steady,' Matt touched my arm.

In the past I would have been touched by his concern, but a little ball of anger had lodged. I fidgeted from his grip. Envious of the girls, increasingly irritated at him for not toasting me.

Annie knocked the table as she stumbled to her feet. She kicked off her heels and proceeded with a string of words that made no real sense. She lifted her chin into the air in that way people do to overcompensate for being pissed.

'I've got something else to say!'

'What's with all these toasts? It's fucking intense, don't you think?' Cameron cut in. 'Let's crack on with the eating and drinking.'

He reached for the wine, barging Angela as he did so.

'Hey! Careful!' Charles waded in.

'Relax, for fuck's sake. Are we having a party or not?'

Annie stood there for a moment, swaying and then, to everyone's surprise, she obediently sat back down.

Ting ting. This time it came from next to me. Matt. Wow. He'd finally found his voice.

A wave of groaning rolled around the table.

Matt rose to his feet, fanning down everyone's impatience. 'Don't worry, what I have to say won't take long.' He took in a deep breath and moved his body to face mine.

'I can't stop smiling.' He shook his head a little. 'This grin, it's been stuck on my face ever since I arrived. Laurie, you've made me such a happy chappie.' He laughed again. 'Look at me, you've turned me into a grinning idiot.'

It wasn't exactly Shakespeare, but it was sweet and heartfelt.

'I know things haven't been plain sailing.' He cleared his throat. 'OK, let me try that again . . . I know I've been an utter dick and you've been through shit, stuff you should have never had to go through, but I hope I've been able to show you how much you mean to me and how sorry I am for everything.'

'I thought you said you were going to keep it short,' Cameron ribbed.

'Hear hear,' Charles echoed.

Matt masked his irritation with a strained smile. He went on. 'Having the chance to come on *The Villa* and prove myself to you has been . . . It's almost impossible to put into words . . . But here goes . . . the best decision I've ever made in my life.' He locked eyes with me. 'You know me. You know how cynical I can sometimes be.'

I smiled.

'I didn't believe second chances existed until now.'

I should have been glowing. Beaming from ear to ear. I'd been waiting for this for what felt like an eternity of self-doubt and depression. Yet something was casting a shadow over our special moment. *Someone* was taking the shine off my turn in the spotlight. *Jess*. I didn't have to turn my head to know, I could feel her drilling holes into me. I swallowed hard.

Matt lifted his glass. 'So! Without boring you any more with stories of how much I love this girl' – he moved his eyes back to me – 'I'd like to make this toast to Laurie. The girl I should have never left. The love of my life.'

The champagne stung as it slipped down my throat.

'All right, all right. Enough. It's time to eat.'

Cameron began lifting the silver domed lids from the platters before Matt had even sat down. He revealed what could only be described as a medieval feast. Whole roast chickens, legs of lamb, pork, entire salmons nestled in a sea of chargrilled cherry tomatoes. Honey-glazed roast vege-tables. There was enough food to feed us three times over.

The noise of cutlery, glasses being filled up, knives searing through flesh, replaced everything that had gone before. And then there was her voice, carving through the excite-ment, sharp and fiery.

'I have something to say!' said Jess.

She removed her napkin, placed it beside her plate and, just in case anyone hadn't heard, stood up.

Jess was wearing an almost identical red dress to mine. My instinct told me it was deliberate. Someone had wanted d, her voice rasping. 'TELL HER.'

me with her cruel stare.

ng for months, *Laurie*. While you were
sofa in your shapeless jogging bottoms,
up in the gym.'

ere Matt met me. I stopped bothering
se, I suppose, I got comfortable in our
hen my anxiety became too impossible
thought of working out exhausted me.
ow – where the anxiety had come from.
me.

to me how you'd let yourself go. How
ecause all you did was sit on it.'

hand to her neck, sweeping her fingers
ain. In such a pronounced way – she
e.

miled. 'Matt gave it to me. His way of
we'll be together soon.' She shook her
He's only here because he thinks he's got
ng with you. He's skint.' She laughed.
ey. He doesn't love you.' She tilted her
voice. 'Aww, you really thought he did.'
g now. Nowhere near as sober as she'd
be.

't move a muscle. Not even a brush of
way the perspiration. I could feel the
ping down my back, between my breasts.
n right. Those niggling gut instincts that
nething wasn't adding up. The ones *he*
had made me feel insane. Panicky.

us to look the same tonight. But around her neck was a
ring of strange purple marks. They looked a bit like bruises.

'I also want to make a toast.' She stared directly at me.
'And don't give me any flak for it because this is something
you'll all want to hear – I can promise you that.'

Knowing looks fired up, darting back and forth between
Annie and Becky. Annie smothered a laugh, while Angela
looked troubled.

What's going on?

I turned to Matt but all the colour had drained from
his face.

'Matt?' I whispered.

He pulled my hand into his lap.

'Hey, what's going on?'

His palm was suddenly clammy.

Jess raised her glass, the muscles of her arm tensing. 'To
Laura and Matt. Because there couldn't be a more perfect
couple.'

There was a fresh tension in her voice. Her tone had
become tinged with something else.

'Perfection. Matched in every way – in looks, in charisma,
you have the chemistry . . .'

Venom.

'I look at you two and I think . . . I wish that could be
me, with your perfect little everything . . .'

Her words were poisonous. It wasn't so much what she
said but *the way* she was saying it.

The smell of meat, the heat, the claustrophobia of our
intimate gathering was suddenly making me feel queasy.

She took a deep, restorative breath. The sort you took

when you were building up to something. With the light of the sunset behind her, and her face in the shadows, her eyes appeared entirely black.

'You're so perfect together,' she said, 'it almost doesn't ring true.'

She paused, allowing her statement to marinate. It had the desired effect, as our party hushed to a silence. The last clink of cutlery subsided as everyone turned their attention to Jess.

Glances were criss-crossing the table like gunfire. I felt my cheeks flush with nerves.

'Laura, you must believe me when I say I'm doing this for your own good,' Jess continued. 'You see, *your Matt* was fucking me while you were together.'

She should have just punched me in the stomach. It would have felt the same.

'While you were working late at your trashy paper, he was taking me from behind over your kitchen table. It always made me smile as I looked across at your *Home is where the heart is* plaque.'

She took a sip of her drink, the corners of her mouth curling as she did so.

I was too winded to fully register the sharp intakes of breath; the whispers swirling the table. I was just trying to keep breathing.

We'd bought that plaque together at a fair. Our first Christmas in our flat in Ealing. It was a rental, a bit of a dump, but it was ours. I must have gone to every single craft fair London had to offer that winter, searching for small glittery things that would make our place sparkle. It

Anxious. There'd been moments when I thought I was actually losing my mind. All those times I'd apologized for being overly suspicious. *Fuck*, I gasped.

Everyone was staring now. Matt was pleading with his eyes. His skin was ghostly white. He was opening and closing his mouth, stupid, incapable of getting his side of the story out.

I didn't need to hear what he had to say, it would only be more lies. Jess could have been making it all up, but I knew she wasn't. She was simply confirming everything I'd suspected.

The world was holding its breath. I could feel it, as if I was with them in their living rooms. Watching them watch me. I think I was having some out-of-body experience. Millions of people were studying me just as they would an insect under a microscope. The viewers tickled by my humiliation, waiting for me to react. *Fuck*.

Inside the little bubble I'd been shocked into, time had stood still. I stared numbly at the carving knife spearing the chicken carcass, thinking things I never could have imagined a week ago. Before I came on this demonic show. Ghastly, evil thoughts.

Twisted bitch. You deserve everything that's coming to you.

CHAPTER FIFTY-FIVE

THE VIEWERS

NINETEEN MILLION VIEWERS

In Birmingham, Kat and her housemates were getting ready for a night out at the university bar. Now *The Villa* was back online they'd gathered in the living room.

'What the actual fuck?' said Evie.

'If I were Laura, there'd be no stopping me now, I'd tear Jess apart,' said Lou.

'Matt cheated too,' Allie pointed out.

'But Jess is the one broadcasting it to the world,' said Lou. 'She's gone on the show to humiliate Laura. Deserves everything that's coming to her. Make the bitch pay.'

'What would you do?' asked Caz.

'Babe, you don't even want to know. What would you do if you found out some girl was shagging Mark behind your back and then told the world?'

'I'd kill her!' said Caz.

'Shh, there's an announcement,' said Kat.

'What is it?' said Lou.

us to look the same tonight. But around her neck was a ring of strange purple marks. They looked a bit like bruises.

'I also want to make a toast.' She stared directly at me. 'And don't give me any flak for it because this is something you'll all want to hear – I can promise you that.'

Knowing looks fired up, darting back and forth between Annie and Becky. Annie smothered a laugh, while Angela looked troubled.

What's going on?

I turned to Matt but all the colour had drained from his face.

'Matt?' I whispered.

He pulled my hand into his lap.

'Hey, what's going on?'

His palm was suddenly clammy.

Jess raised her glass, the muscles of her arm tensing. 'To Laura and Matt. Because there couldn't be a more perfect couple.'

There was a fresh tension in her voice. Her tone had become tinged with something else.

'Perfection. Matched in every way – in looks, in charisma, you have the chemistry . . .'

Venom.

'I look at you two and I think . . . I wish that could be me, with your perfect little everything . . .'

Her words were poisonous. It wasn't so much what she said but *the way* she was saying it.

The smell of meat, the heat, the claustrophobia of our intimate gathering was suddenly making me feel queasy.

She took a deep, restorative breath. The sort you took

when you were building up to something. With the light of the sunset behind her, and her face in the shadows, her eyes appeared entirely black.

'You're so perfect together,' she said, 'it almost doesn't ring true.'

She paused, allowing her statement to marinate. It had the desired effect, as our party hushed to a silence. The last clink of cutlery subsided as everyone turned their attention to Jess.

Glances were criss-crossing the table like gunfire. I felt my cheeks flush with nerves.

'Laura, you must believe me when I say I'm doing this for your own good,' Jess continued. 'You see, *your Matt* was fucking me while you were together.'

She should have just punched me in the stomach. It would have felt the same.

'While you were working late at your trashy paper, he was taking me from behind over your kitchen table. It always made me smile as I looked across at your *Home is where the heart is* plaque.'

She took a sip of her drink, the corners of her mouth curling as she did so.

I was too winded to fully register the sharp intakes of breath; the whispers swirling the table. I was just trying to keep breathing.

We'd bought that plaque together at a fair. Our first Christmas in our flat in Ealing. It was a rental, a bit of a dump, but it was ours. I must have gone to every single craft fair London had to offer that winter, searching for small glittery things that would make our place sparkle. It was Matt who noticed the plaque on the stall next to the guy selling ostrich feathers and baubles. The memory was suddenly so vivid it could have been yesterday.

'Matt would tell me how desperate he was to end it with you, but he was afraid you'd do something crazy.'

She twirled her finger next to her temple, mouthing *crazy* while looking at me.

'He pitied you,' she continued, laughing. 'I even started to feel sorry for you. And then I was pissed off. Because you were trapping him. Keeping him from being with me. How selfish can you be?'

'Enough, Jess,' Matt said.

'Tell her, go on. Tell her how we fucked in every room in your house.'

'Stop it!'

Cameron clapped his hands. 'No, carry on. This is epic.' He cast around. 'Laura needs to know the truth, right? Good one, Jess!'

Jess slid her gaze to Cameron, her face a picture of revulsion. 'Why are you even here?' She glared at him. 'Nobody wants you, not even Laura. You're invisible. When will you realize – you don't matter.'

Cameron fell silent but the look in his eyes – it was more menacing than anything he'd shown me.

There was mania in Jess's expression as she returned to Matt. 'Tell her how only last week you were going down on me in the taxi back to yours.' She smiled at me. 'He likes doing it in public. You didn't know that, did you?'

'Oooh, classy,' Becky said.

Matt glared at Jess.

'Go on,' she said, her voice rasping. 'TELL HER.'

She returned to me with her cruel stare.

'We were fucking for months, *Laurie*. While you were curled up on your sofa in your shapeless jogging bottoms, he was chatting me up in the gym.'

Jesus, that's where Matt met me. I stopped bothering with the gym because, I suppose, I got comfortable in our relationship. And then my anxiety became too impossible to manage. Just the thought of working out exhausted me. It all made sense now – where the anxiety had come from. He *was* cheating on me.

'He complained to me how you'd let yourself go. How your arse got fat because all you did was sit on it.'

Jess brought her hand to her neck, sweeping her fingers across her gold chain. In such a pronounced way – she wanted me to notice.

'Oh, this?' she smiled. 'Matt gave it to me. His way of saying *be patient, we'll be together soon.*' She shook her head in disbelief. 'He's only here because he thinks he's got a chance of winning with you. He's skint.' She laughed. 'He needs the money. He doesn't love you.' She tilted her head, lowering her voice. 'Aww, you really thought he did.'

She was swaying now. Nowhere near as sober as she'd been pretending to be.

And still, I didn't move a muscle. Not even a brush of my hand to dab away the perspiration. I could feel the beads of sweat slipping down my back, between my breasts.

All along I'd been right. Those niggling gut instincts that kept telling me something wasn't adding up. The ones *he* snuffed out. Matt had made me feel insane. Panicky.

Anxious. There'd been moments when I thought I was actually losing my mind. All those times I'd apologized for being overly suspicious. *Fuck*, I gasped.

Everyone was staring now. Matt was pleading with his eyes. His skin was ghostly white. He was opening and closing his mouth, stupid, incapable of getting his side of the story out.

I didn't need to hear what he had to say, it would only be more lies. Jess could have been making it all up, but I knew she wasn't. She was simply confirming everything I'd suspected.

The world was holding its breath. I could feel it, as if I was with them in their living rooms. Watching them watch me. I think I was having some out-of-body experience. Millions of people were studying me just as they would an insect under a microscope. The viewers tickled by my humiliation, waiting for me to react. *Fuck*.

Inside the little bubble I'd been shocked into, time had stood still. I stared numbly at the carving knife spearing the chicken carcass, thinking things I never could have imagined a week ago. Before I came on this demonic show. Ghastly, evil thoughts.

Twisted bitch. You deserve everything that's coming to you.

THE VIEWERS

NINETEEN MILLION VIEWERS

In Birmingham, Kat and her housemates were getting ready for a night out at the university bar. Now *The Villa* was back online they'd gathered in the living room.

'What the actual fuck?' said Evie.

'If I were Laura, there'd be no stopping me now, I'd tear Jess apart,' said Lou.

'Matt cheated too,' Allie pointed out.

'But Jess is the one broadcasting it to the world,' said Lou. 'She's gone on the show to humiliate Laura. Deserves everything that's coming to her. Make the bitch pay.'

'What would you do?' asked Caz.

'Babe, you don't even want to know. What would you do if you found out some girl was shagging Mark behind your back and then told the world?'

'I'd kill her!' said Caz.

'Shh, there's an announcement,' said Kat.

'What is it?' said Lou.

'Shhhhh. QUIET,' Evie yelled. She turned up the volume.

The girls quietened as the presenter of *The Villa* made an announcement.

'*Contestants – the rules have changed.*'

'Stop it! What's going on?' Caz exclaimed.

'*We have the right to change the rules at any time.*'

'They can't be doing this now!' said Allie. 'That's not how it's meant to go. We have three days left. What about our votes?'

'Spit it out, woman!' Evie yelled at the screen.

'*You no longer need to be in a couple to be crowned winner of* The Villa. *Only one person will be leaving the island with the prize money.*'

One million pounds appeared on the screen.

'*Who wins? You decide . . .*'

CHAPTER FIFTY-SIX

THE CONTESTANT

Aruna, Balearic Islands

DAY FOUR, *THE VILLA*

'I'm *dumped*?' Annie broke into a pantomime laugh. She tried to stroke Adam's arm. 'Don't be silly, darling.'

He shrugged her off. 'I'm not feeling it. Sorry.'

Adam didn't look the least bit sorry.

An unevenness entered her voice. 'For goodness' sake. We're perfect for each other.'

'He's not interested, love, take the hint.'

It was Cameron, once again the first to stoke the fire. He'd slouched into his chair. Right leg stretched out in front. Arm slung over the backrest. Bedding in for the finale.

Annie flung her arms around Adam's neck and pressed her lips onto his. He kept his mouth tightly shut.

'Baby?'

He recoiled as she stroked his face.

'What's the problem?'

'He doesn't need you any more to win, that's what's going on. You're making a tit of yourself.'

Annie's smile tightened as a look of desperation took hold. She began slipping down the straps of her dress, revealing more cleavage. As if she thought it would change his mind. It was toe-curling and sad in equal measure.

I'd found sanctuary in quietly watching everyone around me fall apart. The presenter's announcement had detonated an emotional bomb. The declarations of love made barely an hour earlier were cracking apart. The humidity had become infused with anger, resentment and a sense of danger.

Matt had started on his excuses. He was bleating something in my ear but nothing he was saying was registering. I'd slipped into a daze. Unable to speak, to move – cry, I couldn't do anything, except watch.

'Laurie, are you hearing me?' Matt said. 'Look at me.'

I could sense Jess looming behind us, preparing to strike again. But there was nothing else she could say that would hurt me more.

Matt seized my arm. Jolting me out of my bubble.

'Ow! What are you doing? Let go!'

'Not until you hear me out.'

He squeezed my wrist. My hand looked so fragile caught beneath his whitening knuckles, like it might snap at any moment.

'Stop it.' I tried to tear myself free, but his grip was firm. 'Seriously, Matt, you're hurting me.' I'd never seen him behave like this.

'The lady has asked you to leave her alone,' Cameron yelled from across the table. He seemed tickled by the irony of what he was saying. 'When a woman says no, she means no.'

Sick bastard.

'Keep out of it, mate,' Matt fired back.

'Watch your tone, *mate.*'

'Laurie, fuck's sake, look at me.' He shook me so hard my whole body juddered. 'You have to hear me out.'

'She wants you to back off, look at her!'

'Oi! Piss off!' Matt turned, glowering at Cameron.

Cameron shot to his feet. He drained his glass and headed over. The air strained with tension and the threat of what was coming.

Blake dived into Cameron's path.

'Leave it,' he said, pressing his hand into Cameron's chest. 'It's not for you to get involved.'

'Look at you, being the hero,' Cameron sneered. 'Why don't you fuck off out of my way.'

They bumped shoulders as he lunged for Matt.

I heard the crack. So loud it sounded like a bone snapping.

'Matt!' I screamed. Cameron had him in a headlock. 'Someone help us!' I searched around. 'Help!'

Next thing, plates were crashing around me. Glasses shattering. Blake had wrenched Cameron off Matt and thrown him down across the table. The legs caved in and what was left of our feast slid the length of the surface onto the floor.

Smash.

'Holy shit!' I cried out.

I felt his hand lock around my wrist again. I looked up and there was blood smeared around his mouth and nose.

Things were breaking all around us, but Matt wasn't

looking. He barely noticed because he wouldn't take his eyes off me, not even for a second. The intensity of his behaviour was scaring me.

'Ouch!' I tried twisting myself free again.

'Matt?'

It was like he wasn't really there. 'Let me go!'

Finally, with almost a look of confusion, he released his grip.

I stared at the red marks on my wrists, still in shock at how physical Matt had been. But then tonight had shown me – I didn't know my ex at all. Or what he was capable of.

'Sorry,' he said, but I could tell he didn't mean it.

More fighting broke out around us. Blake and Adam had Cameron pinned to the ground. Cameron's legs were scissoring through shards of glass. I winced as I noticed blood seeping through his white shirt.

'Let's get out of here.'

Matt took me firmly by the hand, pulling me away from the chaos.

'Don't touch me,' I said, snatching my arm away. 'I don't need your help.'

We did need to leave but not like that, not with him controlling me. I stood up, hitched up my dress, stepping over the carnage. Glass crunched beneath my stilettos. I hopped over the cascade of profiteroles that bowled into my path.

Becky and Annie had ringed the boys. Becky was pleading with them to let Cameron go. Annie was revelling in the drama, egging them on. Angela and Charles must have scarpered. Jess, where was she?

Matt hurried down the steps, in what looked like the direction of the swimming pool.

I was concentrating so hard on my footing, I didn't notice how far I'd travelled from the main ring of lights, nor did I see there'd been another announcement.

It was Matt who drew my attention to the screen with: 'Bloody hell! Laurie, look!'

Laurie! How dare you. I was spitting under my breath as I drew my gaze up.

Oh my God.

I blinked. And again, just to make sure I wasn't dreaming. But it was still there.

The leader board was up and *my name* was at the top.

What the . . . ? How did I end up being the favourite?

As if someone saw me looking, the lettering was instantly replaced by numbers.

£1,000,000.

With all the drama, there hadn't been time to let it sink in. A whopping one million was now in play and I was first in line to win.

I searched the darkness for answers. Stunned and bewildered. How? Because of Jess's cruel revelations? It must be. The nation was rallying around me.

There was another shuddering crash from behind us. Raised voices. A scream.

'Come on,' Matt insisted. 'You can hate me all you want but let's get somewhere safe first, away from those nutters.'

Fear started me off down the steps again but as we neared the pool, I stopped abruptly. It was so dark; I couldn't even see where I was placing my feet.

'Come on!' he said.

I stared at Matt's silhouette up ahead and an uneasy feeling began to burrow. Suddenly, I regretted leaving with him. I wasn't thinking clearly. The violence at dinner had made me cling to what I knew – Matt. The reality was, I didn't know him at all. The memory of his grip around my wrist came crashing into view.

He noticed I'd stopped following and turned around. 'Hey, let's go.' His hands on his hips. A little out of breath.

I looked back at him, suspiciously. *Why was he making me feel so uneasy?* Being a cheating shit didn't make someone dangerous, and yet that was the vibration I was picking up on. As if Matt had been wearing a mask the entire time I'd known him.

'Laura?'

I needed to think. The shock of it all was blinding. *Come on, Laura. Think.*

You're live on air. You're safe. There're cameras everywhere. Millions of people are watching. The production team are on standby. Nothing bad can happen.

But doubt had been planted. Fear was taking root.

Matt started making his way back to me.

Listen up, he's not going to hurt you. Matt would be crazy to try anything. And it's Matt, for heaven's sake, Matt!

'OK, stop right there,' I ordered. 'Anything you have to say to me . . .' but my voice wavered as I noticed the normally lit up pool area was in darkness. The screen had been shut down. It was as if someone wanted us to be thrown into the shadows.

'This is weird.' I searched around us. I turned to face

Matt. In the failing light I could no longer read his expression. 'I'm going back; this doesn't feel right.'

He stepped into my path. 'Hang on a minute, let me explain—'

'I don't like it here.'

He held up his hand to block me. 'Two minutes. You're going to give me just two minutes.'

'Hey! Don't tell me what I'm going to do. Now get out of my way.'

He pushed his body in front of me. 'Please, it won't take long.'

I stepped back, crossing my arms. 'What? What do you want? Nothing you say will make a difference.'

I was frightened. I was angry. I wasn't quite sure what I was any more. I was swinging between being on the verge of breaking down and lashing out.

'Please—'

'Please what? Have you forgotten already? I don't need you to win,' I spat. 'Why don't you just piss off back to your girlfriend?'

'Laurie, I couldn't give a shit about the money. I care about you.'

'So that stuff about you being skint, is that true?'

'Sort of. I lost my job, but I'll figure something out, I always do. That's not why I'm here, though—'

'Do you have any idea how I'm feeling? To hear those things, to find out in that way? I know she's telling the truth, so don't bother trying to say she's lying.' I couldn't even bring myself to say her name. 'How many times was it? In *our* home. Come on, how many?' I shook my head.

'Actually, don't answer that.' The tears were starting to prick, I'd crossed over the line into pain.

'Ask me anything. I'll tell you what you want to know.'

'Why should I believe a word you say when everything that's come out of your mouth has been a lie, huh? All those times you made me feel like *I* was in the wrong . . .' I felt my stomach tighten with the memory.

'Yes!' he shouted so loudly I jumped. 'The answer is yes, I slept with her. Yes, I cheated on you. It's not an excuse, but we weren't having sex at the time. In fact, all we were doing was arguing. You were always getting at me about this that and the other. I felt like I couldn't do anything right and then— look, I'm a fucking bastard,' he hissed, 'but you have to know, it's not like she said. Jess is crazy, she's mental.' He tapped his temple. 'She became obsessed with me. After I broke things off, she wouldn't leave me alone. And then when she couldn't have me, she became fixated by you. I had no idea that she'd been looking through your things—'

'What do you mean?'

'Jess, she started wearing the same clothes as you, styling her hair the same as you, wearing your perfume!' he exclaimed. 'Your perfume, for fuck's sake, she even copied that.'

Jesus, the perfume. My mind slipped back to how she hugged me on the beach. That haunted stare of hers. A shiver convulsed down my spine.

'I don't know why, maybe she thought that if she smelt like you, I'd fall in love with her, I'd take her back. Christ only knows!'

'OK, so let me get this straight. Jess is so sick in the head you had to fuck her last week. Was she lying about that?'

'Yes – I mean no – I mean, that's what she's like, she gets inside your head, infects your thoughts. I'd been telling her to stay away for months, and then she turned up outside my place and . . .' he shook his head . . . 'I was feeling down about being fired, I'd had two job rejections that morning, she caught me at a weak moment and I momentarily got sucked in by her seduction act. What can I say? I fucked up. I let her back in.' Matt grabbed me by my shoulders. 'But I immediately regretted it. I wished I could take it back – all of it. I'm such an idiot.'

'Take your fucking hands off me!'

'Sorry.' He released his grip. 'Sorry, I didn't mean to frighten you, I just want you to understand.'

'You're scaring me, Matt.'

'No, shuuush, don't be frightened,' he said, reaching around to hug me, sending me lurching backwards. I almost lost my footing.

My chest ached. The shock of the revelations was wearing off and had been replaced with something much more painful.

'You're wanting me to feel sorry for you?' I was on the cusp of bursting into tears. 'You left me for *her*. You did that, didn't you? You chose her.'

He dropped his eyes. 'Because I was caught up in her spell and then I found out what she was really like and . . .' Matt rubbed his face. 'Arrrgh, she's done it again. She's infecting everything. Jess followed me into *The Villa*, she's trying to destroy us, she's scaring you and . . .' His eyes widening.

'And what?'

'. . . and I'm afraid.'

'Afraid?' I narrowed my eyes. 'Afraid of what, *Matt*?'

'I'm scared she's going to do something really crazy . . .' His eyes opened some more . . . 'That she's going to harm you.'

His words hung in the night.

'You need to be careful . . .'

There was a sudden flash of movement between the trees. At first, I thought I'd imagined it. But the shadow moved again.

'Hey, who's there?' I called out.

Matt turned around. He glanced back to me and then shouted: 'Is someone there?'

We heard twigs snapping underfoot.

'Hello?' Matt was frowning as he turned to face me. 'Wait here, I'll be back in a minute.'

He took off in the direction of the noise. Within seconds, the night had swallowed him up and all I could make out was a shadowy smudge moving around the edge of the pool.

I was completely alone with the darkness wrapping around me. My heart was pumping hard.

Thud. Thud. Thudding in my ears.

And then, from out of the silence, came her voice.

'Laura . . .'

Hissing into the night.

CHAPTER FIFTY-SEVEN

THE CONTESTANT

Aruna, Balearic Islands

DAY FOUR, *THE VILLA*

'Laura . . .' she repeated.

She was everywhere. Haunting me.

'Laura, the viewers have spoken. They want *you* to play in the next game.'

Even though she'd revealed herself, I couldn't stop trembling.

'You and you alone have been asked to carry out their next request.'

'What request?' I asked the night. I spun around, half expecting someone to appear out of the shadows carrying further instructions.

'What request?' I said again, angrily. I was done with these sick games.

'Our viewers are enraged by the way you've been treated. They're horrified Jess took delight in revealing Matt's infidelity. They are appalled by her determination to cause you harm. They now want her to experience pain,' she paused. 'Just as you have.'

Pain. She stressed the word.

'It was wrong of Jessica to make you suffer. It was wrong of her to humiliate you. Our viewers want Jessica to be punished for her actions – and they want you, *Laura,* to take your revenge.'

'Revenge?'

'It is up to you to decide how Jessica should be punished.'

'OK, seriously, what is this?'

'You have the option to play your safe word and not enter into a game. But a quick reminder – Laura, you are in the lead. One million pounds is now up for grabs. And failure to comply with the viewers' wishes could see your popularity fall.' There was another pause, long enough to count five thuds of my heart.

'But the decision, as always, is yours . . .'

Revenge. Punishment. Revenge. My mind had become an echo chamber.

This had to be a joke? Were the viewers actually wanting me to hurt Jess? That's insane. Or maybe it's a game? A test, to see if I fall for this crap. I mean, nobody in their right mind says shit like that. To make you want to hurt someone else? I shook my head. This couldn't be legal? Christ's sake – this was supposed to be an entertainment show!

As for the safe word – well, I already knew there was no such thing.

I heard something. Footsteps.

'Matt?' I called out.

He'd been wearing flip-flops. That's not what the noise sounded like. I squinted into the thick pool of black.

Something was moving. A dark smudge slipping through the night.

'Who's there?' I couldn't hide the tremor in my voice.

On hearing me, whoever it was stopped dead. I held my breath. Braced. And then gasped as they started moving again. More quickly this time. More determined.

It was an outline of a woman and she was heading right for me.

It's Jess. She's come for me.

She drew closer.

'Hey?' My heart was thundering.

'Laura? Is that you?'

I felt an intense burst of relief as I recognized Angela's blonde wig. I hadn't realized I'd been holding my breath until the air rushed from my lungs.

'We need to talk,' she whispered. 'Urgently.'

'What the hell is going on?'

'We heard about the new game.' She looked nervously over her shoulder. 'The girls have been talking. They've come up with a plan to win the show.'

'So it's really true?' I laughed, like a crazy person. 'I'm not imagining it, then?'

'We all heard.' There was fear in her voice. 'Jess is *freaking* out. Like really acting weird. It's scary. Everyone's seriously pissed off you're in the lead. I've come down here to warn you—'

'Little Laura.' Annie's clipped vowels were unmistakable. 'Little Laura does it again.'

Angela froze. Like a hunted animal. 'Don't tell them anything,' she said so quietly I almost didn't hear.

'What's going on? What do they want?'

'Laura darling! We've been looking for you everywhere,' Annie said.

I heard the click-clack of more heels. Was that Becky trailing behind her?

'Whatever are you doing down here, all by yourself?'

'Angela? Warn me about what?' I hissed.

'Have you been hiding?' Annie sounded amused. 'Nobody would blame you. You poor thing. You must be utterly devastated . . .'

I stiffened, bracing for full impact.

We were suddenly thrown from the darkness. Someone had turned the pool lights back on. I blinked my way through the glare, slowly coming to focus on the hot mess swaying in front of me.

Annie was barefoot. Her dress had slipped from her shoulders. The hem had torn and was trailing behind like a rat's tail. She held a glass of champagne lazily by her side, but her expression was anything but relaxed. Her eyes were bloodshot. Her mouth stained with wine. She wore that same look of determination as when she'd stripped off for couples yoga. When all she wanted was to win.

She smiled knowingly at Becky, who was skulking in her shadow.

'What a brutal way to find out your boyfriend was cheating. Did you really have no idea?'

She was the last person I wanted to explore my feelings with.

'Nothing to be ashamed of, darling. My first husband rather enjoyed visiting prostitutes. I would convince myself I was being paranoid, that his boys' nights were just that, but of course I knew. You always know, don't you? It's that divine intuition us girls have been blessed with.'

She stopped abruptly, her brow crumpling. She planted a hand on Becky's shoulder for balance while she lifted her foot off the ground.

'Jesus!' I gasped. Annie was so drunk she hadn't noticed she'd sliced her heel open on glass. She looked almost excited by the spectacle of blood – and by my reaction.

'Nothing to worry about,' she said, thumping her foot back down. Within seconds it was weeping, little crimson veins creeping out from under foot. 'She'll never be able to do it. Punish Jess, I mean. I told you she was weak.'

'You need to get that bandaged up,' I said.

'We'll complete your task for you, darling. I'll come up with a suitable punishment for Jess.'

I could feel the muscle of my eye pulsating. 'It looks like it needs stitches.'

Annie sighed impatiently. 'We'll sort your mess out for you.'

'Excuse me? I don't need you to do anything for me.'

Staring at me as if I was stupid, she snapped, 'Well, of course you do. You're clearly not up to the job.' She pointed at me with her glass. 'Look at you. You're down here, hiding, instead of showing that bitch who's boss. You need me.'

Becky fired her a look.

'Us, you need us.'

Annie began to pace while she ranted. Stamping blood across the flagstones.

'You may think you've been hurt. But you haven't. Not really. How long were you with Matt? One, two years?'

'Five.'

'You weren't married, though. You didn't have children together. It wasn't multiple affairs.' She drained her glass in one. 'He wasn't violent. He didn't hit you, did he?' Something snapped in her tone. Like a rope that had been hanging this entire time by a thread. 'He didn't smack you around when you questioned him, did he?' The more she said, the more her mouth contorted. 'You have no idea what pain feels like. You think this hurts? Well, it's nothing. It's just a graze.'

Annie stopped; stared straight through me. A small part of me felt sorry for her. What had happened to turn her into *this*?

Annie shook her head, freeing herself from whatever memory had taken hold. Calmly, she said: 'It's up to us to take control now.'

I glanced to Angela; she was shaking her head 'no' at me.

'Don't listen to her,' Annie roared. 'Angela has no ambition.'

I frowned. 'What's ambition got to do with anything?' But before I'd reached the end of my sentence, I'd realized what this entire conversation had really been about – winning. I'd managed to tap into their deranged way of thinking.

Annie had decided that if she hurt Jess, the viewers

would reward her instead. But where would that leave Becky? Maybe she had plans for her, too.

'You need to get that foot seen to.'

I pretended none of this was happening.

Annie swapped glances with Becky, then said, 'We've come up with the perfect idea.'

'Whoa!' I held up my hands. 'I don't want to know. I don't want any part of this. This is crazy. Everyone's gone mad.' I couldn't think. All reason had ceased to exist on this island. 'You can't take revenge on someone, that's just not what happens in the real world. Where is Jess now?'

'Last we saw, she was with Matt,' Becky needled.

'With Matt?' My anger flared.

'She was begging him to sleep with her tonight,' Becky said, through a smile. 'I think she's afraid to be on her own.'

'So she should be,' Annie said.

'Matt pushed her away. He looked really mad,' Angela said quietly to me.

'I don't know why she went running to him. He has more incentive than anyone to hurt her. She's wrecked everything for him,' Annie said.

'I can't handle this,' I muttered.

'Told you she was weak. "*I can't handle this*,"' Annie imitated. 'That's right, you can't. You're a doormat. Pathetic little Laura, only fit for people to wipe their feet on.'

I turned my back on them.

'Oh Laura,' Annie called out.

Ignore them. They don't exist. I began walking away, although I had no idea where I was going.

'Lau-ra,' they sang together.

Block them out. They're crazy.

'I'd be worried if I were you, babe,' Becky shouted. 'If Jess thinks you want to hurt her, she might try and get to you first.'

They cackled like wild dogs.

'You didn't think of that, did you? After what I've seen tonight, I wouldn't put anything past her.'

CHAPTER FIFTY-EIGHT

THE CONTESTANT

Aruna, Balearic Islands

DAY FOUR, *THE VILLA*

Like a hunted animal, I'd sought refuge in my den. All I wanted was to be left alone. To crawl under the blanket and disappear until this was over. Hide from the chaos unravelling outside.

But the weight of expectation was heavy on my shoulders. Jess – what was I meant to do about her? It felt like I was back in the newsroom, crushed under the pressure to perform. To do something I knew was wrong, but I didn't know how to get out of. *Pathetic little Laura*, Annie's words hummed. *Only fit for people to wipe their feet on.*

Why me? What did I do to deserve this?

And why is it so goddamn hot in here? I couldn't check to see if the air conditioning had broken because there was no fucking controller, because *they* were controlling everything.

Calm down. You need to calm down. It seemed almost impossible to think rationally because my brain had congealed with the heat. Those few steps from the door to my bed were like wading through treacle. Everything had become so much effort.

Everything.

I collapsed across the sheets. Breathless. And there I lay, completely still, until I remembered why I'd come rushing in here in the first place. With momentous effort, I hauled myself around so I was facing the door. I propped up my back with pillows so I could be comfortable while I kept watch.

My breathing deepened; my pulse slowed as I relaxed in the knowledge: nobody was coming into my room without me knowing.

It was impossible to say how much time had passed. Maybe an hour. Perhaps two. I shifted and noticed the sheets beneath me were now damp and transparent. I wanted to dive into a cold bath but even the thought of moving left me drained. My eyes burned from the constant staring at the door.

There it was again – another wave of expectation.

I know what you're thinking, I glared into the camera above. *That I'm hiding. And so what if I am? SO WHAT . . .*

My breathing was shallow and laboured as the heat continued to devour all the oxygen left. My eyes were pleading to close.

I tried pinching my wrist, I tried moving about. I stood up but the inferno quickly forced me back on the bed. Eventually, I gave in and shut my eyes. A two-minute rest couldn't hurt.

The combination of the heat and emotional exhaustion

should have sent me to sleep. Instead, the darkness only ignited my imagination. What followed was a series of vivid, distressing images. One after the other.

Bam. Bam. Bam.

Jess, naked, folded over my kitchen table. Matt was taking her from behind, wearing the same excited look as when he'd kissed her playing Spin the Bottle. I envisaged her head turning to face me. Her mouth rising once she knew she had my attention. 'Harder!' she said through a smile. 'Harder.' Her gaze never breaking from mine.

I screwed up my eyes, then blinked them wide open.

My heart was thudding at such a rate that I had to get off the bed. I stood, rubbing my face, trying to scrub the filthy images away.

But within seconds, she was back, crowding my thoughts. The bright lights of the bedroom weren't enough to scare her away.

It was the same location, same time of day, same everything, only this time I imagined her wearing a short summer dress. The muscles of her legs shifting under her tanned skin as she opened herself for him. Matt with his favourite Levi jeans bunched around his ankles. He tugged at her ponytail, stretching out her neck, which made her squeal with delight. Her eyes were gleaming as she cast me her sideways look.

Bitch.

And all the while this was playing out, the whisper in my head grew louder.

You don't need him. You can win without him. A million pounds could be yours.

Again.

You don't need him. You can win. The words thumped in my head like a drumbeat. A tribal chant. Warriors psyching themselves up for war. *You can do this all by yourself. You can win.* YOU CAN WIN.

ONE MILLION POUNDS COULD BE YOURS.

There was a brief pause and then my subconscious spoke to me: *All you need to do is take revenge.*

Maybe the viewers were right. Jess did deserve it. If millions of people thought so, it must be true. It didn't need to be that harsh a punishment, just something to show I wasn't a mug. That I wasn't a doormat for people to walk over.

My thoughts were back on the prize. A million pounds. *A million.* Imagine what I could do with that sort of money. It would buy me a new life. One without Matt, Ben, the newspaper. I could start over. I snorted as the next idea hit me. I could even become Iris. Change my name by deed poll and become *her.*

Or maybe . . . I might actually enjoy the fame that came with winning. Just like all those girls who came away from these shows with endorsements and sponsorship deals.

This is my time to shine.

Something was happening to me. I was becoming strangely disconnected from my feelings. All sense of right and wrong was becoming skewed.

I needed to get out of this sauna before I drove myself insane.

I slipped on my flip-flops, moved across the room and placed my ear to the door, listening out for voices, for any movement, but there was nothing. In fact, it had been eerily quiet since I'd locked myself away. Not even Matt had come knocking with more excuses. It was almost as if the villa had been evacuated or, worse . . . were they waiting outside to ambush me?

Jesus, my imagination was running wild. Everything would be OK once I got some air. But as I turned the door handle, I hesitated. Something had come back to prick me. Becky's parting words:

Jess might try and get you first.

CHAPTER FIFTY-NINE

THE PRODUCER

Madrid, Interview Room One

NOW

The blood found on the other side of the pool was a match for Annie Gardner. *Surprise!* Not really. I knew she was a pisshead, but I thought she had a bit more sense than to run barefoot through glass. Before she lived off her divorce settlement, she was an accountant – she's meant to be able to put two and two together.

'The situation outside is escalating, sir,' says an officer, entering the room.

Sanchez looks concerned but shoos him away.

'What should we do?' he presses the detective for a directive. 'There's hundreds of them.'

'Has the statement gone out?' Sanchez asks.

They're speaking in English so I can understand. They want to frighten me into a confession. That's one of the first skills I learned in media. Embellish. He's decorating the truth with drama. *That's my job, Sanchez.*

'You need more officers out there,' the detective says.

'We're understaffed as it is.'

Sanchez frowns. Now he's irritated. 'Make a call to El Pilar, see if they will send some of their team over.'

Wow, all this fuss, for me. Come on, I'm not buying it.

The door closes and Sanchez's eyes return to me. He looks exhausted. Join the club. We've been at it for hours. So long, I've lost all track of time.

He glances down. *Tap tap.* The tip of his biro makes contact with his pad.

'The air conditioning system in the villa was switched off on Day Four at 11.40 p.m.' *Tap*, on the time.

I might as well get in there first. 'It wasn't my decision,' I announce.

'Don't tell me: it was the viewers?' Sanchez says, mockingly.

'Yes, actually!'

He harrumphs so hard his shoulders rise.

'The viewers wanted the contestants to suffer?'

'I don't know if *suffer* is the right word.'

'Why else would you order that during a heatwave?'

Not again. He just won't listen.

'You planted the idea in their head?'

'No.'

'So where did it come from?'

'Our team of researchers gathered data from across our social media platforms while the show streamed. Comments left on Facebook, discussions on Twitter, postings on forums, Instagram – you get the idea. We compiled the three top trending suggestions and then fed it back to the audience in a multiple-choice format. From what I remember, they opted for option A. For the air con to be switched off.

'We didn't influence the process,' I continue. 'We were simply feeding their own thoughts back to them.'

Why can't Sanchez see that? I won't give up, but I'm struggling to get him to come around to my thinking.

'Anyway, what's the big deal? A bit of heat's never killed anyone.'

'I'm afraid that's where you're wrong. The heat was used as a device to flush Laura Peters out of her bedroom.'

'It wasn't deliberate. How could I have predicted that?'

'And if Laura hadn't left her room, what happened next might never have occurred.'

CHAPTER SIXTY

THE CONTESTANT

Aruna, Balearic Islands

DAY FIVE, *THE VILLA*

Her bedroom had been ransacked.

The door was ajar, drawing my gaze inside. Necklace beads were scattered across the floor. Clothes were strewn. In the half-light, they appeared like animals that had curled up to die. Someone had pulled apart Jess's things. They'd slashed her sheets. The bedside lamp had been knocked over – shards of bulb glinted across the pillow.

What the hell had happened in here? And where was Jess?

My chest tightened.

I hurried down the stairs and into the night. Bursting into the garden as if I was coming up for air after being held underwater.

But there was no escaping it. The heat, it was relentless. The air was thick with humidity and it smelled different. Briny, as if something rotten had been washed onshore.

All the lights in the villa were out. Everything was still and quiet and hidden in the shadows.

Luckily, I still had the moon. As my eyes adjusted to the dim light, I was able to see the carnage that lay before me.

Meat, bones, the leftovers from dinner had been tossed about in what looked like some sort of food fight. Bottles and overturned glasses besieged every surface. Someone's entire suit was slung over the back of a chair. Limp and waterlogged. An orphaned shoe lay on its side close by.

Chairs had been chucked in the pool. The inflatable flamingo had been punctured, a shrivelled raft of pink left floating on the water. By the looks of the strewn silver wigs and feather boas, the dressing-up box had been raided.

Something crunched. I'd stepped into a puddle of glass and alcohol. The tart smell of warmed-up wine and decaying food rose up all around me. And something else. Something sharper. It was a pool of vomit – lumpy and pale in the moonlight – making me retch.

What had happened here? And where was everyone?

There was a whisper of sunrise on the horizon. I must have nodded off for longer than I thought, while somebody trashed the villa.

I stood perfectly still, listening for voices. But all I could hear was the distant hiss of the ocean.

There was an eerie tension about the place – as if something terrible had happened.

I wrapped my arms around myself, heading to the kitchen. Desperate for something cold to cool me down.

But as I reached for the fridge door, I startled.

It was much more obvious in the moonlight. From the way the shadows fell you could clearly see the mark of each individual knuckle. Undulating grooves that made me shudder. I imagined the rage as he punched the fridge. The hate behind his eyes. The same look of entitlement he'd cast me right before he forced me under the covers. The memory as raw now as it was then.

And to think he was only the start of the abuse. The last four days almost didn't seem real. I'd been on a rollercoaster, jerking between extreme emotions. Fear. Anger. Betrayal. And now I was careering into something else. A bitter and rancid force was taking over my body.

I found a glass and poured myself some milk. The cold alkaline liquid instantly eased the burn in my stomach, but did nothing to cool my systemic anger.

I tried to soothe myself with some deep breaths but all I could take into my lungs was the warm stench of the party. Vomit, food and . . . there was something else.

So familiar, yet I couldn't quite place it. I inhaled again. Sweet, floral . . .

It was the lingering scent of perfume. *My* perfume.

Jess had been here.

The images of them instantly resurfaced. Their groans of ecstasy. Matt's hands gripping her hips. That gleeful smile Jess served up at dinner. Thrilled, knowing she'd crushed me. My anger, triggered.

If Jess wasn't in her room, and she wasn't here any more . . . I cast around – then where was she? And where was Matt? Were they together?

Of course they are, I thought with absolute conviction.

I felt my features harden. My mind had never been clearer.

I opened the drawer and began rummaging. Bottle opener, can opener, cutlery – all the usual kitchen utensils were stashed inside. I picked up a knife but immediately put it down again.

I yanked at the next drawer and continued the search. The red mist was descending. A dangerous, untamed anger which I was uncertain I could control.

And that wasn't all – I was feeling increasingly detached from my emotions. Like I could say or *do* anything, and I wouldn't give a shit.

My fingers settled on a pair of scissors. They were sharp and jagged, the type that would cut through meat. I pushed down the wave of doubt.

You don't need to do anything crazy. Destroy something of hers. Something she loves. Cut up her clothes. I don't know, chop off her hair. That would teach her. All those beautiful curls – gone. The audience will fucking love that. And then something much darker crept in.

Jesus, I couldn't believe I was thinking like this. Where was it coming from? *You're blinded by anger. Sleep on it, things will seem different in the morning.*

But it was impossible to shelve, not when the feeling was so unexpectedly satisfying. The thought of hurting Jess was giving me pleasure.

And now I'd taken the step of selecting them and holding them, I was actually questioning if I could do enough damage with the five-inch blades. My knuckles were white, I was gripping the scissors so tightly. I scanned the kitchen to see if there was anything else I could use to complete my game. That would please the viewers. What else? My eyes shifted across the surfaces. What could I use to carry out my revenge?

And that's when I noticed. Because I too was searching for them.

The knife rack – it was empty.

CHAPTER SIXTY-ONE

THE VIEWERS

TWENTY MILLION VIEWERS

In the factory security office in Exeter, Devon, Joe and Damien were keeping themselves entertained while on the night shift.

'Go on, love, get her!' Joe cheered Laura on. 'I didn't think she had it in her, to be honest. Not the mug I had her down for.'

'Good on yer, girl, you've found your backbone,' Damien said. 'Now finish the job.'

'Jess is bricking it after what those boys did to her, her heart rate is through the roof!' Joe said.

'She's got a knife, though,' Damien pointed out.

'Who has?'

'Jess, she took it from the kitchen earlier, didn't you see?'

'What?'

Damien hopped to camera three.

'Jesus fucking Christ. Laura, watch your back!' Joe yelled at the screen.

323

'What's happened? Hey, turn it back on, you bellend.'

'I haven't done anything,' said Joe.

'It's not working.' Damien struck the keyboard. 'You've broken it!'

'Let me have a look at it,' Joe nudged Damien out the way. 'The internet's working fine, it's not the computer.'

'It's the show, then. It's gone offline. Hey, what does that say?'

An announcement had appeared on the screen. Bold gold letters on black.

**Due to unforeseen circumstances,
content is not available at the moment.
We'll be back soon.**

'You don't think . . .' Joe said.

'Think what?'

'Jess had a knife. You don't think she's gone loony tunes and stabbed someone?'

'Don't be daft, she's being filmed,' said Damien.

But the men fell silent, passing a wary look between them.

'It's nothing to do with us,' Damien proclaimed.

'You voted for Laura to take revenge. I saw you!' said Joe.

'Not me!' Damien wrinkled his nose. 'Turn that thing off . . . it's irritating me now.'

'You did!'

'Stop making things up. I'm bored of this. Let's have the telly back on.'

CHAPTER SIXTY-TWO

THE PRODUCER

Madrid, Interview Room One

NOW

He pauses the film. 'What do you see when you look into those eyes?'

I tilt my head as I consider his question carefully.

Sanchez zooms in on her face.

'You see what I see, don't you?' he says.

I continue blinking at the frozen image. His eyebrow lifts as he waits for me. 'That's the look of fear. Someone terrified for their life. And you, Michelle Jessop, are responsible for what she did next . . .'

I was being honest when I said I created *The Villa* because I wanted to help people find love.

There wasn't much of it about, growing up – love. I'd earmarked a happy marriage as the pinnacle of everything. *The endgame.* Most of the women on my estate were single mums in complicated, mostly abusive relationships, who'd grown up watching and evolving into something similar.

That's so often the case, isn't it? Well, not me, I was going to break those chains. I was determined I'd be nothing like my mother. *That whore*.

So, that's what I did. I left her as soon as I could wrench myself free of her emotional blackmail, the 'who's going to look after poor old me' act, and would-you-believe-it, landed a job as a runner. It was a crappy TV show that aired at 1 a.m., but it was a huge break for someone like me. Unlike some of those posh kids working there, whose daddy knew such and such arsehole on the board of something, I never once took my job for granted and worked my fucking arse off. Whenever I felt too exhausted to lift my head off the pillow – because, let me tell you, my work hours were savage, and the diva demands of a certain TV personality, not mentioning names, were almost too much to bear – I'd remind myself of how bad things used to be. I'd replay the punches and the abuse, and quickly realize that I never, EVER wanted to end up back there.

So I sucked up the shit that was shovelled my way. I swallowed the put-downs and the tantrums and histrionics. And yes, I'm not proud of it, but I even sucked someone off to inch myself a little further up the career ladder to assistant researcher. Up and up I clawed, and I never looked down because the thought of staring that gutter in the face terrified me more than anything.

And then, one day, all my networking paid off. I met Harry King. My secret investor. Yeah, he wasn't kosher – he'd made his fortune from strip clubs, loan-shark investments and shady deals I didn't want to know about. A self-made man who, like me, came from nothing. And, yeah, I had to fuck him, on numerous occasions, but he knew a good business opportunity when it came his way.

He was the first person to believe in me. He made me feel seen. Can you imagine what that feels like after a lifetime of being passed over?

We weren't just going to transform the reality show landscape, we were going to be leaders in it. We'd fucking own it! Our little island, our beautiful villa. Goodbye, reality TV, with your one-hour round-up transmission and your non-existent audience interaction. Hello, livestreaming. The future belonged to us. Sponsorship deals, funding, so much money we wouldn't know what to do with it.

And then, I suppose, watching love blossom on the show triggered hate within me rather than happiness. It was so unexpected. I'd be in the control room, watching the screens, when all of a sudden rage would overwhelm me. Within minutes my skin would feel on fire and I'd be glaring at the contestants, wanting to destroy what they had – what I'd never had. I know it's wrong, I KNOW, but it was fun being the voice of the show, playing God with their lives. I got off on watching Jess dismantle Laura and Matt. I hated seeing Angela and Charles all cutesy together. I shouldn't have tipped off the paper about Angela's whoring past, but I couldn't help myself. The bitterness inside was too virulent. I guess, the evil of my mum lives on in me. *Bitch*.

'We have the footage,' Sanchez announces. 'You didn't make it easy for us.'

The tapes were encrypted. But I handed them over.

Throughout this 'investigation' I've never hidden anything. I've been the one trying to help them see.

But the fight I had in me when I first arrived at the police station has dimmed.

He's referring to the recordings after I cut the live feed. I had no choice but to pull the plug on the show – things had got too far out of hand, even by my standards. It was a crying shame though, because the ratings had rocketed to twenty million. *Twenty million!* I can't tell him that, though. He wouldn't understand.

His finger hovers over the pause button. 'Ready?'

I stare at him, my gut twisting at the thought of having to walk through that night again.

His deputy is suppressing a smile. She's been waiting for this. I nod and the tape begins.

CHAPTER SIXTY-THREE

THE PRODUCER

Madrid, Interview Room One

NOW

Sanchez has rewound the footage by forty-three minutes. The image pauses on Jess, cowering outside her bedroom as she listens to it being ransacked.

Play.

Annie's lost the plot. She's grabbed a knife from the kitchen and is carving up the sheets. Laughing her head off as she does so. Becky is tearing apart Jess's wardrobe. She keeps looking over her shoulder, checking with Annie that she's doing it right. Desperate to secure her approval.

Smash.

Annie smacks over the lamp. Crazy woman, that fitting cost me, or rather Mr King, £5,000. I feel as irritated watching it now as I did then.

'Come on, let's find the bitch,' Annie shouts as they leave.

Camera 45. We're back to Jess. She's dived into Becky and Blake's bedroom and her face is a picture of a woman on the edge. All that bravado she'd served up at dinner is gone. She's behaving in a way even I didn't foresee. I had her down as impulsive but not unstable.

I knew my viewers would turn on her after the truth came out, but not like this. Revenge – those were *my* thoughts. I wanted to break them. I thought it would make me feel better. Hurt people, hurt people. What can I say?

Laura is in her room, hiding from the pressure and the decisions she needs to make. True to form. I'd written her off at this point. She looks weak and pathetic.

Camera 57. Things are kicking off by the pool. The lads are necking the beers and Blake has stripped off. He lifts his hands up to a cheer and a 'Go on, son', and then fires into the water like a cannonball. Cameron's bitching about Matt and blaming Laura for screwing up his chances of winning. He seems really pissed off, like he wants to hurt someone. I underestimated the anger in him. It's almost as big a ball of rage as my own. Or maybe I didn't, and subconsciously I was drawn to him because of it. Like attracts like, and all that. I'd fuck him. All that fire would make for great sex.

The girls have moved outside in their hunt for Jess.

Camera 5. Matt is climbing the stairs, drunk and slovenly, in slow pursuit of his beloved Laura. His grand plan of wooing her back and taking the prize money fell through spectacularly. He was on track for winning a cool million. It's no surprise he despises Jess, like *really* hates her.

He shouldn't have shagged her then, should he? The past always catches up with you. I should know.

The detective has moved his chair right around the table

so he can be close to me while I watch. He's assessing me again with those big, brown eyes. He knows. He can tell my armour is wearing thin. But I will not be intimidated. I've worked too hard for this; I've waded through so much shit to get here. Mr King is waiting for me, we've made plans. Something bigger, even more spectacular than *The Villa*.

He needs me, and as soon as I get out of this sweatbox we can get cracking. He promised me, so I'll keep my promise to him.

Matt doesn't make it to Laura's room. Jess is waiting to pounce. Manic and hysterical, she quite literally sinks her claws into him, clutching at his shoulders.

It's painful to watch.

'Please, Matt, you have to protect me,' she begs.

He tries to prise her off. 'You deranged headcase,' he sneers. 'What are you on about?'

'Laura is out to get me. Annie's got a knife! *An actual knife!* I don't want to be alone, I'm frightened. Matt, please help me.'

'Jesus, you'll stoop to anything to try and get me back, won't you?'

He's mad. Oh boy, he's had it with her.

Sanchez's eyes dart between me and the screen. He's saying, *Look at them.*

I am looking, Sanchez, don't you worry about that. I've seen how this plays out. My hand moves to my throat, trying to loosen the imaginary noose that's fastened there.

Matt pulls Jess off and shoves her against the wall, hard. We hear the thud. The air thumping out of her lungs. She's sobbing. She's begging him. Christ, it's like watching a car crash in slow motion.

He's showing this to upset me. To provoke a confession. I know I should be distressed, but something's getting in the way. Watching the drama play out on the small screen makes it seem far less real. In fact, I can't help but feel mesmerized by what I'm seeing. Even though I know how this ends, I'm on the edge of my seat. How can that be?

And that's when it hits me, really smacks me in the face – I realize what a brilliant job I've done. I've created a show you can't look away from.

Jess's legs pack in and she slumps to the floor, sobbing, while Matt turns his back on her. Leaving her to fend for herself.

Barefoot, she belts down the stairs and into the open, right into their lair.

The lads are howling with laughter because Cameron's chucked a chair into the pool. *Genius*. They're smashing through the beers. They're wasted. It's obvious they're spoiling for another fight.

Doesn't she realize she's playing into their hands? She pleads with them for help but she's only feeding their appetite. The car crash has slowed to one excruciatingly painful freeze frame at a time.

My skin prickles as I watch Cameron turn.

He laughs. 'Why would we help *you*?'

He says it in such a way, Jess could be the shit he's scraped off his shoe.

'You deserve it. Everyone thinks so.' He looks from the boys to the cameras, playing to the gallery. 'What did you say I was? Invisible? You can see me now, though, can't you?' He approaches. 'Are you scared?'

Her eyes flare wide.

He strolls up to her with drunken confidence. His shirt is shredded and stained with blood.

'Shhh, don't be frightened.'

He grins and smashes the beer bottle at her feet.

She shrinks backwards.

'Hey! Where you going?' he says. His eyes are cold and unfeeling. He stares at Jess as if she's a curious object. Something to play with.

Adam and Blake aren't joining in, but they're not doing anything to help. They drink and watch, just like the rest of the world.

'The people want to see you get yours, huh? What would be a fair punishment?' He smiles. 'For a tramp like you.'

Her cry rings out. She's stepped on the broken bottle. Jess cowers, desperate to reach down and pull out the glass, but too terrified to take her eyes off Cameron. She edges away, wincing with every step. Then, she turns and runs.

My body instinctively shrinks at the thought of what that must feel like – glass being hammered into you.

'See what you've created with your games and your viewers,' Sanchez says. 'Nothing more than a spectator sport. You know what this reminds me of? The bullfighting in my country. If you goad the bull enough, eventually it will attack.'

Attack. Kill. The words hum.

'Meanwhile, everyone enjoys the spectacle, relishing the bull's pain, baying for more blood.' His mouth straightens into a hard line. 'It's sickening. Your show is nothing more than a gladiator sport.'

'That's crap!' My reply burns in my throat.

'Money has the power to turn people into monsters,' he continues. 'As you said yourself, everyone has a price, a number they will do almost anything to get their hands on.'

I've been wasting my time. Nothing I've said has gone in.

'Jessica is scared for her life, believing she is being hunted by everyone. You have created a masterpiece, señora. Congratulations.'

Jess shrinks into a ball, hiding behind the garden chair, listening to the taunting, to the wolf howling. To the foot-steps of Annie and Becky as they hunt for her with the knife. They stumble about, only metres from her hideaway.

I know Jess is trembling. I know she's holding her breath; she's doing everything in her power to stop herself from breaking down. I recognize that look all too well.

The playback has taken a surprise turn. It's now evoking all kinds of emotions. But not about her – I'm thinking about *me*. It's busted open the lock on my past. I keep seeing myself, recognizing my past pain in the arena I created.

Sanchez skips through the next half hour. Fast-forwarding until the group disintegrates. It's musical beds. Blake folds into the hammock. Cameron skulks upstairs; he seems to be heading for Laura's room, but then makes a detour to the toilet. Adam falls onto a daybed outside, not realizing that Jessica is hiding nearby. Becky has climbed into bed with Annie, and Matt has stumbled into Annie's room by mistake.

Camera 45. He sways in the doorway. Matt's body is loose and unsteady. But his expression is one of arousal as he stares at the two half-naked women on the bed. The door clicks shut behind him.

Down the hallway, Laura peels open her door.

CHAPTER SIXTY-FOUR

THE PRODUCER

Madrid, Interview Room One

NOW

Sanchez stares at me suspiciously.

'You can't deny me my rights.'

Several beats pass and then he nods to the armed officer at the door to let me pass. 'Garcia will escort you.'

I don't even look at her as I cross the room. I pass through the fan's wind tunnel and remember what it's like to feel a breeze on my skin. The sick feeling swells.

The corridor is a ghastly sight. More strip lighting. Shrivelled public service posters wallpaper the noticeboard. There's no attention to detail here. The lino floor curls where it meets the skirting. It reminds me of dry-cured meat. Of flesh.

The image of her dead body strikes. Sanchez and I were just getting to that part. The thought of what's to come. I'm going to throw up.

I quicken my step and I feel Garcia's grip around my arm tighten.

There's an officer manning the toilets. He's waiting for someone. A suspect like me, who needs to be watched.

Garcia lets me go and I dive through the door and into a cubicle. My body convulsing, retching, and up it comes. Bile and instant coffee. I fold over the filthy toilet seat and spew my guts out.

I've always been a noisy puker. I sound like an animal dying while I retch. The vomit scalds my throat and sits in my mouth. I slump to the floor, wiping my lips with the back of my hand. A string of saliva follows, crossing the air like a spider's web.

The sound of a toilet flushing next door makes me jump. Oh great, somebody's heard my orchestral vomiting. I wrench myself back onto my feet and slide the lock open.

She catches me in the mirror reflection.

'Are you all right?' she says, massaging a soapy lather through her hands.

It feels weird, seeing her in the flesh. She doesn't recognize me but I know everything about her.

'I heard you being sick. This place will do it to you.'

'Yeah,' is all I can manage. I'm a little afraid to look her in the eye. To let the monster I created stare back at me.

'Oh! You're also English?' she says.

I smile weakly.

'What a shithole, huh?'

She manages to lock me with her stare and for a split second I panic. She knows who I am, I think. But her eyes travel past me as she gets lost somewhere far in the distance, a place beyond the sterile tiled walls. They're bloodshot from crying, the skin beneath is purple. She dries her hands on a paper towel. The snap of the metal bin closing its jaws makes me jump again.

'See ya, then,' she mumbles, before slipping out the door to be met by her police escort.

'Bye, Laura,' I whisper.

CHAPTER SIXTY-FIVE

THE CONTESTANT

Madrid, Interview Room Two

NOW

'State your name for the tape, please.'

'Laura Peters.'

I settle back into the hard plastic chair. My body is here, but my mind is still flying me across the ocean.

I can still hear the whirr of the helicopter blades. I can envisage the calm black sea. The moon on the horizon shooting silver across the water. I tried to stop myself looking back but the pull of the island was too powerful. By the time I turned my head there was barely anything left of paradise. Aruna was a speck in the ocean. I blinked and then it was gone.

Numb. That's how I felt as we flew back to the main-land. 'In shock,' was Dr Alexander's explanation as he put his arm around me. He said something else, softly in my ear: 'Everything's going to be OK now.'

Detective Perez is stunning. She reminds me of Jennifer Lopez with her lustrous hair, chiselled cheekbones and plump lips. It's a habit I've adopted from the newspaper, comparing everyone to celebrities. She must have the officers drooling every time she walks past.

But she has a quiet assertiveness that says *Don't even think about trying it on just because I'm a woman and I'm hot*. I like her instantly.

She opens her notebook and clicks the end of her biro. Even though I'm being recorded, she wants to take notes. Thorough.

'We have the tapes. But I want to hear in your own words what you did after the transmission was severed.'

There's no warm-up. No offer of a glass of water or a cup of coffee. She's dived right in.

I blink at her. 'It was severed? I had no idea.'

'At 3.45 a.m.'

'I didn't know about that,' I said, looking around. 'And I have absolutely no idea what's going on.' My voice has a tremble to it now.

'The live transmission was cut eleven seconds after you picked up the scissors from the kitchen. We have you on film carrying them into the garden.'

The flush of heat rushes to my cheeks.

'Where were you going with them?'

Tears of guilt start to form.

'What were you planning to do with them?'

I can't look at Detective Perez, I feel so deeply ashamed.

She puts her pen down and gently says, 'It's OK, Laura. You're safe now.'

She tries to connect with me. Her eyes are nets, desperate to reel me in. 'Take your time. You're safe,' she repeats.

What did I do in my moment of insanity? When all reason left me. When I felt that overwhelming urge to destroy Jess. I went hunting for her with five-inch serrated blades, that's what.

'Have you ever felt possessed?' I say.

The detective looks at me strangely.

'Like someone has hijacked your body?'

She frowns. If she hadn't thought I'd lost the plot, she must now.

'Yeah, neither have I,' I laugh a little. 'But that's what that show did to me. I stopped thinking for myself. All I could hear was what the viewers wanted me to do. Their thoughts became my thoughts and by the end I didn't know what to think.'

I feel my lip quiver. I wipe the tear that's fallen down my cheek.

Perez's beautiful, bright eyes soften.

'Walk me through those final moments,' she says.

'I hadn't thought it through when I picked up the scissors. All I cared about was wiping the smirk off Jess's face. Matt was as much to blame, but I hated her so much more. She was the one who humiliated me. She was the predator. She was the one they were telling me to hate.

'Jess wasn't in her room so I figured she must be with Matt, fooling around on one of the daybeds at the back of the garden. I went to find them.'

I close my eyes as I retrace my steps.

'Past the pool, right to the end where all the trees are. And that's where I heard it.'

The detective leans in. 'Heard what, Laura?'

'Crying. I stood there for a while, trying to work out where it was coming from and then . . .'

'What happened?' she says, insistently.

'I remember looking down at my hand, at the blades and thinking *what the actual fuck*! Even though all the lights were out, it was like someone had turned them back on. I could see again. I don't know who it was but just the sound of someone being so upset shocked me out of whatever madness I was in. I remember shaking my head, actually going like this' – I show the detective. 'I despised Jess, but I couldn't hurt her. I'm not programmed like that. No amount of money or the promise of a new life is worth that.'

She nods carefully.

'The thing that scared me most was . . .' A shuddering breath leaves my lips.

'Yes, Laura?'

'I thought about it . . . hurting her. That frightened me more than anything, and I bolted.'

'Where did you go?'

'To the only person I could trust.' I close my eyes as I think of him. My skin still tingles where he touched me. 'I went to find Dr Alexander.'

She nods again.

'He knew I was coming. They all knew, everything we were doing. He was waiting in the therapy room, behind the door. He scared the living crap out of me.'

'He was trying to frighten you?'

'No, no. He was trying to warn me.'

'How?'

'He signalled to me to keep quiet while standing with his back to the camera.'

'He was keeping secrets from his boss?'

I lift my eyebrows. 'Yeah, you could say that.'

She notes it down.

'Once he was certain I understood, he guided me into the room and ran through the same stuff as before. How was I feeling? Would I like a drink? The whole time warning me with his eyes. I didn't know what was going on. I was screaming inside, desperate to get the guilt off my chest.

'The more he looked at me in that way, the more anxious and panicked I became. What was he hiding? Could I even trust him? So then' – my hand automatically clutched my heart – 'I had a full-blown panic attack. Worse than anything I'd had before. I literally couldn't breathe. Next thing, I'd dropped to my knees, I was wheezing . . . I . . .' I look up at the detective. 'Can I have a minute?'

'*Si.*'

She gets up and glides across the room to where there's a misty jug of water on a table. The beads of condensation are carving rivulets. She pours me a glass. The glugging sound is soothing.

Who was that strange woman I met in the toilets? My mind wanders. She seemed in a bad way, hectic and jittery. Her face, red and pockmarked with acne scars. Poor thing. I wonder why she was here?

'Are you OK to carry on?'

I take a sip. 'Yes.'

'You were telling me about Dr Alexander.'

'He was kind to me,' I say. 'He rubbed my back and

343

told me to breathe in time with him. I must have looked a complete state, on the floor, panting like that. I don't remember him getting me back on my feet but the next thing I knew, he was taking me through the secret door.'

'The secret door?'

'The one which he'd disappear through to fetch me stuff during our therapy sessions. He announced he was grabbing me some medicine. That was for the benefit of whoever was watching us.'

'What was he really doing?'

'Getting me the hell out of there! As soon we were away from prying eyes, he reassured me everything would be OK. We were in a corridor, some sort of rabbit warren running underneath the villa.'

She notes that down, too. 'What could you see?'

'Not much. There were a few lanterns fixed to the wall. I could see the actual bedrock. It looked like a wartime bunker. The darkness helped calm me and finally I was able to confess. I told Dr Alex I was scared of who I'd become. That if I hadn't stopped when I did, I was certain I would have harmed Jess. I told him the show was twisted. The way the viewers were controlling what we do, what we think, it was all MESSED UP!' I run both hands across my face. 'Honestly, I thought I was losing my mind.

'I asked Dr Alexander if he thought I was a bad person. And then immediately regretted it.'

'Why?'

'I was terrified what he'd say. He's a psychologist, he might have seen some dark evil side to me . . .'

Perez looks at me expectantly.

'He said no,' I tell her. 'He explained I'd been manipulated. Apparently, I'm someone who is susceptible to
coercive control. I didn't know what that meant, at the time
I didn't care, I was just so relieved I wasn't a psychopath.
Pretty soon after that . . . it happened.'

'What happened?'

I blush.

'It was weird, we just started kissing. I know that sounds
messed up and . . .' I find myself trying to conceal a smile.
'But we were caught up in a moment. It was like we needed
to get all that stress out of our system and that was the
natural way to deal with it.'

She smiles knowingly. I wonder if Perez has also experienced that stress-lust scenario. What I don't confess is how
far it went.

I can still feel the grains of sand. The stones crumbling
behind me as he pushed me against the wall. No cameras
this time, just him and me and the darkness that smelled
of earth. The soft glow from the lanterns turning him
golden.

I remember feeling the muscles of his back working hard
to lift me up and imagining how they must have looked.
Taut and rolling under his skin like sand dunes drifting in
a storm.

He pushed my dress up to my waist. I heard the rip,
but I was too lost in his touch to care. He kissed me while
moving his fingers inside me, and the next thing I knew,
he'd ripped my underwear away and something much bigger
was thrusting inside me.

I'd been wanting him for much longer than I realized.

All that intimacy shared in our therapy sessions had been cranking up the sexual tension.

The sex was as frantic as what I used to have with Ben but so, so much better. It wasn't painful. It wasn't dirty. Dr Alexander knew exactly what he was doing. Slow then fast and then slow. He locked me with those eyes, binding me further into the moment. Vivid blue and shining. His breath, hot across my neck as he fucked me until I came. Me first, then him.

As soon as it was over, he apologized. Knowing he'd crossed a line. Taken advantage of me. I noticed the tips of his fingers were trembling. He brushed the sand from my thighs and helped straighten my dress.

'Stop fussing,' I'd said. 'Really, I'm fine.'

I remember grinning goofily because I was better than fine – I was buzzing. My insides were tingling for more. We started kissing again. Until his phone ringing broke us apart.

'He must have messaged the helicopter pilot while I was having my panic attack,' I explain to the detective. 'It was go go go after he got the call. We ran through the tunnel. I was trying not to trip up. We came out on the other side of the wall.'

'Where?'

'I don't know, maybe ten metres from the villa.'

'Can you be more precise?'

'It was dark, I couldn't see so well. I remember the escape door being solid wood. It looked new. At a guess I'd say the passage had been built at the same time as the villa. For whatever reason they wanted a secret tunnel in and out.'

She underlines something I've said.

'We ran. It was so hot and humid I could barely breathe. I kept stumbling. Alex was stressed out; he was checking over his shoulder and saying something about the dogs.'

I remember how my feet fell away on the uneven earth; a minefield of rocks and clumps of dry grass.

'We hid behind a boulder next to a clearing and waited for the helicopter. Alex kept muttering, saying how he hadn't signed up for this and she'd taken things too far.'

'She?'

I shrug.

'Did he mention a Michelle Jessop?'

I shake my head.

She frowns again.

It's strange, I can't picture the helicopter landing, or getting on board. But the feeling of my stomach lurching as we took off is vivid. I remember closing my eyes and gripping onto Alex, playing some stupid song over and over in my head to calm my vertigo.

'We barely spoke for the entire journey,' I say. 'I was so exhausted. I don't think I'd slept or eaten properly for the entire four days and it all suddenly hit me.' I remember my shoulders relaxing into his arm. Falling asleep resting on his chest.

'Everything else you know,' I say.

The flashing blue lights lit up the sky. At first, I thought it was the coast guard. But as we drew closer to the mainland, it became clear they weren't there to warn us.

The pilot had been ordered to divert his landing to the seaside town of Balerma. Where dozens of armed officers were waiting for me.

I sobbed as they pulled me from Alex's arms, as they frogmarched me to the police car. His voice, telling me to stay calm, fading away. I had absolutely no fucking clue what was happening. Not until they told me I was wanted for murder.

I take in a deep, shuddering breath. 'Am I still under arrest?'

'We had no choice but to arrest you, Laura,' the detective says coldly. 'You were last seen carrying a dangerous weapon in pursuit of the victim.'

Victim. I still can't get my head around the fact that she's dead.

'You had motive. Intent. And were seen fleeing the scene. We've since recovered the missing footage which proves you had no involvement. She died while you were in the tunnel with Señor Alexander.'

While we were fucking – she was dying. It makes me feel even guiltier.

The detective slides a piece of paper across. 'We need you to sign your statement.'

I stare at the bright white sheet and all of a sudden the band that's kept me strung together snaps. The thought of her drowning is pulling me under.

I've been told some of what happened. The bare details, so as not to compromise their case against the real murderer.

I know Jess drowned. My imagination, filling in the blanks, has taken me to a dark place. One where I can see her arms thrashing. She's coughing. Gasping as her lungs fill with water. Trying to fight him off, but he's too strong. He plunges her head back under. It's *him.* I know it is.

I start sobbing. Hot tears stream, dropping down onto the page, where I'm meant to sign.

'It's OK, Laura,' the detective says, trying to soothe me.

But it's not OK. It could have been me that killed her. Those were *my* thoughts.

CHAPTER SIXTY-SIX

THE VIEWERS

Gavin from Milton Keynes has travelled to Madrid to be closer to her.

Thanks to the media, the villa's secret location has been revealed.

He checks the lock on his hotel room four times. He taps the door handle three times. He counts the number of steps it takes him to cross the room – seven.

The camera is in position on the tripod. He presses record and takes a seat in the armchair.

Gavin scratches at his beard. He hasn't changed his clothes in days, not since he started watching the show. But he likes the smell. It's comforting.

Before he begins, he must check one last thing. He looks to the mirror opposite. Instead of his reflection, Gavin is met with the image of *her*, dozens of pictures wallpapered across the glass.

'What have you done with her?' he says. 'It's a conspiracy,

the government are working with the show to manipulate our minds. They're controlling us. It's all a conspiracy. They're out to get us. They want to kill us. They want to kill Jess. Beautiful Jess. Where is she? I love her, where is she?'

Round and around his sentences spin. He gets up, paces the room, returns to the armchair and screams into the camera. His anger, blooming to the uncontrollable level it did last time they took him away and put him in 'the hole'. The psychiatric unit, another government conspiracy.

Someone is banging on his door.

'They're in on it, too, don't listen to them,' he whispers. 'Trust no one.' He stares into the camera. 'Someone needs to pay. Someone *will* pay for Jess.'

CHAPTER SIXTY-SEVEN

THE PRODUCER

Madrid, Interview Room One

NOW

Clutching the scissors, Laura heads to where Jess is hiding.

I can almost hear her fear through the recording. Short sharp puffs of air into her chest. Swallowing down her pain. Her eyes straining as she stares through the holes in the rattan chair, searching for movement. Ears pricked for sound.

Since that night, I've often found myself wondering, *why*?

The scissors clatter as she drops them to the ground.

What makes Laura suddenly stop and turn back? I really thought she was going to go through with it. Riddles like that eat me up.

Jess seizes her chance and runs back inside the villa. She's in the bathroom, turfing out the dressing-up box. She picks up the platinum blonde wig.

'A desperate attempt to disguise herself,' Sanchez says.

She stops, she starts. Freezing when she hears a sound,

charging when she thinks the coast is clear. It's jerky, it's frenzied, the movements of someone who's not in control of herself. She reminds me of a trapped insect, hurtling into windowpanes in a bid to escape.

The tragedy is, no one is chasing her.

Cameron has fallen asleep in Laura's bed. Angela and Charles checked out hours earlier. They're snuggled into each other's arms. Along the hall, Matt is making the most of his time left in the villa, grabbing his chance to get laid. He's repositioning Becky onto all fours. The three of them have been fucking since he stumbled into their room, and Becky's clearly his favourite. That's the problem with threesomes, there's always one who's overlooked, isn't there? It's only a matter of time until Annie snaps. Someone with an ego as fragile as hers. I don't know if I'm relieved or gutted this never made it on air.

The fear she's being hunted has become the monster in Jess's head.

She slips back downstairs, this time wearing the wig. She returns to the kitchen, where she pulls the last remaining carving knife from the block. It's like some old horror film. The blade catching in the moonlight.

It sounds muted in the recording. A faint *tap, tap, tap.*

Sanchez freezes the footage on Jess pounding the entrance door. He catches my eye. 'Why didn't you let her out?'

He presses play for two more seconds. 'Help!' she cries, faint as a whisper.

She then pulls back, remembering.

Her safe word was where she'd meet Matt for a quick fuck after he finished work. The name of the alleyway that ran behind the supermarket. She confessed everything to me before going on the show. Genius touch at the time, but now it didn't seem so funny.

'Fairview,' she sobbed. Repeating the word again and again.

'Well?' says Sanchez.

'We were in crisis talks!' My reply comes out sharper and angrier than I intend. I'm trying to cover my back but there's not much material left.

It's the truth, though. We were in crisis talks, me and the skeleton night crew, panicking around the boardroom table. I was having a nervous breakdown, screaming for someone to find Alex.

'We were trying to contain the situation while someone tracked down our therapist. If anyone could calm the situation it would be Dr Alexander. Letting Jess out of the villa in her hysterical state to run around the island like a headless chicken was not a good idea. I was thinking of *her*,' I hiss through my teeth.

'Who was watching the screens?'

'That wasn't my job,' I say quickly.

'Whose job was it?'

'The research staff.'

'The ones that were in the meeting with you?'

I don't answer.

'You had a duty of care to your contestants. They were your responsibility and you failed them.' Sanchez checks the file. 'Where was your therapist?'

'Very good question,' I fire back.

'Would it surprise you to know he was with your

contestant, Laura Peters?' He pauses. 'Did you know they were romantically involved?'

I laugh. 'Bollocks!' *My* Alex was not involved with Laura.

'The news is upsetting you?'

'No,' I snort.

'Are you sure, you look distressed?'

'You're lying.'

I push into the back of my chair. Arms folded. I feel another episode brewing. The familiar rage rising. The way it always does when I see control slipping away from me. And this time it's sullied with something else – jealousy.

He wouldn't have done that, he wouldn't. There's an outpouring of fury, straight into my veins. *If he's done anything with her, I'll kill him myself.*

Sanchez stares at me, enjoying the moment, and then resumes the playback. I park Alex for now as I brace for the finale.

When the door doesn't open, Jess sprints for the sea wall. There's a brief moment, as she stares over the drop, when it looks as if she'd rather risk death than stay in the villa. Her dress billows like a ship's sail as she sets off again. One last journey. The knife blade held out in front of her.

Jess skims the edge of the swimming pool. She stumbles, tripping, crashing onto her hands and knees. She manages to get up, and then . . .

I wince. I can almost feel the shard of glass puncturing her foot. It was bound to happen again with all the bottles those idiots smashed.

The pain throws her off balance. She slips and falls,

smacking her head on the corner of the pool, a wet cracking noise before the splash of water.

Sanchez immediately jumps to our underwater camera. It's the first time I'm seeing the footage, but I already know how this ends.

A deathly silence settles in the room as we watch the blood jetting out of the gash in her head. Trailing behind her like a crimson ribbon. As we watch her sink.

It's over – thank God. I look away, relieved. We can move on now.

'Señora,' Sanchez says, directing me back to the screen.

'What?'

I know she's dead, I want to scream.

'Señora,' he says again.

Angrily, I return my gaze, just at the moment Jess opens her eyes.

CHAPTER SIXTY-EIGHT

THE PRODUCER

Madrid, Interview Room One

NOW

It's like a horror film.

Her arms windmilling through the water. Her legs kicking back and forth as if she's climbing an imaginary ladder. Her cheeks swollen as she tries to hold her breath. Her eyes, bulging. She's terrified. She doesn't have the strength to pull herself to the surface. Her body begins to convulse as the last of the air leaves her. It seems to go on and on . . .

I look away, and this time he doesn't force me back to watch.

It was my assistant who raised the alarm. She left the meeting to find me some paperwork and saw Jess in the pool. But by then, it was too late.

'I called the emergency services! As soon as I knew, I did everything in my power to try and save her.'

My voice is strained. I'm properly panicking now.

I've asked for a lawyer. I've had to because I don't like

how they're twisting what I say. It won't be long now until King gets here. He'll set them straight, he'll protect me like I've protected him.

I relive the moment we burst into the villa. The lights back on. Her body slowly sinking. She was caught in a beam of light. Calm and serene for those few tranquil seconds before the tidal splash. Our runner Brett dived in after her.

'It was an accident!'

'It was an accident provoked by you. Jessica would not have died if you hadn't made her fear for her life.'

'You can't blame me! It was the viewers who came up with the games. And the contestants chose to take part. Nobody forced them. They wanted the money.'

Sanchez isn't listening.

'This notion of helping people find love which you've been peddling is a cover story for your real ambition,' he says. 'You created the stage. You gave the viewers authority over people's lives. You gave them the power to choose life or death.'

He holds up his thumb. A parody of the Roman emperor in the Colosseum.

'They were all willing participants! They wanted to play!' I scream at him.

'They were your guinea pigs,' he corrects. 'You took advantage and you neglected to look after them. Where were you when it mattered?' He takes a deep, steadying breath. 'Señora Michelle Jessop, I've instructed that you will be taken to the judge to be charged with corporate manslaughter. Do you know what that means?'

'This is bullshit!'

'You are indirectly to blame for the death of Jessica Carmichael. Under the Ley de Enjuiciamiento Criminal you have the right to remain silent. Anything you say can and will be used in evidence. I've giving you warning against self-incrimination.'

'You're actually arresting me?'

'The judge will decide whether you will be charged. In Spain, that's how we do things.' He says it with pride, with arrogance. 'You will leave now with our officers.'

His entire manner has shifted. His interest in me has immediately faded. If there's something I hate, it's being forgotten.

'Is my lawyer on his way?'

Garcia approaches. 'The number you gave us has been disconnected.' She hands me back the paper with his mobile number in my handwriting.

What? 'Can't be. Try again.'

I try to catch his eye as Garcia escorts me out, but he's busy reading over the file.

'*Hey!*' I say.

He blanks me.

'Hey, Sanchez, look at me!'

Garcia grabs me roughly; the handcuffs catch my skin as she snaps them around my wrists.

'Is that really necessary?' I bark.

She shoves me to where three more officers are waiting in the corridor.

I shout back at the detective. 'It was a fucking accident. What more do you want? Hey! Listen to me!'

I stumble as I'm pushed out the door.

They're lying. King wouldn't cut me off, he wouldn't abandon me, no way, he needs me. He'll be waiting on the other side. Fuck your lies.

And as for the judge, ha, he'll throw this out of court, he'll understand me, just you wait, Sanchez.

Fraught exchanges ping between the officers as they frog-march me along the corridor. I get the feeling plans have changed – my exit from the police station has been revised.

We stop. I'm pushed to the right, and the pace picks up as we storm down another bleached-out corridor. We pass through several more swinging doors and hurry down a flight of stairs, leaving the building through a push-bar fire exit.

The afternoon sun is searing. I squint, adjusting to the blinding light, and in that whitewashed moment I hear the noise. A thunderous tirade of abuse. Blinking rapidly, my eyes return into focus, and settle on the enormous protest that's swelled outside.

Placards wielding *Burn bitch* and *Justice for Jess*. There's more, in Spanish, languages I don't instantly recognize. Hang on, is the whole world here? Someone with pink hair is belting out abuse over a megaphone. A ring of police officers are trying to hold back the crowd but they're tipping over like trees in a storm.

Fucking hell!

I freeze as fear takes hold. I'm not going anywhere near them. I shimmy backwards but the officers flanking me give me a hard shove – in the direction of the marked van.

'Move!' they shout in Spanish.

The officers fire tense words to each other. The realization we've been ambushed is not lost in translation.

Two policemen charge ahead, attempting to burrow a tunnel through the wailing crowd.

'Justice for Jess, Justice for Jess.' The chants ring in my ears.

I'm thumped to the left, elbowed to the right. The noise grows louder.

Hands are everywhere, reaching out to grab me like tentacles. The officers try to bat them away, but some are resilient, snatching hold of my arm. I feel nails dig in and scrape my skin as I wrench myself free.

'Justice, Justice, Justice for Jess.' The red letters drip down the placards like blood.

An intense pain shoots through my scalp. I spin around in time to catch the woman in a yellow vest and denim shorts clutching a clump of my hair. Our eyes lock and after what feels like a long significant pause, she spits, 'Your turn to suffer!'

The megaphone crackles before exploding again. 'Justice for Jess. Justice for Jess.'

Somebody shouts: 'Hope they lock you up and throw away the key!'

The world has gone mental. How could they get it so wrong?

'Get me out of here,' I say. But my voice is brittle.

The officer to my left elbows someone in the face but then comes the blow to my ribs. It's a short, sharp pain that immediately winds me.

'Hey!' I puff. 'Somebody get me out of—' But by the final word, the oxygen has already exited my lungs.

We keep up our struggle with the mob but I'm feeling weaker by the second.

Something warm and wet is spreading around my waist. I glance down to find my strappy vest is stained red. And there's a gash, two inches above my waistband and spurting blood. The surprise of seeing the wound is almost worse than the surge of pain that follows.

My legs buckle and I drop to my knees.

It's from down here that I catch sight of the blade in his hand, moments before he retreats into the crowd and the throng of protestors swallows him up.

Some crazy nutcase has stabbed me. The taste of blood floods my mouth. Bitter and metallic. The pain starts to throb and spreads, up and down, moving across my chest. My vest is now glued to my skin.

My arms feel like they're being wrenched from their sockets as the officers try to haul me to my feet.

All of a sudden, I'm freezing cold. Despite the sun, I'm shivering. A chill that's burrowed right down to my bones. My mouth is thick with blood.

They're yelling, fighting to clear a path to the van, but we're gridlocked. My legs turn to mush. My body becomes slack. A limp ragdoll.

'Justice for Jess.' The chants slow and soften. 'Justice for Jess', so faint it's more of a whisper now. Pretty soon all I can hear is my heartbeat pummelling blood through my ears. Fighting to keep me alive.

The sound has gone. Lips are moving, commands are

being screamed, but the world has fallen beautifully silent. For the briefest of moments, it feels like I'm back in the hub, the show control room, watching the screens on mute. Submerged inside my glorious bubble world. The piece of art that I've created.

I can feel the sand warming the soles of my feet. Hear the hiss of the ocean as it sprays the rocks. The sky is vivid blue. The sea washes its marine scents through the bay. Beautiful Aruna.

And then, there's nothing. Except fuzzy grey and white pixels, moments before the darkness arrives. The screen falls black and the picture . . . it disappears.

CHAPTER SIXTY-NINE

THE SURVIVOR

London Docklands

THREE MONTHS LATER

'If you could move a bit more to the right, yep, that's it . . .'

The photographer snaps away.

'And Laura, love, can you snuggle into his chest . . .'

I slide along the faux-leather sofa.

'Luvely, yep, just like that.'

He takes a few more pictures, then pulls back.

'And Alex, give Laura a kiss . . . Little peck on the lips for us . . .'

Alex smothers a smile as he leans in to kiss me.

'Blinding, yep, bit more, no you got it . . . puuurfect.'

The camera flash goes berserk.

I sigh. 'Can we take a break?'

'All done here, love.'

The entire morning has been swallowed up by the *Hello!* shoot. Various poses on tasteless furniture. I've hated every second of it. Stories like ours are the kind of superficial crap I used to write about for the paper. Plus, since *The Villa*, any camera stirs up deep feelings of mistrust.

But Alex loves it. He's a natural showman. It's hard to believe he was camera-shy when we first met.

I suck it up because the magazine spread will do great things for his new business. He's opened a therapy centre in Harley Street and with all the publicity we've been receiving as a couple, demand for him has gone through the roof.

Celebrity couple. I still can't quite get my head around how, after everything, we've become national treasures. *The couple that got away*. The Villa*'s real love story*. Some of the many headlines still doing the rounds in the press and social media. Three months on and there's no sign of it petering out.

We're not the only ones who've been in the press. Becky's been milking the fame. It feels like she's everywhere I look. Modelling in a bikini or her underwear. I heard through Alex that her diary's back-to-back with PAs – personal appearances. Mostly nightclubs. He's kept in touch with everyone. I think he still feels responsible for us all.

An accident. It doesn't get any easier to wrap my head around. I was convinced Cameron had killed Jess for humiliating him at dinner. I'd seen the way he looked at her – with rage in his eyes. I should know, I'd been a target of his anger, I knew how easily he was triggered when he was made to feel small. When he didn't get what he wanted. The police wouldn't put me straight, so I spent the entire time imagining it was him, holding her head underwater.

All I want is to forget. To pack it away like a bad dream. I know that's not realistic, and I suppose it hasn't *all* been bad. I've been offered decent money to be the face of a hair vitamin treatment, and only this morning the contract for me and Alex to be the ambassadors for the dating app Matched came through.

The couple that got away. Sometimes it doesn't feel like that when we're being hounded for interviews. Not when two people died in the course of making us famous.

We stand to leave and he whispers close to my ear: 'You did brilliantly,'

'I hate this shit,' I hiss.

'You look gorgeous,' Alex reassures me. 'The world needs to see what a lucky guy I am.'

I'm about to say something sarcastic, but I leave it.

I feel the warmth from Alex's chest as he presses into my back. Hugging his arm around my waist, he plants his lips on my neck. I watch the studio staff awkwardly avert their eyes. I love how demonstrative he is with me. Matt was so uptight, he wouldn't even hold hands in public. Alex is proud, he wants to show the world I'm his. His touch quickly softens my irritation and the memory of where he kissed me this morning burns in my mind.

'Alex and Laura,' the woman writing the feature says. 'Just a few questions before you leave. Let's chat over there where it's a bit quieter.'

She leads us across the untreated floorboards. Our footsteps echo into the hollow shell of a room. We're in some trendy apartment in Docklands with bare brick walls and exposed piping. Oversized pieces of modern art and floorboards that will give you splinters. She sits us down on a sofa next to a grey sculpture. I think it's meant to be a couple entwined but it's more a molten mess, at least to my untrained eye.

Annabel Baker crosses her legs, her white trainer bouncing until her foot stills. Her hair is scooped into a messy top bun. She's wearing a wool rollneck and black leather trousers. She places her digital recorder on the glass-topped coffee table in front of us.

I can instantly tell she's attracted to Alex.

I'm not jealous or paranoid – the signs are there to read. The way Annabel smiles when she addresses him compared to the hard stare she delivers me.

I'm getting used to it. In fact, I enjoy it. I'm proud to say he's mine. And unlike Matt, who would play up to the attention, Alex barely notices. Alex is looking particularly fit this morning in a blue blazer, white shirt and jeans. He's been playing squash four nights a week with his new doctor buddies and it really shows. His skin still has a whisper of a tan from the summer. From *that* week.

'Do either of you want a drink?' says Annabel.

'No, I'm fine,' I say.

'OK, fab.' She nestles back. 'This won't take long, all I need is a few lines about life after the show. How in love you are, that kind of thing.'

I'm wary because I used to do her job. Once upon a time, I too had an agenda.

She glances at some notes she's prepared.

'So, you live together?'

Alex smiles. 'That's right. Didn't waste any time. What is it they say? You're better off finding out sooner rather than later.'

His reply sounds well oiled. But I know it's a facade. Alex has shown me his more vulnerable side since we escaped. I know the guilt has followed him, too.

'How are you finding it? Any habits about each other you can't stand?' She follows her inane question with a little laugh.

Alex plays along. 'Well, there is the small issue of stealing the duvet . . .' He smiles at me and I cast him a look.

'Really?' I say.

He laughs, a throaty warm sound. 'Only teasing. Everything is great. Obviously, there're always small things that niggle, but it wouldn't be normal if there weren't.'

The perfect answer. I love how he's taken charge and is keeping her on a leash.

Annabel tilts her head, directing her gaze at me. A much frostier one.

'How are you finding life since the show?' she says. 'With all the attention?' A hint of something else slips into her tone.

'It's fine, I'm getting used to it.'

'And how are you coping with what happened *inside* the villa?'

'Fine.' I clip my reply.

'Have you been following the investigation?'

I feel Alex's hand fold protectively over mine.

The investigation to uncover who else is responsible for Jess's death is ongoing. It's now been handed over to the British authorities. The search to find who murdered the show's producer is still being carried out. Spanish police say it was a revenge attack. A crazed fan whose mind was hijacked by the drama of the show. Alex explained to me that mass hysteria – or collective obsessional behaviour, as it's officially known – occurs when group members feed off each other's emotional responses, causing panic to escalate. Having been a victim of the show's mind games, it's easy to see how the world became obsessed with *The Villa*.

A day doesn't go by when I'm not scanning the news for the latest reports. When I'm not hit with a surge of anxiety. The panic attacks are becoming less frequent and less severe though, thanks to Alex's therapy. Not that I was going to reveal any of this to *her*.

'I stopped reading the news. All I want is to put it behind me.'

She leans forward. Uncrossing her legs. Elbows are on her knees as her eyes latch onto mine.

'So, you haven't been struggling with what happened to Jessica? The part you played in her death.'

I look to Alex.

'How do you feel about Michelle Jessop's murder?'

My heart quickens.

'There's been a lot of controversy over whether she deserved to die for taking the show too far.'

I'm swimming into deep water.

'Was Michelle's death justice for what happened to Jessica?'

'OK, that's enough,' Alex dives between us. He shrugs his shoulders back and unbuttons his blazer. A small gesture but laden with meaning. There was often a hint of something primeval about Alex underneath his polished exterior. He was baring his teeth.

'Do you feel guilty for what you were about to do to Jessica?'

Leave me alone.

Alex stands up. 'I think you have all you need here,' he says, keeping things polite. 'Thanks for your time. And,' he smiles, 'if you could mention my clinic, that would be great.' He fishes out his card and hands it to her.

She looks sheepishly at him.

I get up and his hand moves to my back, guiding me out of the interview.

Minutes later and we're outside in an alley. The rumble of traffic growls nearby. But we're all alone in our little capsule, tucked from sight.

'Are you OK?' Alex asks.

My breath shudders. 'She was trying to get a rise out of me.'

'You handled it well. Will you be OK?'

'Yeah, I guess. But I don't want to do—' I'm about to tell him I'm done with the publicity circus but I stop myself. He needs this, I shouldn't make it all about me. 'You don't need to worry,' I say instead.

Traumatic bonding – another clinical term and the reason we've grown so close in such a short space of time. We haven't spent a night apart since we escaped the villa. Alex says the trauma of the show has bound us together.

Sometimes it drives me crazy, the way Alex has to put a label on everything. The way he always needs a deep psychological analysis when all I want is a hug and a laugh. But that's the only time he irks me. Every other moment, I don't want to be without him.

He slips his arm back around my waist. 'But I do worry,' he says. His hips press against me and small electrical currents fire through me. 'I feel guilty for dragging you into this.'

'Hey, I'm a big girl, and it's not as if I haven't dealt with arrogant reporters before. I'm tougher than I look.'

He kisses my forehead. Holding his lips there for a moment. 'OK. Well, take it easy today. Get a taxi home. I'll see you later.'

I'm exhausted by the time I reach our flat, wishing I'd followed Alex's advice and not taken the underground home. Some days I'm fine. Other days the smallest things leave me drained. Alex says it will take time to recover. Recovering from trauma isn't always instantaneous. It can lie dormant, resurfacing when you least expect it.

We live on the tenth floor in Chelsea Harbour. One of the first to occupy a flat in the new-build overlooking the Thames. There's a concierge manning the entrance. An underground car park, a gym, spa, restaurants and a coffee shop, all included in the complex. It's more of a high-end hotel than anything else.

Modern and ultra-minimalist – some mornings I wake up thinking I'm back in the villa, with all the pale stone surfaces and abrupt interior design. But within seconds, the feeling washes away as I remember this isn't make-believe. It's a *real* home. Somewhere I'm finally happy.

I tap the security code into my mobile app just in time to stop the alarm from triggering. Alex made sure we installed a cutting-edge system after all the threats and abuse we received. It was mainly at the start. Haters trolling me. Chat rooms filled with cruel comments. Threatening letters in the post. It seemed to be coming from a small minority, but for a while, their venom overshadowed all the love and support I was getting from the fans. I've mostly learned to control the effect it has on me. Sometimes, though, during the night, I get jumpy – when the fear finds a way back in.

The lights are also controlled by the app. That's what sealed the deal for Alex when he was house-hunting. The way, with the swipe of a finger, you could alter every surface, from the shower to the coffee table to the cooker top. He says colour affects mood, something new he's been experimenting with in his treatment plan at the clinic.

The soft furnishings are Scandinavian Hygge style. Varying tones of white, cream and grey. I sink down into the cushions of the long low sofa, folding my legs underneath me. I wrap the blanket across my shoulders and gaze through the floor-to-ceiling windows, past the clear-walled balcony, onto London. Usually the room is flooded with light, but today, the city, river and sky have been bleached grey. I want to say I yearn to be on an island somewhere, but just the thought of Aruna stops me dead.

You wouldn't know we were in the heart of London. The hum of the city has been completely snuffed out with the flat's soundproofing. It's so effective it even acts as a dimmer on our own voices. I want to fling open the balcony doors and breathe oxygen into the place, but I can't find the energy to pull myself up.

Perhaps it's the thought of next weekend. There's a memorial service planned for Jess. Angela organized it. We all agreed it was the right thing to do, but I haven't seen any of them since I left the police station, and I'm not sure I want to. Alex doesn't think it's a good idea, he's concerned it will stir up my anxiety. I think part of him is also dreading it. He blames himself for not being there when it mattered. For letting Jess down. For misreading the situation. I feel sorry for him – that's a lot of responsibility to be carrying around with you every day.

Unlike me, he falls quiet when he's low. Walls go up and I feel helpless. There's a part of Alex he keeps locked away. It's sometimes hard to live with, but I understand – that was me until I met him.

I rest my eyes and before I know it, I've drifted off.

The dream is always the same – I've been dropped from a great height into the ocean. I can see the shore in the distance but it's too far to swim. The feeling of creatures brushing up against me returns. Cold and slippery as they weave between my legs. The water is too deep, too dark to see what's lurking. They start biting and the pain feels real. Almost every night I've been waking up in a hot sweat to Alex stroking my back, trying to soothe me.

I escape the creatures today because I'm woken abruptly by the intercom.

I consider leaving it, but it rings again. And again, with barely a breath between buzzes.

'OK, OK,' I angrily mutter as I cross the room.

The intercom is the only device I can't control from my phone. I press *receive*. The small rectangular screen lights up with a security camera image. But no one's there.

Weird.

I'm too tired to investigate. The concierge will handle it. I head for the coffee machine in the kitchen and, while I'm topping up the water, there's a short, sharp knock on my door.

I warned security I don't like unexpected visitors. Not after the threats.

I start the machine. The gurgling fills the uneasy silence as I retrace my steps down the hallway.

My brow is furrowed with irritation as I open the door.

The surprise of seeing him leaves me winded. The same gut punch as when Matt walked into the villa. The past had come knocking.

'What are you doing here?' I hiss.

CHAPTER SEVENTY

THE SURVIVOR

Chelsea Harbour

NOW

'How did you find me?'

Stupid question. He's a journalist.

'How did you get up here?'

'Don't I even get a hello?' says Ben.

My jaw tightens.

'I waited for someone to pass through the gate. For such a plush pad the security is shambolic. Look, it's cold, can you let me in.'

My God, he's still acting as if he has a right to me.

'What do you want, *Ben*?' I'm fighting to keep the emotion out of my voice, but my anger is flaring. Quitting *The Record* was the first thing I did when I got back to the UK. I'll never forgive Ben for making the story more important than my safety. How he told me to shrug off my terror and provoke Cameron to get the scoop.

Fucker. I glare at him. He looks like crap. The rugged,

unshaved, just-rolled-out-of-bed charisma that used to pull me in is now repellent.

I close the door in his face, but he traps it with his foot. 'Hang on, let me say my piece.'

'Hey!' I push back against him. 'I'll call security!'

'Hear me out. It won't take long, I promise.'

He looks agitated and there's something else in his eyes. An expression I've never seen before. Concern.

'Trust me, you want to hear this.'

'Ha! I doubt that.'

'I'm worried about you.'

The anger I've been harbouring for him surges. *How dare he?*

'Worried about me?' I spit. 'Don't pretend you give a shit.'

He looks away.

'Did you know about Cameron's past?' My voice flushes down the corridor. 'When I rang you from the villa, did you know he had previous?'

Cameron's violent history had been splashed all over the papers following the police investigation.

Ben frowns. 'Come on, of course I didn't.'

I glare back. 'I don't believe you.' The fury boils over and I slam the door onto his foot. He winces but keeps his foot there.

'That's it, I'm calling security!'

'He's not who you think he is!' Ben blurts.

It shouldn't, but for some reason it makes me pause. I shake my head. 'Fuck off, Ben.'

'I've been doing some digging and there's things you need to know. Stuff that doesn't add up.'

'What are you on about?'

'All the contestants on *The Villa* were at some point patients of Trinity Hospital.'

I shrug. 'And?'

He pulls a printout from his inside pocket. 'Becky, she was a patient at Trinity's clinic in Kent for six months in 2019. Annie, she was being seen for years and is still a patient at the group's flagship hospital in St John's Wood. Adam – I haven't managed to find the dates for him, but he was being treated in the Cheshire clinic.' He clears his throat. 'Angela—'

'Stop! I don't even know what that means. Why are you telling me this?'

'Angela was also a patient in central London. For drug rehabilitation.'

'How do you even have this information? Isn't there patient-doctor confidentiality?'

'I've got a friendly doctor who put some calls in for me. Favour for a favour.'

'You haven't answered me. What does this have to do with Alex?'

'You didn't know?'

I look at him blankly. 'Know WHAT?'

'Alex Scott was a therapist with the Trinity Group.'

'Why would I know that? He runs his own clinic now.'

'It's a bit of a coincidence, don't you think?'

'What are you implying?' But my heart is thudding.

Ben scratches his chin. 'That the people who were picked out for *The Villa* were being treated for psychological disorders at the clinic where he works.'

'*Did* work, allegedly. And loads of people see therapists. I bet half my friends have been to see a counsellor at some point.'

Ben goes on. 'Did you know that Angela didn't apply to be on the show? They approached her. She told the paper she needed the money, that's the only reason she went for the audition. Did you see the exclusive we ran on her?'

I roll my eyes. 'No.'

'She wasn't the only one. They were all head-hunted.'

'Isn't that what researchers are there for, to find talent?'

'And Annie? Why her? Out of all the people you could pick for a show like that. Hundreds must have volunteered to take part. None of it really makes sense.'

'This has nothing to do with Alex. Why are you even bothering me with this stuff?'

'Because I don't trust him. He's not who he's making himself out to be.' He narrows his eyes and stares. 'You changed your hair back.'

'Alex prefers me natural.'

A shard of spite in my tone because I know Ben preferred me blonde.

'Do you do everything he says now?'

'You're married. I should have never crossed the line with you.'

'Guessing he told you that, too.'

I breathe out sharply. 'You're jealous! Can't you just be happy for me? No! You can't because you prefer seeing me down and insecure. Well, I'm not that person any more.'

I feel the tears blistering. *I'm not pathetic Laura who people can push about.* I can't let Ben see me cry.

'Dr Alexander has helped me see who I can be. I'm happy. I don't need this crap in my life.'

I smack the door against his foot with such force that it makes Ben stumble back. In those final seconds before it closes, a look of something flashes through his eyes that leaves me cold.

'Just think about what I said, Laura,' he shouts through the door.

Now he can't see me, the tears arrive.

'We miss you at the paper. Come back. It won't be like last time.'

Silent heavy sobs, my chest heaving.

Everything falls quiet and I think he's left.

'OK, well, I'm here if you need to talk. You have my number.' There's another pause and a heavy sigh. 'Take care of yourself.'

The footsteps fade and I know he's gone this time.

I can breathe again.

An hour and a half passes and I've only managed to write two lines. The coffee I was nursing has turned stone cold. Perched on my stool at the breakfast bar, I flit back and forth between the tabs on my internet browser. Anything to distract me from working. I almost confessed to Ben about the book. To prove I really have moved on since the paper. It's a novel inspired by what happened to us in the villa. But every time I think I'm finally getting somewhere, I stumble and stop. Perhaps I'm stuck because I don't have the answer. What did they do to us? The past is tangled and now Ben's come along and knotted the threads even more.

I can't shake off what he's said.

Doubt sits on me like a lead weight. I'm furious at Ben for intruding. Meddling. For staining my new life with his filthy insinuations.

I'm watching the ads pop up on the side of my screen, tempting me with another distraction.

The idea he planted is growing.

I begin reasoning with myself. There's no harm in having a look. *Put your mind at rest.*

Alex has a study where he works on his reports. The room is as uncluttered as the rest of the flat. No paintings, no framed photos. No cupboards, fixtures or fittings, not even a lamp. The light beams down from silver orbs pitted in the ceiling.

There are only two things that break the mass of white: Alex's desk with his computer, and the single shelf of psychology books that runs from one end of the study to the other.

The floor is a plush beige carpet that's so thick my feet leave behind imprints. A telltale sign of where I've been.

I call the office his man cave. Even though he wouldn't mind me being here, I feel a tug of guilt for intruding.

I push down my doubt. But it springs back almost immediately. *Why are you checking up on him?*

It's not that I don't trust Alex; it's about extinguishing Ben's voice. I'll prove him wrong. The to and fro in my head takes me all the way to Alex's desk.

Alex's computer is enormous, the size of a widescreen TV. He says it helps him immerse himself in their world – his patients. I nudge the mouse and the screensaver appears. An island just like Aruna. Rocky and barren. It gives me the shivers whenever I see it.

It wants a password. I actually don't know why I bothered trying.

I lean back against the desk. Planting my face into my hands. What am I doing? Ben's filled my head with ideas. He's bitter. He's jealous. Ben wants what he can't have.

I shake myself, trying to shoo him away.

But within minutes, he's back. The doubt, needling.

FUUUUCK. I turn back to the desk.

I have no idea what I'm searching for. Something that links the contestants? Something that connects Alex to the contestants. I don't know.

Think, Laura.

The desk has two drawers and, surprisingly, neither is locked. I carefully slide open the top then let out a guilty sigh.

A wave of relief hits me. I smile. It's so typically Alex to have his stationery neatly compartmentalized. Pens in one area, scissors and a stapler in another. There's a notebook marked with his initials, but it's completely blank inside. Sunglasses. Spare car keys. The drawer below contains a pack of printer paper.

There's absolutely nothing suspect here, or alarming, or out of place. Alex's only crime might be that he's too tidy. Satisfied, Laura? I'm an idiot for even considering what Ben had to say.

I leave his study exactly as I found it and retreat to the living room. I'm overcome with a strange feeling. It's not grief, but it has the same heaviness about it. I'm not really sure what it is I've lost, though. Perhaps a part of myself? The *new me* I've been working so hard on.

For the first time in weeks, I want a drink. Alex has helped me give up my bad habits, my 'crutches', as he calls them. We've been on a healthy vegan diet but, between the *Hello!* shoot, Ben showing up unannounced and now the disgust at myself for not trusting Alex, I'm staring at the bottle of wine in the rack and thinking I need something to take the edge off.

CHAPTER SEVENTY-ONE

THE SURVIVOR

Chelsea Harbour

NOW

Alex comes home to find me on the sofa nursing a glass of red wine.

I'm sitting in the dark because I haven't moved for what feels like hours. I've been staring out of the window, watching the grey sky morph to black. London looks like a constellation of stars when it's lit up at night. I'm not pissed, but not exactly sober. I'm in that no man's land where the alcohol gives you the false courage to shoot your mouth off.

He clocks the bottle on the coffee table and the corners of his mouth drop.

I look away, angrily. I know I'm turning my guilt on him, but I can't help it. Seeing Ben has really upset me and I'm doing a poor job of controlling my emotions. Alex would be disappointed if he knew, after all the therapy we've done together.

'How was the rest of your day?' he asks gently.

Stop being nice to me. I don't deserve it.

'Did you get much writing done?' He touches my arm and I flinch. 'You OK?' He starts massaging my shoulders.

His kindness makes me feel even guiltier for snooping.

'I didn't write a thing.' I'm angry at myself for that, too.

'These things happen. Tomorrow will be better. What would you like for dinner? I'm knackered, and thinking takeaway.'

I look at him apologetically. Appalled with myself for being so selfish. He's working all hours trying to build up his business and I'm sitting on my arse, guzzling wine, feeling sorry for myself.

He kisses me. The warmth of his touch reminds me of what we have and the drama of the day quickly fades. We order Thai food and then curl up on the sofa watching Netflix. Soon the comforting feeling that it's us against the world returns. I rest my head on his chest, feeling him breathing softly.

I should leave it. The evening has turned out perfectly. I honestly don't know what spurs it on. Maybe I'm still a little tipsy? The words come out of my mouth before I have time to think them through.

'Where did you say you used to work again?'

There's a pause, much longer than there should be.

'I don't think I did say.'

'Oh. Um, OK. So where was it?'

I feel his chest rise and sink as he takes a deep breath.

'The Trinity Hospital. Why?'

'Just curious.'

We continue watching the TV but the silence feels heavy.

I'm not following the film because my mind is busy building questions. Ben is back in my head.

'There was something else I was wondering . . .'

'Hmmm . . . yes?'

'Do you know how the contestants were chosen for *The Villa*? Did you have something to do with that?'

I feel him pull away. I turn to look back and I'm met with a look of irritation.

'No,' he says, coldly. 'I don't know. I had nothing to do with the production side of things. That was managed by the producer.' He waits for a moment, as if letting something settle. 'Michelle had the final say on things. I assessed them once they had been chosen.' His eyes narrow a fraction. He's looking at me in that way he used to do in the therapy room. Trying to size me up. 'What's going on, Laura?'

'Nothing's going on.' The words come out a little less confidently.

'Is it the reunion? I knew it would be a bad idea raking up the past, especially as you're doing a great job of moving on from it.' His eyes cross to the table. 'Is that what brought on the drinking today? The thought of seeing everyone again?'

I haven't considered that possibility until now. Maybe Alex is right.

'I don't think it was,' I say. 'I was just curious about it all, about you. We've been living together for all these months, but there's so much I still don't know.'

He almost laughs. 'Ask away, what do you want to know?'

He's thrown me with his directness. My mind falls blank.

'Look, there's never been much to say about my work with the Trinity Group, that's why I didn't mention it,' he explains. 'I did several days a week there and then I got offered *The Villa*, which I thought, like everyone else at the time, would be a unique experience and an opportunity to propel my career to another level.'

'Which it did,' I add.

'But not for the right reasons, or how I set out for it to happen.'

He frowns, as if he's contemplating something, or has been drawn back into that world he often disappears into. A wasteland of guilt that I'm also lost in. He gets up and walks over to the balcony. There's a sudden blast of cold air as he slides apart the doors. I huddle into my blanket, watching him looking out over London. His body is completely still except for the faint rise and fall of his shoulders.

'I'm sorry if I upset you,' I say.

The sex that night is incredible. On the sofa. In the shower and then again in the bedroom. When Alex gets going, he can't stop. His appetite for me seems insatiable. His desire makes me feel wanted and sexy. It's as if I've had a sexual awakening, that I was completely numb until I met him.

We fall asleep so exhausted we don't notice the sheets have knotted around us. Perhaps it's the sensation of being bound that does it. My dreams that night take me back to the island.

This time I'm trapped underwater. My foot has become tangled in rope and I'm fighting to swim to the surface. The air is running out. My body's spasming. I wake up as the water floods my lungs. Gasping. Dripping with sweat.

Alex would normally be rubbing my back, trying to soothe me from my nightmare. But tonight, he's out for the count. Exhausted by our lovemaking. His breathing is soft and even. I carefully disentangle myself from the damp sheets, trying not to make any jerky movements. I unplug my mobile from its charger and clutch it into my palm while I thread my arms into the gown hanging from the back of the door. I slip out of the room.

I keep on my toes, moving lightly from room to room. I fix myself a drink and check the illuminated clock on the microwave: 3.24 a.m.

The nightmare wakes me at the same time. It's become a life force of its own. Controlling my circadian rhythm.

The water is refreshing and soothes the heat that's built up inside me. I lean against the countertop and it's within the calm that a new image swims into view.

The books. The only place I didn't think to look.

I rinse out my glass and place it upside down on the draining board. There's a glow coming from Alex's study, spilling a diamond into the hall. A beacon, drawing me in.

I won't be able to sleep unless I check.

I'm feeling unhinged, the way insomnia intensifies your every thought and emotion. There's something deeply unsettling about being awake while the rest of the city sleeps.

I creep past our bedroom and along the hall, guided by the white light.

It's coming from Alex's computer. His screensaver. The bright sunshine of the Mediterranean illuminates the room. The island, pulling me in.

I keep the lights off so as not to draw attention.

The books run along the wall opposite the door. Ordered by size. In the half-light they appear like the rising crest of a wave. I begin with the smallest, running my finger along the spines. I have absolutely no idea what I'm looking for.

Why Women Love Too Much. Inside the Minds of Angry and Controlling Men. How Men Entrap Women.

I feel chilled faced with all these publications about emotional and physical abuse towards women. I had no idea Alex had a particular interest in this area – *Control*.

My arms instinctively fold across my chest. I continue, but my muscles have tightened.

Facing Love Addiction. Facing Co-dependence. Boundaries.

Less ominous. I relax a little.

Outer Calm, Inner Calm. How to Be Mindful and— My breath catches. *Battered Women Syndrome. Stop Hurting the Women You Love.*

One after the other. The theme of violence and manipulation returning. Then, something else catches my eye.

Alex's name, printed on the spine. He's written a book?

I pull it free, revealing the title: *Coercive Control.*

Jesus!

It creaks as I open it. Almost like a warning. The text is dense and full of medical terms, and it reads like a foreign language. As I flip through the pages, something falls to the floor.

Shit.

I turn on my phone torch and shine it across what appear to be research papers.

Is that odd? When everything else of Alex's is meticulously filed away. *Yes.*

Something doesn't feel right. I crouch down and take a closer look.

It's a much bigger bundle than I first thought. Maybe a dozen stapled sections.

I glide the light across one of the top sheets. There's a logo, and underneath, a name.

The Trinity Hospital Group.

My breath catches.

That's where Ben said Alex used to work.

Anxiously, I turn the page.

At the top in bold letters is PATIENT NUMBER X3456. My breath shudders as I realize the patient has a name. Annie Gardner. Annie from *The Villa*. Age 47. Weight 13 stone 4 pounds. Height 5 foot 5 inches. Below that, a list of the medication she's using: Xanax. Antidepressants. Sleeping pills. A cocktail of mood stabilizers.

Further down, a psychological diagnosis – Narcissistic personality disorder.

Jesus. These are her private medical notes.

But that's not what's most alarming. No. What makes my breath catch in my throat are the notes in the margins. Neat little annotations in red ink.

*Needs to be adored and the centre of attention.
If threatened by another woman she's likely to
go to extreme lengths to throw the spotlight
back onto herself. Becky would be the ideal
contestant to provoke her.*

There's more:

> *Suffered emotional and physical abuse in her
> marriage. Husband had affairs, slept with
> prostitutes. Eventually he divorced her for a
> younger woman. Remarks made about her age
> and fading looks could provoke an entertaining
> reaction.*

Entertaining?

> *She's a functioning alcoholic. Removing alcohol
> or increasing availability will almost certainly
> provoke irrational behaviour. Or, better still,
> yo-yo between the two and you'll likely achieve
> a bipolar effect.*

My God. Whoever wrote this knew Annie's problems
and exactly how to trigger them. I don't why I'm saying
whoever, though. The notes are marked in a precise and
orderly way. In a handwriting style that's all too familiar.
Alex.
There's more.
The rational part of my brain is desperately trying to
find some sort of reassuring explanation. I flit to the next
set of notes.

> *Cameron Walker. Violent. Abusive. Controlling.
> Borderline personality disorder?*

*Likely to repeat violent behaviour. Doesn't
respond well to orders. Has trust issues – likely
to be brought out if he feels deceived. Potential
to turn violent towards Laura when he
discovers she's been lying about her identity.*

Potential?

*Watch for tells such as angry outbursts or
veering between calm and erratic. Couple up
with a contestant who's <u>NOT</u> sexually interested
in him as the rejection will spark his need to
control. Could behave aggressively or force the
contestant to do something against her will.*

It feels like someone's smacked me in the face. Cameron's
chilling words: 'You know you want me' echo.

He knew he would try and hurt me. Alex *knew*. It was
a set-up. I'd been used as bait.

The familiar sensation of my chest tightening returns.
Not now, please no. I need to finish reading. My hand lifts
to the imaginary rope tightening around my throat. Hastily,
I turn the pages.

*Angela. Drug addiction. Could be pushed into
doing things she would ordinarily say no to out
of desperation to pay back debts.*

Some of the files aren't marked with the hospital's logo.
These are notes Alex must have made from his observations.

At the audition? In the therapy room? I know what's coming but I can't deal with it just yet.

> *Rebecca Adams. Low self-esteem. Diagnosis –*
> *body dysmorphia. Addicted to surgical*
> *procedures. Her overly confident persona is a*
> *shield to protect her from her self-loathing.*
> *Potential self-harmer.*

Then in the margin:

> *Easy to make feel old, unattractive/overweight.*
> *She'll respond positively to competition, being*
> *ignored, the feeling of losing out to another*
> *girl. Would ideally be coupled up with a*
> *narcissist or someone who has avoidance*
> *tendency to make her feel invisible.*

Invisible. He wanted Becky to feel like she was nothing. Why? WHY?

> *Charles has inferiority issues due to feeling*
> *overshadowed by his father's notoriety. If made*
> *to feel invisible, depressive tendencies could be*
> *triggered. Make sure alcohol is readily available.*
> *Will lead to emotional distress and confessions.*

I feel like I'm going to throw up.

I can't believe Alex could write something like this. Why? And then, there was me. I don't realize I'm trembling until I notice the paper shaking between my hands. I'm not sure I have the courage to on.

Shit! What's that?

I hear a noise. A patter, like the sound of bare feet. And I freeze.

I switch off the torch and stay perfectly still, straining to listen. My heartbeat rocketing.

When several minutes of silence pass, I realize I'm imagining it. It's my guilt playing tricks on me.

I've been jumpy ever since the hate mail started arriving. The thought that strangers who have it in for me know where we live, has me permanently on edge. Especially after what happened to Michelle. What did the reports say? Stabbed to death by an obsessive fan.

My heart slows, but within seconds the noise returns.

This time, there's no doubt. It's clear as anything. Footsteps. Someone is moving around in our flat.

I'm a rabbit in headlights. The patient notes spread around me like debris from a blast. And it really does feel like a bomb has gone off – everything I've known about Alex up until now has been a lie.

The sound is heading in my direction. The light pad of feet along the hallway.

Move, Laura.

Outside the study.

I scramble around on my hands and knees, gathering the papers together.

Faster. Put the book back where you found it.

It's too late. As I rise to my feet, I see his shadow. He's right behind me.

CHAPTER SEVENTY-TWO

THE SURVIVOR

Chelsea Harbour

NOW

It wasn't loud. It was just the same as always. 'Laura? Are you all right?' Alex's voice – calm and measured.

I'm clutching his notes to my chest. The paper feels like it's the only thing keeping my heart from leaping out onto the floor. I can't bring myself to meet his eyes.

'What've you got there?' he asks.

He knows exactly what I'm holding.

He steps towards me, wearing only boxer shorts. He smells of aftershave and sex. 'Couldn't you sleep?' Caring and kind, the Alex I've known up until now. 'I told you, there's no need to worry about someone breaking in. This flat is secure as a prison.'

Prison.

'Try and relax.'

Relax?

'You're tired, come here,' he says, moving closer. 'You look like you could do with a hug.'

All I want is to fold into his arms. To unsee what I've seen. I'm desperately trying to find some rational explanation for all this. He places his hands on my shoulders. His touch jolts me back to my senses.

'Stop!' The word hurtles out, so aggressively it catches Alex off guard.

'Don't touch me.' I shrug him away.

As I shuffle backwards my foot knocks into something hard and cold. I look down and my heart sinks. My phone – I've left it on the floor.

Shit.

'Laura,' he says, watching me. There's an edge to his tone now.

If I'm quick, I can snatch it up . . .

'Laura . . .'

I lift my gaze and finally our eyes meet. His expression doesn't match his warning tone, though. Alex is smiling, in a consolatory way. Lips pressed together; his forehead creased. He looks deeply concerned, just like when he was counselling me in *The Villa*.

'Those are private patient files,' he says, eyes flicking towards my hands, then back to me. 'You really shouldn't be reading them.' He holds out his palm. 'Hand them back, please.'

I'm gripping them so tightly I can feel the edges cut into my fingers.

'Come on,' he smiles, as you would for a child.

My reply comes out strangled. 'Why do you have them?'

'I'm worried you've misread the situation.'

'There's a psychological report on everyone who was in *The Villa*.'

'That's right, all contestants needed to be thoroughly vetted.'

'This,' I shake the papers, 'isn't about assessing someone's mental stability, this is deliberate. This is about cherry-picking people with serious psychological problems, manipulating them and using them to your advantage.'

He gently shakes his head. 'Laura, Laura,' he sighs, 'you've really muddled things up this time.'

'I've seen your notes. I've read your suggestions on how to trigger them. How to push someone over the edge.' I think about Jess.

'My notes?' He tilts his head.

Why's he even pretending? There's no question it's his handwriting. He probably kept them as souvenirs. Scalps.

'You knew about Cameron, you *knew* he was violent. Jesus, you even suggested he should couple up with me.' The memories of that night come crashing in. 'I sat with you, crying, telling you how he tried to force himself onto me and all along it was *you*. *You* engineered it. You wanted him to hurt me.'

I'm screaming at him now.

'Shhhhh,' he says, holding up his hands. 'You need to calm down. Take a few deep breaths or you'll bring on another panic attack.'

Only the mention of a panic attack triggers a feeling inside me. My chest tightens. How's he doing this?

'Calm down, Laura. You've taken something this small,' he holds an imaginary ball between his palms, 'and you've blown it up into something this big.' His arms move apart. He snaps his hands together. The thunderous clap makes me jump. My heart rockets and my ribs feel like they're crushing my lungs.

'Laura, I'm worried you're regressing back to old patterns and behaviours. Your tendency to mistrust, to be overly suspicious.'

'Matt was lying to me, though!' I scream at him.

I've used up the last of my air. I fold in on myself. My knees buckle.

'The misconception that all the men in your life will hurt you comes from your father and it's simply not true. I won't hurt you.' He grabs under my arms and hauls me back onto my feet. 'Breathe with me, in for one count of four . . . and out . . .'

'Let go,' I shout. His grip tightens, pinching my skin. His muscles tense, reminding me how easily he could overpower me. *Hurt me.*

He clamps his arms, pulling me into his chest for a hug. His cool skin smothers my mouth. He strokes my hair while I put up a pathetic struggle. The papers brush my right thigh and I feel my grip on them weaken.

'That's it, nice and steady,' he says, his tone even and gentle. 'Your brain is tricking you into thinking I'm dangerous, I'm a liar, but I'm not. I love you and I'm here for you.'

He kisses the crown of my head.

'I'm not going to cheat on you or leave you.'

His hand leaves my back for my side. I feel its warmth cupping over mine, trying to ease the notes out.

'You need help and I'll be here every step of the way. We'll get another programme set up for you. What happened in the villa must have affected you much more than I realized.' He sighs. 'That's my mistake. I let you down.'

He tugs at the papers. But something in me refuses to let go.

He pulls again, much harder this time.

I'm clinging on as if my life depends on it.

'Laura . . . let go.'

But I won't. I won't be controlled.

'. . . Laura.' I feel his muscles flexing, strengthening.

And then, before I have time to work out what's happening, he releases me, steps back, and strikes my face.

Pain explodes across my cheek and I'm not thinking about the files any more. I'm cradling my face, trying to put out the fire burning my skin. I look back at Alex and he's stopped smiling. His eyes are narrow slits, angry and cruel. He's holding the papers and he glares, as if he really hates me, like he wants to hurt me.

Adrenaline floods my veins. I look at the door, pitch forward and I make a run for it.

As I try to dodge past Alex, I hear him say: 'Why couldn't you have minded your own business?'

And then *clunk* – there's a short sharp pain to the back of my head that instantly brings tears to my eyes. It's dull, deep and pressurized, like someone's drilling through my skull. I fall to my knees. My head is singing with a high-pitched ringing. *Make it stop*. The room has gone from white to grey and now . . .

CHAPTER SEVENTY-THREE

THE SURVIVOR

Chelsea Harbour

NOW

For a moment, I think I'm back on the island. Dappled spots of white float in front of my eyes. I'm sunbathing. Eyes shut, I'm gorging on the heat. And then I move and a stabbing pain rockets through my skull.

It's more of a pounding. A thump. Thump. Thump.

I can't hear anything except ringing in my ears and a faint noise that sounds like crying.

It's a struggle just to open my eyes. I'm curled on my side, cheek to carpet, but I have a clear view of Alex. He's sitting less than a metre away, resting against the wall. His arms draped over bent knees, sobbing into his chest.

He hears me move and snaps his head around. I sense he's been waiting for some time for me. The anger has dissolved. The whites of his eyes are bloodshot. He stares, without blinking. Sad and defeated.

'Baby, I'm sorry,' he whispers.

His skin looks swollen, grey, dead, in the bright bluish

light from the monitor. The papers are fanned out around him. He's ordered them into a concertina.

His face crumples. 'It was an accident, baby, I didn't mean to hurt you. You wouldn't let go.' He shakes his head, 'I didn't know what else to do.' His voice is thick with tears.

He's staring at me and I'm looking back at him like I'm seeing him for the first time. *Who is this man? How could I have so misjudged you?* We've been living in each other's pockets for three months and never once did I see a hint of violence. I'm dizzy with confusion, with the strobing pain.

'I wouldn't have had to do it if you hadn't been interfering. Those files, they're personal. My study, the things in it, are private. You can't just come in here and stick your nose where it doesn't belong.'

The edge in his tone returns.

'And then when you ran, knowing confidential things about my patients,' he says, shaking his head more insistently, 'I couldn't allow that. So what am I supposed to do? Hey? You've put me in this position. And now I have to clean up the mess.'

His eyes harden. 'How selfish can you be?'

I open my mouth to speak but it's swimming with blood. Sour, metallic, I imagine it pooling beneath my tongue, snaking between my teeth. I'm scared to think what he's done to me.

'It's just a knock,' Alex says impatiently, as if he can read my mind. He's been doing that all along, analysing me like a lab rat. Implanting thoughts in my head.

I swallow the blood and it makes me gag.

'You'll live, stop fussing. That's a bad habit you've got into. Being a drama queen. Exaggerating every little thing. *"Help me, I can't breathe"'* – he makes a horrific parody of me. 'Half the things you do are to get attention. It must be exhausting being you.' He's shaking his head again. 'Not an ounce of the strength my sister had.'

He notices my frown. 'Michelle, the producer, creator of *The Villa*. She was my sister.'

I swallow hard. More blood clots in my throat.

'Half-sister, actually. Same crack-whore of a mother. Father unknown. *Dad* was probably one of her clients. That's what she used to call them, to try and make herself sound more distinguished.'

I have no idea what he means.

Irritation fills his eyes. 'My mum was a drug addict who fucked anything that moved to feed her habit,' he spits.

A vague memory swims into view. A story I read in the paper – 'From the gutter to the private island – the rise and fall of Michelle Jessop'. I think it might even have been *The Record* that covered that story. My God, they were in on it together. Messing with our minds.

'She was a genius, my dear sister. Much more imaginative than I could ever be. God knows who gave her that gene,' he snorts. 'But I came with other skills. Logic, planning, selecting. I was able to pick out who would be perfect for her show.'

A chill crawls over my skin.

He looks down at the files. 'You were all special, in your own way. And I discovered you,' he says, proudly.

'You didn't find me,' I say quietly.

'What's that, Laura?' He leans forward. 'Ah, but I did find you. Two minutes into your audition and I knew you were going to make TV gold. All those hang-ups. All those insecurities . . .

'When Michelle told me her idea for a reality show where the audience would be controlling the contestants, I knew she was onto something huge. She couldn't do it without me, though. She needed me, *my* expertise, to select the right people to star in it. They had to be malleable. Easily manipulated. Suffering from disorders that could be triggered with a gentle poking. And of course, desperate for money. So much so, they'd be willing to do anything to win. Why?' He smiles. 'I know you're asking, Laura. Because that's what the public want to watch! Chaos and drama. People doing extreme things. They want break-downs, fights, emotional unravelling. People pushed to the edge of reason. Of course, they'll never admit it – their dirty little secret – but that's what they tune in for. *Entertainment*. They want to watch people's lives fall apart because it makes them feel better about their own crappy existence.' Alex laughs. 'Misery seeks comfort and all that.'

He clears his throat.

'I was working at the Trinity so half the job was done for me. All I needed to do was select patients with *issues*.' He commas his fingers around the word. 'It took months to sift through psychological reports. Can you imagine? Thousands of files to read, from up and down the country. But I did have some buzz words to help narrow the search. Addictive personality. Obsessive personality. Confidence issue. Body dysmorphia. That Annie, she was a prize gem.

What didn't she have? And the remaining contestants, I sized them up at the audition. You,' he smiles, 'particularly caught my eye.'

I cough. A spray of blood hits the carpet.

He looks at me sympathetically. 'Easy, baby, easy.'

For the briefest of moments, I think he's about to get up and come over, but something changes his mind. Instead, he sighs loudly and presses back into the wall.

'I'm tired, Laura. You're not the only one who hasn't been sleeping. And you didn't even lose someone you love. It was *my* sister who got murdered. I'm the one who's had to silently grieve all these weeks. What you went through on the show is nothing compared to my pain.'

I'm trying not to meet his eyes but the sound of him sobbing makes me look.

He's swerving between violent, angry and sad at an alarming rate. Who is he now? The gentle Alex I once knew or . . .

'It's my fault,' he says more loudly. 'She died because I was careless. If I'd been watching Jess instead of fucking you down some rancid tunnel, she'd still be alive and so would Michelle.' He pauses again. His eyes narrow as he turns and looks directly at me, holding me in place with hate. 'Actually, I've changed my mind.' His lip curls. 'It's not my fault. It's *you*, you're to blame.'

I want to scream at him – *you sick fuck*, but I can't. I barely have the strength to open my mouth. I'm back in the ocean with the rope pulling me under. There's something about Alex that makes me feel weak. He has this inexplicable power to silence me.

'Ah, I don't know.' He breathes heavily. 'Maybe it was her fault, too. We had something amazing. Dreams as big as . . .' He shoots his hand through the air. 'We were going to turn *The Villa* into the greatest franchise the world had ever seen. We had a plan. We had the Agenda. For our next show we'd introduce our mood-enhancing drug Viacon. A little something I created that amplifies your personality. Can you imagine how entertaining that would have been?

'Why did Michelle have to let it all get out of control? I told her, don't push them too far, not yet, but she couldn't help herself. You see, as brilliant as my sister was, she wasn't quite right in the . . .' He taps his head. 'Me, I know about self-control. Everything in moderation. Michelle was blinded by money and her obsession with constantly bettering herself.'

He sounds bitter.

'In some small way, you remind me of her. All she ever wanted was to be seen. She thought Harry King cared, that he needed her, but King was like all the other men in her life: he didn't give a shit about her. He was in it for the money.

'Just like your Ben. He was in it for the story. He threw you to the wolves and then washed his hands of you. If only Michelle could've learned to not take things so personally. It was just business.

'If only she'd given me the time I needed to diagnose Jessica properly. What a mistake, parachuting her into *The Villa* like that, without allowing me to assess her mental state. I would have foreseen her breakdown if only Michelle had let me . . .'

Really bitter.

'So, it was hardly a surprise that the whole thing imploded.' He breaks away. Clears his throat. 'As it turns out, things worked out for me anyway, and, well, I have you partly to thank for that. The media love us. We're the golden couple. Alex and Laura . . .'

'I didn't help you,' I say.

He laughs. 'You were the biggest surprise of all.' He gets up. 'I really did miscalculate your strength. You hid that well. I'd never have guessed someone like you would find the courage to stand up to the viewers.'

Alex looks almost excited.

'I love surprises. Not many people can do that . . . prove me wrong. Congratulations. But . . .' He looks down at me with contempt. 'You've regressed, haven't you? Back to weak, simpering Laura. Blaming everyone but yourself for your unhappiness.'

He selects a file from the floor and slips open to the first page.

'Laura Peters.' He begins reading.

Oh God, make it stop.

'*What she fears most in life is rejection. Suffers from a string of insecurities including fear of failure. Low confidence.*' He looks up at me, reciting his words by heart. '*Make her feel unloved. Remind her of what it's like to feel worthless, and she'll become destabilized. The more she's kicked, the harder she'll try to please.*'

I feel the tears arriving.

'You thought you were better than the rest of them, didn't you?'

'No,' I whisper as I start to cry.

'You marched into that villa with your nose turned up at what we'd created and the type of people who star in reality shows. You weren't superior to them; you were all the same. Greedy, broken individuals.'

I'm not broken. But the words I'm telling myself are hollow.

He grins. 'I was wondering how long it would take you to cry.'

'You won't have a career left when everyone hears what you did,' I say through my sobs.

He walks across the room and crouches over me.

'Baby, your threats are turning me on.' He grabs my hand in his and places it on his crotch. I can feel him, hard, beneath my fingers. He closes his eyes as if he's getting off on my touch. 'You like turning me on. Don't lie to yourself, Laura, I know you do.'

'You're sick,' I hiss.

'Me? Sick? You've got things the wrong way round, my dear. I'm the doctor and you're the patient. I helped you, you ungrateful bitch. I showed you the path out of your self-pity. I taught you how to live again. You should be thanking me.'

He wraps his hand around my neck and then leans in to kiss me. I recoil but he squeezes my throat.

'Shhhh, don't be frightened.' He brushes my cheek with his lips.

His mouth glistens with my tears as he pulls away.

'I'll take care of you,' he says. 'Don't worry, I'll fix you.'

My eyes feel like they're rolling into my head.

'Starting tonight, we'll get you on a nice course of tranquilizers. Ah, don't move!' He squeezes my throat. 'There's nothing to be frightened of. They'll calm you right down. I've got the perfect therapy programme in mind, tailored just for you.'

Images of being trapped in his soundproofed flat, drugged up to the eyeballs, flash in front of my eyes. I've got to get out.

As he strokes my cheek, I imagine freedom. I'll pick myself up off the floor, I'll bulldoze past him and out the door. I won't take the lift. No, the stairs will be better, two at a time. I can hit the fire alarm on the way down, I can . . .

'Come on, let's get you back into bed, shall we?'

He peels my head off the carpet.

What am I even thinking? There's no way I could overpower or outrun Alex. I sob again, a guttural wailing that provokes Alex to handle me even more roughly.

'Oh, shut up!'

And then, in a moment of madness, I do the only thing I can think of, I raise my fist and pound it down, as hard as I possibly can, onto his bare foot.

The surprise is enough to make him drop me. My head thumps back to the floor. I roll over.

'Fuck you!' I spit while I crawl on my hands and knees for the door, my head pounding.

'Where do you think you're going?' he laughs.

There's another sudden sharp pain to the back of my head as he grabs me by my hair. My scalp feels like it's being ripped off as he drags me across the room.

I'm kicking, I'm screaming. My arms are flailing but there's nothing in his study to grab on to. Nobody will be able to hear my cries through the soundproofing.

'Pathetic little Laura. Someone people wipe their feet on. Isn't that what Annie said?'

He's still laughing. He throws me to the ground.

'Let's try this again,' he says. He wedges his hands under my armpits, his thumbs spear my skin as he hauls me to my feet. I'm a broken doll strung up on hooks. He sticks his face right into mine. His eyes are emotionless. Black, gleaming orbs.

'We're going to have to double your dosage. Don't look at me like that, it's for your own good,' he says in a sing-song way. 'I'm your doctor, trust me.'

Trust. A word Dr Alexander has referenced countless times during my therapy. And now he's using it again, to bait me. Such a small, harmless word but it's my *trigger*. Finally, that inner strength he alluded to shows up.

The rage I've harboured for years swells. *I'm not broken. There's nothing wrong with me.* As he looks at me with pity, I scream to myself: *Fuck you, I'm not weak.* I then hinge my head and sink my teeth into his shoulder.

'Biiiitch!' he cries and punches the side of my face. I hear the wet crack as his fist meets my cheekbone. The blow is so powerful, it sends me flying. Pain explodes as my lower back hits his desk.

'You actually bit me.' He studies the blood from the wound and then takes big strides towards me, every single muscle on his abdomen inflated to bursting.

If I hadn't been snooping, I'd never have known it was

there. Instead of trying to get to my feet, I arch back, contorting my right arm, stretching, reaching.

He leans over me. His entire hand slips around my throat. His always perfectly fresh breath is sour on my face.

The tips of my fingers make contact with the handle. I'm not even sure I have a grip on the scissors as I pull them out. I can't feel my fingers any more, I just hope I've got them, that I don't drop them – as I draw an arc through the air.

It doesn't even make a sound when the blade breaks the skin. Alex simply looks at me with big, confused eyes before staggering backwards.

I roll off the desk and fall to the floor. Across the room, Alex does the same. There's a long streak of blood from where he bumped the wall and slid down.

With one hand, he clutches the scissors I plunged into his neck. There's no dramatic blood spurt, it's much gentler, flowing out of him like hot lava. Forming small streams that diverge around his muscles. In the blue light, the blood looks black. It's beautiful, I think, and then I realize I must be in shock.

'Laura,' he gasps, in a way that suggests he's been trying to reach me for some time. 'Call an ambulance.'

His breath is shallow and ragged and fading.

'You need to get me help – now.'

He coughs and black droplets spray into the air.

'Laura . . . please.'

CHAPTER SEVENTY-FOUR

THE SURVIVOR

ONE WEEK LATER

The warm amber glow from the country pub is summoning me.

I've been hiding in the dark of my car for ten minutes, watching the rain hammer the windscreen. The windows are steamed up from my rapid breathing. The air is icy. I can't stay here, like this, and yet I can't build up the courage to go inside.

What is there left to say to one another that hasn't been said for us? Our lives have been laid bare in the media. And then I remind myself that this isn't about me or them – it's about Jess.

I've dressed all in black out of respect for her. The thick woollen scarf snaked around my neck barely covers my bruises. I tighten the tie belt of my coat, hoping that will somehow hold me together. Three more shuddering breaths, misting in the cold night air. Three more and then I pull open the catch on the door.

It was Charles's idea to meet in The Greyhound in Amersham. Tucked away in the Buckinghamshire countryside down twisty hedgerow lanes – somewhere we were less likely to be recognized. Where we could discreetly pay our respects.

The pub looks uninviting from outside. Wooden picnic tables, saturated to black by the storm. Forgotten ashtrays collect water. Folded umbrellas parked up against the crumbling stone wall.

But I can see the warmth waiting for me inside. Steaming up the windows.

I tug open the entrance door and I'm hit with a blast of heat and noise.

The pub is heaving, much busier than I thought it would be and I immediately feel panicky. I've become wary of crowds and anyone who thinks they know me.

I feel the stares, I hear the gasps, I notice the look of horror from the guy working behind the bar. I've lost count of how many I've had this week, starting with the young doctor who stitched up my face at the hospital.

'Barrett-Jones?' the barman calls out Charles' surname.

I nod, avoiding his eyes.

'Through there,' he thumbs to the backroom.

I shuffle through the pub, keeping my gaze low. I imagine everyone watching me weave through the candlelit tables. By the time I reach the door I've forgotten how nervous I am. I'm just relieved to return to the shadows.

There they are, all eight of them. Squashed together in two adjacent booths. Angela is the first to notice me arrive.

'We didn't think you'd come,' she says, getting to her feet. She studies my face and smiles compassionately. 'But

I'm glad you're here. It wouldn't be the same without you.'

We'd all fallen under his spell. That morning I'd seen Angela leaving Alex's therapy room, she'd been to see him about her anxiety. Not understanding it was him that was making her unwell.

She gives me a careful hug, but even the slightest touch sets off the pain. My bones feel like they're being crunched.

Over her shoulder, I notice how the rest of the group quickly lower their eyes. Nobody, not even Matt, wants to be caught staring at my battered face. They don't need to ask how and why. It's been covered a thousand times in the press. My face, his face, splashed across every media platform. *The curse of* The Villa. *House of Horrors, the match made in hell.* 'I finally got a front page,' I tried to make a joke of it with Mum, but when she saw my injuries, she burst into tears.

I've moved back in with her until I find somewhere to live. I could have stayed in Alex's flat for a while, but just the thought of it made me sick. Even if I'd managed to get the blood out of the carpet, the stain that night has left will never fade.

Three officers and a female detective found me curled in a ball hugging the phone into my chest. They moved me to the living room where they took my statement. I remember nursing a cup of tea until it turned cold. It's hard to remember the rest. The words I used, the sentences I formed. Shock took me into its clutches. My wounds and the patient files they found did most of the talking for me.

After an intrusive forensic examination at the station, the detective was satisfied with a ruling of self-defence. I do remember one thing clearly from that night, though. The sunrise over the early morning frost. When the paramedics opened the doors of the ambulance at Chelsea and Westminster Hospital, London looked like it was made of diamonds. At that moment, it felt like the most beautiful thing I'd ever seen.

Matt shuffles along the seat, making room for me. Annie is opposite, dressed in hot pink. 'How are you, darling?' she says.

I let out a little laugh. 'I'm not going to lie, I've been better.'

It's enough to break the ice. A ripple of laughter moves through the group.

'You're doing great, babe,' says Blake. 'Chin up, stay strong.'

Angela's been to the bar; she returns with a glass of red wine for me. The smell of cheap alcohol turns my stomach. You'd think I'd be downing everything in sight after what happened, to take the edge off life, but for some reason I can't touch a drop without wanting to be sick. My body is telling me – it's time to change.

I learned a lot about Alex from the news reports. How he grew up on the same council estate as Michelle. How he suffered horrific physical and sexual abuse at the hands of his mother's regular lovers. Neighbours came forward and told how Alex was a shy, bruised boy who barely spoke. He'd always play alone – they remembered how he'd kick the ball against the wall for hours, long past dark. One lady, now in her seventies, said she was certain he'd rather have slept out in the cold than go back in *there*.

It was clear Alex was as driven as his sister to fight for a better life. But neither of them could erase the memory of violence. I often find myself wondering if there was anything genuine about the Alex I knew. I like to think so. Other times I convince myself it was all an act, a staged performance like the television show he'd created.

I do this to help ease the guilt.

I touch my phone and it lights up. But it's not the missed calls from my mum or the messages from friends checking I'm OK that I notice. It's the crack, running right through the middle of the screen.

We both saw it at the same time. While Alex was pleading with me to save him, our eyes fell onto my phone, which I'd left on the floor. All he needed to do was reach out and it would be his.

I could have stayed where I was and let him call 999. I could have picked it up and rung the emergency services for him. With the last energy I had left, I staggered to my feet and dragged myself across the room to where he was slumped.

The blood had pooled beneath him, bleeding into his pristine carpet.

Without feeling, I observed him, his pained expression as he stretched and strained and then, just when he was about to make contact with his lifeline, I kicked my mobile out of his reach. So hard, with such hate, it smashed against the skirting board.

I stare at the crack now, remembering his face in those final moments, as I watched him bleed to death.

Someone clears their throat and I look up to find Cameron has moved from his booth to be beside me.

His eyes are shadowed. He's exhausted, as we all are. I brace myself for some shitty comment, but for the first time ever, he actually looks ashamed.

'Hey, for what it's worth,' he says, 'I'm sorry.'

I'm so taken aback, I let out a sharp breath.

'I'm back in counselling. I think it's helping this time – working through stuff. There's a lot of things I regret and want to fix.' He lifts up his glass. 'Lemonade,' he states. 'I've been teetotal for three weeks now.'

'That's really great,' I say softly. Our eyes lock with some kind of mutual agreement of peace and then Charles taps his glass. We obediently hush.

'I wish we could have met today for different reasons,' he begins. 'I don't have much to say, other than this never should have happened. Jess, us,' he casts around, 'we were all used. There's so many more out there who should be held accountable. It wasn't just us, others have blood on their hands. Like all those people who got off on watching us suffer.'

There's a rumble of 'hear hears'. Others shift in agreement.

'The reality is, nothing will be done about it as long as people keep watching shows like *The Villa*. As long as there's people desperate enough to take part. The entertainment world is too powerful.' He pauses, gathering himself while a current of anger washes through the room. We all feel it. 'So let us not dwell on things we can't change. But give us the strength to accept them and the courage to move forward.' His voice, now uneven, continues: 'One day at a time.' He lifts his glass. 'To Jess, we'll never forget.'

'To Jess!' we say in chorus.

As Charles takes his seat, he swaps looks with Angela. It's discreet and brief but unmistakable – the tenderness in their exchange. It's clear they're still very much together. All that gossip in the news about him about faking his love for Angela was bullshit. He'd rather have her than his inheritance. At least one good thing came out of *The Villa*.

There's so much I'm still processing. Only yesterday I remembered the car journey from the hotel to the helicopter and the strange feeling that I'd been drugged. I'm certain that was Alexander's doing. Knowing I was a journalist reporting back to my paper, he and Michelle would have tried to hide the villa's location from me. And knowing what I do now, I don't think there was any length they wouldn't go to in order to protect their investment.

I think about my therapy sessions in the villa, how I always seemed to leave them with a new fear implanted. Alex pretended to listen, to calm me down. When all he was really doing was stoking the fire.

I suppose some questions I'll never find answers for. It's something else I'll have to learn to live with.

As we chat and drink, I study the group, each one of them in turn. They're not bad people per se. Not evil, just flawed. And *The Villa* brought out the worst in them. The feeling I had when I first walked into the villa returns. A sense of camaraderie. We will never really be friends, but we're bound by some inextricable force which I know will tie us forever.

The mood is dark but there is something else. A feeling hiding with us in the shadows. A realization that we all have a lot of work to do on ourselves. A commitment to change, however small that might be.

Perhaps I do have Alex to thank for that, for showing me the way, the beginnings of the path at least. I've come to realize that I don't need saving. I don't need a boyfriend or a marriage proposal or even a one-night stand to make me feel I'm worth something. For the first time ever it's just *me*, and I'm fine with that.

I've even started writing again. After Alex died, the words began to flow. Slow at first and then gathering pace as I finally broke through the wall. It's because it all makes sense now – what happened to us. Writing has become my therapy.

As I feel the comfort of their company, in my mind's eye I'm dragged back to the ocean that's been haunting me in my dreams. But, for the first time, I'm not drowning. I'm not fighting for air. Nothing is pulling me down. I'm surfacing towards the light from deep underwater.

CHAPTER SEVENTY-FIVE

THE INVESTOR

New York

NOW

In the heart of New York lies the prestigious new development of One Central Park South. A skyscraper made up of luxurious apartments and duplexes designed by leaders in their field of architecture. Harry King owns the entire building, which includes a rooftop pool.

He lifts himself out of the water and wraps a towel around his waist. Raking the hair from his face, he picks up the Bloody Mary which has been carefully prepared for him.

The air feels still this high up. Sounds are muted and there's only the faint noise of traffic from below.

King looks out across the city, admiring the view of Central Park, taking the crisp winter air into his lungs like he's drawing on a cigarette. He misses smoking, although he still has the occasional cigar with whisky.

He has a sip of his drink, savours it, then picks up his mobile. His lawyer and adviser Ms Wilson answers on the second ring.

'Arabella, morning.'

'Morning, sir.'

'There're some things on my mind I need your reassurance with. You've seen the news; things have got messy. Can you confirm all our Villa investments have been dealt with?'

'We've sold off the production company and moved the ownership of the island to our Omega group.'

'So, it's secure?'

'The transactions are hidden in a series of shell companies.'

'To confirm – anyone looking into our accounts won't be able to connect us to *The Villa*.'

'Absolutely.'

King smiles.

'Good. Pity about Michelle, but she was becoming too much of a liability. Fate worked in our favour. It's time to pivot to our next investment.'

'Yes, Mr King.'

'Get Christopher Philips on the line. He was our architect for *The Villa* and will be leading our Miami project. Inform him that testing for Viacon can commence. We have Alexander Scott's prototype to work from and it shouldn't be difficult to replicate. As soon as Project Icarus is in the air, we can invite our associates and begin the auction.'

'Of course, Mr King.'

CHAPTER SEVENTY-SIX

THE VIEWERS

Emma is on the bus home from work. Her head pressed up against the window as she watches London go by in a blur. Every inch of her body is aching after another manic week at her chambers.

Remind me, why did I ever get into law? She's been asking herself this question on repeat recently. Since her caseload doubled. She's not even sure she wants to make partner any more.

Thank God it's Kylie and Lauren's turn to cook tonight. She can't wait to put her feet up and relax. A long weekend of doing nothing is stretched out in front of her.

The bus pulls in at the next stop and something catches her eye. The billboard above the Tesco Express has been replaced.

There's now a gleaming image of beautiful women in thong bikinis and men with six-packs partying around a pool.

The sun is shining. The water is a glistening aquamarine. She can almost hear the DJ music coming out of the poster. She wishes she was there right now, not under the grey sky pressing down on the city.

The engine roars and the bus lurches back onto the road. Emma snaps her head around – she didn't catch what the advert was for.

THE HOUSE PARTY begins on ITV.
This Saturday 9 p.m.

Dive into the UK's first interactive dating show.

Our contestants will be waiting for you to join.

Jesus, after everything that happened with *The Villa*! Emma was certain these sorts of reality shows would have been shut down. Instead, it's moved across to national television. How did that happen?

Emma feels a spike of adrenaline.

At first, with outrage, at the horror of what happened to that poor girl. Have no lessons been learned?

But slowly, another feeling creeps in. Guilt.

She'll keep it to herself. The girls needn't know. It'll only be for half an hour or so. Just to help her relax and switch off.

Emma feels guilty because she knows what she'll be secretly tuning in to this weekend.

ACKNOWLEDGEMENTS

Firstly, a massive thank you to my editor, Alex Saunders, for bringing *The Villa* to life. Thank you for your incredible eye for detail and all your enthusiasm and encouragement along the way. I couldn't have done this without you!

Thank you to the whole team at Pan Macmillan – so much goes on behind the scenes and I'm truly grateful.

A big thanks to my agent Jordan Lees for your unwavering confidence in my writing. Your positivity and reassurance shine through and make it so much easier to navigate the highs and lows of being a writer.

To my family, my dad, my brother and all my friends, who I constantly badger for feedback about my ideas. Endless walks along Amsterdam's canals nursing cups of coffee, chatting through plotlines. A special thank you to Kate Imbach for your invaluable help with my first draft, and to Allie Steemson for always being there whenever I get stuck and making me laugh so hard.

To Michael, my rock. Your support means everything.

And Judy Potts, for all your kindness when I needed it most.

And lastly, but no means least, to Mum. My greatest cheerleader, my inspiration, the strongest woman I know. My best friend. Mum sadly passed away during the edits for *The Villa* but I take comfort in knowing how proud she was and I have no doubt she'll be smiling down from above when *The Villa* is published and hits the shelves. Mum – thank you for encouraging me to do what I love most. Thank you for everything you've done for me.